"Gabrielle Meyer's story of time-cr... pelling and kept me turning the pag... Christian romance with a twist of the unusual, I encourage you to try *For a Lifetime*."

Tracie Peterson, best-selling author of
PICTURES OF THE HEART series

"Gabrielle Meyer takes us on a time-travelling adventure complete with two love stories and a fresh, innovative plot that is impossible to put down. Unpredictable, clever, and heartfelt, *For a Lifetime* is a fantastic addition to the TIMELESS series."

Elizabeth Camden, RITA Award–winning author

"An inspiring tale of faith, hope, and love. Meyer's magical pen draws out what it truly means to discover one's path when trusting God."

J'nell Ciesielski, bestselling author of *The Socialite*

Past Praise for the TIMELESS Series

"A fresh and innovative twist on time travel, each book of the TIMELESS series features clever heroines, emotionally charged love stories, and unpredictable twists that will keep readers engrossed until the last page."

Elizabeth Camden, RITA Award–winning author

For
a
Lifetime

Books by Gabrielle Meyer

TIMELESS

When the Day Comes
In This Moment
For a Lifetime

TIMELESS · 3

For *a* Lifetime

GABRIELLE MEYER

BETHANYHOUSE
a division of Baker Publishing Group
Minneapolis, Minnesota

© 2024 by Gabrielle Meyer

Published by Bethany House Publishers
Minneapolis, Minnesota
BethanyHouse.com

Bethany House Publishers is a division of
Baker Publishing Group, Grand Rapids, Michigan

Printed in the United States of America

Library of Congress Cataloging-in-Publication Data
Names: Meyer, Gabrielle, author.
Title: For a lifetime / Gabrielle Meyer.
Description: Minneapolis, Minnesota : Bethany House, a division of Baker
    Publishing Group, 2024. | Series: Timeless ; 3
Identifiers: LCCN 2023051312 | ISBN 9780764239762 (paper) | ISBN 9780764243134
    (casebound) | ISBN 9781493446520 (eBook)
Subjects: LCGFT: Christian fiction. | Time-travel fiction. | Novels.
Classification: LCC PS3613.E956 F67 2024 | DDC 813/.6--dc23/eng/20231102
LC record available at https://lccn.loc.gov/2023051312

Unless otherwise indicated, Scripture quotations are from the King James Version of the Bible.

Epigraph Scripture quotation is from the New King James Version®. Copyright © 1982 by Thomas Nelson. Used by permission. All rights reserved.

This is a work of historical reconstruction; the appearances of certain historical figures are therefore inevitable. All other characters, however, are products of the author's imagination, and any resemblance to actual persons, living or dead, is coincidental.

Published in association with Books & Such Literary Management, www.BooksAnd Such.com.

Cover design by Jennifer Parker
Cover images Rekha Garton, Dmytro Baev, Ildiko Neer / Trevillion Images

Baker Publishing Group publications use paper produced from sustainable forestry practices and postconsumer waste whenever possible.

24 25 26 27 28 29 30   7 6 5 4 3 2 1

To my daughters,
Ellis and Maryn.
You bring hope and grace
into my life every day.
I love you with all my heart.
~ Mama

So teach us to number our days,
that we may gain a heart of wisdom.

Psalm 90:12

PART
One

1

GRACE

It was a strange reality to be on the precipice of tragedy and not be able to stop it. Stranger, still, to live two simultaneous lives and know that one day I would have to choose one and leave the other forever. But this had been my existence since birth. A gift, my mama had called it, though I am certain she only said that to placate the fears of a child.

A child born with the mark of a time-crosser.

As I kneaded sourdough in the kitchen of my father's tavern, my hands and wrists covered in flour, my mind slipped from the harsh conditions of Salem Village in 1692 to my colorful life in 1912. It was the only way to cope with the drudgeries of my work and the foreknowledge I had about the witch trials that would soon be upon us. Reverend Parris's daughter and niece had been ill for the past six weeks, and the whispers had

11

already started—soon the accusations would fly and the event I had dreaded for a lifetime would be at my doorstep.

Bringing with it the revelation of my own dark secret.

I glanced up as rain slashed against the leaded windowpanes in the small kitchen and pushed aside the blonde hair that escaped my white cap. It seemed that no amount of daydreaming could keep me safe from the life I was currently living.

Outside the tavern, a storm had been blowing for the past six days, bringing relentless wind, rain, and sleet. The real storm, though, was picking up strength in the clouded minds and hearts of Salem's inhabitants, who were always on the lookout for an attack—whether from the Abenaki Indians or from the spiritual realm, which was much more frightful and heinous to battle.

My twin sister, Hope, entered the low, timber-ceilinged kitchen at the back of Eaton Ordinary and snatched a dried fig from the worktable. The tavern was the only home we'd ever known in Salem Village. It was the center of the community, and our father, Uriah Eaton, the tavern's proprietor, was the most beloved man in the county. Generous to a fault—when it served him well. Ruthless and shrewd when it did not.

"Sarah Good is here begging again," Hope said.

I shaped the loaf of dough and laid it into a bowl before setting a linen cloth over the top. Without a word, I wiped my hands on my apron and reached for a few sweet biscuits and baked potatoes, fresh out of the brick oven.

"You're not going to give her food, are you?" Hope frowned. "She'll keep coming back if you feed her."

I sighed. "She has two small children to feed, and they're homeless. What else are we to do? Especially with weather like this?"

"You're far too kind for your own good, Grace. You know Father wouldn't like it."

"Father isn't here." I laid the items onto a square of linen and tied it shut, pushing aside the guilt that propelled my generosity. If Hope only knew the secret that had been burning in my chest for the past few years, she would not call me kind.

I started to leave the kitchen, but Hope put her hand out to stop me. We were identical, though anyone who knew us well could tell us apart immediately. Hope was a little taller, a little slimmer, and more talkative. She had a beauty mark to the left of her full lips that I did not. But we both shared the same brown eyes, the same curly blonde hair tucked under our white caps, and the same delicate features.

"They're whispering about her," Hope said quietly so our indentured girl, Leah, did not hear from the hearth where she tended the fire.

"Everyone is always whispering about Goody Good," I responded, trying to move past her.

Hope shook her head, and I could see the concern in her eyes. "Reverend Parris's daughter and niece are worse—and now young Ann Putnam and Elizabeth Hubbard are showing signs of affliction. They claim that Sarah Good is one of the women who has bewitched them."

I continued forward, but Hope took hold of my arm.

"Let us leave," she pleaded. "You know we can change history and forfeit this path. 1912 is vibrant and promising—we could stay there forever and not have to return here."

I stared at my sister, younger than me by fifteen minutes, apprehension tightening my mouth as I said, "'Tis dangerous to change history. Mama has warned against it our whole life— especially for selfish reasons. Something catastrophic might happen, and it would be our fault."

"But we would not have to endure this godforsaken path any longer," Hope insisted. "We could leave the hardship and the trouble behind us. You know it's going to get worse."

How many times had we fought about this issue?

Our mother in 1912, Maggie Cooper, was a time-crosser and

had passed the gift on to us. Hope and I had been born with Mama's mark on the backs of our heads that sent us between 1912 and 1692. When we went to sleep in 1692, we woke up in 1912, and when we fell asleep in 1912, we woke up in 1692 without any time passing while we were away. On our twenty-fifth birthday, October twelfth, we would choose which path to keep and which to forfeit forever.

We both knew we would not stay in 1692, but Hope had always wanted to leave early, and the only way to do that would be to knowingly change history in 1692. If we did, we would forfeit our lives here. Our physical bodies would die in 1692, and our conscious minds would stay in 1912.

But it was much too dangerous. It would be easier—and safer—to bide our time.

"We cannot change history," I whispered as I clutched the bundle of food. "It could set into motion events that are not supposed to happen. We could cause wars or famines—or worse. It's not worth it, Hope. Not when we only have seven and a half months left to endure."

She let out a weary, frustrated sigh. "Fine—but if anyone accuses me of witchcraft, you won't be able to stop me."

My heart fell at her words, opening the gaping darkness inside me.

I could never tell Hope that it would be *me* who accused her one day. I had foolishly allowed my curiosity to get the best of me four years ago in my other path. While studying the witch trials, I saw words that had haunted me ever since. *Hope Eaton, daughter of the ordinary keeper Uriah Eaton, was yet another casualty of the Salem Witch Trials when her sister, Grace Eaton, became her accuser.*

How could I ever call my sister a witch? It was unfathomable, but history did not lie.

Or did it?

I had slammed the book closed before I could learn more.

What had it meant by "yet another casualty"? I couldn't bring myself to look, and I vowed I would never search for answers again.

"Don't talk like that," I whispered, trying to cover the anxiety in my voice. "You know what people already think about us."

I stepped past Hope and walked through the connecting door into the main room of the tavern. It was past the noon hour, but there were several men and women sitting at tables with their pints of ale. The weather had made all outside work impossible, so people had come to the ordinary to visit, hear the latest gossip, and stay warm.

John Indian, Reverend Parris's enslaved man, was tending the bar today for Father. He worked at the ordinary several days a week and kept an eye on things when Father was away. John glanced up at me and nodded toward the crackling hearth, where Sarah Good stood with her back to the room. Her worn and tattered dress had probably not been washed in a year. She carried her young son on her hip, while her four-year-old daughter, Dorothy, clutched her mother's skirts. Neither of the children were properly clothed for the February weather.

I acknowledged John and moved toward Sarah and her children. Hope followed me out of the kitchen.

Several people in the room were watching Sarah, whispering to each other. Salem Village was a small agricultural community about five miles north of Salem Towne. With fewer than a thousand inhabitants, almost everyone knew everyone else's business. Surely they all knew of the afflicted girls and the rumors swirling about bewitchment.

When Sarah saw me approach, she turned and snatched the bundle out of my hands, grumbling under her breath. "Is this all?"

Her unwashed body and sweat-stained clothing sent off a putrid smell. It was well known that her husband, William Good, had abandoned her. She and the children were left to the charity of neighbors, but they were cast out of one house after the other because of Sarah's foul mood.

15

"'Tis all we can spare," I told her. "Stay and warm yourself as long as you need."

"All you can spare?" Sarah snorted. "You aren't so high and mighty as you think, Grace Eaton. They may be whispering about me, but they've been whispering about you and your sister much longer."

Hope took a protective step forward. "We've given you what we can—"

"You've given me nothing but leftovers," Sarah spat.

The other patrons quieted, and John stepped out from behind the bar.

Sarah looked between Hope and me. "'Tis the likes of you who should be begging. With those strange marks of yours and the mysteries surrounding your birth. The only reason no one questions you is because your father owns the ordinary." She took a step closer while Dorothy tripped along. "Do you ever wonder about your mother? Why no one knows her name or where she came from?"

Hope drew closer to me, and I inhaled, lifting my chin.

"You should leave," I said. "We've given you what we can."

Sarah snarled at me and then turned and left the ordinary, Dorothy trailing behind her.

The other patrons remained quiet as they stared at Hope and me.

What Sarah said was true. People did whisper about our marks and the mysteries surrounding our birth mother in this path—yet Father forbade anyone to speak of her.

Hope turned her back to the others and met my troubled gaze. "Don't mind Sarah. No one listens to her, anyway."

John returned to his place behind the bar, and the others slowly returned to their drinks and gossip.

The front door blew open, and Father appeared in a black cloak.

"Gather some food and firewood," he said to Hope and me.

"We've been summoned to the parsonage. Reverend Parris's girls have worsened. Something must be done."

The storm had intensified. Hope and I bundled up in our thickest coats, mittens, scarves, and caps to walk the quarter mile from the tavern to the Parrises' home. Our properties abutted one another, but trees stood between them, so we took the road to Andover, trying to avoid puddles even though it was useless. Sleet pelted my face, so I kept my head down.

The hem of my blue gown was caked with mud, and my shoes were sodden with cold rainwater. I toted a basket of food for the Parris family while Hope carried a bundle of firewood. We followed Father like dutiful daughters, though Hope was mumbling under her breath.

She would much rather be in 1912. We both would. But God had chosen this path for us, as well, and we had work to do here.

Soon we turned off the road and onto a drive that led up to the parsonage. We were met by the family's dog, who was soaking wet. He wagged his tail in greeting and followed us up the path.

The brown house was tall and narrow, with two rooms on the main floor and two above. A central chimney allowed for a fireplace in each room. The church had built the house many years ago, and it had been the home of several parish ministers. The Parris family had moved in three years ago, but from the start, Samuel Parris had been a source of division for the village. He preached strict adherence to Puritan laws with little to no mercy, but many of the congregants were supporters of the Half-Way Covenant, a partial church membership that allowed more freedom of thought and behavior. Because of this, half the town disapproved of him and refused to pay his wage or supply him with firewood. The winter had been long and cold for the family.

Father rapped loudly upon the front door, and it was opened immediately by Tituba, the Parrises' enslaved woman and John Indian's wife. She lowered her gaze and opened the door further to allow us to enter.

"Mister Eaton," Reverend Parris said as he stood from his chair near the hearth. "Welcome."

Three other men were in the cold room, their dour faces filled with concern. Two of them were Putnams, the wealthiest and most powerful men in the village. The other was a deacon of the church, like Father.

"Take the supplies to the kitchen," Father instructed us. "And be useful."

Tituba closed the door behind us, and we followed her through the main room to the kitchen lean-to in the back. There, Mistress Parris sat at a table, looking through the window at the bleak world outside.

Though there was a fire in the hearth, each of the rooms was chilly and shadowed. An eerie, foreboding feeling penetrated the dark walls and made the air feel thick.

Where were the girls?

"Good day, Mistress Parris," I said. "We've brought food and wood."

She looked up at us and blinked several times as if pulling herself from a daze. Deep worry lines and circles under her eyes betrayed her exhaustion.

"Bless you," she said as she rose. "Just when I think we shall run out of food and wood, God doth provide more."

Tituba went to the hearth, where she removed bread from the brick oven. Mistress Parris glanced at her with a look of such distrust, I felt a shiver run up my spine.

I set my basket on the table, and Hope placed the firewood near the door. She startled at the sound of a knock.

"Who hath come in this violent weather?" Mistress Parris asked. "Not another man to gape at my poor child, I pray."

Tituba opened the door, and a man stood outside. His wide-brimmed hat was pulled low on his forehead, but I immediately recognized him.

"'Tis Isaac Abbott," I said with a smile, instantly feeling better.

He looked up and met my smile, just as surprised and pleased to see me. His kind blue eyes immediately took in the room, and he nodded at Hope. She nodded back, though she didn't seem nearly as happy to see our old friend.

"Goodman Abbott," Mistress Parris said, seeming relieved herself. "What brings you to our home today?"

He stepped into the small kitchen and took off his hat, closing the door behind him. "I've come with a load of firewood. 'Tis not much, but it should get you through the week."

"Bless you," the older woman said with tears in her eyes.

"Mistress Parris?" came the stern voice of Reverend Parris. "Bring Tituba and the girls to us."

She briefly closed her eyes, as if saying a prayer, and then nodded at Tituba to follow her.

They left the kitchen, and I moved closer to Isaac. He had been tall and broad since his teenage years but had grown stronger since taking over his family's farm. His steady presence was comforting, though I wasn't sure what he could do to ease my concerns.

"Are the rumors true?" he asked me, speaking in low tones.

"I know not," I replied. "I haven't seen the girls myself."

Isaac glanced in Hope's direction, and I could see the longing in his handsome gaze. He clutched his hat and said, "You look well today, Hope."

She busied herself stacking the firewood. "Thank you, Isaac," she muttered, though she didn't bother to look at him.

He'd been in love with my dazzling sister since he was thirteen, but she had never given him reason to speak of his feelings. On the contrary, she had tried to discourage him for years.

And for good reason. We didn't intend to stay in 1692 and had turned down anyone who tried to pursue us. It wasn't hard, since women outnumbered men in the community because of the casualties of King William's War and the influx of female refugees from Maine.

But even if we had planned to stay, I doubted Hope would have been interested. Isaac was steadfast, kind, and dependable.

In other words, *boring* in Hope's estimation.

To me, Isaac was the very best friend I'd ever had outside of my sister. If we were to stay in Salem Village, I could easily love him. Though he had never seen me in that light, since I lived in Hope's shadow—both here and in 1912.

A commotion in the main room made me jump. Wails and screaming rent the air as something hit the wall.

Hope looked up at me, her usually fearless gaze full of trepidation.

"I will unload the firewood," Isaac said, then quickly left the kitchen, allowing a burst of cold air to enter the house.

The door leading into the main room was cracked open, so I approached to see the girls for myself.

"Come," Father said when he saw me. "See what witchcraft hath brought upon this home."

I opened the door farther and stared at the scene before me.

Nine-year-old Betty Parris lay writhing on the floor, her body contorting in inhuman ways. Her twelve-year-old cousin, Abigail, sat in a chair, alternately crying out in pain and swatting at the air as if someone were attacking her.

"They have grown worse," Reverend Parris said in a severe voice. "Five nights past, Tituba made rye bread with their urine and fed it to the dog. Her white magic has increased the girls' sufferings."

The girls' wails grew louder, and Abigail threw herself to the ground like her cousin, Betty. They both began to writhe and jerk upon the floor.

I was familiar with the white magic Reverend Parris spoke of. After the dog ate the bread, it was supposed to point to the person responsible for afflicting the girls. All it had done, according to the reverend, was make his daughter and niece's afflictions worse.

"Who doth afflict you?" Thomas Putnam demanded. His own daughter, Ann, was suffering similar afflictions in his home. "Speak their name!"

"Tituba doth afflict me," Betty cried.

"No." Tituba shook her head and stepped back.

"And Goody Good doth afflict me," Betty continued.

"Anyone else?" Mister Putman asked, not questioning but accepting their claims to be true.

"Goody Osborn," Abigail wailed. "Goody Osborn doth afflict me."

"There is nothing else to be done," Mister Putnam said. "My daughter Ann and Elizabeth Hubbard doth name these same women."

"We must bring them for questioning," Reverend Parris said, "or my daughter and niece will continue to suffer."

"We will have them brought to Eaton Ordinary," Mister Putnam said, "to be held there for questioning on the first of March. Do you agree?" He looked to the men assembled, and each of them nodded.

I glanced at Tituba, who silently shook her head. She looked at the girls and then the men, terror in her eyes, but she said nothing.

It had begun.

2

HOPE

1692 was far from my mind the day after we took firewood to the Parris home. Whenever I was in 1912, I purposely cast thoughts of Salem aside. I had no time or patience to lament our lives there—especially today. My pulse thrummed with excitement, and I couldn't contain the wide grin that had been on my face all morning.

"Are you ready?" Lucas Voland asked me. His French accent turned the simple words into a bouquet of sounds that never failed to make my heart flutter.

I nodded, knowing my brilliant smile was irresistible—at least for most people. Luc was the one man who hadn't fallen for my charms—yet—and perhaps that was why I had been enamored with him for the past seven months. That and his fearlessness.

"You do not have to go through with this," Luc cautioned me

as I pulled my leather gloves over the wrists of my flying suit. "The wind is strong from the northwest. Perhaps too strong for—"

"You've already been up there today," I told him as I fixed the brown silk scarf tied in a bow around my neck. "And you've taught me everything I know." I laid my gloved hand against his forearm, loving any excuse to touch him. "I'll be fine."

He studied me with his intelligent blue-green eyes, and I knew he was contemplating the wisdom in my plans. He'd warned me that if he didn't think I was ready, he wouldn't let me take his Blériot aeroplane up for my first public flight. I had started taking lessons from him in secret last August in New York and had flown until it became too cold in November. I planned to test for my pilot's license this week before leaving Florida to return to New York, but I had been invited to join the Glenn Curtiss Exhibition team today and said yes. I would be the first woman to fly in Florida.

It was colder and windier than we had hoped, but fluffy white clouds marred an otherwise pristine blue sky. Nothing could dim my excitement or enthusiasm—except Grace's displeasure in me, but I would worry about that later.

Thousands of spectators sat in the grandstand nearby, and many more watched the skies from the surrounding fields. At the front of that crowd, Grace waited with our parents, Graydon and Maggie Cooper. Grace had talked her editor at the *New York Globe* into sending her as a correspondent to cover the event, and we had invited our parents to join us.

What they didn't know was that I was going to fly in the air show, too.

Luc's Blériot aeroplane stood nearby, the mechanics waiting for me to step into the French machine before they could start it. Though aeroplanes had been invented by the Wright brothers in America, the French had quickly taken the lead in technology. To learn how to fly from a French pilot—a daring and handsome one, at that—was to learn from the best.

23

"Are you nervous?" Luc asked, his gaze intense. "Because if you are nervous—"

"Not even a little." My grin became wider. I had survived living in Puritan Massachusetts. Nothing in 1912 made me nervous.

He shook his head, admiration in his handsome gaze. "I've never met a woman with less fear than you."

"Fear is a waste of time," I said flippantly with a shrug. "Life is too short to worry about what *might* happen."

I moved toward the Blériot waiting on the end of the runway and put my canvas jacket on over the dark brown flying suit I wore. It protected the suit from any castor oil that might spray from the engine as I flew. The suit was made of silk and matched my eyes. I'd had it made in secret by my dressmaker in New York. It was a clever little ensemble that had buttons up the inside of the legs, and if I unclasped them, my suit turned into a dress.

Now, however, all the buttons were holding the material in place, creating pant legs, which allowed me to climb over the tail and into the cockpit, holding onto Luc's hand. It wasn't easy or graceful, but I made my way to the metal chair without falling—which was my only goal.

The pants might shock most people—but so did female aviators. A new era was dawning, though, and I was determined to lead the way.

The aeroplane was a feat of human imagination, only nine years old, that still left me awestruck. Mama had lived in 1941 and 2001, so she knew about the invention and had told me about it as a child, but it was still hard to imagine until I saw it for myself. The machine was made of lightweight wood, wire, and canvas stretching over the fuselage at the front.

Luc came up to me as I positioned the flying goggles over my eyes, nodding as he ran through last-minute instructions. He still looked uncertain, and I knew what he was thinking. Each week we heard about the death of another pilot. It was one of the most dangerous undertakings in human history—but I couldn't resist the urge to be at the forefront.

I just knew I was born for this.

He finally backed up and then motioned to the mechanics.

Four mechanics held the tail of the aeroplane as a fifth turned the propeller and I flipped the ignitor switch inside the cockpit. The timing was crucial to prevent a reversal of the propellor that could break a hand or wrist.

The motor began to roar as the propeller spun, going faster and faster by the second. The men held the machine steady, waiting for a signal from me that I was ready.

When I lifted my hand, they let go of the tail, and the machine began to move across the uneven field. I pushed the throttle lever forward, causing the plane to move faster, and I began to feel the lift under the wings. The lever had a sort of wheel at the top and came up between my legs. If I turned it one way or the other, it allowed me to warp the wings to adjust the balance and create the lift that my plane—and my heart—desired.

The moment the wheels left the ground, I felt weightless, and a sense of freedom overcame me. It was a heady sensation that I had become addicted to over the past seven months. No matter how many times I experienced it, it was never enough.

Pylons stood on either end of the airfield, used for racing. I pointed my aeroplane toward one now and warped the wings, causing the plane to start turning. I banked my machine and circled the first pylon, then headed toward the second.

Luc had made me promise I wouldn't do anything dangerous my first time up in public, so I circled the second pylon and then brought the aeroplane to the ground and cut the engine. As soon as the roar of the motor quieted, the sound of the deafening crowd filled my ears.

I took off my jacket and stood in the cockpit, raising my arms above my head. Hundreds of handkerchiefs waved at me from the audience, showing their appreciation. I was used to applause on stage, but nothing compared to this.

Soon, Luc was at the aeroplane, reaching for my hand. He helped me climb out, putting his hands at my waist. When he lowered me, I smiled up at him, happier than I had ever been.

He just shook his head, a rare smile tilting his lips.

I could live off that smile for weeks, but I would soon have to face Grace and my parents, which dimmed my enthusiasm. When I started walking toward the grandstand, Luc held back.

I turned to him, admiring the way the morning sunshine played with the sculpted features of his face. He was one of the handsomest men I'd ever met. He had all the trappings of a hero and was famous across Europe and America for his daring aviation exploits and his record-breaking skills. When I witnessed him flying in New York last summer, I had experienced love at first sight, something that had never happened to me before—and that I was certain would never happen again.

"Don't you want to meet my family?" I asked.

He glanced toward the crowd, and I could see the aversion in his gaze. For a man who had captured the attention of the world, he didn't seem to enjoy the fame.

"I should get ready for my own flight," he said as he backed toward the hangar where his other Blériot was waiting.

The thrill I had felt moments ago crashed with disappointment, and I turned to face my family—alone.

The closer I walked to the grandstand, the more I lifted my chin and pretended I was as confident as they expected me to be. Grace stood beside Mama and Daddy. Despite being identical twins, we couldn't be more different. She was an early riser, and I loved to sleep in. She was practical and thoughtful, and I was rash and headstrong. She loved baking and housekeeping and gardening, and I would be happy if I never had to cook or clean again.

And Grace was kind, often shining a light on my own selfishness, though she would never know it. She saw me for who I was and loved me regardless. It was her greatest strength and sometimes her greatest weakness. People could hurt Grace easily—me, the easiest of all, though I never did it on purpose.

"Hope!" Mama said, her eyes wide with shock as her mouth slipped open.

Grace and I had the same first name in both paths. It was part of the gift. Mama said that God inspired our names, so our father and mother in 1692 had been inspired to call us Grace and Hope, just like our parents in 1912.

Mama was seventy-one, though no one would guess it, with her slim figure and pretty face. She had been a time-crosser, as well, and had chosen this path—and my father—fifty years ago. She had also lived in the 1940s and the early 2000s and had taught me everything I knew about the time-crossers in our past. Her mother, Libby, had lived in the 1770s and the early 1900s, and her father, Henry, had occupied the same years. It was a strange existence, but I had become accustomed to it when I was young and didn't give it much thought on days like today, when all I could think about was the here and now.

"Surprised?" I asked as I jogged the last few yards to their sides. People in the stands called out to me, but I focused on my family.

Mama pulled me into an embrace. "How could you have kept this a secret?"

I hugged her tight, trying to avoid eye contact with Grace. "I took lessons at four-thirty in the morning almost every day for eight weeks last summer and fall."

Mama held me at arm's length and examined me with her bright blue eyes, her dimples shining as she smiled. She was a doctor and seemed always to be assessing me. I was surprised she didn't feel my bones to see if anything was broken. "You never cease to amaze me."

Daddy took me in his arms next. He was tall and strong, a few years older than Mama. His hair was gray, but his brown eyes were still alight with intelligence. He'd been a Pinkerton agent, working with President Abraham Lincoln in the White House during the American Civil War, and had gone on to help form the Secret Service. He'd retired ten years ago, but he still looked capable and ready at a moment's notice.

"You're not going to fly again, are you?" he asked.

"I'll be flying with the Glenn Curtiss Exhibition team this year. I have several events already booked."

"What about your work? Aren't you in a show right now?"

I sighed, wishing we didn't have to have this conversation. Grace and I had moved to New York from Washington, DC, five years ago for her to pursue a career in journalism and so I could be on the stage. While Grace had gone to every newspaper and magazine office in the city looking for someone to give her a shot, I had auditioned for countless productions. She had finally landed a position as a journalist for the *New York Globe*, though she wasn't taken seriously until recently. I had found work in secondary roles and minor speaking parts, making just enough income to survive. But the passion and determination I'd had for the stage was now eclipsed by flying.

"I finished my last show two days before we came here," I told him. "I plan to fly now."

Mama and Daddy looked at one another. I knew that look. It often came seconds before one or the other began to lecture me. So I took my chances and turned to Grace, my hands on my hips.

"Well?" I asked her, ignoring my parents' concern.

Grace stood before me, beautiful in a white blouse, black coat, and black, nine-gored skirt. She wore a large hat, shading her face, though her blonde curls peeked out from beneath it.

Her brown eyes, so much like Daddy's and mine, stared at me, but I couldn't determine if she was mad, surprised, or disappointed. She held a black Kodak camera and wore a brown leather shoulder bag, where she kept a notebook and pencil handy for her writing.

"Why?" she asked me.

I lowered my arms. "Why, what?"

"Why are you doing this?"

I laughed and motioned toward the airfield. "It makes me feel alive and excited and—" I paused, not sure how to say that my disappointment on the stage was now overshadowed by my enthusiasm for something new. I didn't have to compete with other women for a role—this one was all mine. I simply said, "It's fun."

"It's dangerous," Grace countered. "And foolish and irresponsible."

"I know." I smiled and looped my arm through one of hers. "That's why I love it."

She was stiff beside me, but what could she say? I had made up my mind, and she knew she couldn't change it.

Perhaps Grace had the upper hand in 1692, but here in 1912, I oversaw my destiny, and nothing my responsible sister could say would persuade me otherwise.

"Is this why you asked us to come?" Grace asked, frowning.

"Of course." I grinned at her. "I wanted to surprise you. And give Mama and Daddy a much-needed vacation from the orphanage."

Our parents shared another look—and this one had nothing to do with me.

Something was wrong.

Grace must have noticed it, too, because she moved away from me and put her hand on Mama's arm. "What is it?"

"Nothing," Mama said, forcing a smile.

"Is it the orphanage?" Grace asked.

Mama put her hand over Grace's. "We didn't want to say anything now—especially here."

I moved closer, forgetting about the large crowd. Our parents were strong, intelligent, and hardworking. I rarely worried about them. What could be wrong?

"Our landlord approached us before we left Washington with unexpected news," Mama began. "A buyer has offered to purchase the building we've been leasing for the past twenty-five years."

"At a price we could never match," Daddy added.

I frowned. The orphanage was ideally situated in the heart of Washington, close to where they lived. It was just as much our home as the house we grew up in. And it was home to dozens of children and the matrons who cared for them. Mama and Daddy would never be able to find another building like it.

"How could Mr. Lorenz sell the building to someone else?" I asked. "Why wouldn't he sell it to you?"

Again, my parents shared a concerning look—and my worry mounted. What weren't they telling us?

"The buyer is J. B. Thurston," Daddy said, directing his words toward Grace.

My heart stopped for a second, and I looked at Grace.

J. B. Thurston was the wealthy owner of several shirtwaist factories in New York. Grace had gone undercover to reveal the abuse and neglect in his buildings and had written an exposé article that created trouble for Thurston. Change had been slow in New York, even after the catastrophic fire that killed over a hundred and forty employees at the Triangle Shirtwaist Factory a year ago, but Grace's article had stirred things up. The success of the story had gotten her a raise and a bit of notoriety at the *New York Globe*. It had also encouraged her editor to agree to her trip to Florida as a correspondent.

"It can't be a coincidence," I said to Grace.

Her face had gone pale. "J. B. Thurston?"

Daddy nodded.

She shook her head. "I'm so sorry," she whispered. "I had no idea."

"It's not your fault," Mama tried to assure her.

"He must have done his own investigation to know right where to strike me," she said. "He can't take your orphanage. I won't let him."

"I'm afraid Mr. Lorenz can't turn down Thurston's offer," Daddy said, heaviness in his voice. "He's offering three times what the building is worth."

"Is there nothing we can do?" I asked.

"I can approach Mr. Thurston and tell him to leave my family alone," Grace said, indignant.

"I don't want you anywhere near Thurston," Daddy replied, his voice filled with warning. "He's a dangerous man and would never listen to you anyway."

"Then what will we do?" she asked him.

Mama let out a sigh. "Mr. Lorenz has agreed to sell us the building at the price Mr. Thurston has offered, but we must provide half the money as down payment by May 1st and the other half by September 1st."

"Since our lease is up in September, it's more than he's obligated to offer us," Daddy added, "but I don't know where we'll get the money."

"There's time," I said, trying to sound cheerful.

Grace frowned at me. "Where will we come up with that kind of money by May?"

"Let's not ruin today with more talk of the orphanage," Mama said. "This is our problem, not yours."

"It *is* our problem," Grace said. "It's my fault."

Daddy put his arm around her. "Don't ever shy away from telling the truth, even if it's risky. We'll figure something out."

The next pilot took off behind me, and we all turned to look.

"Let's talk about this later," I said, forcing a smile to make them forget about our troubles. "Grace, come with me. I'll introduce you to some of the aviators. It will be good for your article."

She didn't look ready to meet anyone—not after the news about J. B. Thurston.

"Enjoy the rest of the show," I said to Mama and Daddy as I pulled Grace away. "We'll meet up with you later." I blew kisses at them as we moved toward the hangar.

"I can't believe what Thurston is trying to do," Grace said, almost in denial. "It's all my fault."

"Stop that," I told her as I tugged her along. "We can talk about this later. Right now, I want you—"

"How will we come up with the money? And what if Thurston doesn't stop at displacing the orphans? What if he tries to get revenge in other ways?"

My own concern was making me feel frustrated, but I couldn't do anything about it right now. "I'll come up with a plan. I promise."

I had to change the topic or she'd ruin the whole day with her worry.

"I know you're mad at me about flying," I said, though I hated to remind her. "You might as well get it out now."

"How could you be so foolish?" she demanded, quickly shifting her focus, as I knew she would. "Flying is dangerous."

"Living in Salem is dangerous," I countered. "Getting in an automobile or on a train has risks. *Life* is a constant chance. Why not live it to the fullest?"

Grace scowled as we walked over the grassy field toward the hangar where Luc would be preparing for his race. "This is different, and you know it. You seem adamant on breaking every rule and pushing every boundary."

I hugged her arm. "God knew what He was doing when He made me this way. He'll take care of me." I wasn't a hundred percent certain I believed that, but I said it anyway.

Grace rarely rolled her eyes, but she did so now. "A ridiculous excuse for your carelessness."

"I'm not careless," I protested with a laugh. "Just exciting and spontaneous. It's the only way I can survive the unending days in Salem."

I hated to even think about waking up there tomorrow. I loathed the hard work and drudgery and abhorred the strict rules and confining expectations. I couldn't wait for our birthday in October when I would never have to return there again.

"There he is," I said the moment I saw Luc. He was attractive in his dark blue suit and tie, a flat cap on backward. Even if I hadn't been in love with him, he would have stood out to me in a crowd.

"Who?" Grace asked.

"Lucas Voland. You've heard of him, haven't you?"

"Who hasn't? We saw him at the air show in New York last summer."

"That's right. He taught me to fly."

"*He's* the one responsible for your carelessness?"

"Don't take your frustration out on him. He's simply my teacher."

We hadn't been able to get close to Luc at the air show last August, but I had gone to Delmonico's after one of my performances that night, and Luc had been at the restaurant with a table of other men. I walked right up to him and asked him to teach me to fly. And he had agreed.

Luc glanced up at our approach, and his gaze slipped from me to Grace. I had told him I had a twin sister, but the look on his face revealed his surprise. Most people who met us for the first time couldn't tell us apart, but it didn't take them long to distinguish us from each other.

Of course, in my flying suit, he couldn't mistake us now.

"Luc," I called out and waved.

He was standing next to his Blériot, a wrench in hand, but he tossed it into a wooden toolbox and pulled out a handkerchief to wipe off the ever-present castor oil.

Grace looked around, taking in the mechanics, the hangar, and the aeroplane in one sweeping, appraising—and irritated—glance.

When we were finally standing in front of Luc, I wrapped my arm around Grace's and stood proudly beside her. My two favorite people were in the same place for the first time, and I couldn't hide my joy. "This is Grace," I said to Luc. "And, Grace, this is Lucas Voland."

"How do you do?" Grace asked, her voice cool. Was she truly upset at him for teaching me to fly? More than anything, I wanted her to like him.

Luc stiffened. "*Bonjour, mademoiselle,*" he said with a slight bow and a tight smile.

"Hope tells me you are the one who taught her to fly," Grace continued, showing no qualms at meeting one of the most famous men in the country. "Are you not concerned for her safety?"

Luc lifted his chin and took on a supercilious expression that he usually reserved for annoying aviation fans—and, apparently, bothersome older sisters.

"She is an adult, no?" he asked as he crossed his arms.

"Yes, but does she understand the dangers involved?"

It was my turn to roll my eyes. "Grace."

Luc glanced at me for a second and then looked back at Grace. I couldn't tell what he thought of her—but he didn't seem impressed. "It is not my job to tell her how dangerous it is. She should know for herself."

Grace opened her mouth again, but one of the mechanics approached Luc and said something quietly into his ear. He nodded and then straightened before he offered us a slight bow, his expression hard to read. "I must fly now."

He walked away from us, and my heart sank for the second

34

time that day. He didn't like Grace—and one look at Grace told me she didn't like him, either.

"He's arrogant," Grace said, under her breath. "Why do you like him so much?"

"How do you know I like him?"

"It's written all over your face. Oh, Hope. You're in love with him, aren't you?"

I couldn't hide the truth from Grace. She knew me better than anyone else—sometimes better than I knew myself. So all I did was offer a pathetic shrug and smile.

She might know me well, but she didn't always know what was best for me.

And right now, that was Luc.

3

GRACE

I hacked at the ice in the water bucket with more force than necessary that morning, my thoughts on the orphanage, J. B. Thurston, Hope, and Lucas Voland. We'd spent the evening brainstorming possible solutions for the orphanage during dinner, but any option we could imagine would take time—something we didn't have.

Daddy told me I wasn't to blame—but we all knew the truth. I hadn't knowingly caused this to happen, yet it was because of me that the orphanage was at risk. If I hadn't exposed Thurston's illegal and dangerous business practices, he wouldn't be coming after my family.

That wasn't all that was on my mind this morning. Hope had invited Luc to join us for supper to meet our parents, but he hadn't shown—a fact that had left Hope melancholy and me irritated. How could he stand up our parents? And why did Hope like someone so self-important?

I jabbed at the ice harder, and it finally broke, splashing cold water against my apron and face.

The winter morning was sullied by a thick blanket of clouds blocking the sunrise and dropping more sleet upon our village. I was usually the first to rise, with our servant girl, Leah, next; Father after that; and Hope last of all. My physical body rested while my conscious mind was in 1912, and I was usually refreshed and ready to face the day when I woke up in either path. I had two identical bodies, one in 1692 and one in 1912, but it was my consciousness that moved between them. If something happened to my body in 1692, it didn't affect my body in 1912. I could have an illness in 1692 and be perfectly healthy in 1912. It was the same for Hope.

If I fell asleep and then woke up before midnight, I would wake up in this same time and space. I never crossed over until after the midnight hour. If I stayed awake past midnight, as was common in 1912 when I attended the theater with Hope, I would remain in that path until I fell asleep.

When Hope and I were younger, we had tried to stay awake for as long as possible in the 1900s, hoping we could skip a day in our 1600s path, but it never worked. As soon as we fell asleep, we woke up the next day in the 1600s. Unless we purposely changed history in the 1600s, there was nothing we could do until our twenty-fifth birthday. On that day, whatever timeline we wanted to remain in forever was the one we could stay awake in until past midnight—and we would never wake up in the other one again.

There was a noise on the stairs, and I turned, expecting to see Father coming down from the rooms above. But it was Hope, adjusting the white coif on her head, yawning.

"Still mad at me?" she asked.

I poured water into a kettle and set it on the iron crane over the open fireplace to warm for our tea. I had laid the fire when I first came downstairs, and it had begun to warm the kitchen. Sleet blew outside the ordinary, promising another miserable day of cold. My hands were chapped and red, but I didn't mind the work. It passed the time and kept me occupied while distracting me from the trouble swirling around us.

I glanced at the lean-to door where Leah slept, just off the large kitchen. She was mute from her trauma in Maine, but she listened to everything we said.

Reaching for the tin of tea leaves, I kept my voice low. "I don't want to talk about it here." We had agreed, long ago, that we wouldn't discuss our 1912 life in 1692 unless necessary. It was a dangerous risk, given the mystery of our birth mother and the spiritual turmoil in Salem. We didn't need to provide more reasons for them to be suspicious of us.

Hope sighed as Leah's door opened and she entered the kitchen in her dark dress and white apron—pausing for a moment at the sight of Hope, probably just as surprised as me that she had woken up so early.

We were soon busy preparing the morning meal for the three lodgers who had slept in the rooms above the ordinary and those who had come for breakfast. Our rooms were in the attic over the kitchen, separate from the rest of the public spaces in the large home. The size of the building was a testament to Father's wealth and standing in the community.

The smell of baked oatmeal pudding, fried venison sausage, doughnuts, and fried potatoes filled the kitchen and made my stomach rumble. Hope enjoyed serving the food more than I did, so she lifted the platters and took them to the dining room. Father was there, sharing and receiving news as he oversaw the meal.

When the food had been served, Leah and I took our plates to the table in the corner of the kitchen. Leah was no older than fifteen, though she had never spoken her age. She'd come to us

38

as a war refugee from King William's War, which was raging between the colonists and the Abenaki Indians in Maine. The bloody battle had lasted for four years already. Leah had been orphaned during one of the massacres, and she had no family to care for her. She'd fled to Salem Village with other refugees and become Father's servant. Though Hope and I had tried to draw her out, she had remained mute since her arrival, the terror of her experience locked tightly in the recesses of her mind.

We ate our fried potatoes and venison sausage silently as Hope entered the kitchen and filled a plate. She brought it to our table and sat next to me.

There was tension between Hope and me—though it would soon blow over. I wasn't angry at her for flying—or for keeping it a secret. I just hated when she took unnecessary risks. She'd been doing it her whole life.

Secretly, though, I wished I was more like her. Hope's recklessness had forced me to be the dependable one. Mama and Daddy worried about her, so the last thing I wanted them to do was worry about me, too.

The door opened again, and Father entered. He wore expensive clothes befitting his station. A long white shirt, gathered at the cuffs, with a black doublet over it. Black breeches and white stockings clad his legs, with black buckled shoes on his feet. His long hair was worn back and off his forehead. He wasn't handsome, but he was commanding, his emotions swinging like a pendulum. Merry and gregarious one moment—harsh and moody the next. I had done my best not to exacerbate his bad temper, but Hope didn't care if she darkened his moods. They often stood toe-to-toe, and she refused to back down unless he used physical force.

"Sarah Good hath arrived," Father said. "She will be kept in one of the upstairs rooms with her children until she can be questioned tomorrow. Take her and the children food when you are done eating."

He was about to leave the kitchen when he paused and turned back to us. There was uncertainty in his brown-eyed gaze—something I didn't see often—but resolve soon filled his face. "I will marry Susannah Putnam nine days hence. Because of the recent difficulties, Reverend Parris has agreed to waive the reading of the banns to allow us to marry in a timely manner."

My mouth slipped open in surprise, but he wasn't finished.

"As the Word of God says, 'It is not good that the man should be alone.' 'Tis past time I take a wife. She will join us for supper this evening."

And with that, he left the kitchen, not waiting for our response.

My gaze sliced to Hope's, whose mouth hung parted, her fork half-risen to her lips. Shock pulsed through me, followed by denial and confusion.

"Susannah Putnam?" Hope asked as she slowly lowered her fork. "She is naught but a child."

I rose, my legs weak beneath my heavy skirts. I wanted to demand that Father explain himself, but he would never answer to me.

Leah looked up at us, her curious face filled with a hint of fear.

There was nothing to recommend Susannah but her beauty. She had never treated me well, though we rarely spoke. At the age of eighteen, she was six years younger than me.

And she was soon to be my stepmother.

The storm finally cleared late that afternoon, and for the first time in a week, the clouds broke and a pale blue sky appeared. Though it was cold and I had supper to prepare, I stood outside making kindling, raking the fresh air into my lungs.

Father's announcement had turned my world upside down,

and I needed time and space to contemplate the ramifications. An eighteen-year-old stepmother? And Susannah Putnam, of all the spoiled, selfish girls. Unfortunately, it wasn't uncommon for an older man to take a young bride. As long as Father could provide well for Susannah and Susannah could give him a male heir, both parties would be satisfied.

Hope walked through the back door and joined me in the snow-covered yard. There were horses hitched to the posts out front, owned by men who had come to discuss the witch accusations against Sarah Good, Tituba, and Sarah Osborn. Tituba had joined Sarah Good in the upstairs room, awaiting their questioning tomorrow. Magistrates from Salem Towne had been contacted and would join Father and the others.

A cold wind sliced through my cape, ruffling the edges and drawing a shiver along my spine.

Hope wrapped her arms around herself and glanced across the road to where the watchhouse tower stood. Guards were stationed there around the clock, on constant alert for an Indian attack.

"I hate this place," Hope said as her breath fogged out of her mouth.

"'Tis not all bad." I tried to sound convincing, though I struggled to believe it myself. "Their hearts are in the right place."

"Are they?" Hope looked back at the ordinary. "They long to control everything we say and do. If Father didn't need us so much and men weren't so scarce, he would have forced us to marry long before now. The elders are simply looking for more ways to control us. They will use the witch trial to their benefit."

"We saw Reverend Parris's daughter and niece. There is something causing their affliction, whether mental or physical. The leaders don't yet know about disease and mental illness like we do. They must blame it on something, and witchcraft is all they know."

"I think the girls are faking."

I shook my head as I gathered the kindling. As a journalist, I longed to look deeper to find the root cause. "I think they suffer from mental turmoil, which has brought on the attacks. The constant threat of war, hunger, and God's wrath has overcome them. Reverend Parris's family has lived from meal to meal for months, always wondering when their next load of wood will be delivered. It must take a toll on them."

"If men like Isaac would stop bringing them wood, perhaps they'd leave."

My loyalty to Isaac made her words sting. "He thinks he is doing what is right."

"He cares too much about the elders' opinion of him. He follows their rules blindly."

"'Tis not that he agrees with their strict beliefs or that he bows to the Putnams, but he does not like to see the Parris family suffer. Isaac is good, and he cannot help but be kind to them."

"He should take a stand against them. Half of the village has refused to pay Reverend Parris's wages, and they are decrying this witch-hunt. Why can't Isaac be more like them?"

The color was high in Hope's cheeks, but before she could go on, a movement along the road brought our conversation to an abrupt end.

Susannah Putnam had appeared with her friend Mercy Lewis. Both were in their late teens. Mercy had been orphaned, like Leah, and worked as a servant in the Putnams' home, though she had freedom to come and go.

My stomach dropped at their arrival.

A self-satisfied smile lifted Susannah's lips, and she tilted up her chin at the sight of us. With confidence, she strode across the lawn, Mercy following.

"Your father hath told you our news?" she asked us.

I nodded, trying to hide my displeasure. What good would it do if she knew I was unhappy?

"We have heard," Hope said, "and we believe it to be foolish."
I wanted to groan.

Susannah eyed Hope from the hem of her gown to the coif on her head and lifted an eyebrow. "It matters not what you think, for I shall be the mistress here, whether you like it or not."

Hope pressed her lips together as she stared at Susannah. I put my hand on her arm to still her retort.

"Are all three accused women abovestairs?" Susannah asked, turning her gaze to me.

"Just Sarah Good and Tituba," I said, "for now."

"They will be examined on the morrow?"

Hope nodded, crossing her arms. "Though 'tis the accusers who should be examined."

"Hope," I said sharply.

"The Holy Word says, 'Thou shalt not suffer a witch to live.'" Susannah studied Hope. "Some say that is why your mother was killed."

I caught my breath and shook my head. "Our mother died in childbirth."

"She was not a witch," Hope added, defiantly.

"Was she not?" Mercy asked, her keen gaze just as calculated as Susannah's. "'Tis not what I heard. Some say she was hanged in Boston and that witchcraft doth run in your veins, Hope Eaton. Mayhap you should be abovestairs with the others."

Hope clenched her teeth. "Those women are no more a witch than me."

I squeezed her arm to still her words. "Hope is just as concerned as the rest of us." I tried to reassure them and calm the tension that had coiled around us. "We want the truth to be known."

"'Tis what we all want," Susannah said, her words laced with accusation. "The truth about *all* the inhabitants in Salem

Village. The hand of the devil is at work here, and we must root out evil, especially generational witches who perpetuate the darkness."

Did she truly believe our mother was a witch? Did others? It couldn't be true. Father did not speak of her, but he would have told us if she had been hanged as a witch. Wouldn't he?

I motioned to the ordinary. "We must get supper ready."

"And I must hasten to my betrothed's side," Susannah said to Mercy. "Come."

They walked toward the front of the ordinary and entered the building as Hope and I stayed by the woodpile.

"They are nasty girls," Hope said with spite. "I cannot wait for this day to end. I long to be in my aeroplane again."

"Aren't you afraid of their accusations? Surely they're spreading the rumor that our mother was a witch. If others believe them, we will be treated with suspicion."

I had been so preoccupied with the idea that I would accuse Hope, I hadn't wondered if I was to be accused, as well.

"We have always been treated with suspicion," Hope said. "'Tis nothing more than rumors and gossip."

"Not anymore." I gathered the last of the kindling. "We cannot let the rumors spread or we will be accused with the others."

"How will you stop them?"

"By finding the truth. There must be someone who knew our mother and will vouch for her innocence."

"Why do you care?" she asked. "We are almost done with this place."

"We have several months to endure. I don't want to spend them rotting in gaol, only to be hanged."

"At least we would hasten to 1912."

I let out an exasperated sigh.

As we returned to the ordinary's kitchen, I couldn't stop thinking about our mother. What if the rumors were true? What did that mean for us? And what did that mean for the accusation I would make about Hope?

It was a puzzle with pieces that didn't make sense. But I would not rest until I knew the truth—and somehow, in the process, change the history books.

I could not accuse my sister of witchcraft—or let anyone else.

4

HOPE

FEBRUARY 29, 1912
JACKSONVILLE, FLORIDA

The drama in Salem couldn't reach me in Florida—nor could it dim my happiness as Grace and I entered the lobby of the Seminole Hotel in downtown Jacksonville after the air show. My skin was still warm from the afternoon sunshine, tinged pink with joy. I had set an altitude record for women, reaching three thousand feet, and had won a five-hundred-dollar prize. My head was still spinning, especially with thoughts of the reception and dance being held in the aviators' honor at the nearby Windsor Hotel later tonight.

More importantly, the prize money had given me an idea, and I wanted to share it with Grace, though she wouldn't like it.

"I'm starving," I said to Grace as I tried to look through the crowded lobby toward the Indian Room. The lavish dining room was famous in Jacksonville for its décor and menu. "I need to fortify myself for the dance this evening."

Grace opened her leather bag and looked inside. "I have an article due to my editor tomorrow. I'd like to polish it before I wire it to him."

"I don't want to eat alone."

"Then order room service and join me."

Mama and Daddy had left the air show earlier that afternoon to board a train back to Washington, DC, and start looking for donors who might help save the orphanage. They had told us not to worry—but how could we not? I didn't know two less selfish people, and they deserved all the help we could give them.

Which was why I was so excited about my idea.

"I don't want room service," I said, trying to see if my guest had arrived in the dining room. "I have a surprise for you."

"I've had enough surprises lately."

I took her by the arm. "Come with me. Please. I have someone meeting us in the dining room—and I want them to tell you about my plans."

She studied me, a small frown on her forehead. Finally, she sighed. "I hope this isn't something dangerous."

I lifted my eyebrows as I led her toward the Indian Room.

As soon as we walked into the paneled room, I saw Luc at a table in the corner near a large potted fern, partially hidden from view.

"There he is."

Grace paused—clearly not pleased to see Luc again. They had avoided each other all day at the air show.

"Hope . . ." she said, letting my name trail off.

"Come with me," I pleaded. "I want you to hear what he has to say."

She reluctantly followed me as the maître d' led us to Luc's table. A distinct Seminole Indian theme graced the room. Painted canoes hung from the ceiling, feather headdresses flanked the doorways, and peace pipes hung crisscrossed on the walls. I thought of the Abenaki Indians at war with the colonists in 1692 and wondered what they would think of the Seminoles' culture being reduced to restaurant décor.

When Luc saw us, he rose from the white linen–covered table and nodded at me with a smile. When his gaze slipped to Grace, it became guarded.

"Bonjour," he said as he held out a chair for me while the maître d' held one out for Grace.

"Thank you for agreeing to meet with us," I said anxiously. It would take a bit of convincing for Grace to agree to our proposition.

Grace said hello, but her voice was lost in the din of the room. The sounds of conversation, clinking silverware, and laughter filled the air.

The maître d' handed us menus and then bowed at the waist before leaving.

There was an awkward pause before Grace and Luc picked up their menus, busying themselves with perusing the options. I tapped my heeled boot impatiently on the wood floor. I couldn't wait another moment.

"I have a plan to help Mama and Daddy," I blurted.

Grace lowered her menu and looked over the top edge, her brown eyes filled with curiosity—and a little surprise.

Luc also lowered his menu, but he didn't look curious or surprised. Perhaps he was used to my abruptness.

"The plan involves Luc," I continued quickly, offering him a grateful smile. "That's why I asked him to meet us here." Since talking to him about my idea earlier today, he had already set the plan in motion.

Grace lowered her menu farther, laying it on the table, and glanced between me and Luc. She was clearly skeptical of this man—yet he was just as uncertain of her. He was probably wondering how much trouble she would cause my career—and him.

"What is the plan?" Grace asked as she folded her hands on the menu.

I licked my dry lips before I began. "It's going to take a lot of work, but I know I can do it."

"What is it, Hope?"

I took a deep breath. "I'm going to be the first woman"—I lowered my voice, afraid someone might overhear and ruin my plans—"to fly over the English Channel."

Grace stared at me and blinked a couple of times before her mouth started to form her disapproval.

"Please listen to my plan—our plan," I said, nodding at Luc. "When Louis Blériot flew over the channel for the first time in 1909, he became the most famous man in the world. No woman has made the flight—which means if I do it, I will have the same fame, and it will open all sorts of doors—"

"Hope—"

"After I take my licensing test tomorrow," I continued, not letting Grace interrupt me, "we will return to New York. Luc has already wired friends in France and is looking for a Blériot aeroplane I can borrow. On March seventh, we'll board a ship for England."

Grace lifted a hand to stop me. "It sounds like a very expensive endeavor. So many things could go wrong, and then how would you be helpful to Mama and Daddy?"

"What can go wrong? Several men have successfully made the flight after Blériot—"

"And several have died attempting it," she interrupted, her irritation rising. "Not to mention that someone else could get there before you, and then what? Your money and time will be wasted."

"Luc has already started making the plans. There are dozens of companies that would pay me after the flight to endorse their products, and dozens of exhibitions that pay well, too. But we must not waste a single moment. Luc wants to return to America on the maiden voyage of the *Titanic*, which leaves France on April 10th. Some of the wealthiest people in the world will be on the ship. What better place to find sponsors and support? It will give us a couple weeks on the journey to raise the first part of the down payment for the orphanage."

"Mama and Daddy would never approve—"

"They won't know anything until after I've made the flight. But think of how much money this will raise for the orphanage."

I knew the prospect of helping Mama and Daddy was hard for Grace to ignore. Her lips twitched as if she was trying to form a good argument to keep me from making the flight.

"I have offered to finance and manage this flight for Hope," Luc said to Grace, his voice almost monotone, not inviting debate. "I have also started to form the best support crew of mechanics in the world. Blériot flew from France to England, so Hope will fly from Dover, England, to Calais, France, a flight of only twenty miles."

"It will be simple," I said to Grace. "Just twenty miles."

"Over open water," she reminded me.

"Softer landing than grass and dirt," I said with a saucy smile, trying to get her to laugh.

She frowned harder. "Do you honestly think you have the skill to fly over the English Channel?"

"Shh." I put my finger to my lips and looked over my shoulder to see if anyone was listening. "No one can know our plan," I said quietly. "If word gets out that an American woman is attempting the flight, one of the European women will beat me to it. I'm surprised no one has thought to attempt it, yet."

"Perhaps because it's too dangerous," Grace countered. "The weather is often unpredictable and treacherous over the channel."

"Hope is one of the most talented aviators I know." Luc's voice was low and serious. "I would never encourage her to make this flight if I didn't think she could do it."

My chest filled with affection. His opinion mattered more than anyone else's.

Grace studied him, as if trying to find some hidden agenda in his words.

"And we want you to come," I said, intending to pull her into the plan, hoping she'd agree. "As a reporter for the *New York Globe*. I want you to take pictures and be the first to report my successful flight. Just think how it will advance your career." I reached across the table and laid my hand over her clasped ones. "I want you by my side."

She didn't speak for a moment as Luc and I waited.

"You're going to do this whether I agree or not, aren't you?" she asked me.

She knew me well. "I want you there—but I'll do it, regardless."

Grace let out a slow breath. "Fine. I'll go."

I couldn't help jumping up to give her a hug.

Luc didn't look as pleased. After all, it was my idea to invite Grace. He wanted to do it without her.

The ballroom at the Windsor Hotel was warm and crowded as I danced with Luc several hours later. Grace had stayed behind to finish her article for the *Globe*, though I suspected she didn't want to be in Luc's company. It gave me the opportunity to be alone with him—if being alone in a room of three hundred people counted.

"Do you think Grace will change her mind?" he asked as we danced to "The Merry Widow Waltz."

"I don't think so." I smiled at other couples as they spun around the room with us. There were a dozen aviators gathered, all guests of honor, though I was the only female pilot. We'd spent over an hour listening to speeches by the mayor, a congressman, and other important Jacksonville citizens, all thanking us for bringing the air show to their fair city, before the dance had started.

But now it was just Luc and I for a moment, and I didn't want to talk about Grace.

"Do you truly think I am one of the most talented aviators you know?"

He was at least a head taller than me, and he looked down at me now, studying me with his blue-green eyes in the dim light from the wall sconces. It was hard to concentrate when I was this close to him.

"I don't say things I don't mean."

I smiled, wanting him to know how deep my feelings ran. I couldn't hide it from my face or my voice. "Your belief in me has gotten me this far. I owe everything—"

"You owe me nothing, Hope. I'm simply doing my job."

I shook my head, loving the feel of his arms around me as we waltzed across the dance floor, my skirts trailing after me. My gown was made with tiers of magenta silk, overlaid with metallic lace extending to the hem. It shimmered under the chandeliers and was designed for elegance and attention.

I moved closer to Luc, as close as our dance would allow, not knowing how to make him aware of my feelings. I didn't usually struggle to communicate how I felt. After years of being on stage, even in minor roles, ardent admirers sent flowers and made advances. Not to mention Isaac's interest in me since we were young. But there was no challenge in that, so I had dismissed each of them. I had always known that one day I would meet someone like Luc who didn't fall over himself to be with me. And *there* was the challenge.

The song was ending, and I didn't have much time left to convey my feelings. "Thank you for bringing me to the dance," I said. "I know how much you detest these gatherings."

He'd been eyeing the door like a caged animal almost since we arrived.

"I knew it would be important to you," he said.

My heart fluttered.

"If you want to make a name for yourself," he continued, "and you want to make a living at aviation, you'll need to attend events like this until your name is well-known. As your new manager, I could do nothing less."

I looked away, trying not to feel disappointed. Tonight was all business? "You're more than a teacher and manager to me," I said, my voice hushed. "Surely you must know that by now, Luc."

He was quiet, and I couldn't bring myself to meet his gaze. I was both frightened and hopeful at what I might see there.

"Of course," he said. "We are friends. Though, if I will be your manager, then we should keep our relationship professional, should we not?"

I finally looked up at him, and his eyes had softened just enough for me to see that he did regard me with some affection—but was it the kind I dreamed about?

It took a lot of courage to muster a smile. "Of course."

When the song ended, Luc pulled away. "Are you ready to return to the Seminole? We don't want to be late for your licensing test in the morning."

I nodded, still unable to find my voice. I rarely cried—not like Grace, who seemed to tear up at the least provocation—but I was dangerously close now. Could it be that Luc truly didn't return my feelings? He had agreed to put his own exhibition flying on hold to be my business manager for the flight across the English Channel. Surely that meant something. Didn't it?

The Windsor and Seminole hotels were less than four blocks apart, so Luc offered his arm to me when we stepped outside, and we headed south on Hogan Street. Darkness had fallen on Jacksonville, but the winter tourist destination was still alive with activity. Magnificent lights lit up the streets and buildings, and music could be heard coming from inside several establishments we passed.

If I was going to spend the next several weeks with Luc, the last thing I wanted to do was make it awkward. Instead of *telling* him I loved him, I would have to *show* him how I felt.

The new goal brought my head up and banished any threat of tears. If I showed him how I felt, he couldn't deny me, could he? I would find a way to convince him that we were meant to travel the world together.

Feeling better, I clasped his arm a little tighter and felt the bounce return to my step.

But Luc was silent beside me. He dipped his head as people passed us, allowing the brim of his stylish fedora to cover his face.

"If you don't enjoy their attention," I asked, "why do you pursue aviation? It's one of the most compelling things that has ever happened to the world and begs for attention."

He paused to look in the window of a dark store as we passed. I could see our reflection in the glass. He studied himself as if he didn't recognize the man before him. It made me wonder. Was he happy?

We made a striking couple, he tall, dark, and devilishly handsome in his black tuxedo. Me, delicate, fair, and elegant in my evening gown and long velvet coat.

He turned away and continued walking. "Does it matter why I fly?" There was an edge to his voice, though it wasn't directed at me. "I must be the best, and if that means gaining the attention of the world, then it's something I must endure. If I could fly without notice, I would choose that."

I wanted to ask him why he must be the best, but I didn't want to push him. It was more than he had ever revealed to me.

At the Seminole Hotel, the doorman greeted us as we entered the opulent lobby. Luc led me to the elevator, and we stepped inside. There were so many things I wanted to say, but I remained quiet. Part of me was still in awe of Lucas Voland, the world-famous aviator—and probably would be for the rest of my life. He remained untouchable—even to those closest to him. What were his secrets? Why did he hold them so close?

And why was I afraid to ask?

When the elevator stopped at the fourth floor, I stepped forward, but Luc took hold of my hand, and I turned, surprised. It sent a jolt to my heart because he rarely touched me when it wasn't necessary—and never so intimately.

"I will pray for your test tomorrow," he said. "I believe God has created each of us for the times we live, and you were created for this purpose, for this time. But we are responsible to use the talents and abilities He gives us wisely. If you do everything the way you've been taught, you should succeed admirably tomorrow morning."

I stood for a second, both surprised and touched by his words. All I could say was, "Thank you."

"I'll meet you in the lobby at six." He let go of my hand and took a step back into the elevator, his walls rising up again as his emotion cleared from his face. "Goodnight, Hope."

"Goodnight, Luc." I took another step back, and the elevator doors closed.

I was alone in the hallway, my breath coming quickly.

Luc had never spoken of God before. His promise to pray for me not only surprised me but tugged at my own complicated relationship with God.

Grace's faith seemed to come naturally to her, despite the differences of beliefs and dogmas between 1692 and 1912. Somehow, she knew and understood God in a way that evaded me and transcended time, religion, or doctrine.

As I walked toward our room, my lifelong spiritual debate warred within me.

Our Puritan teachings were strict and full of rules, an extension of the authoritarian Church of England. The harsh lifestyle had not taught me how to be good and righteous—it had only taught me how to hide my sinful heart and defy my elders. It had made me afraid to do the wrong thing instead of longing to do the right thing.

Whereas Mama and Daddy had taught us that God's grace allowed more freedom. People were given independence to follow their dreams—women in particular—which was why I was able to pursue flying and theater, while Grace was a photographer and journalist. It was a prosperous time, with crusading reformists tackling child labor, factory conditions, women's right to vote, prohibition of alcohol, and more. But did that freedom allow more justification for sins?

The differences were jarring, especially as a child. Which one was right? I believed that God existed—but who was He? Was He the Puritans' God of strict rules and regulations who predestined people for salvation? Or was He the God of my parents who offered grace and mercy and provided salvation to repentant sinners?

I slipped the key into my hotel room door, uncertain if I would ever understand. It was easier to float, untethered to something that might not be right.

What I did know was that God had created me for this time and place, as Luc had said. That was irrefutable—especially with the time-crossing gift I had inherited. And I would live this life to the fullest.

It was harder to accept the same about Salem.

5

GRACE

All morning, as I served the patrons in the ordinary, I could think of little but Hope's astonishing announcement the day before. I could still see the excitement on her face—her pure joy at the prospect of being the first woman to fly over the English Channel—and I felt guilty for being a naysayer. But someone had to talk sense into her. Mr. Voland should have discouraged her, but he appeared to be the one who planted the idea—or at the very least watered it. What would he gain from Hope making the flight? Money? More fame? Would he not rest until *everyone* in the world knew his name?

My initial dislike of him grew each time I was in his arrogant presence—and Hope's lack of discernment where he was concerned alarmed me most of all. The whole thing was a foolish idea. I scrubbed the tables in the dining room harder than necessary, wishing I could wipe away their plan.

Yet—would Hope have considered the flight if it weren't for J. B. Thurston's threats? If Hope was successful, this might be the only way we could save the orphanage. For that reason alone, I had agreed to go along.

I tried to focus on Salem and what was troubling me here. Father stood on the other side of the dining room, instructing John to haul two barrels of ale up from the cellar. I had not had the opportunity to question him about our mother's death, but even if I had, I doubted he would tell me the truth. With the oncoming witch-hunt, it was more important than ever that I learned what had happened. I knew how I might find out, but I would need help.

I was so wrapped up in my thoughts, I almost missed the moment Sarah Osborn entered the ordinary with the constable.

It was cold in Salem, despite the bright sunshine. An eerie silence fell over the occupants in our large dining room as Goody Osborn was helped into the building by one of her servants.

Hope was clearing dirty dishes as I washed tables. The ordinary was full of patrons who had flocked here, knowing today was the first day of questioning the accused women. Though John had little choice about being there, since Father paid Reverend Parris for his labor, I suspected he appreciated being close to his wife, who had slept upstairs, under guard, the night before with Sarah Good and her children.

"Grace," Father called to me, motioning for me to join him near the door where he had greeted the constable who brought Goody Osborn. His face was stern as I approached. The weight of today's proceedings was heavy upon his shoulders—though he didn't mind the business it brought his way. "Escort Goody Osborn upstairs."

Sarah Osborn turned her heavy gaze to me, pain and confusion in her every move. She was in her late forties and had been bedridden with melancholy for years. She was wobbly on her feet, requiring assistance, and looked as frail as a newborn colt.

"Yes, Father," I said as Hope came to take the rag and bucket from me. "Come with me, Goody Osborn."

"Do you not see me?" Goody Osborn clutched her servant's hands as she looked from Father to the rest of the silent gawkers. No one spoke. "I am more likely to be a victim of witchcraft than to be a witch. I have not strayed far from my bed in years, afflicted with a malady that cannot be cured. How could I afflict anyone else?"

"Pray, silence your tongue," Father said to her, his voice a hushed rumble, "if you know what is good for you."

Father nodded at the servant and the constable, and they followed me up the narrow stairs to the guest room above. A guard stood outside the smaller of the two upstairs rooms.

I did not realize that Father had followed us until the constable opened the door and Goody Osborn passed by me, making more room in the upper hall.

"You're to examine the accused," Father said to me. "You're to look for images or devil's marks upon their bodies."

"Father?" I frowned. I'd heard of such things, but I didn't know what they might look like. More importantly, I didn't believe they existed.

"Witch's teats," he hissed under his breath, causing the guard to look our way. "Preternatural excrescence of flesh where the devil or his familiars doth suckle."

Revulsion turned my stomach. Familiars were small spirit animals, like toads, birds, snakes, or most commonly, cats, sent by Satan to aid witches in their cruel acts. People believed the familiars sucked blood from the witch to gain nourishment, especially where they might have warts or other skin imperfections.

My first instinct was to run—but where would I go? Hope and I had discussed leaving Salem Village many times, but two single women in Puritan Massachusetts would be destitute and turned away from paying jobs. Besides, there were few places where Father couldn't find us.

"Please do not ask this of me." I swallowed, my throat dry. "I cannot do such a thing."

"You will aid the magistrates in this way," Father said, taking an intimidating step forward.

It struck me that if I didn't examine them, then someone else would. I could not ensure their dignity if the examination was undertaken by someone who did not care for their plight.

I nodded and cast my eyes down.

"It must be thorough," Father warned. "Every inch must be inspected."

I entered the room where Goody Osborn was being lowered to one of the hard beds. Tituba stood by the window, cradling her right arm, and watched everyone with a wary expression.

Goody Good, standing defiant in the center of the room, turned her steely gaze on me in a sort of challenge. She held her baby boy on her hip, and her daughter, Dorothy, sat in the corner of the room, quietly playing with the frayed hem of her gown.

"Grace will examine each of you," Father said as Goody Osborn's servant was escorted out of the room by the constable.

All three women stared at me.

"The magistrates will be here to start questioning them soon." Father gave me a pointed look. "Be quick but thorough."

He strode out of the room, closing the door behind him with a thud.

My hands trembled as I faced the three accused women. I wanted to weep for them—and for what I knew was to come. How could I stop this madness without willfully changing history and forfeiting my place in time? It was a risk I couldn't take, no matter how much I wished to save these women.

But I could not degrade them by examining their bodies for something that did not exist.

"Well?" Sarah Good asked as she lifted her chin at me. "What will you do, Grace Eaton?"

Each woman was in a precarious position, and though I knew them to be strong and capable, they were filled with fear—and rightfully so. Tituba was a black slave from Barbados in Reverend Parris's home. Goody Osborn was a widow who had purchased the contract of indentured servant Alexander Osborn—and then scandalized the village by marrying him. She had been related to the Putnams through her first husband and was in a legal battle over the land her husband had left in a trust for her sons—a legal dispute the Putnams were still embroiled in. Sarah Good was married, though she had been betrayed by her husband and was destitute. It was no wonder the afflicted girls had accused them. Tituba, Sarah Good, and Sarah Osborn were already outcasts in Salem Village—ostracized and feared. The type of women historically accused of witchcraft throughout the ages.

"I will wait here for an appropriate amount of time," I told them, keeping my voice low so the guard didn't hear, "and then I will go below and tell the men I have found no markings on you."

My disobedience could not possibly change the course of events that would play out in the coming weeks and months, but perhaps it would spare these women a small amount of shame.

Tituba merely turned back to look out the window while Sarah Osborn wept quietly in her bed, but Sarah Good revealed a morsel of respect for me in the glint of her eyes.

It was the very least I could do for these falsely accused women.

An hour later, I descended the steps and entered the main room. The inhabitants had doubled since I'd gone upstairs. I knew that this heinous event would be the catalyst for the end of the Puritans' rule in Massachusetts, but I couldn't begin to understand God's sovereignty or why He had chosen to do it this way. I prayed that God would stop this thing from happening. But if He would not, I asked for strength for everyone who would endure it.

Hope saw me and moved through the crowded room with a stack of dirty dishes. It was hot and loud and smelled of unwashed bodies.

"Have the magistrates arrived yet?" I asked, taking some of the dishes from her.

"Just now. Father took them outside to speak in private." She studied me. "Did you examine them?"

I glanced over my shoulder to make sure no one was close enough to hear. "I couldn't do it."

"What will you tell Father?"

"The truth. Those women do not have the devil's marks on them."

Hope smiled—a beautiful, approving smile. But then it dimmed. "The afflicted have arrived. They are being cosseted in the corner." She nodded toward the space where the four afflicted girls sat with their families and close friends. Susannah was there with her cousin, Ann Putnam. The girls were quiet—no signs of affliction at the moment.

The sight of Susannah made the hair on my neck rise. She smiled at me with the same look she had given us outside when she'd accused our mother of being a witch. As if she knew something I did not. Had Father told her about our mother? *Did* she know something?

As we moved from the dining room into the kitchen, my eye caught on Isaac, who sat at a table not far from the afflicted girls. His large hand curled around a cup of ale while he spoke earnestly with another man. His face was serious as he finished speaking and then glanced up, meeting my gaze. He nodded briefly, acknowledging my presence, before his gaze slipped to Hope.

Always Hope.

But I didn't have time to lament his affection for my sister. I was just happy he had come. I needed Isaac's help to learn the truth about our mother.

When the kitchen door closed behind us, I asked, "How long has Isaac been here?"

Hope sighed. "He is always here."

Her response angered me. "Why do you do that?"

"What?"

"Treat him as if he's a nuisance. Isaac is one of the best people in Salem—and he's in love with you. You should be flattered."

"He's a rule-follower, Grace. He bows down to the elders without question. He is content to stay on his farm, attend meeting, and work himself to death. I would shrivel up and die if I had to submit myself to such a life. I want more than Salem Village can give me, and you know that."

My heart ached at her words, and I set the stack of plates on the worktable. If only Isaac would look at me the way he looked at Hope.

We returned to the dining room as Father and the magistrates entered the ordinary, and everyone quieted.

Magistrate John Hathorne was a formidable man in a black suit of clothes with a stark white collar and long white hair. He stepped forward. "We have decided to move the questioning to the Meeting House. There is not enough room in here for the accused to join us."

A low murmur filled the room as people began to rush to the door, hoping they might be the first to the Meeting House for the best seats—or afraid they wouldn't get a seat at all.

"I think I might go," Hope said.

I frowned. "Why?"

"I cannot stop the hysteria, but I have this strange fascination to see how it unfolds. Aren't you curious?"

"No." I had no desire to watch the accused being tortured

and mocked by fickle teenage girls and frightened grown men. I had read enough in the history books—too much.

"There will be no business during the questioning," Hope said. "Father wouldn't mind if we go."

"I won't go," I told her, resolute in my decision.

"I'll tell you what happens, then." She touched my arm before following the others out of the building.

"Daughter?" Father approached with the magistrates, and all eyes were on me. "What did you find when you examined the accused?"

I forced myself to remain calm. "I found nothing."

The men were silent as they exchanged surprised, concerned glances.

"It will be hard to convince a jury without physical evidence," Magistrate Corwin said to Hathorne and Father, his voice low.

Hathorne nodded. "Do not fear. We will uncover the devil in each of them and have an abundance of evidence for the grand jury when the time comes. I do not doubt that the devil is afoot here in Salem Village. And it is our job to bring this evil to an end."

A shiver ran up my spine as the men passed by me without another glance, calling for the accused to be brought to the Meeting House by the guards and constable. In their eyes, the women were already guilty. They just had to prove it.

They stopped near the afflicted and created a sort of barricade around them, pushing aside others who stood in their way. Susannah sidled up to Father, and he gave her a heated glance that made me sick to my stomach. How was I supposed to watch them live as man and wife when I couldn't even stomach seeing them in the same room together?

And what if she perpetuated the rumors about our mother? I had to find the truth—and Isaac was the only person I trusted to help me.

As everyone departed the ordinary, I approached Isaac. "May I have a word?"

His gaze went to the door Hope had just exited. I had to glance away from the lovelorn look in his eyes, not wanting to acknowledge what my heart already knew. It made me feel lonely in a way that nothing else did.

"Aye," he said, hiding his impatience, though I knew he wanted to be with Hope at the questioning.

But this could not wait. I looked around the room one last time and saw we were alone.

"What is bothering you?" he asked, concern furrowing his brow.

"There has been talk of my mother," I told him, my voice low. "Rumors have begun to circulate again, and I am afraid that if they continue, it will put Hope and me at risk."

"What rumors?"

"Have you not heard?"

"People do not speak to me about you and Hope," he said. "They know I would defend you."

His words warmed me, convincing me I had come to the right person.

"They are saying our mother was a witch—and claiming that Hope and I have witchcraft in our blood."

His lips parted at the accusation. "What doth your father say?"

"He refuses to speak of her. But someone must know. It occurred to me that a midwife must have been present at our birth, and she might know what happened. But we were born in Boston."

"Ann Pudeator hath been a midwife for decades," he said. "She came from Boston. Mayhap she knew your mother. Have you thought to ask her?"

I nodded. I had thought of Ann, which was why I needed

Isaac's help. "But she lives in Salem Towne, and I cannot get to her on my own without raising suspicion."

"Are you asking me to help you speak to Goodwife Pudeator?"

My pulse thrummed. "Will you?"

"I would do anything for you and Hope. I long to make her happy. . . ." He let the statement go, but I knew what he meant.

I wanted to reach out to him, to tell him that Hope would never care for him the way he wanted, but that I would love him—did love him—and could make him happy.

It was on the tip of my tongue—but for some reason, I felt like I was betraying Hope by speaking the truth.

And it would be a fruitless confession, since I was not staying in 1692. I couldn't bear to win Isaac's love only to lose it when we left.

6

HOPE

MARCH 7, 1912
SS *AMERIKA*, ATLANTIC OCEAN

The sky was gray, though my mood was anything but cloudy. Excitement, anticipation, and energy coursed through me as I stood at the rail of the SS *Amerika*, a beautiful passenger liner, speaking to a group of journalists. Twin smokestacks rose into the heavy sky as passengers, crew members, and visitors mingled on the massive deck.

"What's it like to be one of the first American women with a pilot's license, Miss Cooper?" a reporter from *Leslie's Illustrated Newspaper* asked me, an admiring smile on his face.

"It's like nothing I've ever experienced," I told him honestly, grinning as another journalist lifted his camera to take my picture. "I'm thrilled to have the honor, and I know I won't be the last."

Grace stood off to the side, watching quietly, her face hard to read under the floppy brim of her large hat. She looked beautiful and stylish in a brown traveling suit with wide lapels and a long coat. She knew a few of the reporters interviewing me, but she didn't compete for my attention, since she had already written an article—the first—after I earned my pilot's license in Florida. I was the third woman to be licensed to fly an aeroplane in America, and it was causing a sensation, as I knew it would. It had boosted her reputation with her editor, as well.

"What takes you to Europe?" a man from the *New York Times* asked. "Especially so soon after earning your license. I would think you'd like to stay in America and fly with the Curtiss Exhibition team for a while."

I continued to smile, not wanting to reveal even a tiny hint of why I was sailing to England. If anyone knew, I was certain someone else would beat me to the flight. As it was, there was a chance that another female aviator was already planning the same trip. I had to get to Europe as soon as possible.

"My sister and I have always wanted to travel to Europe," I said, glancing at Grace.

"Yes," the *Times* reporter pressed, "but why now? Is this a pleasure trip, or do you plan to fly in Europe?"

My smile did not dim, but I said, "If there is a story to be had, I'm afraid my sister will get first opportunity, gentlemen."

There were groans from the reporters, and Grace offered me a real smile for the first time in days. With her unhappiness about her part in my parents' orphanage dilemma, my plans to fly over the English Channel, and the darkness of life in Salem, there had been little reason for her to smile lately.

After being questioned by the magistrates at the Meeting House on March first, Tituba, Sarah Good, and Sarah Osborn had been transferred to the Salem Towne gaol and would be held there until they could be tried by a jury, though they were questioned several more times in the gaol by the magistrates. I had never studied the witch trial history and had no idea what was to come. I just knew it wasn't good, and the sooner we got out of there, the better.

My gaze caught on Luc as he boarded the *Amerika,* a single leather suitcase in hand.

The reporters turned to see what I was looking at, but there were thousands of people moving about the docks and ship. They couldn't possibly know I saw Luc.

"All visitors ashore," called a steward as he walked along the deck. "All visitors ashore."

"I'm sorry," I said to the reporters, "but it appears the ship is about to embark."

Luc walked toward me, but I wasn't sure if he saw the reporters. He hated speaking to the press and wouldn't like to be spotted by them. But how to stop him from moving toward me without drawing attention to him?

I glanced at Grace, hoping she might read my expression. Would she know to stop Luc?

She studied me, and I tilted my head in Luc's direction—just enough to let her know to look for him.

She turned toward the direction I had indicated, and I knew the moment she saw Luc. Her shoulders tightened, and the line of her mouth hardened. But she walked in his direction to stop him.

"One more picture, Miss Cooper," said another reporter. "Do you mind?"

"Of course not." I smiled and struck a pose with my hands on top of my closed parasol. I turned one way and then the other, happy to oblige.

"Beautiful," said the reporter as he put down his camera. "Stylish, talented, *and* lovely."

"Not to mention adventurous and intelligent," I said with a light laugh, knowing it would draw a chuckle from the reporters. I'd learned in my acting career that a smiling audience was a happy one. "Thank you, gentlemen."

I kept one eye on Grace's progress. Since the journalists would have to walk in the direction Luc had just come from, they would cross paths if Grace didn't intercept him. Would she get Luc out of the way soon enough?

I wasn't just worried about his discomfort. If the reporters knew he was with me and Grace, they might ask questions I didn't want to answer. There could only be a few reasons two single women would travel with the most famous aviator in the world: romantic reasons or business. I didn't want them to prematurely link Luc and me romantically, knowing it would only push him away. And I didn't want them to guess at what kind of business we would be undertaking together, such as a historic flight.

Luc paused when he saw Grace, his body becoming rigid—but he continued walking until they met at the railing. They were too far away for me to hear what they said, but Luc nodded, and the two of them disappeared into the crowd of passengers and visitors saying good-bye.

I let out a sigh of relief and walked the reporters toward the gangplank to see them off the ship. As soon as they were on shore, I searched for Grace and Luc, finally spotting my sister's large, tan hat. She was standing at the rail, facing Hoboken, New Jersey, where the ship had been docked. At her side stood Luc. Though it was crowded and people were pushing for a spot at the rail to wave to friends and family, they stood with space between them, looking in opposite directions.

Their dislike of one another was palpable.

No one could be as close to me as my time-crossing twin sister. If she didn't approve of Luc, how could I continue to pursue him? I had to convince her he was worthy of my love.

I pushed my way through the crowd, breathless, determined to make them like each other by the end of this voyage.

"There you are," I said, trying to sound pleasant.

They both turned at the same time.

Grace looked relieved at my arrival. "Finished with the reporters?"

I nodded. "Are you two getting to know one another?"

They glanced at each other, but there was no sign of comradery or blossoming friendship. Just mistrust.

Neither responded to my question.

Instead, Grace said, "I think I'll go to our room to write a little before supper."

Luc also pulled away from the rail and lifted his bag as he addressed me. "I should find my room, as well, and then we should meet to discuss our plans. We cannot overlook any detail."

"But what about saying good-bye?" I indicated the shoreline and the waving passengers. "This is the most exciting part."

"We cannot lose any time," Luc said. "Nothing should stop us from returning on the *Titanic* on April 10th. That gives us less than five weeks to accomplish our goals."

"Five weeks should be plenty of time," I said, trying to make him relax. This trip wasn't just about the flight but about convincing him he was in love with me—and that my sister was worthy of his friendship. "We have six days onboard the *Amerika*. Can't we take a little time to enjoy ourselves?"

"I don't have the luxury of enjoying myself," Grace said. "I plan to spend every available minute writing articles for the *Globe*. Each one is another paycheck for Mama and Daddy." She nodded good-bye to Luc and then looked at me. "I'll see you later."

As she left, Luc watched her go with an expression I couldn't read. Then he turned to me. "Enjoy the departure, but we must meet soon to go over the plans I've made since we spoke last. I'll get settled in my room and find you when we're out to sea."

He didn't give me time to respond but walked in the opposite direction and disappeared into the crowd.

This was going to be a long voyage.

The Ritz-Carlton Restaurant on the SS *Amerika* was one of the finest dining establishments on the high seas. The lavish decorations and the attention to detail were impressive. A gray-and-yellow stained-glass skylight dominated the ceiling, which was held up with four large chestnut columns. Seated around the tables of white linen and fine china were some of the wealthiest and finest-dressed passengers I had ever seen. They laughed with ease, eating and drinking the best cuisine to be had on an ocean liner. The ship boasted the first à la carte restaurant at sea, and it was a raging success. If the captain of the ship hadn't invited Luc and me to dine with him, we would have been eating with the other passengers in the regular dining room, since it was almost impossible to get a table in the Ritz-Carlton.

The ship was buzzing with excitement on the first night out to sea. With over three thousand passengers, between guests and crew members, it was easy to see why.

Luc and I had been given seats of honor at the captain's table. Captain Barends sat at the head, while I was seated to his right and Luc to his left. Grace had been given a spot next to me.

The captain peppered both Luc and me with questions about aviation until my mind was spinning. Though Luc didn't like attention from crowds, there was nothing he loved more than talking one-on-one with someone who was truly curious about aviation. His handsome face lit up, and he was unhindered and unashamed as he talked about his flying pursuits, slipping into French on accident in his excitement. This was the Lucas Voland I had fallen in love with, the one who was so alive and vibrant—and accessible. Did Grace notice? She had told me she thought Luc was arrogant and self-centered. Was she noting this different side to him?

"You make me want to fly," Captain Barends said almost

wistfully. "I could see myself in an aeroplane. That is, if the sea didn't hold my heart."

"Ah, but if you could go into the clouds," Luc said, his French accent filled with passion, "the sky would steal your heart. *C'est l'amour.*"

It is love.

Warmth filled me at the sound of his voice and the emotion in his words. Flying *was* like falling in love.

"Perhaps." The captain sighed. "But flying is for young men. I am too old and set in my ways."

"You are not too old," I told him, though he appeared to be in his early sixties, with a gray beard and sea-wizened wrinkles around his eyes. "I believe that one day almost everyone will fly." Mama had told me about airplanes, as she called them, from her life in 2001. It was hard to comprehend, but even in 1912, many people believed that flying would become accessible to everyone someday.

"Surely the aeroplane will not replace ocean liners," Captain Barends said with a good-natured laugh. "There is no finer or faster way to travel from America to Europe. Even now, the largest ship in the world is preparing to set sail in just over a month. I see no future in which ocean liners are not the safest way to travel."

Grace and I shared a smile. There were things we knew that we could never tell a soul, but I was happy we had each other to share the knowledge.

"You speak of the *Titanic*?" Luc asked.

"Indeed." Captain Barends took a sip of his wine. "A feat of engineering genius."

"We hope to travel home on her maiden voyage," Luc told him.

"You will be one of the lucky ones."

As the meal progressed, I kept my eye on Luc and Grace. They were not rude to one another but remained guarded and cool. I wished Grace would speak up to show Luc she wasn't prudish and critical. Ever since she met him, she had been just as aloof as him. I wanted her to show him her kind, thoughtful, and wise side.

But she didn't appear to care what he thought of her.

"I do hope everyone plans to stay for the dance tonight," Captain Barends said, looking around the table. "Monsieur Voland?"

Luc laid down his fork, finished with his grilled salmon. "I do not believe I will attend the dance."

Disappointment pinched at my heart, but I put a smile on my face when the captain turned to me.

"And you, Miss Hope? Will you save a dance for me?"

I didn't want to stay at the dance if Luc wouldn't be there. Yet I couldn't refuse the captain.

"Of course."

"And you, Miss Grace," Captain Barends asked my sister. "Will you attend the dance?"

Grace looked beautiful in a cream-colored satin gown with a lace bodice and sleeves. She wore long white gloves, and her blond curls were caught up in a low chignon with a wide lace band around the crown of her head. Pearl earrings dangled from her ears, and strands of pearls were draped around her neck. She was stunning—and her ensemble complemented her gentle spirit. As a child, I hated how calm Grace seemed. I often bullied her into a temper so I wouldn't always be the one getting in trouble. Neither of us had changed much, and her gentleness was still one of her best qualities—one I had grown to appreciate over the years.

"I'm not certain," Grace said. "I have a lot of writing to do."

"Oh, yes." Captain Barends's kind blue eyes took on a shine. "I heard you are a journalist for the *New York Globe*. How marvelous."

The conversation shifted to Grace and her writing as dessert and coffee were served. The captain had just as many questions for my sister as he'd had for Luc and me, and the rest of the captain's guests seemed intrigued by Grace's work. Just like aviation, it was strange for a woman to work in a position usually dominated by men.

I listened as Grace described her articles and the undercover work she had done to unmask the corruption and danger in J. B. Thurston's factories. Even as she talked about the man, a knot formed in my chest, and I was happy she was defending her work—despite his attempt to bully our parents. We still had until May 1st to come up with the down payment for their orphanage, and I was more determined than ever to succeed at our goal.

As she spoke, pride swelled within me. I glanced at Luc, hoping he appreciated this side of her, but it was hard to read his expression. His gaze was riveted to her, as if he wasn't aware of anything else.

"You are a brave woman, Miss Grace," Captain Barends said, shaking his head in awe. "I don't believe I would have the courage to stand up against a man like Thurston."

"If no one is brave enough to challenge powerful people, then nothing will change," Grace said, conviction in her voice.

"Aren't you afraid?" Luc asked her, watching her intently.

I glanced from him to Grace, eager for them to interact.

She looked at him, her expressive eyes full of conviction. "Not when I think of the fear that some people face as they enter a factory or go home to a dilapidated tenement. My fear of being bullied by powerful people could not compare to the daily life-or-death situations they face. I only hope I can continue to write investigative pieces that bring attention to their plight."

"You speak of powerful people who would like nothing more than to silence you," Luc continued. "Or hurt the people you love."

He knew of Mr. Thurston's plans to take our parents' orphanage. Was he goading her? Or truly concerned?

Grace looked down at her plate, the first hint of fear in her brown eyes, and I knew she was thinking of Mama and Daddy. But when she lifted her face, I saw steely resolve. "I know the risks I take. And if my parents have taught me anything, it's to fight for what I believe to be right. If I can make a difference in the lives of people who do not have a voice, then it is worth the risk. I will deal with the bullies as they come."

They held each other's gazes as the table grew silent under the weight of Grace's comment.

"All of us make sacrifices," I said, almost too quickly, my cheeks warming when everyone looked at me. "W-what I mean is that each of us must sacrifice something for our callings. Just think of aviation. It's one of the most dangerous jobs in the world—even President Taft has applauded the death of pilots as a necessary sacrifice for the advancement of aviation. But we know how important it is to keep flying, don't we, Luc? If we don't take the risk, aviation will never be safe for anyone. And that is our hope. That everyone can fly one day."

Grace turned her heavy countenance to me. She hated it when I reminded her about the dangers of flying.

"Very well said, Miss Hope." Captain Barends smiled.

The sound of violins drifted in from the connected dining saloon where the dance would be held.

"I do hope you will honor me with the first dance, Miss Grace," Captain Barends said. "I would very much like to talk to you about the third-class passengers and what we might do together to improve conditions for those traveling in steerage. I've wanted someone to report on it for a long time but haven't known who to ask."

Grace smiled, relieving a bit of the tension around her mouth and eyes. "I would be honored to discuss it with you."

As the diners stood and started moving away from the table,

the captain offered Grace his arm. Luc watched them go, giving me the opportunity to approach him.

"I wish you would stay." I smiled at him. "Can I persuade you to stay for just one dance with me?"

He studied me, his eyes dark in the dim lights of the restaurant. "*Oui*. For you I will stay for one dance."

I couldn't hide my smile.

Taking his arm, I allowed him to lead me into the dining saloon. The captain was introducing Grace to an important-looking group of people, his eyes glowing as he regarded her.

We watched them as the musicians began the first waltz of the evening. Captain Barends bowed to Grace and then took her into his arms to start the dance. No one else was on the dance floor as they spun to the sound of the music.

Grace was lovely. She personified her name perfectly.

Everyone looked on for several seconds before they joined in. Colorful gowns and sparkling jewels twinkled from the ladies, while freshly pressed tuxedos and crisp white shirts complemented the men.

"Will this waltz do?" Luc asked with a smile that went straight to my heart.

He was a different man when he wasn't being bombarded by crowds of adoring fans, though he still hid behind an invisible wall I couldn't seem to climb over. I'd known him for months—but did I really know him?

I lifted the train of my gown and nodded, and he whirled me away onto the dance floor. He was an impressive dancer, so sure on his feet and confident in his grasp of me. All else faded as I lost myself in his eyes. Was he growing to care for me?

What might it take for him to realize he loved me?

The song ended, and the captain led Grace to the side of the dance floor. Luc and I followed, and when we reached them, the captain turned to me and extended his arm. "May I have this dance, Miss Hope?"

I nodded, glancing back at Luc and Grace as the captain led me away. Would Luc ask my sister to dance? It would be the polite thing to do.

They stood awkwardly on the edge of the dance floor for a few moments—and then Luc turned to Grace and said something I couldn't hear.

Whatever she said in response made him nod with stiff shoulders.

Then he left the room.

7

GRACE

MARCH 8, 1692
SALEM VILLAGE

I slowly opened my eyes. Morning darkness blanketed our cold bedroom above the kitchen. The slanted ceiling in the attic room was close to my face. Hope was still asleep in the bed next to me, her breath coming slow and steady. I closed my eyes again and sighed, drawing warmth from her body, not wanting to greet Father's wedding day—though hopefully by the end of the day I would have more answers about our mother in this path.

If my plans with Isaac worked.

My mind drifted to the previous day onboard the *Amerika*. After the dance, Hope and I returned to our stateroom, and she had talked about Luc's attributes for the rest of the night. I knew she was trying to make me like him, but actions spoke louder than words, and he had yet to show me he was a man of good character. I appreciated how he had warmed up when he spoke to Captain Barends about aviation, but that was no indication of his nature. He even asked me to dance, though I knew it was out of obligation, nothing more. I spared him the trouble and told him no.

When he wasn't talking about aviation, he was cold, distant, and proud.

The very opposite of what I loved about Isaac.

A groan came from Hope, telling me she was awake.

"Father is getting married today," she said as she rolled over with a dramatic tossing of her arm across her face.

"I know. I've been lying here, trying to avoid the inevitable."

She moved her arm and looked at me in the darkness. The small window in our room revealed the first hint of morning light as it lined the horizon, offering just enough glow for me to see her clearly.

"I really do wish you'd give Luc a chance."

It was my turn to groan. "You are the most single-minded person I know."

She laughed. "That's because I know what I want. And sometimes it takes stubborn determination to get it."

I shook my head but couldn't disagree with her. "What makes you think I'm not giving him a chance?"

"Besides refusing to dance with him?" She pursed her lips and raised an eyebrow. "You hardly acknowledge his existence—let alone speak to him." She turned all the way to look at me. "Just try, please, for my sake. Our time in Europe will be unbearable if you can't be friendly."

With another groan I said, "Fine. I will try to get along with him."

A beautiful smile tilted the edges of Hope's lips, and she hugged me tight. "Thank you."

I didn't respond, not knowing what to say. Hope was passionate and knew what she wanted in life. When she didn't get it, her disappointment often turned into anger or bitterness.

Sometimes it was easier to give in to her than deal with her moods.

My only consolation was that she seemed aware of this character flaw, though she did little to stem it.

We dressed in our best black gowns, since black was the most expensive color of fabric in the colony. The gowns befitted the daughters of a successful tavern owner. With the witch-hunt underway, Father's wedding would be a somber affair, but there would still be a celebration. The magistrates had questioned the accused women, and both Goody Osborn and Goody Good had claimed innocence—while Tituba had confessed to everything.

According to Hope, while Sarah Osborn and Sarah Good protested their guilt at the Meeting House, the afflicted girls had writhed and cried out vile things until the constables had taken both Sarahs away to the Salem gaol. When Tituba had entered, the girls had continued—until Tituba confessed that she had seen the devil in the lean-to kitchen at the parsonage, and he had told her to serve him.

Had she not confessed, the witch-hunt would have most likely ended with her going to gaol, and the event would have blown over. But while she confessed, the afflicted girls had become silent, almost in awe that she agreed with them. The more leading questions the magistrates asked, the more Tituba admitted, to the great alarm of those present. It was as if her confession unleashed the floodgates and made others believe there was real witchcraft underfoot—and that perhaps they too were afflicted. Fear spread like wildfire. A week after Tituba's confession, several more girls and women had become afflicted with strange and painful convulsions, hallucinations, and tremors—and many more people were accused.

Including little Dorothy Good.

My heart was heavy for the four-year-old child. I didn't know what would become of her and the others, since I had not allowed myself to learn all the details about the witch trials in my 1912 path. I already knew too much, and daily I wondered when and where I might accuse Hope. Would learning the truth about our mother help us or hurt us? It was still unimaginable to think I would call Hope a witch, so I tucked the foreknowledge into the depths of my soul, hoping and praying it would not come to pass. I had control, didn't I? No one could force me to accuse her—even if the history books claimed it would happen.

By midmorning, the kitchen was hot and smelled like baked bread, roasting lamb, and apple cobbler. The wedding would take place at noon since there was a town meeting later that day. All the guests would be invited back to the ordinary for a midday meal, which Hope and I would serve with the help of Leah and John.

I hadn't spoken to Father about his marriage to Susannah because I knew he wouldn't listen to my concerns. Over the past few days, he had been in the best mood I'd seen in years, and it was obvious he was pleased with the match. It appeared that Susannah was, as well, though it was hard to fathom how a girl her age could be happy with a man twenty-five years older than her.

Father didn't come into the kitchen until half past eleven. He was wearing his best clothes; his face was freshly shaven; and his damp hair was combed away from his face. Baths in Massachusetts were an uncommon occurrence, though the Puritans valued cleanliness. Sponge and hip baths were used, if people could afford them, and clothing was cared for with diligent hands. Hope and I bathed as frequently as we could, knowing that cleanliness was essential to good health. Mama had taught us that from her 1941 and 2001 paths. No one else in Salem Village knew about germs, but Hope and I did.

"'Tis time to go to the Meeting House," Father said.

The meal was warming in the hearth. Leah would stay behind to finish the last-minute preparations.

I didn't want to witness my father's vows to Susannah, but I had no choice. I nodded and changed my soiled apron for a clean one. Hope did the same and set a steeple-crowned hat over her coif.

Without another word, we followed Father out of the kitchen, through the taproom—where John was serving travelers who were passing through Salem Village—and into the clear, bright day.

It wasn't a long walk to the Meeting House, which was one of the reasons people came to the ordinary between morning and evening meetings on Sundays to eat their meals and warm themselves. The ordinary was in the center of the village on the road to Andover and easily accessible by everyone in the area.

"Susannah's relatives will move her possessions into the house after the wedding," Father said, breaking the silence as we neared the Meeting House. "I expect both of you to treat her with the utmost respect as your mother."

"My mother?" Hope asked, disgust in her voice. "She's but a child."

Father stopped, steel in his voice and eyes, clearly in no mood to put up with Hope's opinions. "Until you see fit to marry and leave my home, she will be your mother."

Revulsion filled my stomach, and for the first time in my life, I could not keep quiet. "Susannah is younger than us. You cannot expect us to treat her like our mother. We had a mother—do you not think of her today?" She was all I could think about, knowing what Isaac and I had planned.

A flicker of emotion passed through Father's brown eyes—and for a moment, I could see the depth of his pain. He'd never given any indication that he loved our mother or that he missed her. It was almost as if she hadn't existed. Yet now I wondered.

"Do I think of her?" he asked, his voice low. "Not a day goes by that I do not think of her. But *thinking* will not change anything. She is gone, and life hath moved on. Today I am choosing a new wife, something that is long overdue. If you do not like the arrangement, you may find yourself a husband and move on yourself."

Hope crossed her arms. "'Tis fine for you to say now when you are about to replace us. You haven't once encouraged us to marry before."

I wanted to roll my eyes at Hope's impertinence. I had encouraged Father to finally speak of Mother for the first time—and all she could focus on was her anger at him.

He instantly shuttered his emotions and glared at Hope. "I will do as I see fit," he said as he began to walk again, "and I will not answer to you."

I could think of nothing now but our mother. Could Ann Pudeator finally answer the questions that had been burning in my chest for two decades? The witch hysteria was growing, and I could no longer wait.

As an investigative journalist, I wanted answers. As a sister, I needed them soon.

It took everything I possessed to keep my face free of emotion as Hope and I served the wedding meal later that afternoon. Susannah was a radiant bride, sitting next to Father, her friends and family nearby. It seemed like the entire Putnam clan had shown up for the celebration; even the afflicted Ann Putnam was in surprisingly good spirits despite all that she had endured the past few weeks. Reverend Parris and his wife were also in attendance, though they had sent their daughter, Betty, to stay with a friend in Salem Towne after Tituba and the others were questioned.

Neither Hope nor I were given time to sit and enjoy the meal we had prepared, though I wouldn't have wanted to join the festivities. There was no joy in the occasion for me, and I couldn't celebrate my father's decision to marry Susannah.

Thankfully, the meal didn't last long, since the town meeting was set to begin at two. Father would not attend the meeting. Instead, he and Susannah were going on a wedding trip to Boston for a few days, where she would purchase items befitting a new bride—a luxury not every bride was afforded.

Their absence would give me time to visit with Ann Pudeator.

As the last of the guests were leaving, Hope and I brought a stack of dishes into the kitchen to begin the arduous task of cleaning up the wedding meal.

The door opened and Susannah appeared, wearing her fine wool gown. I couldn't deny she was beautiful, as were most of the Putnams. She carried herself with the confidence born of entitlement and excess—something that was hard to come by in Salem Village.

Hope and I looked up. I held my breath, unsure what Susannah would say. Had she come to thank us for the meal? Ask us what her duties would be now that she was the mistress of the ordinary? Tell us that she and Father were leaving for Boston?

Or make another insinuation about our mother?

"My things have been brought up to my room, and I expect them to be unpacked by the time I return from Boston."

She was about to leave the kitchen when Hope spoke.

"I'm not touching your things. If you want them unpacked, you can do it yourself when you return."

A steely smile thinned Susannah's mouth. "Your father told me you would be difficult to manage. But it doth not concern me. I have had a lot of practice disciplining servants."

"I'm not your servant," Hope replied, her smile full of just as much venom as Susannah's.

Susannah lifted an eyebrow. "As the mistress of this establishment, I will have my way. As your father's wife, I will have his ear, both day"—she let the word drag out—"and night. Do not underestimate me. You will not like what you find."

With those portending words, she slipped out of the kitchen, letting the door slam behind her.

Hope shook her head, her mouth twisted in a mocking smile. "If she thinks—"

"You would do best to bide your time, sister."

"Bide my time?" Hope scoffed. "Say the word, and we can be done with this place."

Thankfully Leah had gone out to fetch water and had not returned, so I said, "You know the cost."

"Hang the cost." Hope slammed a stack of plates onto the table. "This is ludicrous, Grace. Let us leave."

I didn't want to argue about this again, so I didn't say another word.

The truth was, Hope didn't need my approval. If she wanted to leave Salem, she could find something to change in history and forfeit this path without my help. I would remain here and be in 1912, as well, even if she was just in 1912.

If she was desperate enough to do it, she would.

But she hadn't yet.

Within the hour, Father and Susannah left for Boston. Thirty minutes later, Isaac returned with his wagon.

My heart sped up, but I wasn't sure if it was because of him or the visit we were about to make.

"Is Hope ready?" he asked quietly so the occupants in the taproom wouldn't hear.

"I haven't asked her yet." We had been so preoccupied with the wedding in 1692 and the trip to Europe in 1912, I hadn't had a chance—or maybe I hadn't wanted to talk to her about my plan. It was something Isaac and I shared—just the two of us. "We'll meet you out back."

He left the building while I told John and Leah that Hope and I were going to visit a neighbor. I didn't tell them *who* we were visiting, and they didn't ask.

Hope was sitting at the kitchen table, reading a book. She glanced up at me, a frown on her face when she saw me wearing my cloak. "Where are you going?"

I took a deep breath. "Isaac is here."

She sighed and looked back at her book.

"He has come to take us to Ann Pudeator's home."

Hope frowned again as she looked up. "Why?"

I moved across the room and stopped near her. "She is one of the oldest midwives in Salem, and she came from Boston. Surely she must know something about our mother. I'm determined to find the truth. If she doesn't know, then mayhap she knows someone who does."

For several seconds, Hope studied me. "Do you think she'll tell us? No one has ever spoken of our mother."

"Maybe not, but I must try and stop the rumors about her death. If someone accuses us of having a witch for a mother, we will need to know the truth so we can deny the charges."

"Why is Isaac helping?" Hope looked out the window to where he had appeared with his wagon.

"It would be difficult to do this alone—and he cares about us. He is the only person I trust. Will you come with us?"

Finally, she nodded and stood.

A few minutes later, we approached Isaac.

"Good day, Hope," he said as he took her hand and helped her into his wagon.

She paused and smiled. "Thank you for taking us to Ann."

The look on his face was pure joy—as if this one comment from Hope would warm him for weeks to come.

I had to tear my gaze away, wishing with all my heart that he would look at me the way he looked at her.

We said little to each other on the way to Salem Towne. If

Father and Susannah had troubles of any kind, we would come across them on the road. I kept my eyes open for any sign of them, but to my relief, we made it to Salem Towne without encountering them.

Ann's home was on the common in the heart of town. She was a wealthy widow in her early seventies, though she was still strong and agile. She had spent much of her life as a midwife and healer, coming to Salem Village often.

"I'll wait for you," Isaac said as he helped us from the wagon. "Take your time."

"Thank you," I told him, putting my hand on his arm. "We will be as quick as possible."

As it was, it would be dark before we returned to Salem Village. And though I wasn't convinced there were witches among us, some of the reports had started to alarm me. Ever since Tituba's confession, there had been other sightings and strange occurrences. The night of the first questioning, William Allen and John Hughes had come across the form of a beast on the road—but when the beast saw them, they said it split into three women who fled so quickly, it was as if they vanished. The next day, a creature followed William home in the dark, and then both men reported animals visiting them in their bedchambers in the dark. Their sightings, along with the strange affliction that still plagued the girls, was creating mass hysteria.

I tried pushing the troubling thoughts aside, though it was impossible. It was all anyone could think about or talk about.

Salem Towne was a bustling harbor community, much bigger and more active than the rural village we occupied. The seaport was full of ocean-going vessels of every kind, bringing items from all over the world. I loved visiting but didn't get away from the ordinary very often—and at the moment, enjoying the town was the last thing on my mind.

I took a deep breath as Hope knocked on Ann Pudeator's door.

A servant answered and said that Goodwife Pudeator was at home. She showed us into the main room of the large house, and we waited for Ann to appear. When she did, she had a welcoming—if somewhat curious—smile on her face.

"Good evening," she said. "I didn't expect to see you here. Your father was married this day, was he not?"

I nodded. We didn't have much time, so I needed to get to the heart of the matter.

"We are here to ask you a few questions," I said, swallowing my nerves. "About our mother."

Ann frowned. "Your mother?" She didn't take a seat or offer one to us. "Why would you ask me about her?"

"Did you know her?" Hope asked.

Ann's face was lined with wrinkles, and her brown dress was in stark contrast to her white hair and pale skin. But her blue eyes were sharp and clear. "Yes. I knew your mother."

My breath hitched in my throat. "What was her name?"

"You don't know her name?" Ann took a step into the room, concern and empathy on her age-worn face. "My poor child. Everyone should know their mother's name."

I tried not to let my emotions show as I waited for her to continue.

"Her name was Tacy Howlett—before she married your father."

Tacy Howlett. I let the name roll around in my mind. It was a foreign name, one I'd never heard before.

"How long did you know her?" I asked.

"Only a few months. She visited me when she learned she was pregnant, and I helped bring you into this world. But I came to know her well in those months." She pursed her lips—as if she'd said too much.

I took a step closer to her. "What can you tell us of our birth? How did she die? Was it instantaneous? Did she live for a few days afterward?"

Ann studied me, squinting. "I know your father doth not allow anyone to speak her name—and for good reason. But hath he told you nothing?"

Hope and I shook our heads. "We know nothing," I confessed.

She took several moments, and then said quietly, "Your mother did not die when you were born."

Silence fell over the room as the information hit both Hope and me. My heart pounded hard. Were the rumors true?

"Father said she died in childbirth," Hope said.

Ann shook her head. "Your mother's death had nothing to do with your birth."

With that simple sentence, everything I'd ever believed about our mother in this path shifted. She hadn't died when we were born? Then how *had* she died?

A noise in the hall startled all three of us, and we looked toward the sound. It was simply the maid, who had dropped a tea tray, but it had shattered the moment, and when I looked back at Ann, I could see she was worried. It was in the creases of her eyebrows and the set of her mouth.

"I've said too much." She took a step back. "If your father knew what I've told you—" She paused and took a deep breath, shaking her head. "I mustn't say more. I cannot say more."

"You can tell us whatever you like," Hope said, moving toward Ann.

Ann continued to shake her head and back up. "I know what happens to widows who step out of place." She moved to the front door and opened it. "Pray, leave me. I cannot risk making Uriah Eaton angry. He hath the ear of the Putnam family." She was trembling. "I've said too much. Do not tell him what I've said."

I looked at Hope, and she was just as confused and upset as me.

"We won't breathe a word," I promised Ann.

"No one must know you've been here." Ann looked out her door as if searching for prying eyes and ears. "No one."

"Please," I said, "if you want to tell us more, contact Isaac Abbott, and he will get word to us. We won't tell anyone what you've said."

Ann shook her head and closed the door as soon as we were outside.

It was clear she wanted us gone, though I had a hundred more questions.

This changed everything.

8

HOPE

MARCH 23, 1912
HARDELOT, FRANCE

The tramcar was crowded with families heading to the beach for Easter vacation. My ears rang with the shrieks of excited children, reprimands of overwhelmed parents, and grumblings of crabby grandparents. There were so many of us packed into the tramcar, Luc, Grace, and I could not find a place to sit. We had been standing for over an hour and a half, since leaving Boulogne, changing cars once to reach the famous resort town of Hardelot.

In moments like this, when I could not talk about my up-coming flight with Luc, my mind traveled back to Salem. I still couldn't believe what Ann Pudeator had told us. Our mother hadn't died in childbirth. But how had she died? *When* had she died? Was she hanged as a witch as Susannah had claimed? Grace and I didn't even know who to ask, and once Father and Susannah returned to Salem, we didn't have the ability to travel to Ann again. Even if we did, I doubted she'd tell us more. I tried to put it out of my mind as much as possible—though Grace wouldn't let it go so easily.

"You've been to Hardelot before?" I asked Luc, who stood sandwiched between two rambunctious little girls playing peek-aboo around him. He was smiling at their antics, allowing them to continue, even after an hour and a half of weary traveling. He joined in from time to time, moving to one side or the other, surprising the little girls and making them giggle.

It was a side of Luc I'd never seen before. He was playful, even in a crowd of people—though they didn't know his identity. What would happen if I told everyone he was the famous aviator Lucas Voland? He was an international hero—but here in his home country, he was a legend.

Grace stood behind Luc, watching the little girls. Since the morning of Father's wedding, neither of us had brought up Luc's name in 1692 again. But to Grace's credit, she did appear to be more friendly with him. She was polite—almost too polite—and tried to engage him in conversations, when necessary. But she still regarded him with caution, which was painfully obvious to me—and probably obvious to Luc, as well. He treated her with the same politeness, answering her questions, though he only spoke to her when required.

When we arrived in London, Luc had traveled ahead to Paris with no time to lose. While he met with Louis Blériot to arrange the use of an aeroplane, Grace and I had met with the editor of the London *Daily Mirror*. After telling him who we were and why we had come to Europe, he had agreed to hire Grace as the *Mirror*'s representative for my flight.

It was her first international job.

After we joined Luc in Paris, he had told us that Louis Blériot's monoplane—the one I would use—was in Blériot's hangar in Hardelot where he summered. Luc recommended I test-fly the aeroplane before we had it shipped to Dover, England, for the flight.

So nine days after arriving in Europe, we found ourselves on a packed tramcar to Hardelot, watching Luc entertain children. I was anxious to test-fly the Blériot. We only had eighteen days before the *Titanic* would depart, and I didn't want to miss our opportunity.

"Luc?" I asked, trying to gain his attention.

"Oui?"

"You've been to Hardelot?" I asked him again.

He finally looked away from the little girls. "No."

I frowned. Hardelot was a popular seaside resort town a hundred and sixty miles north of Paris. "You didn't come as a child with your family?"

"No," he said again but did not expound. Instead, he returned his attention to the children.

My frown deepened. I had assumed he was from a wealthy family because he spoke flawless English and was a pilot. Flying was an expensive endeavor. Perhaps I had been wrong. But every time I asked him about his past, he brushed aside my questions, just like now. Why didn't he want to speak about it? What was he hiding?

One of the little girls tried to move around Luc, but he blocked her, making her laugh. She fell backward into Grace, who caught her and smiled down at the child.

"*Merci*," the little girl said with more giggles.

Grace glanced up and caught Luc's eye. He smiled at her, and she returned the smile.

My heart soared at that small gesture. It was a start.

Children weren't drawn to me like they were to Grace, and I tried not to feel jealous as the girls included her in their game. It wasn't that I didn't like children—they were fine. Some of them were even cute. I had thought about having my own children, but I wasn't sure if I wanted to pass on my time-crossing gift. Not all children born from time-crossers carried the mark, though. Mama had a brother and sister in her 1941 path who weren't marked. But I didn't know if I was willing to take the risk. Maybe if I had only been given one path, the idea of having children wouldn't feel so daunting.

Darkness had fallen on Hardelot by the time we pulled into the station. Grace and I had left our steamer trunks in Paris and only brought essentials in the bags we now carried.

We were the only passengers who got off in Hardelot—which surprised me.

"The resort should be to the west," Luc said as the tramcar pulled away, the little girls waving at Luc and Grace through the back window.

We all turned west, expecting to see the lights from the resort in the distance.

All we saw was darkness.

The entire town felt deserted.

"I thought this was a popular seaside resort town," I said to Luc.

"It is." He frowned and nodded to a little café across the street. "Let's see why it's so quiet."

Grace and I followed him across the empty street. It was cold and windy with thick, heavy clouds overhead. There wasn't a star in sight, and the moon was nowhere to be seen.

The café was a warm and welcome respite after the noise of the tramcar and the chilly outdoors. Soft candlelight filtered from the tables, and the smell of fresh baked bread and spices made my stomach rumble. There were about a dozen other people in the café, most of them unaware of our entrance.

Luc found us a table, and the waitress arrived to take our order. Their words flew back and forth so quickly, I couldn't look from one speaker to the next before the other was talking again. The French language was beautiful, though I only understood a handful of words.

I didn't know what was being said, but it was easy to discern something was wrong. It was written all over Luc's face, and the waitress kept shaking her head.

When she finally left the table, Luc sighed. "The resort does not open until May."

"Even with the Easter holiday approaching?" Grace asked.

Luc nodded. "There is one hotel open, but the waitress doesn't know if we will find a room there."

"What will we do if we can't find a room?" I asked, frowning.

"I don't know." Luc shrugged. "We will hope and pray for the best. The closest town is Calais, thirty-two miles north. I do not know if they will have a hotel available, and there are no tramcars running there tonight. Besides, the monoplane is here in Hardelot."

The waitress brought lobster bisque and crusty bread to the table. The soup was warm and creamy, and the inside of the bread melted in my mouth.

"Do you like oranges?" Luc asked as the waitress waited for our reply.

I grinned, and Grace chuckled beside me.

"They're my favorite," I said. They were almost impossible to come by in Salem. Though they were grown in Florida in 1692, there was no way to transport them efficiently to the northern colonies without great expense. The only time I could enjoy them was in 1912, which I did whenever possible.

Luc nodded at the waitress, who left the table and soon returned with large, juicy oranges for us to enjoy.

A girl, perhaps ten or eleven, bussed tables nearby and watched us with curiosity. Her interest was so obvious, I finally leaned over to Luc and said, "Who is that girl?"

He looked in the direction I pointed and shrugged. "I do not know."

The next time the waitress appeared, Luc spoke to her, and the woman turned to the girl.

"She is the owner's daughter," Luc said to me. Then he spoke in French to the waitress again, who motioned for the girl to join them.

The girl was pretty, with dark brown eyes and hair. Her gaze shifted between Grace and me. "*Sœurs jumelles?*" she asked, her shy face tilted down as she looked at us.

"Oui." Luc smiled. "Twin sisters."

"*Sont-ils Américains?*" she asked.

"Oui. They are Americans."

"Doesn't she know who you are?" I asked Luc.

He shook his head. "I am not here as an aviator. I am here as your business manager. It does not matter who I am. This is all for you."

His words warmed me, and I wanted to repay his thoughtfulness.

"Do you know Lucas Voland?" I asked the girl.

The girl's eyes grew wide. "Monsieur Lucas Voland?" She prattled off a slew of French words I did not understand, though I did catch *grand aviateur*. Great aviator.

I nodded. Even if she couldn't understand my English, she knew Luc's name. I motioned toward him, appreciating his attempt at humility, though it wasn't necessary. He deserved all the applause and accolades he could get.

Luc shook his head, and his shoulders grew stiff. What little relaxation he was enjoying a minute ago vanished, and his face shuttered.

"Lucas Voland?" the girl cried out. She shouted something toward the rest of the café, and all the patrons turned their heads to see.

Soon everyone, even the cook, was at our table, showering Luc with French words I could not understand. Finally the owner of the café broke up the group, and they began to return to their chairs, their faces bright with excitement.

The only person who didn't look pleased was Luc.

By the time we arrived at the hotel, Luc had become cold and distant again. He answered my questions, but with one- or two-word responses. Grace had become quiet and withdrawn, as well—though whether she was upset at me or Luc, I couldn't tell.

I tried to shake off their moods. I had learned my lesson and wouldn't tell anyone who Luc was again. But as soon as we walked into the hotel, I knew someone had called ahead from the café and told them who we were.

"Monsieur Voland!" the proprietor said with a hearty voice. "*Bienvenue. Je suis honoré.*"

Luc's cool voice was not as lyrical as he spoke to the proprietor in French. It was easy to tell there was a problem here, too, though the proprietor looked very unhappy and uncomfortable. Luc said *no* several times, and the proprietor seemed to be trying to convince him to do something he didn't want.

I hung back with Grace, trying to stay small and out of the way in the corner. Luc was probably very angry with me already. I didn't want to irritate him further.

"He asked you not to tell anyone who he was," Grace said under her breath. "It's clear he doesn't like the attention. Why did you do it?"

"I thought he was attempting to be humble. Why fly if you don't want attention?"

"Not everyone does it for the applause, Hope. I don't write for applause but to shed light on injustice. Perhaps Luc flies for reasons other than fame."

I turned to her, surprised. "Does this mean he might have a noble character, after all?"

She sighed. "I don't know *why* he doesn't like the attention—perhaps he's a notorious criminal and doesn't want his past to come to light." A small smile tilted her lips at the absurdity, but then she became serious again. "Instead of assuming you know what's best for people, try to listen to them. Try to honor their wishes. He's not happy with you right now."

"This coming from the woman who has assumed the worst in him since you met."

She shook her head and looked down at the bag in her hand. "I admit I have not given him the benefit of the doubt, but he's so hard to get to know. All I can base my assumptions on are his behaviors, and he's often indifferent and withdrawn—if he's not being arrogant and aloof."

Finally, Luc turned, frustration in his hooded eyes. He crossed the lobby to join us. "There is only one room available. Monsieur LeBlanc is trying to give us his family's apartment, but I cannot put his children or his wife out of their home. So I have agreed that we will take the single room. I hope that is satisfactory."

"Yes." I nodded quickly, not wanting to make more trouble for him.

Luc was guarded as he spoke to Grace. "Will that be acceptable?"

She nodded. "Of course."

He turned back to the proprietor, and after several more minutes of debate, Mr. LeBlanc finally gave Luc a key and pointed toward the stairs.

Grace and I followed Luc up a narrow staircase and down a hallway to a door at the end. He unlocked the door to reveal a small, cold room with a single bed, a washstand on an old dresser, and a straight-backed chair in the corner. There were no rugs on the wood floor, only one small pillow on the bed, and a narrow window near the corner of the room.

When Luc turned on the lamp, it did nothing to improve the quality of the room. If anything, it looked more threadbare and uncomfortable.

Luc looked at Grace as if expecting her to complain.

Instead, my sister smiled and said, "At least we have a room and can be out of the night air. I'm thankful for that."

For the first time since the café, Luc smiled—and the tension I'd been feeling in my chest eased.

"Monsieur LeBlanc said he will have his son bring up extra blankets and pillows," Luc said. "I will sleep on the floor."

"You can't sleep on the floor," I told him.

"Of course I can. I grew up in much worse conditions."

It was another reference to his childhood. Did I take advantage of his comment and ask him to tell me about his past? Would he want to talk about it?

I opened my mouth to ask, but someone cleared their throat behind us, and I turned to find a teenage boy holding a stack of blankets and pillows. He stared at Luc as if seeing Zeus on Mount Olympus.

"Merci," Grace said as she took the items and then stepped between the boy and Luc. She gently closed the door, making the room feel much smaller.

"Hope and I will share the bed, and Luc can sleep on the floor," Grace said, her efficient, no-nonsense voice filling the room. "We will ask the proprietor to tell us as soon as another room opens."

She set the blankets and pillows on the bed and placed her bag next to them. After taking off her hat and gloves, she surveyed the room.

Luc and I watched her. She was taking charge, as she often did, and it was hard not to turn to her.

"There isn't a lot of space," she said with a nod, "but there's enough for a pallet here in the corner near the window." She picked up the blankets and walked over to where Luc was standing. He moved aside, and she began to layer the blankets on the floor.

"I believe one or two of those are for you and Hope," he said, his voice quiet. "The one on the bed is threadbare."

"We'll have each other to keep warm," she insisted without looking at him. "We're used to sharing a bed."

He took one of the blankets off the floor and handed it to her. "I insist."

She paused as their gazes met. Finally, she took the blanket and nodded, then went back to our bed to spread it out.

At least they were talking to each other. Kind of.

All I wanted was to go to sleep. Tomorrow I would test-fly the Blériot aeroplane, and then we could ship it to Dover, where I would make my flight. The sooner it was done, the better.

The only trouble was that I would have to endure an entire day in Salem before I would be back in Hardelot to fly. A difficult day of hard work, Susannah's constant whining, and the growing tension with the witch-hunt.

A knock at the door startled me.

Grace motioned for me to stay where I was and opened the door. It was Mr. LeBlanc.

"Pardon," he said in a thick French accent. "I have news about the weather."

Luc stepped forward and spoke in his native language. When the conversation ended, he turned to me with frustration and defeat on his face. "I asked Mr. LeBlanc to get the weather forecast—and it is not good. A storm is moving in, and they expect several days of wind and rain."

"What does that mean?" Grace asked.

"It means we will be here for a long time before Hope can test-fly the Blériot aeroplane. A week, perhaps, but it must be done. She cannot fly over the Channel without being familiar with the aeroplane."

"If it takes a week, then it takes a week," Grace said. "We will still have plenty of time to get to the *Titanic*."

Luc let out a sigh. "The other bad news is that the hotel is full until after Easter. There will not be another room available unless someone leaves early."

"It will be cozy," Grace conceded as she tried to assure him. "But we can make do."

Despite her optimism, my disappointment mounted.

I had to get over the Channel as soon as possible. The future of Mama and Daddy's orphanage depended upon it—and J. B. Thurston could not win.

9

GRACE

**MARCH 24, 1692
SALEM VILLAGE**

Nothing had changed since Father married Susannah—except that we had one more person to care for, and we had to be extra cautious about what we said and did. She slept late, came down to the dining room during the busiest social hours to visit with friends and family, and then returned to the room she shared with Father for the remainder of the day.

Whenever Hope or I asked her to assist with one of the chores, Father was quick to quiet us. He made it clear he had not married Susannah for the extra help.

In truth, I was thankful she wasn't under our feet, trying to change the way we operated the ordinary. Life went on as before, just with a little more work now that Susannah lived in Father's room.

I had far more important things to worry about. The breakfast hour was upon us, and Hope, Leah, and I were busy serving the meal while John tended the bar. With the uncertainty of the examinations and accusations, people flocked to the ordinary to get up-to-the-minute reports. If Tituba's ongoing and consistent confessions were to be believed, there was a coven of witches in Salem—at least nine, and they were being led by a powerful man. So far, Sarah Good, Sarah Osborn, and Martha Corey had been arrested and questioned, along with Tituba. That supposedly left at least six more women and a man on the loose. *Who were they? Did they reside among us? Eat at our tables?* Rumors and accusations swirled.

As suspicions grew, more people became afflicted, and everyone was remembering old disagreements, unsolved mysteries, previous witch accusations, and individuals with Quaker connections. In their minds, these things could easily be explained by witchcraft.

But it wasn't just Salem on my mind as I served the morning meal. As much as I hated to admit it to myself, I couldn't stop worrying about Hope's upcoming flight—or her relationship with Luc.

I had been surprised at his silliness with the children on the tramcar to Hardelot and his protectiveness as we navigated a foreign country. After the incident in the café, I started to question his reasons for flying. He didn't seem to do it for attention and fame, as I'd first thought. So then, what drove him?

He was still reserved, but I had begun to see that he wasn't being aloof so much as watching, assessing, and studying those around him. I suddenly wanted to know more—and not because I had promised Hope I'd try to get along with him. Perhaps it was the investigative journalist in me, but whatever it was, I felt a pull to understand him. He was a complex man who didn't allow others to get close. Did anyone know the real Lucas Voland? Did my sister?

Father went from table to table, visiting with his patrons, while Susannah sat with her friends, Mercy Lewis and Mary

Warren. Both were orphaned refugees from the war and were now working as servants, though they had more freedom to come and go than Hope and me. And both were now dabbling in affliction—and whispering behind their hands every time Hope or I passed their table.

As I served two patrons, I glanced at Father and saw that he was smiling indulgently at his new bride. He wore a perpetually pleased expression of late—in stark contrast to Hope's scowl.

"He does not notice your anger," I said to Hope as I met her near the kitchen door with a pitcher of cider in my hands. "You could frown all day and he wouldn't stop to ask what troubles you. All it does is make your face look sour."

"I don't care how my face looks," she said, her brown eyes sparking. "The less likeable I am, the better."

I wanted to roll my eyes. Hope could be dramatic on the best of days. It served her well on stage—but in day-to-day living, it was exasperating. "There's no need to draw more censure."

"Hope," Susannah called out across the busy room, "I need you."

Hope ignored Susannah's bidding and walked into the kitchen.

I followed her. "She will not be happy if you ignore her, especially in front of her friends."

"I care not what she thinks. She can scream and demand all she wants, but I refuse to serve her."

I set down the cider and sighed. There was no use pretending that Susannah was going away. Instead, I reentered the dining room and walked to her table.

All three young women looked up at my arrival. "What do you need?" I asked.

Susannah narrowed her eyes. "I need Hope to obey me."

The two other girls giggled, eyeing me to see what I would do.

"Hope is busy. I can help you, if you'd like." I ignored the girls. It didn't pay to give them a show. "Do you need something to eat or drink?"

As Susannah pondered my question, the front door opened, and the constable entered with Rebecca Nurse and Dorothy Good.

The entire room quieted, and my heart sank. Rebecca Nurse was one of the oldest and dearest women in Salem Village. In a time when the Half-Way Covenant had been adopted to try to draw more people into the church without all the responsibilities of a fully covenanted member, Rebecca had stood firm in her Puritan faith and become fully covenanted. She was a woman to admire—though now she was pitied.

Her thin, pale skin looked whiter than normal. She had been frail for years and had recently been ill. Her dress hung off her emaciated frame, and the circles beneath her eyes were dark and sunken. At her side, holding her hand, was four-year-old Dorothy. She had been sent to live with her father when her mother was put in the Salem gaol with her son. Now she was being brought in for questioning—and her father was nowhere in sight. What could a four-year-old understand about any of this? And why would Ann Putnam accuse her? Why would she accuse either of them? They did not fit the stereotypical qualifications for witches. They were not widowed, religiously questionable, cantankerous, or destitute.

I had heard about a legal squabble Rebecca had with the Putnams years ago, but that was the only issue I could think of. Perhaps that was the only one necessary. I'd also heard that Dorothy had bitten Ann not long ago when the little girl was being teased. Was that the cause of her accusation?

"Constable Herrick," Father said as he nodded at the newcomers. "Take the accused upstairs. I will send Mistress Eaton up to examine them for the devil's mark."

Susannah rose from the table with importance. Now that she was the mistress of the ordinary, she had been tasked with examining the accused—perhaps the only job my father had given her since their marriage. But it saddened me that I could not protect Rebecca or Dorothy from the shame.

Everyone in the room looked toward the door where Rebecca and Dorothy stood, but *I* looked at the afflicted girls. How could they sit there and watch this happen? Some whispered it was because they were servants and orphans past marrying age, seeking attention. Others said it was because the atrocities they had seen in the Indian wars had addled their brains.

It didn't matter to me. I couldn't abide either of them.

Suddenly, Mercy stood and pointed toward a corner of the room and screamed. All eyes turned to her.

"I see the specter of Goody Proctor!" she cried. "She hath come to hurt us and demand we sign the devil's book."

Mary's eyes grew large. Elizabeth Proctor was her mistress. What would happen if Goody Proctor was brought in for questioning? Would her husband John turn Mary out?

For a split second, Mary seemed to vacillate—but with all the attention on her, she had no choice. She began to cry out, as well. No one looked at Rebecca or Dorothy any longer.

People rushed to Mary and Mercy's side, trying to calm them. They writhed and screamed, shouting as if they were being pinched and pricked by needles.

I stood, motionless, unsure what to do.

Hope stepped out of the kitchen and quickly took in the scene. She walked over to Mercy and put her hand on Mercy's shoulder, her knuckles white as she pressed upon the young woman.

"Stop this," Hope said in a firm voice, silencing the whole room—including Mercy and Mary. "There is no specter. Quiet yourself, Mercy Lewis, or leave the ordinary and take your antics elsewhere."

Mercy looked up at Hope, her mouth slipping open in surprise—and my breath caught. Had Hope angered her? Would she accuse Hope next?

Slowly, a smile tilted Mercy's lips, and she began to laugh. "We must have some sport, Hope."

Several people gasped at this declaration, but Father quickly stepped in.

"Away with the accused," he said to the constable who ushered Rebecca and Dorothy up the stairs.

Susannah pressed her lips together in disapproval. She scowled at Hope and then strode to Father's side. Sidling up to him, she whispered into his ear. He nodded and looked toward Hope as Susannah left the room and walked up the stairs, presumably to examine Rebecca and Dorothy.

I followed Hope into the kitchen.

She crossed her arms and paced, anger radiating off her. "This is absurd. Those girls are taking advantage of this situation—"

Father slammed through the kitchen door, his face distorted in rage. We both jumped.

"You have no right to question the afflicted," he said, getting close to Hope. "They suffer unimaginable torments—things we cannot see or hear."

"Mercy admitted she doth this for sport," Hope said incredulously, not backing away from him. "She's lying for attention, and you believe her. The hysteria is growing because of fear, and the Putnam family is using it to their benefit. When will it end? After all their enemies are accused?"

"Hold your tongue," Father said, leaning forward until his nose was inches away from Hope's face. "You are accusing my wife's family."

"*I* am your family," Hope cried. "Yet you care little about what I think or feel."

Father breathed heavily. "You embarrass me with your disrespect, especially in front of our patrons. Leave the questioning to the elders. You are a mere girl who knows nothing."

Hope stared at him, her eyes hard. "I am a woman with a mind that God gave to me."

"Then use your mind to keep your mouth shut." Father glared at her for another heartbeat and then left the kitchen.

"I will not stop questioning the afflicted," Hope said, pushing away from the worktable to pace again. "I believe Reverend Parris's daughter was afflicted with an illness that cannot be explained—but the others have been driven by fear, attention, or revenge. Mercy Lewis is only doing this for show. You saw how she acted out there. She is a troubled young woman who loves having control. Nothing more."

I moved closer to Hope and put my arms around her. "You're afraid, too," I said as I hugged her.

She was stiff in my arms. "I'm not afraid."

"It's okay to admit your fear, Hope. All of us are afraid from time to time. It's only natural."

She shook her head and pulled back. "1692 can't touch me. I'm only here for a few more months. I won't be afraid of this place. I won't let them get to me."

I tilted my head in sympathy, thankful there was no one in the room to hear her. I spoke quietly. "1692 is a part of you, Hope, whether you like it or not. God doesn't make mistakes. He placed us here because it's supposed to be a part of us—for good or for bad. We are a product of our lives, of the people and events that shape our experiences, our personalities, even our hopes and dreams. The things we're learning here will help us in 1912."

"I'm not learning anything helpful here," she protested. "Just anger and bitterness—and what *not* to do."

"That is a valuable lesson. Learning from other people's mistakes helps us grow. Hardship deepens our faith. Nothing is wasted."

"I don't think my faith is deeper because of this place." She shook her head. "Mayhap people like you and Isaac have good hearts and desire to live pure, godly lives—but the rest struggle under unrealistic expectations and rules that no one can possibly follow."

"The rules that are hard to follow are the manmade ones," I said.

She stared at me for a long time, then said, "I wish I could understand these things as easily as you do."

"I don't always understand—I question and wonder, too. We all do."

"Why would God allow this to happen here? What's the point?" Her eyes pleaded for an answer.

Four years ago, I wanted to know the answer to Hope's question—a question I'd had since I was a child—and that was how I learned that I would accuse her of witchcraft. I'd been researching the trials to make sense of them. Once I discovered the unthinkable, I had stopped. But I knew enough to answer her.

I leaned in and whispered, "The witch trials will undermine the Puritan religion. Highly respected ministers of the faith, like Increase Mather and his son, Cotton Mather, who control every aspect of this colony, will align themselves with the magistrates and defend their decisions." I studied her. "Puritanism will begin to die after the witch trials—and laws will be enacted to protect people accused of witchcraft. It will no longer be a hanging offense."

Hope nodded slowly. "'Tis a tough price to pay, but at least something good can come of this misery."

I wouldn't tell her what else I knew about the coming witch trials. Not all of it was good, though perhaps I was wrong. Perhaps there was a reason I would accuse Hope—something I could not possibly understand yet.

The day wore on, and I grew more and more anxious to be done so Hope and I could wake up in 1912. Even though I was nervous about her flight over the Channel, I was eager to see her test-fly the new Blériot. It was the most innovative of all the aeroplanes that had come before it, and if she could fly it well, it would ease my worries.

Darkness had started to descend upon Salem Village, and the ordinary had closed for the evening. There were two travelers staying overnight, besides Rebecca and Dorothy, who were being held in the other upstairs room under guard. I had brought them a warm meal and extra blankets since the night was cold. I tried to comfort Dorothy, but she huddled alone on the floor and wouldn't let me hold her.

Hope was fixing a hem at the table. We were the only two awake. Father and Susannah had already retired for the evening, and Leah had gone to bed, pale and presumably ill.

I looked out the lone window in the kitchen as I finished wiping a dish. Fog blanketed the cold ground, swirling in the early moonlight. The trees still held their winter gloom as gnarly branches clawed toward the heavens.

A shadow crossed the yard, causing me to pause.

"What is it?" Hope asked. I hadn't realized that she'd been watching me.

"Nothing," I said, knowing my eyes were playing a trick on me. It was easy to be afraid, given the rumors about bewitchment. Everyone seemed to have a story about apparitions, specters, and wild beasts prowling in the night.

Hope joined me at the window. "Did you see something?"

I shook my head, not wanting to get caught up in the drama and hysteria.

But then a burst of panic quickened my heart. Was that why I would accuse Hope? Would I give in to the hysteria?

It couldn't be possible.

"It was nothing," I said, pushing the panicked thoughts away. "Just a shadow. Mayhap a cloud passing in front of the moon."

Another movement caught my eye, causing the hair to rise on the back of my neck. Someone—or something—was out there.

"I saw it, too," Hope said cautiously, reaching for a rolling pin.

A knock at the back door made both of us jump.

My hands shook as I turned to face the door. "Who could be here at this hour?" I whispered.

"Let's find out." Holding the rolling pin, Hope walked to the door and motioned for me to follow.

"Hope?" a male voice whispered through the door. "Grace. Are you awake? I saw the candle still burning."

"'Tis Isaac." With relief, I reached around Hope and yanked open the door, wincing when it creaked on its hinges. "Come in," I whispered with a warm smile, though my heart still pounded.

Hope backed up, clearly relieved to see Isaac, as well, though she probably wouldn't admit it.

"Are you alone?" Isaac asked quietly.

"Yes," I said, "everyone is abed."

Isaac nodded and then held up his hand, asking us to wait, and disappeared into the darkness again. Cold air filled the kitchen and made the flames flicker in the hearth.

I frowned and exchanged a look with Hope.

Within seconds, Isaac was back—and this time he was not alone.

"Ann," I said, surprised to see Ann Pudeator on Isaac's arm. "'Tis too cold to be outside. Come in."

She entered the kitchen slowly, looking around, as if to make sure we were alone. Her hands showed signs of arthritis, and I could only imagine her knees and other joints also ached in the damp night air.

I put several more logs on the fire, though it was late and Father would hate the excess. He'd probably hate to know Ann was here, as well, but we wouldn't tell him.

"Warm yourself," I told her as I pulled a chair closer to the fire.

Isaac helped her sit. She was much too old to be out this late at night, and at such a long distance from home.

"Is it true they've arrested Rebecca?" Ann asked, her brows wrinkled.

I nodded. "She's upstairs now."

Worry lines creased her eyes and mouth. "I've known Rebecca my whole life. She is no more a witch than I."

"She's under guard," I said, "or I would suggest you visit with her."

Ann lifted her hands to the fire. "I cannot stay long. Isaac was kind enough to fetch me when I sent word, but I must get home as soon as possible. If anyone knows I've come here . . ." She let the words trail off.

I pulled chairs over to the fire so we could sit with her. "What brings you all this way?"

The firelight danced in Ann's eyes as she looked from me to Hope. "I could not live with myself since your last visit. There are things you must know, and it wasn't right that I withheld them."

"You were afraid," I said, understanding. Whatever she had to tell us had brought her out on a cold, dark night. It must be very serious.

"Fear is no excuse for doing the wrong thing. In my desire to protect myself, I have deprived you of the truth. That isn't right."

I put my hand over her arthritic one. "I do not want you in harm's way."

"What I have to say will put all of us in harm's way—you most of all."

Her words sent a shiver up my spine.

"You can tell us," Hope said. "Your secrets are safe with us."

"If only that were true." Ann took a deep breath and glanced at Isaac, uncertainty on her face.

We had told Isaac what Ann said in Salem Towne, so I wasn't surprised when Hope said, "Isaac is safe. You can trust him."

He sat up straighter at Hope's comment. Did she realize the power she held over him?

Ann seemed satisfied with Hope's reassurance. "I told you

that your mother didn't die in childbirth. But I didn't tell you how she died." She glanced over her shoulder toward the stairs that went up to our private rooms. She dropped her voice and said, "Your mother was hanged in Boston."

My mouth slipped open. "Then 'tis true?" I couldn't believe it. "As a witch?"

Ann shook her head. "As a Quaker."

No one spoke as we absorbed this information.

"Our mother was Quaker?" Hope whispered in shock.

The Puritans did not tolerate other religions in the Bay Colony —but they had a special hatred for Quakers. The Quakers, like the Pilgrims, had broken away from the Church of England and promoted democracy among its people—whereas the Puritans hadn't broken away. They were still part of the Church of England, attempting to purify it from afar. Unlike the Pilgrims, the Quakers were pacifists and believed that God existed in each person. They also practiced spiritual equality between men and women, allowing women a voice in the church. This enraged the Puritan elders. At one time, a person could be sentenced to death for giving a Quaker directions from one town to the next. Other religions were banned from Massachusetts—and stayed banned. The Quakers refused to leave, however, even under penalty of death. It was no longer legal to kill them for their faith, but they were still hated.

"Yes, your mother was Quaker," Ann said. "And she was warned twice by the authorities to stop preaching. She was arrested on both occasions. When she met your father, they were so in love, she thought she could abandon her faith—and her family—and follow the Puritans. She changed her name so no one would connect her to her former life. That was when I met her. They lived in Boston when you were born, and no one knew her real identity.

"She tried to conform to the Puritan faith, but her conscience got the better of her. When you were only six months old, she began to preach under her old name again. Your father wanted to move her out of Boston and bought the land here in Salem Village to build the ordinary. But she refused to go with him and would not let him take you. This time, when they arrested her, they sentenced her to death by hanging. It was within their legal rights at the time. She pleaded for your father to save her—but he had started to build this establishment and did not want her crimes to follow him. He was angry that she had left the Puritan faith, and he knew that if he aligned himself with her beliefs, he would face ruin."

"So he let her hang?" I breathed in disgust and disbelief.

Ann nodded. "He went to Boston to retrieve you from the prison, but he refused to speak to her. He came back here and told everyone that she had died in childbirth and that you had been staying with family until he could get the ordinary built. I begged him to save her, but he threatened me for interfering. I knew if he could let his own wife die, he could do the same to me."

We were silent again as the information seeped into our hearts and minds.

Father had let our mother die without a fight, afraid people would learn that she was his wife—and he hadn't even said good-bye to her.

"No wonder he hath never wanted us to speak of her," Hope said.

"He hath been living with the guilt his whole life," I whispered.

"*If* he feels guilt." Hope shook her head. "I doubt it."

"Did her family live in Boston?" Isaac asked Ann.

"If I remember correctly," Ann said, "Tacy was from the town of Sandwich. There is a large Quaker colony there."

"Thankfully, it's no longer legal to hang a Quaker," Isaac assured us.

"No," I agreed, "but 'tis legal to hang a witch, and some Quakers are accused of witchcraft as a means to destroy them."

"Do you think her family still lives in Sandwich?" Isaac asked Ann.

"I cannot say. Their name was Howlett, I remember that much. I never spoke to Tacy's family. I only knew what she told me."

"She must have trusted you," I said. "Thank you for being a friend to her."

Ann's smile was weary, but she nodded. "Tacy was a special woman, and I'm blessed to have called her a friend. I still miss her."

"I do, too," I admitted, even though I didn't have any memories of her.

"Is there anything else you can remember?" Hope asked.

"I'm afraid that's all I know about her." Ann sighed. "I wish I knew more."

"Thank you for coming to us," I said. "It gives me hope that mayhap we can find her family and learn more about her."

"Sandwich is over eighty miles away." Hope frowned. "How will we learn if her family is still living there?"

"Let me help," Isaac offered. "After planting season, I can make a trip there on your behalf."

"You don't need to take time out of your busy life to help us," I said to Isaac. "You've already done so much."

"I want to help." His voice was serious. "I hope you'll let me."

I glanced at Hope, and she nodded.

"Of course." I smiled at Isaac, knowing how much it meant to him to help us—or rather, to help Hope.

Ann looked at both Hope and me intently, fear in her gaze. "Your father threatened my life if I ever breathed a word of your mother's story to anyone. All these years, I thought he had at least told you the truth. When I realized he hadn't, I decided I must say something. But if he learns what I've done . . ."

I took Ann's hand again. "I promise we won't tell him. You have our word."

She nodded, but the fear did not leave her eyes. "I'm afraid

I've put you and your sister at risk. If anyone knows you have ties to a Quaker—one hanged for sharing her faith—you will not be safe."

I took a deep breath and said, "None of us are safe right now. Not after they arrested Rebecca and Dorothy. If they are willing to question them, they are willing to arrest and question anyone."

As long as they weren't a Putnam.

It wasn't long before Isaac helped Ann back to his wagon. I closed the door behind them and turned to look at Hope. As I did, I noticed that the door to Leah's room was cracked open—and she stood on the other side, staring at us.

"Leah?" I stepped forward, my heart racing.

She slowly closed her door and did not say a word.

10

HOPE

It was four o'clock in the morning when I rose from my bed at the Lord Warden Hotel and went to the window to check the weather. Fog blanketed the streets, causing my heart to fall. We had waited for a week before I could test the Blériot in Hardelot, and then another week for the aeroplane to be shipped to Dover. For the past two days, a dense fog had sat thick over the Channel. But today was the last possible day I could make the flight if we wanted to arrive in Cherbourg in time to board the *Titanic*.

The hotel room was dark and silent as I began to pace. Last night, Luc and Grace had taken a ferry to Calais in case the weather improved and I could make the flight. Grace wanted to be on the field with a camera to photograph my arrival, and Luc wanted to be there to manage the press. Before he left, he had said to be ready for his phone call at four to let me know if the flight would happen this morning.

118

I glanced at the clock. It was now five minutes past four, and the phone was still silent.

As I paced and waited, anxious thoughts shifted between the flight and my life in Salem.

It had been over two weeks since we learned the truth about our mother in 1692. We had tried asking Leah what she heard or understood, but she said nothing. If Father knew Ann Pudeator had visited and told us the truth, there was no telling what might happen to her. I prayed that Leah's mutism would continue—at least in this regard.

Since it would be impossible to get away from the ordinary—and Father—long enough to travel to Sandwich, we had to wait for Isaac to go on our behalf. It wasn't like him to subvert our father's authority and look for answers that Uriah Eaton wanted to hide. It gave me a newfound respect for Isaac. I had always thought he was a rule-follower, but perhaps he bent the rules when the rules were unjust.

As for Rebecca Nurse and Dorothy Good, both had been questioned and held in the Salem gaol for further trial. Rebecca claimed innocence to witchcraft. Little Dorothy Good was another story. She confessed that her mother, Sarah Good, was, in fact, a witch. And when Susannah found a small red spot on Dorothy's hand, no bigger than a flea bite, Dorothy claimed her mother's familiar, a little yellow bird, suckled there. The magistrates were elated to have the confession and physical evidence.

I was angry. Who would take the word of a scared and suggestable four-year-old? Thinking about it made my blood boil, and I began to pace with new energy.

The phone rang, and I raced across the room to answer it. With a pounding heart, I said, "Luc? Is it time?"

"Oui."

That one word, once so foreign and strange, filled me with inexplicable feelings.

"A driver will arrive in twenty minutes to take you to the aerodrome," he continued. "The mechanics are on their way there now. It is still foggy over the Channel, but if you stick true to the compass, you will have no trouble finding Calais."

"What if I don't?" I asked, the first hint of trepidation filling my heart.

Just yesterday, Luc had shown me how to use a compass when it became clear we were running out of time. On a clear day, I should be able to see the French coastline from Dover. But with the fog, I would be flying blind. If we wanted to get to the *Titanic* in Cherbourg by tomorrow evening, a nine-hour train ride from Calais, then this was the only way.

"You have no choice," Luc said, his voice grave. "Even if you get just a few miles off course, you could be lost in the North Sea. That is not an option."

I swallowed my nerves. There was no time to be afraid. Fear clouded the mind and created trouble where there was no trouble. I was capable of this flight, and I needed to keep believing it to be true.

"Hope?"

"Yes?"

"*Je prierai pour toi.*"

"What does that mean?"

"I'll be praying for you."

He hung up, and I took a deep breath.

Everything hinged on the next few hours. My parents' orphanage, Grace's work as a journalist, Luc's faith in me—and my life in 1912.

I quickly dressed, putting on my brown flying suit with two pairs of long underwear underneath. I also wore a long wool coat, a sealskin stole, and two pairs of long gloves. Luc had warned me that it would be frigid over the water, so I was taking extra precautions.

A maid brought hot tea up to my room, as Grace had requested for me last evening before she and Luc left for Calais. I forced myself to drink it, even though it was scalding as it ran down my throat.

I hated being alone—especially now, as so many thoughts raced through my mind—but I hoped Grace and Luc had used the time on the ferry and at the hotel in Calais to get to know each other better. They had not become friends over the past two weeks, since Luc spent most of his time away from the hotel and Grace spent most of her time writing, but they had a newfound respect for each other. If that was all I could get from them, it would have to be enough.

Thirty minutes later, I arrived at the aerodrome and was surprised to find a whole crowd of people waiting for me. The *Daily Mirror* had sent representatives and movie cameras to record my historic takeoff after Luc phoned to tell them today was the day.

The aerodrome, which was simply a flying field, sat on the White Cliffs of Dover with a straight, clear shot of the Channel and Calais. There was a sense of urgency since rain was forecasted to start later that morning. The mechanics quickly wheeled the Blériot out of the hangar. It was such a frail contraption of wood, fabric, and wires.

Again, apprehension and fear wrapped around my heart, and I had to take several deep breaths to calm myself.

Dense fog covered the water. There was no wind, which would make flying easier, but it wouldn't help remove the low-lying clouds.

"Are you ready, Miss Cooper?" one of the mechanics asked as I stared at Dover Castle. Luc had told me that I needed to fix my eyes on the castle, fly over it, and head straight on to Calais.

"Yes." I nodded. "Let's go."

The mechanic knelt beside the aeroplane and allowed me to use his thigh as a step to climb onboard. It was harder to maneuver in so many layers, but I was able to make my way to the metal chair in the cockpit. The instruments and layout were a little different than I was used to, but I had familiarized myself with them and was confident in my abilities.

But what if my abilities weren't enough? I wished Grace and Luc were with me on this side of the flight. What if I didn't make it across?

I shook the thought from my head. It wasn't an option.

As I started the motor, six mechanics held the fifty-horsepower engine at bay. I wished I'd had more time to test-fly it before attempting to go over the water, but it didn't matter anymore.

The mechanics let go and dove out of the way.

I was off.

Within seconds, I was fifteen hundred feet in the air, but Dover Castle was banked in fog and hard to see from this height. I had promised the *Daily Mirror* representatives and movie men that I would fly straight over the castle, so I set my sights on it and did as promised.

Before I knew it, I was out over the water.

The wind rushed past me, giving me chills—but I smiled. Nothing made me feel more alive than flying. Behind me, the imposing White Cliffs of Dover disappeared into the fog, and I was all alone with nothing but thick, white clouds and the sound of the aeroplane for companions.

It was an eerie feeling. I was moving, but nothing around me changed. The only thing that marked my progress was the pocket watch I pulled out from time to time.

The engine sputtered castor oil and sprayed me in the face, covering my goggles. The fog was full of misting rain, adding to the trouble. I ripped off the goggles, keeping my eye on the compass, adjusting the aeroplane to stay on course. I was going sixty miles an hour, which meant I should land in Calais in twenty minutes.

Twenty short minutes felt like a lifetime.

I didn't give myself the opportunity to think about the fact that I was flying over the tempestuous English Channel or that the North Sea was just a few miles away. At this point, it was all instinct and routine. I couldn't see the water below me because of the dense fog, so I climbed to three thousand feet, hoping to get above the misting clouds. But the air was so cold up there, and the fog was still dense. After a few minutes, I decided to go lower to see if I could break through the fog closer to the water.

The visibility was better the lower I went—but a sudden jolt of turbulence rattled the aeroplane, and its tail snapped up at a steep angle. I grabbed the edges of the cockpit to keep myself from being thrown out of the aeroplane, and a rush of adrenaline coursed through me. It was like a large, invisible hand had reached out and flicked the aeroplane's tail.

I barely had time to react before the plane had righted itself again—but in that brief moment, my engine had filled with gasoline and started to sputter.

If the fuel didn't burn off the engine in time, I would go down.

Panic seized me as I tried to keep control of the aeroplane.

My mind raced with possibilities as the engine continued to sputter and the plane lost altitude. What would I do if I hit the water? The waves were treacherous. Would anyone find me before I succumbed to drowning or hypothermia?

It all happened in seconds, but it felt like an eternity as I said a prayer under my breath, trying to remain calm. My only hope was to try to land on the water and use my aeroplane as a buoy until I could be rescued.

As I watched the oncoming water and my engine continued to sputter, disappointment gripped me like a vice, sucking the air from my lungs. All I could think about was the money and time we had wasted. How would I tell Mama and Daddy that we couldn't save their orphanage? How would I pay back Luc? Or Mr. Blériot?

With no choice left, I looked over the edge of the plane, trying to find a smooth patch of water.

Seconds before my wheels touched the first wave, the gasoline burned off the engine, it stopped sputtering, and my plane started to rise again. I was so close to the waves that a spray of water hit my face, but relief overwhelmed me as I threw my head back and yelled with excitement.

Perhaps I wouldn't fail, after all.

I climbed the Blériot higher. I was so close to reaching my goal, I could feel the anticipation growing.

The aeroplane was now at about two thousand feet, and the clouds finally parted, allowing me to see the white, sandy shores of France.

My heart soared, and I briefly closed my eyes to offer a prayer of thanksgiving. I never felt closer to God than when I was in an aeroplane. Here, it didn't matter which religion was right or wrong—it was just me, God, and the sky. No one to answer to. Nothing to analyze or explain. Just a weightless peace and an assurance that I was doing what I was created to do.

And right now, I needed to find the field in Calais where Grace and Luc were waiting.

It didn't take long. There were hundreds of people waiting for my arrival. Photographers, movie cameras, reporters, and curious citizens. Louis Blériot had made the first successful flight across the English Channel just three years ago, and many other men had followed. I was the first woman to attempt the flight—and I had made it.

Joy filled my heart to bursting.

Thankfully, there was a clear path for me to land the plane. I did it with ease—almost second nature.

The first person I saw was Luc. He was grinning as he sprinted toward me. He had never looked more handsome or attractive. The sunshine made his eyes sparkle.

I removed my gloves and canvas jacket and started to climb

out of the aeroplane, but Luc reached up and put his hands around my waist, lifting me out. When he set me on my feet, we were face to face.

He shook his head and continued to grin. "*Félicitations,* Hope. You will be the most famous woman in the world when news gets out about your amazing feat." He motioned to the surging crowd. "This is just the beginning."

I couldn't contain my excitement—so I threw my arms around Luc and kissed him.

When I pulled back, I hoped to see surprise or wonder on his face—but all I saw was his unadulterated excitement.

He hadn't realized my kiss was romantic.

I didn't have time to contemplate his reaction or dwell on my disappointment because I was swarmed by cheering Frenchmen who lifted me onto their shoulders, chanting, "*Courageux! Courageux!*" Laughing, I tried to keep my balance and look over the heads of the crowd to find Grace.

She was there in the distance, behind her camera. When she saw me looking at her, she lowered the camera and ran across the field, a brilliant smile on her face.

"Let me down," I said to the men holding me. "Please!"

The second my feet hit the grass, I started to run toward Grace. My heart was pounding, and I couldn't remember being this happy before. The force of our hug took my breath away, and I felt like we were one, sharing this moment.

"Hope!" Grace cried as she held me tight. "You made it! You're alive!"

I laughed as I squeezed her back.

I had made it—and this was just the beginning.

The second part of our plan would start when we boarded the *Titanic.*

APRIL 10, 1912
CALAIS, FRANCE

I was still grinning the next day when we woke up in our hotel room in Calais.

Grace was in the single bed next to me, sound asleep. After my accomplishment over the English Channel, it had been difficult to keep my excitement contained while we were in Salem the day before. Spring had begun to bloom, but darkness still hovered over the New England village like the dead of winter.

But I wouldn't let that dim my joy—not today. Not in France.

"Grace," I said as I reached across the small space and tapped her shoulder. "Wake up."

She moaned and turned to her other side. "Let me sleep."

We'd been awake until the wee hours of the morning. Hundreds of people had heard about my flight and had come to the hotel to celebrate as only the French could. There had been laughter, cheers, dancing, and champagne. Grace's physical body still needed to recover.

But I couldn't stay in bed another second.

I dressed as quickly as I could and slipped out of the room. The hotel lobby was quiet as I went to the front desk to look for today's newspaper—and there I saw it.

L'Aviatrix américaine est la première femme à survoler la Manche.

The article was in French, but I knew what it said. *American aviatrix is the first woman to fly over the Channel.* My name was below the headline with the picture Grace had taken.

"There you are," Grace said a moment later as she found me in the lobby, her eyes still sleepy. "I called to you as you were leaving the room, but you didn't hear me."

"Look," I said, showing her the newspaper. "Your picture."

She smiled. "I wired another article to the *New York Globe* last night, and I received messages from half a dozen newspapers across America wanting me to send them articles about the flight. They're all clamoring to know more. I'll be busy writing on the ship as you wine and dine with the wealthy passengers. I've heard the Astors will be on board. John Jacob Astor is the wealthiest man in the world, and his young wife, Madeleine, is fond of aviation."

I hugged Grace, happy that I didn't have to hide my excitement here.

We returned to our room and quickly packed our bags. The train would leave at eight for Paris, where we would retrieve our luggage and then board another train for Cherbourg. We would need to be there by six in the evening to purchase tickets for the *Titanic*, which departed at exactly eight o'clock.

Luc met us in the lobby with his bag twenty minutes later. He looked just as sleepy as Grace had.

"Bonjour," he said, his languid voice stirring butterflies in my stomach. Ever since kissing him, I'd been a wreck around him—especially because he hadn't mentioned it once. How would I sit on a train for hours on end and not let him know how I felt?

We were soon at the station, and Luc paid for a private compartment.

"We don't need to travel first class," Grace said to him. "The parlor car will do fine."

"You need to write, no?" His blue-green eyes studied my sister's face.

"Yes—but I can write in the parlor car."

Luc shook his head as he accepted the tickets for our first-class compartment. "It will be quieter," he said as he motioned for us to follow him. "If anyone discovers who we are, they will not leave us alone."

The porter showed us to our compartment, with its plush, red velvet seats and generous windows to watch the passing countryside.

I took a seat next to the window, Grace sat beside me, and Luc sat across from us.

Nothing had seemed to change between them, and when I had asked if they'd had a chance to talk while in Calais, Grace had simply said no.

She quickly pulled out her travel desk and began to write as the train left the station. Luc settled back on his bench and crossed his arms, looking out the window, his thoughts far away. Soon he closed his eyes.

The only sound in our compartment was the grinding of the wheels against the rails beneath the train. So much had happened, but we'd already said a lot yesterday, so I lay my head against the window and fell into a light sleep.

When I opened my eyes again, the French countryside was passing by. Luc was awake, unguarded, sitting quietly—his gaze intent upon Grace.

I slowly sat up and looked at my sister. She was still writing diligently, lost in her work. Her brow was furrowed, tendrils of her blond hair were brushing her cheeks, and she had ink stains on her right hand. It took her a moment to notice that I had woken up, and when she did, she looked at me and smiled.

As I turned back to Luc, he was looking outside again, his emotions shuttered.

A while later, a porter knocked at the door and told us that we were approaching Paris. The train was running a little late as we pulled into Gare Saint-Lazare. We still had to return to the hotel where we'd stayed two weeks ago to retrieve our luggage, then get back to the station to board the next train at one o'clock. That left us only half an hour.

"We must rush," Luc said as he looked at the station clock. "We cannot miss the train."

Grace and I followed him through the busy station to the street outside, where he hailed a taxicab to take us to the hotel.

The Paris streets were crowded with pedestrians, omnibuses,

automobiles, carriages, and wagons. It was cool and cloudy with a light drizzle as we passed the Square Louis XVI and then followed a road that bent one way and then the next past the Palais Garnier, where the Opéra national de Paris performed. Our hotel was close to the opera house, but the minutes were ticking by, and Luc was stiff beside me. He spoke in French to the driver, who seemed to be just as anxious as Luc.

We finally arrived, and Luc spoke to the driver, who nodded and waved him inside.

"He'll wait for us," Luc said, "but we must hurry."

We left the taxi and ran into the hotel lobby. The desk clerk was busy helping another customer. Luc tried to wait patiently, but he finally interrupted them.

"*Pardon,*" he said and spoke in rapid French. The other customer didn't look pleased, but Luc seemed to communicate we were in a great hurry.

After an eternity, all the luggage was brought out to the taxi, and we were on our way back to the station. The traffic soon became so bad, we were at a standstill, and Luc was saying things under his breath in French.

I pulled out my pocket watch and my heart fell.

We only had five minutes left.

Grace glanced down at my watch, and her face revealed her disappointment.

"We won't make it," I said to Luc. "It's already too late."

"We have to try," he said. "Perhaps there is another train leaving for Cherbourg that can make it on time."

His optimism was inspiring, but it wasn't realistic.

The taxi driver helped with the luggage, but when we got to the ticket counter, the agent shook his head.

Luc's shoulders fell, and he let out a frustrated breath as he forcefully pushed away from the ticket counter. When he looked back at me, I could see his defeat. "I am sorry. We will have to find passage on another ship."

"It will be okay," I said, stepping close to him to put my hand on his arm. "I'm sorry we'll miss the *Titanic*, but it doesn't diminish my success. There will be other opportunities."

He nodded. "Oui. Of course. This is just a little setback. We won't let it stop us from our goal." He glanced at Grace and said, "I am sorry I could not make this happen."

She offered him a beautiful smile. It wasn't forced or feigned, and it communicated her respect for him. "You have done so much for us. You have nothing to be sorry about."

A weight seemed to lift from his shoulders, and he returned Grace's smile before he went back to the ticket counter to purchase our fare to Cherbourg for a later train.

I was relieved they had finally moved past their dislike of one another—yet something else pinched at my heart. Ever since I'd woken up on the train, I had observed something disquieting.

Luc looked at my sister much differently than he looked at me.

11

GRACE

APRIL 19, 1692
SALEM VILLAGE

The sun was warm upon my shoulders as I worked in the garden outside the ordinary in Salem Village. Rich, black soil moved easily beneath my fingers as my thoughts drifted to the alarming news we'd learned three days ago in 1912. It was all I had been thinking about in both paths.

The *Titanic* had struck an iceberg in the Atlantic Ocean and sunk, taking the lives of over one thousand five hundred people. We were still onboard the *Oceanic* in 1912, making our way back to New York, and that made it even more troubling. There was a somber stillness on the ship as everyone grappled with the news. The knowledge that we should have been on that ship, and that Hope, Luc, and I could have died, still left me numb. Our disappointment at not reaching the boat on time had turned to gratitude that God had protected us from a tragedy. But it had diminished coverage of Hope's flight, since all the newspapers were filled with articles about the sinking.

Sweat ran down my back as I worked the ground and planted cabbage, carrots, turnips, squash, and more. I loved the smell of the soil and the feel of the cool dirt under my fingernails. Mama said that her grandmother, Theodosia, loved to garden. Had I inherited her green thumb?

A noise brought my head up. The wind ruffled a loose tendril of my hair as I saw Father walk around the side of the ordinary with Susannah. She wore a pretty new dress she had fashioned from fabric obtained in Boston with a silk scarf and gold buttons—something that would have been frowned upon had she not been married to a man of wealth and social standing.

Father glanced toward the road and then lifted Susannah off her feet and pressed her into the corner between the back of the building and the lean-to. He kissed her long and hard.

My cheeks grew warm as I looked away, squeezing the soil beneath my hands. My stomach felt queasy. Intimacy between married couples was not only approved by Puritans but encouraged from the pulpit. Yet to do it in plain sight could fetch Father a fine or time in the gaol. It was more proof that Susannah had beguiled him. He would never put himself into such a position if he were in his right mind.

Susannah giggled as she returned Father's kisses. I didn't want to see them—or hear them—but I had nowhere to go. If I moved, they'd know I was there, so I remained absolutely still.

The back door opened, and Hope exited the ordinary. Father pulled away from Susannah, and there was an awkward silence as Hope stared at him. He left Susannah's side and pushed past Hope into the building.

Susannah lingered, a taunting smile on her face as she righted her dress and coif, then she, too, pushed past Hope and went inside.

Hope scowled at them and crossed her arms as she walked

across the yard to join me. She wore a brick-red dress with a white apron and white coif over her blond curls. Even in her simple clothing, she was beautiful. It was such a strange reality that she was one of the most celebrated women in 1912, but here she was simply a servant in her father's home. Overlooked and underappreciated. What would Father and the others say if they knew how important Hope was in a different time and place? How she had broken barriers for women everywhere? They wouldn't know how to fathom such a thing.

"They're questioning Mary Warren today," Hope said as she squatted next to me and moved some of the soil around with her finger.

Mary had been one of the afflicted girls, but she had recanted and said the others were dissembling or pretending. The afflicted girls didn't like her confession—and so they had begun to see Mary's specter attacking them. Mary had been arrested and was now facing questioning by the magistrates.

More and more people were being accused every day, including men like John Proctor and Giles Corey. The afflicted also grew in number and now encompassed older women and men—including John Indian. He had begun to have fits and saw specters that tormented him. He was brought in to testify against several of the accused, though all denied witchcraft.

I sighed. "Will you go to Mary's questioning?"

"I think we should both go."

I hadn't been to a questioning, though I had heard about them from Hope. "Why?"

"Mary Warren is the first of the afflicted girls to admit they are playacting. Don't you want to hear what she has to say? She's the only one courageous enough to stand up and put an end to this."

I knew this wouldn't be the end—but I *was* curious about Mary. "Mayhap I will go."

"Good." Hope stood and wiped the soil from her finger. She

hated working in the garden even more than doing the inside chores. I'd much rather be in the sunshine, even if it meant getting my hands dirty.

Hope continued to stand near the garden as I worked, and I sensed she had something else on her mind. I finally stopped planting the carrots and looked up at her.

"What?"

She squatted so we were eye-level. "Do you think Luc is in love with me?"

I couldn't meet her gaze because the truth would hurt her. "Why do you ask?"

"Because I kissed him."

"You kissed him?" I sat up straight. "When?"

"Right after the flight—didn't you see?"

I shook my head, shocked. "Why haven't you mentioned it before now?"

And why did it bother me that she had kissed him? It shouldn't matter to me—but for some reason, it did.

"I assumed you saw."

"Why would you kiss him in front of so many people?"

"I was overcome with the moment."

I thought back to the past few days since Hope's flight. I hadn't noticed any difference in Luc's behavior toward my sister. If anything, he seemed more reserved, quieter, more contemplative as the *Oceanic* made its way to New York.

"Has he mentioned the kiss since then?" I asked, almost afraid of the answer.

She shook her head. "Not once."

Relief surprised me, and I masked my response by wiping my hands together to remove the soil.

"What do you think it means?" she prodded.

How could I tell my sister the truth without injuring her? "If a man loves a woman, he wants to be with her, sit with her, talk to her—return her kisses if he's invited to. She's all he can think about, and he does everything in his power to be at her side." I studied her and gently said, "Luc treats you with respect and admiration, but I haven't seen anything that tells me he's in love with you."

The look on her face shifted, and she became defensive. "You're only saying that because you've never liked him. You don't want me to be in love with him."

I frowned. "That's not true—"

"I thought that you were starting to like him."

"I do like him," I said, feeling defensive, too.

"Then why would you say such horrible things?"

"You wanted the truth, so I'm giving it to you." I stood, wanting her to understand. "I don't want to discourage you— but I also don't want you to get hurt. He either loves you or he doesn't. You can't force him to care for you."

She looked down at her calloused hands, and I could see she was fighting the truth.

"Do you even know him?" I asked. "His hopes and dreams? How he feels or thinks or what he believes?"

Hope shook her head. "He doesn't open up with me about personal things."

"Then perhaps," I said quietly, "that's another sign. If he loved you, he would be willing to share those parts of himself with you."

She finally lifted her face, determination in her gaze. "I can't give up. I'm in love with him, and I want him to love me, too."

I sighed, knowing there was nothing more I could say. I didn't want to talk about her feelings for Luc or his feelings for her. I'd rather not think about it.

Instead, I said, "We should probably not speak of him here." I looked at the ordinary with a pointed glance. "You never know who is listening."

We still didn't know how much Leah had heard or understood the night Ann Pudeator visited. She didn't say a word—

not to us or anyone else. I wanted to ask others what they knew about our mother, but it was too great a risk. We would have to wait until Isaac could travel to Sandwich and see what he learned.

Hope was quiet for a moment, then walked away from me.

Would Luc ever return her feelings? And if he did, how would that change things—for all of us?

The Meeting House was so full, I could hardly breathe. There had been several questionings before now, but Mary Warren's would be the most important thus far. Since she had been an afflicted girl and was now accused of being a witch, people were curious. Would the truth come out? Would the magistrates believe Mary?

So many people had assembled that there wasn't enough room for everyone to sit. Spectators stood at the back of the room, in the balcony, and outside, peering in through the open windows.

Hope and I had come early and found spots on a bench near the front of the room, just behind the afflicted victims. John Indian was there, sitting off to the side.

The noise in the room was so great, I could barely hear Hope as she whispered in my ear with laughter, "What would they think if they saw me flying? Would they think me a witch, too?"

"Hush," I warned her. "Don't say anything you wouldn't want repeated."

I couldn't help but think about what I had read four years ago. We only had six months left in Salem—at what point was I supposed to accuse Hope? And how would it come about? I still couldn't believe it was possible. I didn't *want* to believe it was possible.

The afflicted girls sat quietly in front of us. Mary Wolcott and

Abigail Williams were knitting while Mercy Lewis, Ann Putnam, and Elizabeth Hubbard whispered in each other's ears. There were several others now, but these five led the accusations—and seemed to thrive on the attention and power.

Susannah arrived beside Father. Seats had been saved for them near the table where the magistrates, John Hathorne and Jonathan Corwin, were sitting. Reverend Parris had been appointed to take notes. Several of the Putnam family were there, as well.

After Reverend Parris led a prayer, the magistrates called Giles Corey to the stand. He was the second man to be questioned. His wife, Martha, had already stood in his place and was now in the Salem gaol awaiting her trial. Giles was coarse and angry, and he refused to put up with the absurdity of the trial. His answers made the magistrates livid, and the afflicted had such violent fits, it was hard for the magistrates to keep order.

I watched in both horror and fascination as John Indian convulsed in front of us, acting just as possessed as the young girls. What could drive anyone to such behavior—especially a grown man? Fear? Resentment? Retribution for his enslavement?

It was terrifying to watch. Their spasms and seizures looked real—and perhaps they were. Mama had told us about studying mental health in her 2001 path. The mind was a powerful thing. Could it be that the afflicted were under some kind of mental delusion that caused real fits?

Was that John's trouble? Or was he so afraid that if he wasn't one of the afflicted, he'd become one of the accused?

Eventually, the magistrates ordered Giles to be removed to the Salem gaol to await further questioning. After a short recess, they brought in Abigail Hobbs, a fourteen-year-old girl from Topsfield who had a reputation for being wild and erratic. For over a year, she had claimed that she had sold her soul to the devil. She had been in Maine during the massacres, but instead of living in fear like everyone else, she ran free in the hills around Topsfield, telling people that the devil protected her.

It was no surprise that she had been accused of witchcraft. And it was no surprise that she, like Tituba, didn't deny the charges.

The strange thing was that the afflicted showed no signs of discomfort when Abigail Hobbs was brought in. They did not have fits or spasms—even when Abigail admitted from the start that she had been wicked. Instead, the afflicted watched with quiet curiosity.

After almost an hour of incessant questions and strange confessions about her connection to the devil and his familiars, it appeared that Abigail was no longer willing to speak. Whether she was tired or bored, she decided to stop answering the questions and stared at the magistrates as if she couldn't hear them.

"I see Sarah Good's and Sarah Osborn's specters!" Mercy Lewis cried out suddenly, pointing at Abigail Hobbs. "They have jammed their fingers in Abigail's ears! They will not let her hear you."

Four of the other afflicted girls cried out the same thing, over and over, as Abigail appeared not to hear any of them.

This satisfied the magistrates, who had Abigail removed from the Meeting House.

"How awful," Ann Putnam said, shaking her head. "Poor Abigail."

"She hath suffered so," Mercy agreed.

"The poor thing," Abigail Williams crooned.

Hope turned to me, frowning. "It appears the girls are only afflicted if someone disagrees with them," she whispered louder than necessary.

Mercy skewered Hope with a glare that would have frightened anyone but Hope.

I pressed my hand on Hope's arm to silence her.

"The court will now call Mary Warren," Magistrate Hathorne said.

Immediately, the afflicted began to writhe and spasm—John included. Several of the girls cried out their alarm, claiming several specters entered the room with Mary.

Mary's face was downcast and pale. She glanced up at the afflicted and then quickly looked down again. Her employers, John and Elizabeth Proctor, had already been questioned and were sitting in the Boston prison awaiting their trials because the Salem gaol had run out of room.

As soon as Mary was standing before the magistrates, John Hathorne demanded, "What do you say for yourself? Are you guilty or not?"

"I am innocent," Mary claimed.

"You were a little while ago an afflicted person. Now you are an afflicter. How comes this to pass?"

"I look up to God and take it to be a great mercy of God."

"What? Do you take it to be a great mercy to afflict others?"

Mary's eyes opened wide at the accusation, and she shook her head, but Elizabeth Hubbard quickly stood up to testify that after Mary recovered from her afflictions, she said that the afflicted persons dissembled. As soon as she said that, all the afflicted people in the Meeting House, and a couple more who had not yet been afflicted, began to convulse and cry out. The room was in such turmoil, the magistrate struggled to gain control.

Mary wrung her hands and looked like she might vomit. All the color drained from her face, and she crumpled to the floor. The girls started to claim that the Proctors' specters had struck her down to prevent her from confessing, and Mary began to writhe on the ground, unable to hear, see, or speak.

Hope reached for my hand and held it tight as we watched. My pulse was racing. The spectacle was so unimaginable. Eventually, Mary began to cry out that she was sorry and asked God to save her. As soon as she was on her feet, she fainted again. Eventually, the magistrates had her carried out of the Meeting House to recover.

"We will take an adjournment," Magistrate Corwin said as he stood. "We will reconvene in one hour."

Father and Susannah rose and went to the magistrates. No doubt many of the people in the Meeting House would remove to the ordinary for their midday meal.

"Come," I said to Hope. "We will be busy."

We wound our way out of the Meeting House, through the crowd that had gathered around Mary Warren, and made our way back home.

Hope's hands were balled into fists at her sides. "'Tis obvious what's happening," she said with a burst of anger. "If you confess and agree with the afflicted, you are safe. But if you deny their charges and accuse them of falsehoods, you will be punished. Those girls hold all the power, and the magistrates are allowing it out of fear."

"You must keep your thoughts to yourself," I said, leaning close to her.

"I cannot." She shook her head. "I can't stand back and watch this happen."

"You must. We cannot stop this, Hope. You know that. Not only because we have knowledge of the future—but because no one would listen to us. We'll only make matters worse."

"I hate this place," she spat out, kicking a clod of dirt on the road. "Every last bit of it. I want nothing more than to be free to fly away from here and never look back."

Noise from behind us made me pause—my heart in my throat. Who had come up behind us, and what had they heard?

I turned and found Isaac standing not four feet away. He stared at Hope, a strange look on his face. Hope also turned, her red skirts swirling about her legs, her brown eyes bright with passion as the wind ruffled tendrils of her hair.

Hope and Isaac stared at each other for several long moments until I finally said, "Did you come from the Meeting House?"

Isaac nodded but kept his gaze locked on Hope. She stared back at him.

"You do not mean what you say," he said to her.

"What?" she asked. "That I hate this place? I do."

"Do not speak of flying, Hope. It will get you nothing but the end of a noose."

"I don't care," she said, defiantly. "It would hasten my departure from here."

Horror and confusion passed over Isaac's face. He shook his head. "You don't mean that."

I stepped forward, giving Hope a glare before turning to Isaac. "Hope is dramatic and passionate. You know that about her. She's only upset about the questioning."

"She's also foolish to speak such things." He looked over my shoulder at my sister, his gaze penetrating. "You don't mean them."

Hope let out a frustrated breath. "Of course not. I'm sorry, Isaac."

I turned, surprised that she would apologize. Hope rarely apologized.

Isaac nodded, though he didn't look relieved.

"Come," I said to them. "The whole village will soon be at the ordinary, and we will need to feed them." Thankfully, Leah had stayed behind to mind the food I prepared earlier in the day for this very reason.

We would be busy, but that was the least of my worries.

Father and Susannah were not far behind Isaac—and I couldn't help but wonder if they had heard Hope's talk of flying or her conversation with Isaac, as well.

12

HOPE

MAY 12, 1912
NEW YORK CITY

The applause was deafening as I stood in front of an audience at the Globe Theatre in New York. The last time I was on this stage, I had been playing a minor role in the musical *The Slim Princess*. This time, I was the main attraction. After hearing about my success over the English Channel, the manager of the Globe asked me to return and speak about my flight.

The theater had sold out.

The stage lights were bright and warm, but I wouldn't trade this spot for anything in the world. I missed the stage—though I would never give up flying now. It was a part of me. The most exciting thing I'd ever done.

With one final wave, I left the stage as the manager gave me a handshake and then bid the audience farewell.

Grace was waiting for me with a wide smile in the dim backstage. "The audience loved you."

I returned her smile. "And I loved them, too."

A stagehand brought my evening coat, and the manager handed me a substantial check that would be sent to Mama and Daddy. Ever since returning to New York, I had been making appearances all over the city. With my earnings and the money Grace had received for her articles, combined with the last of our parents' savings, we'd come up with just enough for the first payment on the orphanage.

But this was my last scheduled talk. I had several exhibitions planned for the summer, and I hoped to make money from contest winnings, but there was no guarantee. And I had other expenses to consider—like the aeroplane I had ordered from Blériot that would be shipped to me at the end of June.

The second half of the payment for the orphanage was looming.

"What do you think about going to Delmonico's?" I asked Grace as we headed for the stage door. "I'm starving."

She yawned, putting her hand over her mouth. "It's almost ten o'clock, and we shouldn't waste what precious money we have on eating out."

"I don't want to go to bed yet—and I have a little extra set aside." Delmonico's was something I never wanted to give up, no matter how much it cost.

But really, I just didn't want to go back to Salem. There was nothing there, except chaos and heartbreak. Dozens of people now stood accused—including Reverend George Burroughs. He had been a pastor in Salem Village several years before and was being accused by several of the afflicted girls of being the ringleader of the witches. There were claims, from several afflicted people, that he led massive gatherings of hundreds of witches in Reverend Parris's field.

He also owed a large debt of money to the Putnams.

The worst news had come yesterday, though.

Mary Warren was brought back to be examined after a

month in the Salem gaol, and this time she had new people to accuse. Including Ann Pudeator.

Mary didn't even know Ann—and we couldn't help but wonder why she had been accused. Had Father discovered that Ann visited us? Had Leah said something after all? Or had Ann been accused because she was a widow and a healer?

"I don't want to go to bed, either," Grace said to me, stepping through the stage door out onto the street. "But we can't avoid Salem forever."

I followed her out the door and then put my hand on her arm to still her comment. "It's Luc."

Grace glanced in the direction I was looking.

Luc was waiting just outside the stage door. Since returning to New York, he had gone back to teaching aviation and working with Glenn Curtiss. We had not seen him in over a week and rarely spoke about him. I didn't want to repeat the conversation we'd had while Grace gardened, especially because I couldn't deny her comments. Luc did not behave like a man in love with me—yet he was here now. That had to mean something.

"Bonjour," he said, a smile on his handsome face as he looked from me to Grace.

"Bonjour." I couldn't hide the pleasure from my voice. "I didn't expect to see you here."

"I have exciting news."

The street glowed from the Broadway lights. Well-dressed people walked past, some glancing in our direction, a few whispering as if they recognized us, but no one stopped.

What news would bring Luc all the way to the Globe Theatre? It must be very good.

"What is it?"

A group of people stopped, and a lady in a beautiful fur coat looked between me and Grace. "Is one of you Hope Cooper? The aviator?"

I nodded and smiled, though I didn't want to be interrupted

now. Being famous had taken a toll over the past month, and I finally understood how Luc felt when he was bombarded by fans.

The lady's eyes opened wide, and she grasped my hand, tugging me toward her. "How wonderful! No one will believe I've met you."

I gently pulled my hand back, and Luc stepped close to me, wrapping his arm through mine before offering his other arm to Grace.

"Have a good evening," he said to the group as he began to escort Grace and I down the street. "Can we go somewhere to talk?" he asked us once we'd left the group behind.

"We were planning to go to Delmonico's," I said, trying to keep up with him. "Would you like to join us?"

"I would enjoy that."

"I won't be going," Grace told him.

Luc turned to her, disappointment in his voice. "I had hoped to speak to you, as well."

I waited, torn because I wanted Grace to come yet I longed to be alone with Luc.

She shook her head. "I'll let Hope tell me later."

"Is there nothing I can do to convince you?" he asked.

"I'm afraid not."

Reluctantly, he hailed a taxicab for her, though she protested and said she could walk. He won the debate, and after she got inside, his gaze followed the cab.

I slipped my arm through his again. "Can you tell me the good news now? Or must I wait for Delmonico's?"

He put his free hand over mine, his excitement returning as his focus shifted back to me. "You must wait."

It didn't take us long to reach Delmonico's. The opulent restaurant was the place to see and be seen by the upper crust. Rich wallpaper adorned the walls, thick trim graced the doors and windows, and crisp white tablecloths draped to the floor.

The maître d' showed us to a private table in the corner. People looked our way, commenting amongst themselves. Whether they knew me or Luc or us both—it didn't matter. Delmonico's was filled with rich and famous people, and no one bothered each other. Luc could relax, and we would have privacy for our talk.

After the waiter took our order, I leaned forward, smiling. "What is this good news?"

He studied me. "You have an offer from a sponsor."

That was the good news? I leaned back, deflated. There had been several sponsorship offers. Different companies asked me to endorse their products, wear their logos, or agree to be on advertisements. I had said yes to some of them, though they didn't pay as well as speaking or flying engagements.

"It's more than a sponsorship," Luc said, his eyes animated. "William Randolph Hearst has offered a fifty-thousand-dollar prize to the first person who can fly from New York to Los Angeles in thirty days or less. Armour and Company approached me, since they heard that I was your business manager for the Channel flight, and asked if you would be interested in attempting the cross-country trip. They are offering to sponsor you if you agree to paint the logo of their new grape soda, Vin Fiz, on the aeroplane. The flight will require a large support team, so they have agreed to charter a three-car train to follow you on your journey. They would like the press to go along—so I thought perhaps Grace would like to go. And your parents, too, if you want."

My head was spinning, so I put my hand on his arm to stop him. All I could think about was the first thing he had said. "A fifty-*thousand*-dollar prize?"

Luc nodded. "And Armour and Company's president has said that you will get every penny, if you make the flight in thirty days."

I wasn't even sure I knew who Armour and Company was—

but there was another pressing question on my mind. "And if I don't make it in thirty days?"

"They'll still sponsor your flight, since it will bring awareness to Vin Fiz. You might not make any money, but at least you won't lose any."

I put my hands to my head, thinking through the possibilities. Excitement and nervous energy buzzed through me. "And my parents?"

"They could come with you on the train. Grace could write articles about the flight."

I nodded slowly, but then I looked up and met his gaze. "And you? Will you come?"

He studied me. "Would you like me to come?"

My heart soared, and I nodded. "Yes—very much." I went on quickly. "I know you would have to give up your own flying to come with me, so you could serve as my business manager again. And I will share fifteen percent of my earnings—if that's enough."

"Oui." He smiled. "I would do it for free."

I shook my head, wanting to take his hand, but uncertain. He was kind and thoughtful, but he never reached out to me. I couldn't tell if he was helping me because he was furthering aviation—or if his feelings went deeper.

A little voice whispered in my heart that if he did love me, I would know by now—but it sounded an awful lot like Grace's voice, so I pushed it away.

"You could attempt the flight and try for the money yourself," I said. "Why are you letting me do it?"

"You are the one they asked." The waiter brought our meals, and when he left, Luc said to me, "Will you agree?"

I wanted to say yes without hesitation—but I needed to speak to Grace and see if she would come with me. I didn't want to make the trip to California without her.

"I will let you know after I speak to Grace."

At the sound of my sister's name, he looked down at his plate. "Ah, oui." He sighed. "Grace."

"You said—" I paused, confused. Hadn't he suggested that she should come along? "Do you still not like her?"

He looked up quickly, frowning.

I was surprised to realize that part of me wanted him to agree and tell me he did not like her. But I remembered the way he had regarded her on the train to Paris and how he had watched her leave in the taxicab tonight. I wanted to be mistaken about those looks. After all, he hadn't told Grace he cared for her—hadn't pursued her or sought out her company since we'd returned to New York.

"Why do you think I dislike her?" he asked.

"You've been at odds with her from the beginning."

Luc shook his head as he stared down at his plate. "Just because we've been at odds does not mean I dislike her."

"Then why do you seem upset that I want to talk to her before committing to this trip? Isn't that what you suggested from the beginning? That she come along to listen to the offer?"

"Oui." He nodded as he smiled—though there was something in his gaze that I couldn't identify. "Do not mind me. Ask Grace and then let me know what you decide."

I worried my bottom lip as he began to eat his filet mignon. Did I really want Grace on the trip, after all?

It wasn't quite midnight as I walked through the door of the stylish Hotel Victoria in the heart of the theater district with both excitement and trepidation. The hotel boasted two entrances, one on Fifth Avenue and one on Twenty-Seventh Street. It had recently been redecorated and advertised rooms with and without private baths. With our combined incomes, we'd been able to afford a room—but there was little left this week for the rent. Something foremost on my mind.

I took the elevator up to the fifth floor and walked down the hall to our apartment, wanting to talk to Grace about the flight—and not wanting to tell her at the same time.

I opened the door into our apartment and took off my coat and hat. The main room was both a sitting room and a dining room with a little kitchenette. Three doors fanned out from the main room. Two bedrooms and a bathroom.

Grace appeared, wearing a nightgown and hugging her robe around her middle. "Well? What's the good news?"

She looked so excited and happy for me—and I knew that even if Luc cared for her, I had nothing to worry about. She would never return his affection. Not only because she hadn't liked him from the start, but because she knew I loved him.

There was no reason not to invite her.

"I was offered a sponsorship, with the possibility of making fifty thousand dollars."

Grace's mouth fell open as she stared at me. "Fifty thousand dollars?"

It was an extraordinary amount of money—enough to retire on and live comfortably for the rest of my life even after giving a portion of it to Mama and Daddy for the orphanage.

"What do you have to do for fifty thousand?" she asked.

"That's the hard part—but I can do it." I quickly laid out the stipulations for the prize money.

Grace didn't speak for a moment, her frown deepening. "A cross-country flight would be dangerous, Hope."

"No more dangerous than any other flying."

She pursed her lips, and I knew that look. She was formulating her argument.

"And I want you and Mama and Daddy to come, too," I said. "You can come as a *Globe* correspondent. You'll travel in style on the train, and we can spend time in California. You

149

can write articles about my flight and about the states we travel through. The opportunities are endless."

She shook her head. "I don't know . . ."

"Please." I took her hands. I would go without her, but I didn't want to.

"When?"

"I'm not sure. It will take some time to work out the details."

"What if someone else tries it first and beats you to the fifty thousand?"

I hadn't considered that, but there was nothing I could do about it. "Then we'll look for another opportunity—but I won't worry about that now. I'll know more after Luc speaks to the sponsors."

Grace frowned. "Luc is coming?"

I nodded, secretly happy to hear the displeasure in her voice. "He's going to be my business manager again. Will you come?"

"I don't think it's a good idea—"

"Just think how much this would help Mama and Daddy. They would never have to worry about the orphanage again."

Guilt still plagued her over the situation, so when she sighed, I knew I had won.

"Thank you," I said, hugging her, relieved she would say yes—despite my concerns about Luc's feelings. "I didn't want to do it without you."

"I'm not being entirely selfless. I think the *Globe* would be interested in sending me along for the journey. It will help my career as much as it will help yours."

"See? We both win."

"*And*," she added, "I love the idea of inviting Mama and Daddy. They'll enjoy being there with us."

"I'll still have time before the cross-country flight to participate in air shows and compete for prize money."

"We need to get to bed," Grace said as she stood.

"Why have you been so eager to return to Salem lately?"

"Each day I hope Isaac will arrive with news of our mother's family."

Was that the only reason she was eager to see Isaac again? Though she couldn't be with him after we left 1692, what would it hurt if she had his love until then?

I had treated Isaac poorly, hoping he would leave us alone—but perhaps I could be more thoughtful around him and encourage him to shift his attention to Grace.

It was the least I could do for my sister.

13

GRACE

JUNE 10, 1692
SALEM VILLAGE

Everything about today was somber. The weather, with gray clouds and cool temperatures. The ordinary, which had returned to its regular flow of customers since the grand jury had convened in Salem Towne and most of the accused were now in prison there. And my heart, which was heavy with the knowledge that the first person was being hanged on Gallows Hill this morning.

I stayed in the kitchen for most of the day, not wanting to hear the rumors and gossip in the dining room. I had baked all morning, and now our larder was full of pies, breads, cakes, and doughnuts. It was the only way I knew to keep my mind and hands occupied while Hope cleaned upstairs.

"'Tis done," Susannah said as she entered the kitchen. She removed her steeple-crowned hat, having just returned from Salem Towne to watch the hanging. "The witch is dead."

I swallowed the bile that rose in my throat and looked away from the gleam of triumph in Susannah's eyes.

"What say you?" Susannah asked as she held her hat and stared at me. "Did you wish her to live and continue tormenting the afflicted?"

I had learned to guard my words, knowing that anything could be taken out of context or used against me, especially with Susannah's accusations about my mother hanging over my head. "I wish that none of this had happened."

"Bridget Bishop hath been a plague on this community for years." Susannah took one of the sweet biscuits I had made earlier that morning and began to nibble on it. "She should have been convicted and hanged years ago when she was first accused, and mayhap none of this would have happened, as you said."

I was preparing pottage for supper and had a small mound of root vegetables on the cutting board. I continued to cut the carrots, using my chore as an excuse not to engage with Susannah.

The testimonies and evidence against Bridget Bishop were ludicrous—no matter how long she had been a quarrelsome woman in the community.

A new form of physical evidence had been brought into the proceedings called the touch test. When one of the afflicted was in a state of agitation, the court would order the accused—in this case, Bridget—to touch them. If the touch calmed the afflicted person, it meant that Bridget had power over them—thus proving she was a witch.

Worse, the afflicted were now showing physical signs of torture. Bite marks, bruises, and pins stuck into their skin started to miraculously appear in court. Even John Indian cried out with bite marks on his body during questionings.

I recalled the words of the magistrates in the ordinary months ago.

"It will be hard to convince a jury without physical evidence,"

Magistrate Corwin had said to John Hathorne and Father. But Hathorne had replied, "*Do not fear. We will uncover the devil in each of them and have an abundance of evidence for the jury when the time comes.*"

They were so convinced that the devil was at work in the village that they were willing to see what they wanted to see. They wanted to rid witchcraft from New England and truly believed they had found the center of activity. In their minds, if they could purify the village, no matter how long it took, they might eradicate witchcraft once and for all.

"Goodman Abbott hath not been here for several days," Susannah said as she continued to nibble the biscuit, changing the subject.

What could I say? Isaac *hadn't* been here, which made me wonder if he was in Sandwich. His spring planting would be done by now, and at any moment I anticipated his return. Would he have news of our mother?

"I haven't discerned whether his interest lies in you or in Hope."

I finally looked up at Susannah, meeting her calculating gaze. Was she trying to befriend me? Gossiping like she would with one of her friends or cousins? Or was she trying to use me to get information?

"And I haven't figured out whether you're in love with him or not," she continued.

"Isaac is an old friend," I said with a shrug, trying to be nonchalant. "He's very dear to both Hope and me."

"Men and women cannot be friends," she retorted. "One or the other is usually in love."

I wanted to deny her comment—but it was true. At least in this case.

Susannah leaned forward and said, "I think *you* are in love with Isaac." A half smile tilted her lips. "I know how you can win him over. The same way I won your father's hand."

Her words jarred me, so I moved away to retrieve the large

pot I would need to make the stew. "I don't want to win Isaac," I said, trying to make it obvious that I didn't want her advice.

Where was Hope? She'd gone upstairs at least an hour ago. If she were here, Susannah wouldn't be bothering me. The two rarely stayed in the same room together.

"You lie." Susannah chuckled as she brushed the crumbs from her hands onto my worktable. "Get Isaac alone and *show* him you love him. Do whatever it takes to secure his offer of marriage. No man can refuse physical attention—especially if he believes it will continue once the marriage vows are spoken." That smile of hers returned as she laid her hand on her womb in a motherly gesture.

I briefly closed my eyes as I grasped the handle of the pot and let out a breath.

"There will be a babe come December," she continued. "I pray a male heir to carry on Uriah's name and business."

Susannah was going to have a baby—my sibling. At the age of twenty-four, I hadn't expected to have another brother or sister. But I wouldn't be here when the child was born, so it mattered little to me.

"If Isaac is not to your liking," she said, "I know of other men who would be interested in your hand. I can arrange things if you'd like. You're old but not beyond child-bearing years."

"What would you do if we married and left the ordinary?" Hope asked from the stairs leading up to our rooms. She paused, ice in her gaze as she stared at Susannah. "Who would cook and clean for you?"

Susannah's shoulders stiffened at Hope's arrival, and she lifted her chin. "Leah doth a fine job, and there are others your father can hire, girls and boys who need a home and work."

"Leah." Hope practically snorted. "She's a hard worker, but I scarcely think she could manage this ordinary. One must be able to speak to customers."

Susannah moved closer to Hope, her eyes narrowing. "Leah

and I have grown much closer than you realize. She confides in me—talks to me all the time."

"You lie," Hope said, though I could tell she was trying to gauge whether Susannah was bluffing. "Leah speaks to no one."

One corner of Susannah's lips rose, and she shook her head. "You haven't realized yet the power I hold over this house. Or mayhap you have, and you're lying to yourself. A few well-placed trinkets and kind words are all it took for Leah to start speaking to me."

Susannah turned and looked at me near the worktable. "You'll both be surprised to learn what Leah hath told me—though I'm sure you can guess. Time will tell how I might use the information to my benefit."

With that, she left the kitchen.

Hope scowled as she came down the rest of the steps and dropped her cleaning bucket and rags in the corner of the kitchen. "If anyone is a witch, 'tis her."

"Hope," I said in a warning voice, "she's pregnant."

Hope's eyes widened, and then she rolled them. "Another thing she can hold over Father."

"She has plenty already. Do you believe Leah has spoken to her?"

"No." Hope shook her head adamantly. "She's only bluffing to control us with fear."

"I pray you're right." I handed her a plate with a slice of dried apple pie. "Will you take this to Father? He's in the dining room."

Without a word, Hope took the plate from me and left the kitchen.

I began to assemble the stew and was lost in the work when Hope reappeared.

"Father is speaking with Sarah Churchill." She set down a cup harder than necessary. "Why is Sarah here? And why is she speaking with Father?"

I wiped my hands on my apron and left the kitchen to see for myself. As surreptitiously as possible, I peeked around the door and saw Sarah Churchill sitting at a table in the corner with Father. Susannah had joined them. They were speaking in low tones as Father passed a coin to Sarah, who nodded.

Quickly, I went back into the kitchen before they saw me.

Sarah was in her early twenties and was another refugee from Maine. She had been working for George Jacobs, Sr., when she had been overcome with spasms and torments. Goodman Jacobs had reportedly beat the affliction out of her, and she had recovered. Just like Mary Warren, the afflicted girls had then turned on Sarah and accused her of witchcraft. And just like Mary, Sarah had a change of heart and became afflicted again—this time accusing Goodman Jacobs of being a witch.

What was she doing with Father? And why had he given her money?

"I don't like this," Hope said as she shook her head.

"Nor I, especially after what Susannah said about Leah." Unlike Hope, I wasn't so sure that Susannah was lying.

Leah had said nothing to Hope or I since the night Ann Pudeator had come—but that didn't mean she wasn't talking to Susannah or Father. Ann had been arrested once and questioned, then let go because of lack of evidence.

I prayed she wouldn't be arrested again.

Evening had fallen, and with it, a storm had arrived, shaking the windows in the ordinary. The taproom was full of people who had come to get the latest news about Bridget Bishop's hanging. John was back, pouring drinks and telling everyone what he knew about the grand jury trials. He had been called as a witness in several of the cases. His wife, Tituba, was being held in the Boston prison, and there was no talk about her going to trial yet. Only those who claimed innocence were being tried. Those, like Tituba and Abigail Hobbs, who admitted to their allegiance with the devil, were left alone in the gaol. It appeared the magistrates believed they could rehabilitate those who were willing to confess and were not as concerned with them as they were with those they believed to be guilty and lying about their innocence.

I stayed in the kitchen, sewing a torn seam in one of my aprons, since my other work was done for the day. The food had been served, the pots and pans and dishes had been washed, and I would not be needed again tonight. Leah was in the taproom, helping John.

Hope sat near the hearth, reading her Bible, a contemplative look on her face. Despite all the authoritarian rules, the elders encouraged everyone to read the Bible for themselves. There was no other time in history with a better literacy rate than in Puritan Massachusetts for that very reason.

I loved that Hope was searching for answers, trying to understand. But I worried that she was floundering, like a wave tossed in the ocean, uncertain what to believe. If I knew anything about the nature of God, it was that He was a solid rock, a firm foundation to build upon. I hoped she would gain that same understanding. I longed to ask if she wanted to talk about her questions, but I didn't know if I had the answers she needed. Her journey with God was unique and personal—and unlike my Puritan elders, I did not think I could force her to accept what I believed.

The wind picked up, howling like a wild animal around the eaves of the ordinary. I glanced out the window and shivered, grateful for the safety and warmth of our little kitchen— though some of the afflicted had told Susannah that there were specters all around the ordinary. One of the local boys had even tried to defend Abigail Williams when she came to visit Susannah, drawing his rapier to attack the specter of George

Burroughs in the taproom. It was getting harder and harder to believe the whole thing was foolishness. Though I knew some were using the witch trials for nefarious reasons, there were others who were genuinely plagued by mental and emotional turmoil.

A light rapping sounded at the back door, causing both Hope and I to glance up.

I set my sewing aside and rose on unsteady legs. I had been hoping and praying that Isaac would return. Was this him now?

Opening the door, I found him standing in the pouring rain, his clothing soaked through and his hat misshapen. He removed it and placed it over his chest—and he'd never looked dearer to me than in that moment. His eyes shone with warmth, even if he was freezing.

"How do you fare, Grace?" he asked with a broad smile.

"I am happy now." I pulled him into the warm kitchen, shaking my head. "Why have you come on a night such as this?"

"To bring good cheer."

Hope rose, setting her Bible on the chair, a smile on her lips.

"Good evening, Hope," Isaac said, nodding in her direction.

"Good evening," she responded, giving him her full attention.

It was the first time in years that Hope had seemed happy about Isaac's appearance. Both he and I paused for a second, and I suspected that he noticed the change, too.

"Here," Hope said as she moved her Bible to the worktable and pushed her high-backed chair closer to the fire. "Warm yourself while I get you something to eat and drink."

Isaac took a seat on the chair. He watched as she went about the work of preparing a meal for him, pleasure on his face.

I stood back for a moment, frowning slightly. What had changed? Why was Hope so attentive to our old friend? It was I who usually waited on him.

I grabbed a linen cloth for him to towel off his hands and

face, though he would have to sit in his wet clothes until he could get home to change.

He took the cloth and wiped his face before saying, "I have just now returned from Sandwich with news that will encourage you."

Hope paused and turned from the plate she was preparing—her gaze catching mine.

I swallowed the nerves that bubbled up as I pulled a chair nearer the fire to sit beside him. "And?"

He glanced at Hope. "I'll wait until you're both ready."

Hope finished the plate and poured a cup of mulled cider for him before joining us at the hearth. She handed the meal to him and pulled a chair over for herself.

"What did you learn?" she asked, leaning in, speaking in hushed tones.

He set his cup on the floor and balanced the plate on his lap. When he met my gaze, and then Hope's, he smiled. "Your mother's family is alive and well—and there are many of them."

I briefly closed my eyes as I leaned back in my chair, thanking God that we might have answers. Finally.

"I met your mother's sister, Pricilla Baker, and she was eager to learn about you both. She said that all these years, she hath wondered where you were."

"She didn't know our father?" I frowned. "How could that be?"

Isaac shrugged and shook his head. He hadn't touched the food on his plate yet.

"Are they still Quakers?" Hope asked.

"Yes. The whole family, as far as I can tell." He slipped his hand under his doublet and pulled out an envelope. "Your aunt sent this letter for you."

He wasn't sure who to hand it to, so I took it.

"They are eager to meet you," Isaac continued. "I'm sure your aunt will tell you everything in her letter."

Hope rose from her chair and came to stand behind me as I broke open the seal. Isaac began to eat his meal as I gingerly unfolded the damp piece of paper, my heart beating so fast that I put my hand over my chest.

"Shall I read it out loud?" I asked Hope.

"No. I don't want anyone to hear. I can read it from here."

I lifted the paper to the light from the fire so we could both read.

Dearly Beloved Girls,

I cannot tell ye how surprised and pleased I am that Goodman Abbott hath brought word that ye live. It is a long-held prayer answered, and we are giving glory to God Almighty for this blessing. I am certain ye have a lot of questions, and I pray I can answer them. But I am afraid I cannot say everything I want in this letter.

My desire is that ye know that thou art loved and thought of often by everyone in our family. When Tacy married, she left our lives completely. We did not know who she had married or where she had gone, and when she came back to us, with ye in hand, we were so happy to see her, we did not demand answers she was unwilling to give.

Ye cannot imagine our sorrow when Tacy was hanged in Boston, nor our mourning when we learned that her husband had taken ye away. We had no right to claim ye, and no way to know where ye had gone.

Ye can imagine that we have many questions, as well. Questions I cannot ask in this letter. I have spoken to Goodman Abbott and have arranged a time to come to Salem Village. Ye have a cousin who lives in Salem Towne, though she hath left our family much like Tacy did, and we have not spoken to her in two years. I long to see all my nieces when I come, so I shall be in touch

*with Goodman Abbott as the day draws near. We will not
tell ye the time since we understand the danger besetting
ye. When the day comes, Goodman Abbott will see that
we are reunited.*

*Pray, thank Goodman Abbott for his loving kindness.
If it had not been for him, I am not sure we would know
if ye were still alive. He is a truly good man.*

*With all my love,
Aunt Pricilla*

I lowered the letter, but Hope must not have been done, because she took it out of my hands and brought it to her chair on the other side of Isaac. When she finished, she looked up at me, and then at Isaac.

"Thank you," she said, laying her hand on his arm. "This means so much to Grace and me."

He put his hand over hers, warmth in his gaze. "I was happy to meet your mother's kin. They are a pleasing family—you look like them."

Hope smiled as she removed her hand.

"I think we should burn the letter," I told her. "It wouldn't do if someone found it."

Nodding, she leaned forward and put the letter into the flames. "Is there nothing more you can tell us?" she asked Isaac.

He shook his head. "I fear not. Pricilla and I agreed that it would be best for you not to know the hour of her arrival. I will come for you on that day, and you can meet at my home."

"We are grateful for your help," I told him. "If there is anything we can do for you, please let us know."

He moved his leftover stew around his plate with the fork, then looked up at me. "I require nothing from you."

When he looked at Hope, his expression changed, and the longing in his gaze was so keen, so heartbreaking, I rose from my chair to busy myself with gathering more wood for the fire.

My pulse thrummed as I waited for him to speak, but silence filled the room. When I finally looked back, he was handing his empty plate to Hope.

"Thank you for the food. It was delicious," he said as he lifted his cup and drank the cider.

"Grace prepared it." She smiled at me. "She's the best cook in the colony."

Isaac glanced my way. "Thank you, Grace." He stood. "I must return home and change out of these wet clothes."

He said farewell and left the ordinary, walking through the rain and darkness to his horse, tethered nearby.

I closed the door and turned to Hope. "What was that?"

She brought Isaac's plate and cup to the bucket of water on the worktable to rinse them. "What?"

"Your behavior toward Isaac—you were kind."

She frowned as she wiped the plate with a linen rag. "I'm not usually kind?"

"Hope." I stood with my hands on the back of the chair I had been sitting in. "You know what I mean."

She set the plate and cup on the worktable and turned to me, leaning against it. After sighing, she said, "I realized that I've been unfair to Isaac. I have no reason to treat him poorly."

"What brought this realization about?"

She lifted a shoulder and moved her chair back to the table. "A lot of things."

"Have your feelings toward him changed?" I held my breath, wondering what she was thinking.

"I do not love him, if that's what you mean. But we have such little time left here. Why continue to be unkind to someone who has been a good friend?"

I nodded, though I was still leery of her motive. I wasn't sure what had caused Hope's change of heart, but I prayed she would continue being thoughtful toward him. He deserved all the kindness we could give him.

If it wasn't for him, we wouldn't know our mother's name or her family. We wouldn't know that she had been hanged for being a Quaker and *not* for being accused of witchcraft.

And soon we would know much more.

14

HOPE

"Are you sure you don't want a ride in my new aeroplane?" I asked Grace for the third time that day.

"If God had intended for me to fly," Grace said as she shaded her eyes to watch Luc complete a figure eight in the Boston Air Meet, "He would have given me wings."

"That's ridiculous." I rolled my eyes. "He didn't give us gills, yet humans have been swimming since the dawn of time."

She opened her mouth with a retort but closed it and gave me a look that said she had no desire to keep arguing.

Because I was right.

I smiled and returned my gaze to the brilliant blue sky where Luc was entertaining the audience. Over five thousand spectators had come out to the airfield to see the show, and it was in its fourth and final day.

It was estimated that in just two years over seventeen million

165

people had watched Luc fly. He had performed tricks over Niagara Falls, broken and maintained the world's altitude record several times, and perfected a nosedive recovery from three thousand feet in the air. The last of his tricks had brought him worldwide fame. Several other pilots had died attempting the same trick, though Luc had never had trouble performing it for the crowds.

"I hate this one," Grace said as she turned away.

Luc was beginning his climb for the nosedive, and I shared her aversion to it. I had been to several exhibitions with him in the past two months, and each time he did it, I held my breath until he was safe on the ground again.

Yet his fearlessness was one of the reasons I loved him. I couldn't tear my gaze away.

"How many more shows must you attend before we leave for your cross-country flight?" Grace asked, keeping her gaze on me and not Luc.

"A half dozen."

All the plans were set for me to attempt the cross-country trip from September first to September thirtieth. The train cars had been arranged, the route had been mapped out, the painters had been hired to paint the Vin Fiz logo on the bottom of my new Blériot aeroplane, and my parents had agreed to come along.

Since William Randolph Hearst was putting up the prize money, he insisted that reporters from two of his newspapers, the *New York Journal* and the *Los Angeles Examiner*, travel along with the retinue that would follow. Grace would have exclusive rights as a representative for the *New York Globe*, and Armour and Company was sending a representative to coordinate appearances for me to promote Vin Fiz along the route.

Until then, I was performing at air meets, trying to earn as much money as possible. Every little bit helped Mama and Daddy.

"Have you talked to Mama?" I asked. "Did Mr. Lorenz extend the deadline for the second payment to October first?"

If I accomplished the flight by September thirtieth, I would wire the payment to him the next day. If not, then there was no way we could save the orphanage—unless, by some miracle, I could make enough money at these air meets.

Grace let out a sigh. "Yes, he is extending the deadline, but Mr. Thurston has just made a second offer, and it's much larger than the first. Mr. Lorenz has promised to sell the property to Mama and Daddy—but he's asking more now."

"That's extortion! He is already asking more than the building is worth." If our parents hadn't been using the building for over twenty years and it weren't in such a good location, I would have suggested we find another. But no matter where they moved, it would require more money to update and outfit a building than they had.

"I've thought more about visiting Mr. Thurston," she said.

"And say what? That you're sorry you spent months uncovering the corruption in his factories? Or that you're sorry for the fines he's been given by the city? Or the public shaming he's received? Do you think he'd simply forgive you and forget about his revenge?"

"What else can I do? He can't get away with this."

"It would be foolish, as Daddy said, and you might make it worse."

She let out a sigh. "I feel helpless."

I wrapped my arm through hers. "Don't worry. I'll make the cross-country flight, and then Mama and Daddy will never have to worry about money again."

She squeezed my arm and smiled at me.

Behind her, Luc was gaining altitude as the five thousand spectators seemed to hold their breath with me. As soon as he reached three thousand feet, he would point the plane toward the earth and cut the engine—then, at the last possible second, he would restart the engine and pull up on the throttle and glide safely to land.

If the engine failed to start . . . there was no possibility of surviving.

I didn't know why he did it, but it was the thing everyone had come to the air meet to see. The manager of the event, Bill Willard, had paid Luc an enormous amount of money for his appearance here today.

"I know it's not done until I hear the crowd cheer," Grace said as she looked down at our entwined arms. "Then I know it's safe to look up."

We stood next to my new Blériot aeroplane. It had just arrived from France three days before I left New York to come to Boston. I had taken it up a few times but hadn't tested it as much as I would like before debuting it in public.

Tomorrow I would try for the speed record, which came with a thousand-dollar purse and would help pay for the new aeroplane. I wanted to test-fly it a few more times to get familiar with the course before then. I had asked Grace to come up with me, but since she'd refused, I asked Mr. Willard if he wanted to come, and he had agreed.

"You are missing out on the greatest experience of your life," I told Grace. "Will you ever let me take you up?"

"I really have no desire." She shook her head. "I'm not a fan of heights as it is—but add seventy-mile-an-hour speed and unpredictable wind, and I am not interested."

I shrugged as I watched Luc reach his final altitude and then turn his Blériot nose-down. The aeroplane began to buzz toward the earth, gaining speed. There was always a split second when I was afraid that *this* time he wouldn't make it.

I held Grace's arm tight—but then, at the very last second, Luc's plane pulled up and glided to safety.

The crowd roared with approval, and Grace lifted her gaze. Relief was written all over her face.

This was the third air meet she had attended with me this summer. She'd been busy with the *New York Globe* and was working on a piece about the women's suffrage movement, headed by Alva Belmont. When she attended air meets, I tried to avoid bringing her and Luc together. I wasn't sure why, because they seemed to be getting along better, but it was easier this way.

As for Luc, we saw each other often. He continued to be kind and friendly, but our relationship remained the same. I told myself he didn't want to distract me with romance while I had such a big flight on the horizon. I needed to remain focused on the cross-country journey, and he needed to be my business manager—and nothing else. I hoped and prayed that when we got to California, things would change.

Luc stepped out of his aeroplane to the wild cheers of the crowd. The noise was deafening—and made me grin for him. He waved at the audience and then jogged toward the hangar where Grace and I had been watching.

The moment he saw us, his steps slowed. Was it because of Grace? She had only arrived half an hour ago, so he didn't know she was here. I had invited her to watch me break the speed record—and because it felt strange to be in Massachusetts without her. We were not far from Salem Village, though it was now called Danvers. Part of me wanted to visit to see what had changed and what had stayed the same since 1692. The other part of me wanted nothing to do with the town.

"Bonjour," Luc said as he continued toward us. He took off the canvas jacket that all the aviators wore to protect their clothes from the castor oil, revealing a simple dark blue suit coat with matching trousers underneath. The suit made his eyes look bluer than normal. Beneath the coat, he wore a white collared shirt, and on his dark hair was a flat cap worn backwards. He had taken off his flying goggles, and they dangled from his long fingers. His movements were so smooth and even, as if he had mastery over every action he took.

"Hello," Grace and I said at the same time.

"I did not know you were coming," he said to Grace, something gentle yet eager in his gaze.

She glanced at me and then looked back at Luc. "Hope wanted me to watch her break the speed record tomorrow."

"Oui." He nodded. "She will make history again."

"I am going up for a test flight soon," I said to Luc, drawing his attention back to me. "How is the air?"

He pulled his gaze away from my sister. "It is very good. How has the new monoplane handled for you?"

It was a two-seater, since I planned to make extra money taking passengers up with me. I wasn't used to having the added weight of another person in the aeroplane, but it was easy enough to maneuver. "I love it."

"*Très bien.*" He smiled and then looked toward the hangar where they were wheeling in his aeroplane. "I must go. The mechanics need to speak to me." He returned his focus to Grace. "Are you staying in Boston?"

"Yes, at the Copley Square Hotel."

"Perhaps we can have supper there." He looked at me. "The three of us, of course. Just like old times."

My heart warmed at the invitation—but quickly cooled. I didn't want them together. I didn't want to see Luc looking at my sister the way he was right now—the way he had in Paris.

Grace frowned at me, uncertainty in her face.

"I'm not sure if we'll have the time," I told him, a bit curt.

Disappointment clouded his eyes for just a moment, but then he covered his emotions and gave me a nod. "Another time, perhaps."

As he left us, Grace gave me a questioning look.

I ignored it.

The crowd grew more animated as the air meet continued. The heat and humidity didn't seem to dampen anyone's spirits as Blanche Stuart Scott took to the air. Tomorrow she would attempt to beat the speed record with me, but I was confident in my aeroplane.

As I inspected the new Blériot, looking over each wire, bolt, and mechanism, a man called out my name. "Miss Cooper?"

I turned to see the air meet organizer, Mr. Willard, in a thick wool sweater and a flat cap, much like Luc's, worn backward.

I smiled. "My mechanics should be ready to assist us."

Grace was still standing near my hangar, taking notes for another story. She was far enough away that I couldn't introduce her to Mr. Willard, but she'd want to interview him after our flight.

"Have you ridden in an aeroplane before?" I asked him.

"No. This will be my first time. My son wants to be a pilot, so I had to flip a coin with him to see who would go up with you. I should feel bad that he lost, but I don't." He winked at me.

The mechanics pulled my aeroplane out of the hangar and then assisted Mr. Willard into the passenger seat. He was a handsome man, recently widowed, so it didn't surprise me when some of the mechanics began to tease him.

"How does it feel to venture into the sky for the first time with the prettiest pilot at the air show?" one man asked.

"Why do you think I agreed to go?" Mr. Willard replied with hearty laughter.

I climbed into the cockpit of the monoplane and gave Mr. Willard a few instructions, telling him to sit tight and not make any movements, since it could easily cause the balance to shift.

As the lead mechanic spun the propeller and I flipped the ignition switch, my eye caught something strange.

Luc had come out of his hangar and was casually walking toward mine. The engine whirred to life and the plane began to pull, but I waited—did Luc want to stop me? Talk to me?

The mechanics watched for my signal to let go of the aeroplane. It pulled against them, wanting to be free.

And then I realized why Luc was approaching.

He had his eye on Grace.

I couldn't wait any longer, so I lifted my hand to indicate that the mechanics should let go, and the aeroplane sped across the field, taking me away from Grace and Luc.

When the plane took flight and weightlessness came over me, for the first time I felt no joy.

Behind me, Mr. Willard whooped his appreciation, and I forced myself to think about this flight, pulling the throttle lever back to allow the aeroplane to climb higher.

I gracefully turned the aeroplane and flew east toward the Boston Light, positioned on Little Brewster Island. The first lighthouse in America had been built there, and it was an important landmark for the speed contest tomorrow. I would need to fly out to the light, circle it once, and then come back to the air meet—and do it five times. It would be a timed flight, and the person who did it the fastest would win the thousand dollars.

The sky was a magnificent shade of blue without a cloud in sight. I wanted to end my flight soon, to rejoin Luc and Grace and see what they were talking about, but Mr. Willard deserved the twenty-minute flight I had promised him. It was just past five o'clock, so the sun was starting its descent, offering the perfect amount of light for flying. I climbed to two thousand feet before reaching the lighthouse and made a wide arc around it, not worried about precision or timing today.

After circling the lighthouse, I started to lower the aeroplane's altitude, eager to return to earth. I made wide circles around the airfield as I descended. Blanche was entertaining the audience in the distance, while in the shallow tidal flats sat a boat holding two boys, their faces turned toward the sky to watch us.

Without warning, the aeroplane's tail flicked upward, much

like it had when I was flying over the English Channel. I grabbed the edge of the cockpit and yelled for Mr. Willard to do the same. But to my horror, I heard him scream as he went sailing over my head. The aeroplane had tossed him from his seat.

My hands shook as I worked hard to steady the monoplane, which was off-balance from the loss of his weight. Sweat broke out all over my body as my pulse hummed with panic. I tried to think of what I might do to save him, but he was falling so fast, and I lost sight of him.

I looked for him this way and that, but my frantic movements threw the aeroplane out of balance. The tail flicked up again as if a giant, invisible hand had swatted it. I grabbed for the edge of the cockpit, but my gloved hands slipped off the fragile wood and my body was thrown out of my seat.

For a split-second, I was in complete denial as I began to fall through the sky. I could see Mr. Willard flailing through the air below me. Dread and overwhelming terror filled me with a rush, tearing at me with the same force as the wind.

I began to scream.

I plummeted toward the earth—and there was nothing I could do to stop.

PART
Two

15

HOPE

I opened my eyes and inhaled a deep breath, as if I'd been holding it for hours.

"Hope!" Grace cried as she rose from the bed we shared in the little attic room at the ordinary. She crushed me in her arms, weeping. "Hope!"

I stared at the slanted ceiling beyond her shoulder, my heart pounding hard. Why was she crying?

"Hope," she said again as she pulled back and looked down at me.

The sun had not yet risen on Salem Village, though there was a faint glow in the eastern sky. I stared at Grace, trying desperately to get my bearings.

I sat up, forcing her to move back. Putting my hand on my head, I frowned. "What happened?"

She wiped at the tears on her face and sat back on her heels.

"You were thrown from your aeroplane at the Boston meet." Her face crumpled into tears again, and she threw herself at me, hugging me tighter than she'd ever hugged me before.

Slowly, the memories started to return.

The Boston air meet. Luc. Grace. Mr. Willard.

Mr. Willard!

I forced Grace away from me. "What happened to Mr. Willard?"

She shook her head, weeping. "Oh, Hope, it's just awful. Don't you remember? You were both thrown from your Blériot about a thousand feet in the air. Your bodies landed in the tidal flats. You were both pronounced dead at the scene."

I stared at her, a frown tilting my brow. "What are you saying?"

"I'm saying you died, Hope—you died in 1912. I saw your body." A sob shook her, and she struggled to breathe. "It was so awful. They took you away in an ambulance, you and Mr. Willard. It was the most dreadful thing I've ever witnessed. The entire audience saw what happened, Hope. Five thousand people. Everyone was devastated."

I listened to what she said, but I couldn't make sense of it. I had *died*? But I wasn't supposed to die in 1912.

My eyes opened wide, and it felt like my heart stopped beating.

"Grace." I swallowed the dread and grabbed her arms to steady her. "If I died in 1912, that means—" I couldn't finish the statement.

She nodded, fresh tears streaming down her cheeks. "Your only path is 1692."

I shook my head, denial rising within me. "No. Tomorrow, I'll wake up with you in 1912. I must. I can't stay here." Panic overtook me, clawing up my legs to devour me, while grief twisted in my gut like a violent storm. I had to move—to get out of the bed and pace. My entire body shook as I hugged my arms around myself.

Grace stayed on the bed. "You won't wake up there tomorrow,

Hope. There was no pulse, and I saw your body." She looked
down as more tears fell. "I wish I hadn't."

Rubbing my hands over my upper arms, I tried to calm down.
I couldn't solve anything if I was upset and panicked. There
had to be something I could do—there was always something.

"I fell asleep last night on the train from Boston to Washington," Grace said. "When I wake up tomorrow, Daddy and Mama
will pick me up at the train station. Hope—they're destroyed.
But at least they can still communicate with you through me,
and I'll tell them whatever you need me to."

I stopped pacing and tried to take a deep breath to still my
racing heart. I would never see Mama and Daddy again—would
never fly an aeroplane again—would never have the freedoms
I had enjoyed.

And I would never see Luc again.

The grief was overwhelming and all-consuming.

I crumpled over, my face in my hands, and wept. Great sobs
wracked my body as denial washed over me in wave after crushing wave.

Grace stumbled out of our bed and wrapped me in her arms.
She held me tight, crooning reassuring words.

I didn't know how long I wept or how long she held me.
When I finally felt like I had no tears left, I lifted my head and
realized we had moved back to our bed and were sitting on the
edge. The sun was resting on the horizon, sending pink and
purple light into our room.

We were late to start breakfast, and if we didn't get downstairs soon, Father would come looking for us. What would he
think when he saw my tears? How would I explain?

For the first time in my life, I was truly frightened. When I'd
had 1912, there was always an escape available. No matter how
Father treated me or how others judged me, I had the hope that
one day I would be done with this place once and for all. It had
given me foolish confidence.

But now? Tears threatened again, but I swallowed them back and lifted my chin.

I would not let Salem win. I would not give in to the fear and intimidation. I would make my life what I wanted—regardless of what they said or did to me.

Even as I made the resolutions, I knew it was all nonsense. The truth was, I *did* have to play by their rules if I wanted to survive. Because now I didn't have 1912 as a backup. Now, if I was accused of being a witch and sentenced to die, I would truly die.

"Hope," Grace said, quietly, "talk to me."

I pulled back from my sister and wiped my cheeks with the edge of my nightgown.

"What are you thinking?" she asked.

Shaking my head, I shrugged. "I don't know. There are so many thoughts going through my head."

"God has a plan," she said. "He doesn't make mistakes—even if His decisions don't make sense to us. One day, they will."

I pressed my lips together as fresh tears started. "I don't know, Grace. I don't know if I believe that."

She drew me into her arms again and hugged me. She didn't try to make me understand or believe or accept that this was okay—and I loved her even more for it.

I might have lost 1912 and all the people and things I cherished there, but God had allowed me to keep Grace. She had always been my one constant in life.

Everything felt dark and unimaginable. The loss too raw to comprehend. I couldn't even think about Luc right now. It hurt too much.

So I didn't allow myself to think of him or anything else I had lost.

Instead, I focused on Grace. She was all I had left.

As the day unfolded, I felt numb. I went through the motions, served the meals, cleaned the rooms, weeded the garden, and even listened to the horrifying gossip about the witch trials.

Rebecca Nurse, Sarah Good, and three other women had been sentenced to hang and were awaiting the gallows. My heart was traumatized from my own grief, so I took the news without emotion. I wished I had researched the witch trials while in 1912, but I had not thought it would affect me. Now I wasn't so sure. What if I was accused? What then? Would I hang on Gallows Hill, too?

The fear I had felt earlier continued to mount with stunning intensity. I began to think of every misspoken word, every person I had angered, and each time I had defied the elders. Would they come back to haunt me?

Just before supper, I entered the kitchen, where Grace was rolling out muffin dough. She studied me, her face filled with grief and worry.

"Do not look at me so," I begged as I took up several plates filled with mutton cutlets and stewed peas.

Leah was in the kitchen, quietly preparing the supper plates. She glanced at us but remained silent. Ever since Susannah claimed that Leah confided in her, I had felt a deep aversion for the girl. It was Grace and I who had taken Leah in and treated her with kindness—not Susannah. Had Leah really betrayed us? Betrayed Ann Pudeator, who was now rotting away in Salem gaol—accused for the second time by Sarah Churchill? And had Father paid Sarah Churchill to make the accusation? It seemed too coincidental that we had witnessed him paying Sarah. Did he suspect that Ann had spoken to us, or had he paid Sarah to accuse her because she was the only person who knew about our mother?

How many accusations had been made because of long-standing grudges, revenge, or simply to keep a secret safe?

And if Father *had* paid for Ann to be accused and had let his own wife hang twenty-four years ago, what else might he do?

So many people had been accused, I couldn't keep track. Men, women, and children awaited questioning and trials. When would it end?

"How would you have me look at you?" Grace asked as she took a cup and cut out the muffins, then quickly laid them on a hot iron pan to cook.

"The same as usual," I told her, sending a pointed look at Leah to remind Grace that there were ears in the room.

Grace laid some of the recently cooked muffins on the plates I was carrying and offered me a reassuring smile. "We will get through this," she whispered.

I couldn't imagine how. Melancholy weighed so heavily upon my shoulders, part of me wanted to give up completely. But as much as I hated 1692, I was thankful that I still had it. If Grace had let me forfeit this path before now, I would have nothing left.

How odd that while I slept, Grace would have a full day away from me for the first time. She would have to deal with the grief and mourning there, would have to help plan my funeral. It was too much to think about.

It took concentrated effort to serve supper. My mind was so distracted, I forgot what I was doing and had to be reminded constantly by Grace, by the customers, and even by my father. He watched me carefully, though he didn't ask what was wrong.

Susannah watched me as well, but her stare was more calculating—and I wondered how much she hated me. Would she accuse me if I wasn't careful? She had yet to become afflicted, but was it only a matter of time? Her friends and cousins were suffering affliction, and she spent a lot of time in their company.

When the supper dishes were washed and Leah had gone to bed, I finally allowed myself to sit down for the first time that day. I had wanted to stay busy—needed to stay busy—but I was tired. I'd never been so exhausted in my life.

Grace walked into the kitchen with a rag in hand. She had been wiping the tables in the dining room. "Father and Susannah have gone to bed," she said as she set the rag in the bucket.

"Leah, as well."

She stood with her hands on her hips and studied me. "How are you feeling?"

"Tired, scared, and bewildered." Tears came to my eyes, but I refused to cry again. Crying was a waste of my time and energy. I had to face reality—and the sooner I accepted it, the sooner I would find some semblance of normalcy. There was some comfort to the familiarity of the ordinary. It was my home, after all.

Grace nodded. "I'm feeling the same."

A sound outside the door brought both our heads up, and I went to the window. Though it was dark, I could make out the form of Isaac on his wagon, and a wave of affection overcame me. He was another constant in this path—just like Grace. He was steady. Something I could be sure of.

"'Tis Isaac," I said.

"Do you think Pricilla has arrived?"

I felt a quickening in my pulse. Now, more than ever, I wanted and needed answers about our mother. I longed to connect to my family. I had Grace and Isaac, but I had purposely not drawn close to anyone else. I didn't want it to be difficult to leave Salem. But now? Now I needed connections like never before.

I opened the back door while Isaac was still in his wagon and walked out into the sultry July night. It was humid, and the frogs were croaking in a nearby swamp. The moon was starting to wane, but it was still bright and vibrant, casting shadows onto the yard.

Isaac's eyebrows lifted as he secured the reins to the brake, probably surprised that I had come out to greet him.

"Good evening, Isaac." I wished I could throw my arms around him for a hug. I didn't realize how much I longed for physical comfort until this moment. "Have you come with good news?"

"I hope so." He jumped off his wagon and strode toward me. "Are you and Grace able to come? I have a visitor."

I nodded eagerly, wanting to distract myself with something encouraging.

Grace stood in the doorway, her white coif and apron shining bright in the moonlight. She smiled at Isaac, admiration in her gaze. Grace was giving up so much to stay with me in 1692; there had to be a way to convince Isaac to love her. She deserved to be happy with him. I resolved to make it happen—even as my own heart was breaking.

We changed our aprons, blew out the candles in the kitchen to make it appear as if we'd gone to bed, and made our way to Isaac's wagon. He helped us up—Grace first and then me— before stepping up to sit beside me.

It was a tight fit, but we didn't have far to go, and his steady presence beside me reassured me in ways I couldn't explain.

The moon was like a beacon in the dark night, but the shadows it cast made simple objects appear ominous. We had to pass by the watchtower across the road from the ordinary.

"I'll have to explain myself to the guard tomorrow," Isaac said quietly as we passed. Thankfully, the guard didn't stop us as we drove south.

"Hath she been here long?" I asked Isaac as we drew closer to his farm.

"She arrived earlier this afternoon after stopping in Salem Towne to speak to her other niece. I thought it wise to wait until dark to summon you."

"I've been curious about our cousin in Salem Towne," Grace said. "I hope Pricilla tells us her name. Mayhap we already know her."

"How strange that we have a cousin so close," I mused.

Isaac's farm was now in sight. It was one of the most prosperous in the village, and he'd grown it since inheriting it a few years back. He had taken care of his aged mother until her recent death and provided well for his servants. The main house was large and painted red, with a central chimney and a lean-to in back that ran the length of the first floor. Two rooms flanked the chimney downstairs and upstairs, much like the floorplan of the ordinary, with a central front entrance and stairwell.

There had been many improvements to the farm under Isaac's care, and even in the shadowed moonlight, I could see it was well-maintained. Isaac took pride in everything he did, and it was evident in the prosperity of his property.

He pulled up to the front of the house, and one of his indentured servants, Jabez, appeared from around the corner to take the horses and wagon. Isaac jumped down and walked around the wagon to help Grace down, and then he reached up to take my hand.

His grip was firm and steady, and when I was on the ground, he gave my hand a gentle, reassuring squeeze before letting it go.

The front door was opened by a house servant, and Isaac said, "You remember Judith?"

She looked at him tenderly and then smiled at us. She was one of the refugees from Maine, like so many other young women who had come into Salem. Judith had been widowed in a massacre and had come with her two small children. Isaac had given her a job and provided a home for all three of them. She seemed content—unlike Mercy Lewis, who was intent on taking down the whole village.

"Good evening," I said to Judith with a smile. Until now, I hadn't wondered about her feelings for Isaac, but I could see them plainly on her face. Did he know she was in love with him?

Did he know Grace was in love with him?

I followed my sister through the entrance hall. A lantern

burned in the keeping room to the left, and a woman rose from a chair. She was probably in her late forties, but she bore a striking resemblance to Grace and me, with the same color hair, the same shape of face, and the same nose. We had inherited our daddy's brown eyes and our mama's mouth from 1912, but I had always wondered where our other features came from.

Now I knew.

She stepped forward, her hands to her mouth and tears in her eyes. With a shake of her head, she opened her arms, and Grace and I entered her embrace.

The feeling I had for Pricilla Baker was inexplicable. I felt as if I had always known her. Tears pooled in my eyes again, but this time it wasn't from grief. Here was the connection I hadn't even realized I longed for in 1692. Was meeting her a special gift from God on a difficult day?

"Let me take a look at ye," she said as she stepped back, glancing from me to Grace. "Which one are thee?"

"I'm Grace."

Pricilla turned to me. "That means thee must be Hope."

I nodded, wiping away my tears. "And you're our aunt Pricilla?"

"Yes." She took a deep breath, wonder in her gaze. "I didn't know if I would ever lay eyes on ye again. God is good." She looked up at Isaac, who stood by quietly, and said, "And Goodman Abbott is good, as well."

I smiled at him, my heart expanding for Isaac in ways it never had before. He *was* good—though I had never taken the time to appreciate it before now.

"I will leave you in privacy," Isaac said. "When you're ready, let me know, and I will take you home."

He left the room before we could stop him, and Pricilla motioned for us to take seats across from her.

The keeping room was large and full of comfortable furniture. The thick paneled walls were painted a rich, creamy yellow, there were woven rugs on the wide-plank floors, and pictures of magnificent scenery graced the walls.

"I have so many questions for ye," Pricilla said as she looked from Grace to me again. "But the first one hath been uppermost in my mind for almost twenty-five years now."

I waited, wondering what she might ask.

"What other time did ye live in?"

Grace and I stared at her, and my mouth slipped open.

"How do you know?" Grace asked in a stunned whisper.

Pricilla rose and slowly unbuttoned the top of her waistcoat, then lowered her white linen shift just enough that we could see the top part of a sunburst birthmark over her heart.

"Ye are from a long line of time-crossers, and yer mother, Tacy, was one of us." She buttoned up her waistcoat again, studying us closely. "What we never understood was why the marks ye bear are on the backs of yer heads. No one in our family bears a mark there."

I turned in bewilderment to Grace, and she stared back at me, just as befuddled.

Finally, I said to Pricilla, "We bear the mark of our time-crossing mother, Maggie, from 1912." I leaned forward, my voice low. "Are you saying that our mother in *this* path also bore a time-crossing mark?"

It was Pricilla's turn to look perplexed. "Yes." She shook her head. "Mayhap that's why there are two of ye. Ye are born of *two* time-crossing mothers."

I put my hand to my mouth, uncertain what any of this meant.

"Tacy left us when she was only nineteen and still had two years to make her final decision," Pricilla said. "We did not want her to pledge herself to a man in this path before she left her other one. I pleaded with her to reconsider, but she abandoned us without any word so we wouldn't look for her. When she returned to us, she was filled with remorse—not only for leaving us, but for sacrificing her faith. She was hanged just months before her twenty-first birthday, and my only consolation was that she was still alive somewhere."

"If Tacy was a time-crosser," Grace asked, slowly, "when was her other time?"

"She was born in 1869 in New York City."

For the third time that day, I was stunned.

"If she was born in 1869," Grace said, looking down as if trying to put all the pieces together, "that means—"

"She might still be alive in 1912," I finished for her. "She would only be—" I paused to do the math in my head. "Forty-three-years old."

Pricilla's face crumpled, and tears came to her eyes again. "That means ye might be able to find her for me and tell her I'm sorry that I couldn't save her from hanging."

I started to nod—but then realized I could not find Tacy in 1912, because I would never go back there again.

But Grace could.

16

GRACE

I stood with my parents in the Congressional Cemetery in Washington, DC, staring at Hope's closed coffin. Heavy clouds hung overhead, drizzling on the mourners who had come to say farewell to my twin sister. Though I had spent the past couple of days with her in Salem, trying to make sense of what happened at the Boston air meet—and what we learned about our mother, Tacy—I still couldn't believe she was gone from 1912.

Her death in this path was final—and that stung like nothing ever had before.

Daddy and Mama stood under one black umbrella while I stood under another. It was the first time I'd felt truly alone in my entire life. Hope was usually at my side—but I would never see her here again.

A sob caught in my throat as the weight of reality settled on my shoulders.

Mama wept and laid her head against Daddy's chest as the

189

pastor said the final prayer. Hope's coffin was lowered into the ground next to Mama's father, Senator Edward Wakefield.

"Ashes to ashes and dust to dust," the pastor said, sprinkling a handful of dirt onto Hope's coffin. "Lord, we commit our sister Hope unto thee. Amen."

I felt numb as tears slipped from my eyes. Losing Hope in 1912 had created more than just grief. For days, confusion, uncertainty, and fear had overwhelmed me—but now I just felt dull and void.

Mourners walked past the three of us, murmuring words of comfort and consolation.

"I'm so sorry for your loss," one of our older neighbors said as she reached for my cold hand and gave it a squeeze before moving on to Mama and Daddy.

"You must be devastated," said another. "My thoughts and prayers are with you."

"My heart is breaking for you," said a third. "Whatever you need, be sure to ask."

I glanced at each person, but I didn't really see them. I was too bereft. For me, for Hope, for Mama and Daddy. My parents would never see Hope again, and though I would wake up tomorrow in Salem and she would be there, everything had changed.

Now a question repeated with every beat of my heart.

What would happen on my twenty-fifth birthday? Would I continue with my plan to stay in 1912—forsaking Hope? Or should I abandon my plans and stay in 1692 with her?

Neither option appealed to me.

My heart was so raw, I couldn't possibly make that decision now.

I tried not to shiver in my long black dress, which was getting soaked by the rain as it blew against my back. It felt like a hundred people passed, giving me hugs, shaking my hand, or simply nodding, without saying a word.

Until I heard a beautiful and familiar voice. "*Mon cœur est avec votre cœur, aujourd'hui et toujours.*"

I looked up as tears spilled down my cheeks.

Sadness filled the depths of Luc's eyes as rain dripped from the brim of his black fedora. "My heart is with your heart, today and always."

"You came," I whispered.

"Of course I came," he said gently.

He had been there with me when it happened. As Hope was ascending into the sky, my gaze had fallen on Luc. He strode across the airfield, his blue-green gaze intent upon me, his shoulders broad and confident—and I had been speechless, my heart thudding with a strange beat. It was the first time he had sought out my company, and he had come to tell me that he had read several articles I had written. His comments had been thoughtful and intelligent, and I knew he meant every word he said.

I should have been watching Hope—but all I could see was Luc.

There had been a gasp, and I had torn my gaze from Luc as Mr. Willard's body careened through the air. My stomach had dropped, and I couldn't believe what I was seeing. Then, seconds later, Hope had been thrown from the aeroplane, and my world shifted irrevocably.

I had fallen to my knees, unable to think or move or speak. I knew, immediately, that she had died. My body trembled from head to foot, and I began to weep. As everyone ran toward Hope's body, it was Luc who stayed behind to help me to my feet. I wanted to see Hope—needed to see her, to know for certain. He tried to take me away, but I insisted, so he took me to the place where they had laid her, waiting for the ambulance.

I had regretted my decision immediately.

As the ambulance took her away, Luc put his arm around me and protected me from the crush of people who ran onto the field, trying to salvage souvenirs from the wreckage of her aeroplane. Without a word, he brought me back to my hotel and then left to purchase a ticket for me to travel to Washington, DC. At the station, he bid me farewell, promising that he would take care of all the arrangements and would have Hope returned to us in Washington.

And now here he stood, three days later, anguish on his face, looking as if he hadn't slept in days.

"Thank you," I told him, shivering from the cold and my emotions. I put my hand on his. "For everything."

"You're freezing." He laid his warm hand over mine, enveloping it with unexpected tenderness.

"And you're getting wet." I took a step toward him and lifted the umbrella so it would protect both of us. My heart was beating that same strange rhythm it had at the air show, so I gently pulled my hand away from his.

He looked down at me, his eyes a stormy dark blue, matching the weather swirling around us. "I need to have a word with you—if I may. Will you have time?"

"There is a reception at my parents' home after the funeral. I hope you'll come."

"I would like that."

Neither of us spoke for a moment. I wanted to tell him how much he had meant to Hope—how much he *still* meant to her—but I couldn't find the words.

"I hope you are taking comfort in knowing that God is in control, even in the midst of this tragedy." The conviction in his voice told me that this wasn't simply a platitude—he'd experienced God's comfort before.

I swallowed and nodded. "I do take comfort in that knowledge. Thank you."

"Will you introduce me to your parents?"

"Yes, of course." The rain began to fall faster, so I stepped a little closer to him as we waited for my parents to finish speaking to their friends.

It felt strange to stand beside Luc without Hope nearby.

Everything was strange without Hope.

The friends finally moved away, and my parents turned to us in a sort of daze until they saw who stood beside me.

My mother's brilliant blue eyes glistened with unshed tears. Daddy stood straight and stoic, though I knew his heart was breaking.

"Mama and Daddy," I said as Luc and I stepped closer to them. "This is Lucas Voland—Hope's friend."

He glanced at me as a flicker of disappointment passed over his face. Had he hoped to be introduced as my friend, too?

Mama took Luc's hand in hers, gratitude in her every movement. "Thank you, Mr. Voland, for everything you've done to help us. You were a very good and loyal friend to Hope, and we could not be more grateful."

"I wish I could have done more."

Daddy took Luc's hand next. "Nonsense. You've done more than most. We are in your debt."

"You must come to our home for the reception we're hosting," Mama said.

"I've already invited him," I told her.

"Wonderful." She nodded. "Then we'll expect to see you there."

He said good-bye and then left the protection of my umbrella to walk out of the cemetery. My eyes followed him as I wondered what I would have done without him after the accident.

Before he turned the corner, he looked back. There was something in his gaze that made me catch my breath.

It was longing—but for what?

For Hope?

After all the mourners left the cemetery, I stepped into a cab with Mama and Daddy to make our way home to Lafayette Square near the White House. We drove down Pennsylvania Avenue as the rain stopped and the clouds began to break apart.

My parents' orphanage came into view not far from their home. The building was like a second home to me, maintained with love and diligence by Mama and Daddy through the years. It would be devastating to see them lose it.

I didn't want to add more grief to my parents' hearts, yet it couldn't wait.

"Without Hope," I said, swallowing the guilt plaguing me as I tore my gaze away from the brown-brick building, "we have no way to earn the money needed for the orphanage."

My parents shared a sad look, and Daddy finally nodded. "We've discussed this."

I couldn't meet their disappointed gazes. "This is my fault. If I hadn't exposed Mr. Thurston—"

"We've already told you it's not your fault," Mama said. "Mr. Thurston is to blame."

"I plan to return to New York in the morning to speak to him—beg him to reconsider."

"It's far too dangerous," Daddy said, his British accent strengthening with his certainty. "There is no talking to a man like Thurston. He's wealthy and powerful—and will stop at nothing to take his revenge. You cannot approach him."

"What will we do, then?" I asked. "How will we save the orphanage?"

Mama put her hands to her temples, and I knew it was too much for her.

Daddy laid his arm around her shoulders and said, "It's too soon to think properly. We'll find a way, even if we must solicit donations from a hundred patrons."

I nodded to pacify him, though they could never raise the

money they needed by going door to door. But the conversation would have to stop for now.

And when I returned to New York, I would speak to Mr. Thurston, regardless of the risks it posed.

"I can't tell you how much comfort I take in knowing that Hope is still alive with you in 1692," Mama said, changing the subject.

"She misses you desperately," I told her.

"I worry about her being stuck there during the witch trials." Daddy shook his head. "But if anyone can survive them, it's Hope."

I had to look away. They didn't know I would accuse Hope—and I couldn't tell them.

"Any more news of your other mother?" Mama asked.

The morning after I learned about Tacy, I had told them the shocking news. Mama could hardly believe it, though she had always wondered why we were twins. She'd never known of time-crossing twins before. Perhaps we now had an answer.

"No," I said. "But I plan to start looking for her as soon as I return to New York."

"Is that a good idea?" Daddy asked. "Aren't you supposed to avoid other time-crossers? Your mama has been avoiding her own mother all these years."

My grandmother Libby was a time-crosser and was living in New York at that very moment. She was only seventeen and didn't know we existed. I had been warned my whole life not to look for her—and if I saw her, not to tell her who I was. It might jeopardize her journey. If I intervened and told her how her life would play out, she would make different decisions, and ultimately, I might not be born. It was a strange part of our gift, and it made me wonder who else might be crossing my path.

"I don't know anything about Tacy's future," I told Daddy. "I only know about her past. I want to find her, if for no other reason than to tell her what happened to us."

Daddy nodded, and Mama gave me a sad smile.

As the cab pulled to a stop in front of our house, there were already mourners lined up at the door for the reception.

It would be a long day—yet there was the promise of seeing Luc again.

My parents' home was full as I walked from room to room, accepting more condolences and visiting with old friends and neighbors. Everyone wanted to know about Hope's flights and her accomplishments, and I was happy to tell them. She was remembered fondly, though some people had a knowing smile as they recalled her strong will.

I tried to remember what people were saying so I could relay it to Hope. Most people didn't have the benefit of hearing what others said about them at their funeral.

Today was America's Independence Day, and there would be fireworks all throughout the city that evening. Picnics had already been ruined by the rain, but that wouldn't stop people from going out for the evening festivities. I loved the Fourth of July in Washington, but this year would be much different.

The thought saddened me. For the first time, I wasn't sure if I would be here with Mama and Daddy for next year's fireworks display—or if I would be in Salem with Hope. America was still an English colony in 1692, and independence was not even discussed, let alone celebrated.

As I moved from the dining room into the front parlor, my eyes caught on the newest arrival.

Luc had entered the house and stood in the foyer, speaking respectfully to Daddy. I had seen Luc with leaders and diplomats from all over Europe and the United States. They usually looked up to him with admiration, but here the tables were turned. Luc knew my father had been a Pinkerton agent and guard for Abraham Lincoln, and that he had been the head of the Secret Service in later years. Though Luc wasn't American, he had a deep appreciation for our country and history. He seemed in awe of Daddy.

I watched them for a few moments until Mama came up to me and said, "He's a very handsome young man, isn't he?"

My cheeks felt warm at being caught watching Luc, but I smiled.

"He's also very daring and adventurous," she continued in a quiet, knowing way. "And kind and thoughtful and intelligent."

"All reasons Hope is in love with him."

"Ah," she said, quietly. "I didn't know. Was he in love with her?"

Had the longing I witnessed at the cemetery been for Hope? If so, why hadn't he told her? "I don't know—but she's devastated about losing him."

"If they knew each other that long and you're not sure if he was in love with her, then it probably wasn't mutual."

Luc glanced our way and caught us looking at him. My cheeks grew even warmer. He said something to Daddy and then came our way.

"Thank you for coming," Mama said to him. "We are so grateful for your friendship to both Hope and Grace."

When Luc met my gaze, there was a question there. Were we friends? He hadn't liked me in the beginning—and I hadn't liked him—but something had shifted along the way. Something I was just starting to see.

"Grace mentioned that you needed to speak to her," Mama said. "The rain has stopped, so perhaps you should step out into the garden for privacy."

I led the way through the dining room and into the hallway that ran past my parents' office, and out the back door.

It was a small, walled-in garden with a plethora of plants, flowers, and trees. Mama's roses were her pride and joy, and their colors looked vibrant against the backdrop of the lush greenery. Drops of rainwater glistened on the delicate petals, begging to be touched.

A stone path meandered through the flower beds. I started to follow it, and Luc joined me, his hands behind his back. Neither of us spoke, and I was comfortable with the silence. There was peace in knowing that we didn't need to fill the space.

But there were things I wanted to say—and things I wanted to hear, though I didn't know what he would tell me.

"Thank you, again, for coming," I told him. "I wasn't sure if you would."

He was quiet for another heartbeat and then said, "Hope was very special to me." He paused, and I stopped to search his face. His grief was just as strong as his guilt. *Had* he loved her? "There is much I'd like to say." He took a deep breath. "But I must apologize first. I should have tested the Blériot for her before she took up a passenger. She wasn't familiar enough with it to handle it properly."

"It's not your fault—"

"I was her instructor."

"She was done with her lessons."

"But I knew better than she did. She was not used to flying with a passenger. I should have taken her up first to let her get a feel for the differences. I was too preoccupied with—" He paused and shook his head, looking away from me.

What had been preoccupying his mind that last day?

I put my hand on his forearm, drawing his gaze back. "It was not your fault, Luc."

He stared at me for a heartbeat, as if looking for the truth in my words.

"No one blames you—least of all Hope." I desperately wanted to tell him that Hope was still alive in 1692 and that she had not accused him of being at fault. But I couldn't. He wouldn't understand—and perhaps he wouldn't believe me. He'd think it was grief talking.

"I wish I knew that for certain," he said, swallowing his emotions as he looked down at my hand. "Because the guilt is eating me alive. She was too young and—" He paused as his gaze lifted to mine. "I cannot comprehend the loss you must feel. Your twin sister. There was no one she loved as much as she loved you. My heart breaks for you just as much as it does for her."

Grief threatened to consume me as I felt the weight of his compassion and removed my hand. Yet I wanted to ease his guilt. "Hope knew exactly what she was doing when she made that flight. It was an accident. Pilots are killed all the time. If you fly, you know it's a matter of time before something goes wrong. Hope knew that, too."

"You seem very sure of yourself."

Tears pooled in my eyes, and I had to blink them away. "She died doing something she loved. You should take comfort in that."

We walked again, both in our own thoughts. Finally, Luc took a deep breath and said, "I have something to tell you. I wasn't sure if I should wait, but there's not much time."

I paused, afraid of what it might be.

"Armour and Company contacted me yesterday afternoon with a proposition," he said. "They wanted me to convey their condolences to you and your family—and make you an offer."

"Me?" I turned to him, my skirt brushing the edge of a rose bush, sending a cascade of water across the dark fabric. "What kind of offer?"

"Everything is ready for Hope's flight in September—everything but a pilot. They have asked if you would consider making the flight in Hope's place."

My mouth slipped open as I studied him to see if he was teasing. "Me?"

"You are almost as famous as your sister," he said. "With your articles and with your photograph alongside Hope in

199

Calais. Hope's death has grieved the world, and Armour and Company believe that you will bring healing to everyone if you complete her trip."

"It's a ridiculous idea." I shook my head, not even contemplating the proposition.

"It's not ridiculous," he said, slowly. "Perhaps a little unexpected —but anyone can learn to fly."

"Yes, but you must *want* to fly first. Besides, the trip starts in eight weeks. I could never be prepared to fly across the country in such a short amount of time."

"You could if you let me teach you."

I crossed my arms and began to walk again, shaking my head. "It can't be done."

"Armour and Company has not only guaranteed that you'll get the prize money if you complete the trip in thirty days," he said as he stayed where we had been standing, "but they are willing to pay you ten thousand dollars even if it takes you longer than thirty days."

I stopped and turned to him. "Even if I don't make it to California in thirty days?"

"Oui. But you must get there to collect the money."

I wasn't foolish enough to think I could complete the flight in thirty days—but a guaranteed ten thousand dollars would be more than enough to save the orphanage if Mr. Lorenz would extend the deadline again.

I put my hands on my cheeks, feeling torn between fear and hope. Could this be the answer to our problem? Yet how could I even contemplate such a thing? The thought of flying had scared me to death *before* it killed my sister. Now it terrified me.

"So much could go wrong."

"Oui," he acknowledged, "but I will be with you every step of the way."

"You would still come? Even though we've never—" I couldn't finish the sentence.

"Gotten along?" His eyes were now a brilliant green in the sunshine as he smiled at me. How had he known what I was thinking? "I believe we can overcome our differences." His accent had deepened as his voice lowered. "For your parents' orphanage and for Hope's memory."

If he was willing to proceed with the plans, shouldn't I be willing? But there was so much to consider. I couldn't say no without thinking about Mama and Daddy's future. If I was going to leave them in October, I wanted to make sure they were financially stable.

"I will think about it," I promised him, though I couldn't imagine learning to fly and spending thirty days with him, trying to make it across the country.

It *was* ridiculous—no matter what he said.

17

HOPE

It was later than usual when I woke up on Saturday morning, and Grace had already gone downstairs to start breakfast.

Rolling over, I looked out the small window and stared at the leaves on the treetops in the side yard. It was strange to go to sleep and wake up in the same place day after day. For the first time in my life, I had dreams. I knew what they were, of course, but I had never experienced them because my conscious mind was away from my body while I slept. But now my conscious mind stayed in my 1692 body and was filled with dreams. They were strangely abstract and contained bits and pieces from both of my paths, including my last moments in Boston, leaving me bereft and traumatized all over again.

It had been three days since I'd woken up here after the flight, and those days had gone by in a blur. I wasn't prone to melancholy, but there was a pit deep in my stomach that ached ferociously. Thinking about Mama and Daddy's pain made it even worse. They had just endured my funeral. Had a lot of people come?

Had Luc come?

I sat up, eager to ask Grace. I dressed and went down the back stairs to the kitchen. It was hot and stuffy despite the early hour, promising unbearable heat later in the day.

Leah was sitting with the butter churn. She glanced up at my arrival but looked down again quickly. I avoided wishing her a good morning as I walked over to Grace, who was at the hearth, flipping pancakes. A pile sat on a plate near the heat, staying warm, while cinnamon apples stewed in a pot hanging over the fire and venison sausages sizzled on a griddle. A bowl of clotted cream sat nearby, ready to be sent out with the pancakes.

Grace was a wonder at cooking. With a sigh, I realized I should probably take a better interest in it, since I would be stuck here. There would be no Delmonico's for centuries to come.

She glanced over her shoulder and gave me a slight smile before stacking another pancake on the pile and plopping a dab of butter onto her pan to start the next one. "Good morrow, Hope."

"Good morrow," I told her.

"There are customers in the dining room, ready to eat."

"Is it that late?"

"You've taken to sleeping longer than usual." She worked with deft hands. "Father and Susannah are waiting for their breakfast."

I tried not to sigh.

Perhaps it was time for us to leave the ordinary. It wouldn't be easy to strike out on our own as single women, but maybe Father would be amenable to it now that he had a wife. I doubted it, though. Women did not leave home unless they married or their parents died. If Grace and I left, we'd be looked upon with suspicion no matter where we went. We didn't have any money of our own, either. We'd be destitute. But there had to be a way.

Perhaps our mother's family would take us in—though that was rife with complications, too, and Father would never allow it, especially if it threatened the truth he'd kept hidden about Tacy.

We had much to think about.

I wanted to ask Grace about my funeral, but there was no time or privacy. We needed to get breakfast served, and Leah was present. I filled several plates with food and took them out to the dining room. Father was filling cups of ale, and Susannah was sitting at a table with two men. I didn't recognize either of them, but Father didn't seem concerned that she was talking to them.

When I approached the table, she looked up at me, a half smile on her face. I held three plates of food and set one down in front of each of them.

"Hope, these are my cousins," Susannah said, "come from Boston. Nathaniel Putnam and Benjamin Putnam."

"Good morrow, Hope," one of them said to me.

"It's a pleasure to finally meet you," said the other.

I nodded at them and offered a polite smile but didn't engage with them. Was there no end to the Putnam family?

"They'll be staying with us for a few days," Susannah continued as Father brought the ale to the table.

I glanced at the men again, and they were both staring at me intently. They were pleasant enough to look at, tall and handsome like most of the Putnams, but there was nothing remarkable about either one.

There were other occupants in the dining room, so I left to get more food. Susannah followed me into the kitchen.

Surprised, I turned. "It's not often we find you in here. Come to help?"

She made a face at that suggestion and then said, "I've come to tell you why Nathaniel and Benjamin are here."

Grace turned away from her pancakes, a wooden spatula in hand.

"This concerns you, as well," Susannah said to her. "Your father is arranging marriages for the both of you. I've convinced him 'tis time you were on your own, and with the arrival of his new child come winter, we'll need your bedchamber."

I stared at her, speechless.

"Nathaniel and Benjamin are concerned about your ages," she continued, "but they're willing to take you on if the dowry is right. And your father is willing to give what is necessary."

"I'm not marrying one of your cousins," I said, turning from her to fill more plates. "I'd never consent to be a Putnam."

"If not my cousins, then who? You cannot stay here forever. I won't hear of it."

I sighed. "'Tis not your concern."

"As your stepmother, 'tis my utmost concern."

I had my back to her, so she couldn't see my scornful look.

"What about you, Grace?" Susannah asked. "Have you given any thought to my suggestion about Isaac?"

Frowning, I turned to Grace. "What suggestion about Isaac?"

Grace's cheeks filled with color, and she resumed her cooking, groaning as she realized one of the pancakes had burned.

"I suggested that she lure Isaac into marriage." Susannah smiled at me like a pleased feline. "If you won't have him, then what's the harm in her staking a claim? He's wealthy, handsome, and clearly interested enough to come here at all hours of the night." She glanced at Leah, who quickly dipped her head.

So Leah *was* talking to her.

"Mayhap Grace hath already started to persuade Isaac." Susannah's smile didn't waver as she looked at me. "That is, unless you have your eyes on him?"

"Are you trying to put strife between us?" I asked, though

I wondered why Grace hadn't told me about her conversation with Susannah. Had they talked about a way for Grace to win Isaac? Now that we were staying in 1692, would Grace stoop to snaring him?

"I am simply trying to get you two out of my home." The smile fell from Susannah's face. "And the sooner the better. My cousins will be here for three days. They know why they're here. If they like either one of you, they might ask for your hand in marriage. I'm telling you so you're prepared with an answer."

After she left the kitchen, I turned to Grace. "Why didn't you tell me about your conversation concerning Isaac?"

Grace glanced at Leah. "Take that outdoors, please."

Without a word, Leah lifted the butter churn and stepped into the backyard, giving Grace and me a little more privacy.

"I didn't tell you because it didn't matter," she said. "Susannah suggested I coax Isaac with physical attention, something I would never do." She flipped her pancakes and then returned her focus to me. "What will we do about her cousins?"

I shrugged. "I didn't plan to get married, but things have changed." I nibbled my bottom lip, emotions rising to the surface. "Now that we're not returning to 1912 . . ." I let the sentence dangle. She knew what I meant. We needed to consider all our options.

Grace turned back to her pancakes, focusing on them for a few seconds before she said, "What if I don't want to stay in 1692?"

I stared at her back, uncertain I had heard her correctly. Panic hit my heart as I put my hand on her shoulder. "What?"

She turned, her eyes heavy with uncertainty as she whispered, "What if I don't want to stay in 1692?"

"How could you even suggest such a thing?" I shook my head, incredulous. "We go together. Always."

Tears rimmed her eyes, and she blinked to clear them. "This

wasn't the plan, Hope." There was something in her voice I had never heard before. Desperation, resentment, anger? "We weren't going to stay here. I have work in 1912—work I love. And there's Mama and Daddy and . . ." It was her turn to let her sentence dangle.

"And what?"

"And—everything." Her voice rose with passion. "I didn't choose to fly that aeroplane. I told you it was dangerous. Why must I suffer because of your foolishness?"

I pulled back, feeling like she had just slapped me. "I didn't die on purpose."

"But you knew the risks. Now I must throw my entire life away because of it?"

"You mean because of me." I was hurt—deeply. "Are you saying that your life in 1912 is more important than me?"

"Oh, I don't know." She pushed past me and paced across the kitchen, putting her hands on her hips. "I'm so confused—about everything. I wish you had never learned to fly."

"I'm confused, too." We stared at each other for a moment, and then I said, "Would you truly choose everything else over me?"

She studied me for a long time. "I have always bent to your will because it has been the easiest way to please you. But I'm not sure I can do it this time."

My breath caught. "How could you be so selfish?"

Grace's mouth parted as she stared at me. Tears filled her eyes before she pressed her lips together and left the kitchen, going up the back stairs.

I had hurt her. Grace was one of the least selfish people I knew—yet my heart was breaking. We were a pair.

Would she really leave me here alone?

I finished serving breakfast, and still Grace did not return to the kitchen. I watched the stairs throughout the meal, my heart stopping each time I heard a creak—but she did not appear.

Whenever I entered the dining room, Susannah leveled her glare at me. I wasn't sure if it was meant to intimidate me, manipulate me, or just communicate her displeasure.

Her cousins tried to draw me into conversation, but my mind and heart were with Grace. They teased me about being such a pretty spinster, which did nothing to ease the tension, and the more I ignored them, the more I noticed Father and Susannah keeping their eyes on me.

When the breakfast dishes were cleared, I went into the kitchen to clean them, but Father entered.

"Why were you and Grace arguing?" he asked.

"You heard us?" My pulse ticked up a notch. What had he heard?

"I heard your voices raised." He frowned. "'Tis a poor way to make a good impression on Susannah's cousins. No one wants a quarrelsome wife."

Susannah entered the kitchen, a scowl on her face. "I do not think she wants to marry," she said to my father. "She wants to live on your charity for the rest of her life."

"Charity?" I asked, astounded. "I work hard for what I have, little that it may be. A small, cold room that I must share with my sister. Leftover food, after the customers have eaten, and a few simple dresses and underclothes. If I worked for my living, I could at least be my own master." Anger boiled within me, and tears gathered in my eyes, making me angrier still. It was all too much. "I hate this place, yet I am stuck here forever. Once, I had dreams of doing so much more. But now?" The tears spilled over, and I despised them. "I am a prisoner in time, and there is nothing I can do to leave."

Father and Susannah stared at me, their anger melting into bewilderment.

"I know not what you speak of," Father said, his voice low, "but you should watch your tongue, daughter, lest you find yourself at the mercy of the magistrates."

I swallowed the other words that wanted release, knowing he was right. If I lost control, they would think I had also lost my mind—or worse.

"You will make yourself presentable to Susannah's kin and spend the afternoon in their company. If they offer for you—though after the way you've treated them, I doubt it very much—you will heed my advice and accept them."

I turned away from him, unable to agree to his demands. He didn't wait for me to respond but took Susannah out of the kitchen.

Slowly I walked up the stairs, leaving the kitchen in a mess. My heart was heavier than it had ever been, and I didn't know which way to go. Would Grace really leave me here alone? The very thought left me spiraling into despair. But could I blame her for wanting to go? If the situation were reversed, would I stay for Grace?

I wanted to believe I would, but shame washed over me with the truth. I wouldn't stay here for Grace. As much as I loved her, nothing could have persuaded me to stay in Salem if I had a choice. Yet here I was.

Tapping on the door of our bedroom, I said, "May I come in?"

The door opened, and Grace stood on the other side, her face puffy and red. She moved aside, and I entered our room.

It was bare except for the bed, a washstand, and hooks on the wall to hold our Meeting dresses. To think that I was taking charity from my father was ludicrous. What little he gave me was no comparison to how hard I worked. The accusation made my blood boil all over again.

"I heard you," Grace said as she took a seat on the bed, her shoulders hunched over. "I think the whole ordinary heard."

I closed the door and pressed against it, leaning my head back. "I'm not made for this place."

She offered a soft chuckle. "I don't think anyone is made for this place except the magistrates and men like Father."

"Susannah seems to like it."

"She married well."

"Perhaps that's what I should do."

"Don't be rash. We're still reeling from what happened. We have a lot of decisions to make, and we must take our time."

I moved across the room and sat beside her, cautious hope budding in my heart. "Does that mean you're still thinking about staying here?"

"Of course I am." She turned to me. "We both have big decisions to make. I was only speaking out of my own fear and uncertainty."

I tried not to appear too eager at her words. I didn't want to push her into a decision, though it went against my nature to remain quiet.

"I'm just so—angry and sad and—" She sighed. "I need to tell you about something Luc said."

I waited, my heart in my throat. "You saw him?"

"At your funeral."

Had he told her he loved me? That he was devastated I had died? It would be little consolation, though it would carry me through my darkest hours.

Or worse—had he told Grace he loved *her*?

"Armour and Company wants me to make the cross-country flight for you," she said. "They will pay me ten thousand dollars regardless of how long it takes to get to California. And if I make it in thirty days, I'll get the ten thousand *plus* the fifty thousand from Mr. Hearst."

"Grace!" I grabbed her hand, relieved and excited. "That's wonderful. You can still help Mama and Daddy."

"But I don't know how to fly."

"You can learn. I'm sure Luc would teach you."

"He already offered."

"Then why are you uncertain? This sounds ideal."

"Flying frightens me—and—" She looked at me. "What if I died there?"

Neither one of us spoke for a moment.

"You would be stuck here with me." I lifted a shoulder. "Which you said you might do anyway. What's the worst that could happen?"

She nodded, but I could still see uncertainty in her gaze.

"Have Luc take you flying," I said to her, "and you'll never want to look back. It's unlike anything you've ever experienced. I promise. Then make your decision. But consider Mama and Daddy. Just think what all that money could mean for them."

Grace slowly sat up. "I will think about it."

"Good. I wish I could be there to see you fly, but you'll tell me all about it."

"Of course I will."

"And you'll tell me all about meeting Tacy, too, right?" I hadn't forgotten the other surprise from a few days ago. We hadn't seen Isaac since then, and I couldn't help but wonder why he stayed away. Had he overheard us speaking? Did he think we were all mad for claiming to be time-crossers?

"I'm going back to New York tomorrow, and I'll look for her the following morning," Grace promised. "I won't rest until I find her."

"I wish I could be there for that, too."

Grace took my hand and nodded. "So do I."

I let out a sigh. "Father is demanding that we spend the afternoon with Susannah's cousins. He'll pull us downstairs if we don't go on our own."

"I look a fright."

"Good." I smiled. "Mayhap that'll scare them away."

She chuckled, and it made my heart soar. I loved seeing my sister happy.

As Grace and I prepared to meet with Susannah's cousins, I couldn't help but wonder how I might convince Grace to stay with me forever.

Then I realized the answer might lie with Isaac Abbott.

18

GRACE

It had been two days since Hope's funeral. As I entered the cavernous building off West 35th Street in the center of the garment district, my pulse was pounding so hard I could barely hear the traffic on the street behind me. Grief mixed with trepidation as my heels clicked on the tiled floor. I could hear Daddy's voice of caution echoing in my heart. This wasn't a good idea—but it was the only option I had.

The more I thought about Luc's proposition, the more I shuddered. I couldn't learn to fly and take a cross-country journey. It was a foolish idea that would only create more hardship for Mama and Daddy.

A young receptionist looked up from a large desk in the middle of the lobby and pursed her lips. "If you're looking for sewing work, you'll need to go up to the fourth floor."

"I'm here to see Mr. Thurston."

She looked me up and down, not impressed. "He doesn't do the hiring. The superintend—"

"I'm not here for a job." I hooked my hand on the strap of my leather bag and forced myself to look confident. I was wearing a simple black walking suit with a straight skirt and a long suitcoat. The Victorian mourning customs had eased in recent years, and society wouldn't require that I wear black for long, but people would still expect me to honor Hope in this way.

"Is Mr. Thurston expecting you?" she asked.

A man stepped out of an office behind the receptionist. He was tall and thick around the middle. His graying hair was longer on one side and combed over the top to hide a balding spot.

"Miss Frampton," he said, "I'm expecting an important package. See that it's delivered to me immediately upon its arrival."

The receptionist nodded and then said, "This woman is here to see you, sir."

My gaze locked with his. This was Mr. Thurston? I'd been undercover in his factories and had never met him.

"Come in," he said, a bit gruff. "I don't have all day."

My hands trembled as I walked around the desk toward Mr. Thurston's office.

I had pictured a monster, but though he was one of the wealthiest and more powerful men in the city, he didn't look like a monster. He wouldn't even catch my eye if we passed on the street.

"What can I do for you, young lady?" he asked as he stood behind his desk and faced me. "This better not be about a job. I don't do the hiring."

He was taller than I'd imagined—but also older.

I took a deep breath, ready and willing to fight for my parents and the orphans. "I'm Grace Cooper. I'm here to ask that you rescind your offer to purchase the building my parents lease in Washington, DC."

He stared at me for a long time, his placid composure slowly morphing into something more imposing and sinister. A corner of his lip curled up in a contemptuous smile. "So you're the little thing that caused me so much trouble."

I lifted my chin.

"I've paid thousands of dollars in fines because of you, not to mention the thousands I had to invest in my buildings to bring them up to city code."

"I was only shedding light on—"

"You were only causing trouble to boost your own career."

My mouth slipped open, and I frowned. "No. I care about the people you employ."

He leaned forward, placing his hands on his desk. "I would like nothing more than to make you disappear, Miss Cooper. You're like a pesky fly that needs to be eradicated."

I took a step back, but I wouldn't leave without putting up a fight.

"My parents are good people, and their orphanage has saved the lives of dozens of children in Wash—"

"I couldn't care less. Perhaps you should have thought of them before poking about in my business." He glared at me. "It would be too obvious if you showed up missing one day, so I will do anything in my power to hit you where it hurts the most. And perhaps you'll think twice before sticking your nose where it doesn't belong again. Do I make myself clear?"

He still leaned on his desk as he stared, unblinking.

My instincts wanted me to cower, but I refused. Thurston was a bully, but Daddy had told me not to give in to him—or anyone else who threatened us.

"I will not back down," I said, my voice trembling.

"Then you will be the cause of suffering for the people you love. I will call Mr. Lorenz today and up my offer—just to spite you, Miss Cooper."

"What do you want with an orphanage in Washington, DC?"

"Nothing. I'll let it rot and fall to the ground—and I'll smile, knowing it mocks you every time you see it."

"I won't let you get that building."

"Try and stop me. I'll just increase my offer."

Anger pulsed through me as I turned on my heels and strode out of Thurston's building.

The sunshine blinded me as I walked toward Broadway and the nearest subway station. My breath started to even out, but his words still echoed in my mind. I couldn't let Thurston win— but that meant only one thing.

I would have to make the flight.

Anxiety coursed through me as I thought about calling Luc when I returned to the hotel—but that would have to wait. I had another important task to complete today. One that gave me just as much anxiety.

I had to look for Tacy.

Pricilla had told me that her last name in this path was Barclay. Looking through the directories at the *Globe*'s office, I could not find a Tacy Barclay in New York, but I had found several addresses across the city for Barclay families. I planned to start at the closest address, on East 42nd Street, and go from there.

My mind was still spinning from my visit with Thurston when I heard my name above the noise of traffic.

"Grace!"

I paused, uncertain if I had heard correctly. There were so many people that I couldn't see who might have called me.

"Grace Cooper!" I heard again, and I finally spotted Luc as he jogged toward me.

He wore a black pinstripe suit and a straw boater hat with a black band around the crown. He looked like he had stepped off the pages of a fashion catalogue from R. H. Macy & Company Store.

Everything about New York had felt lifeless without Hope—

but in one sweeping moment, a burst of sunshine fell upon it again as Luc's gaze sought mine and he offered me a smile.

Pleasure filled me with surprise. "How did you know where to find me?"

"I came downtown on business and then stopped by the Victoria Hotel. The front desk clerk told me you were heading to the Garment District. I knew that could only mean one thing." He studied me, concern in his eyes. "I hope you didn't confront Thurston alone."

I lifted my chin in defiance.

"Did he back down?"

I pressed my lips together and shook my head.

"I'm sorry, Grace."

"I had to try—but I'm afraid I made it worse." I didn't want to talk about it, so I asked, "Why did you come to see me?"

"I wanted to know how you're doing."

I had to look away for fear I might start crying. It had been two days since Hope's funeral, but it felt so much longer. "I feel adrift."

"I lost my sister, Michelle," he said, "and the hurt still haunts me."

"I'm very sorry."

He nodded and took a deep breath. When he seemed in control of his emotions, he said, "May I take you home?"

Disappointment weighed heavily on my heart. As much as I wanted him to walk me back to the hotel, I wasn't going in that direction. "I am doing some investigative work today and will be traveling all over the city."

His face brightened. "Even better. I have an automobile and would be happy to take you wherever you need to go."

"You don't mind?"

He shook his head, his gaze sincere. "It would be my pleasure."

"You don't have anything better to do?"

"Than spend the day with you?" He smiled. "No."

My pulse ticked a little higher at the warmth in his voice. Anything would be preferable to walking or taking the hot subway—and it would give me the opportunity to tell him about my decision.

He led me down Broadway and stopped at a black Ford Model T before opening the passenger door for me. The top was down, and the leather seat was hot beneath me.

Luc quickly started the vehicle with a crank at the front and then jumped into the car. He pulled onto Broadway, joining the endless sea of automobiles, wagons, and carriages. I gave him the first address on my list, and away we went.

For a few minutes, we rode in silence. For reasons I couldn't identify, I didn't want to talk about the cross-country flight—at least, not yet. I'd had few opportunities alone with Luc, and I had a more pressing question in mind.

"How did you become a pilot?"

"That is a long story," he said.

"We have all day."

He glanced at me, a teasing gleam in his gaze. "I forget you are a journalist, always asking questions."

"And you are a private man, always trying to hide."

He smiled. "You are not interviewing me for an article, are you?"

I shook my head. "No. You would know if I was interviewing you."

"You'd have your little pad of paper and a pencil in hand, no?"

It was my turn to smile. He had seen me interviewing many people over the past few months. "Yes."

"I enjoy your writing."

"As you've said—but now you're avoiding my question."

His eyes were laughing as he turned down 42nd Street, lighting up in a way that made my breath catch.

Who was this man beside me? A man who was so fearless, he would risk flying over Niagara Falls, point the nose of his

218

plane toward the earth at three thousand feet, and continue to fly even after he watched countless friends lose their lives.

Was he fearless or reckless?

"I grew up in Paris," he finally said.

I playfully rolled my eyes. "I know that much."

He smiled at me—and then grew serious. "My father worked in a bicycle factory when I was a small child, and I learned how to ride very early. I loved everything about cycling—until my father died in a factory accident when I was twelve."

His words were heavy upon my heart. It hadn't occurred to me that perhaps he didn't share his past because it was too painful. "I'm so sorry."

He nodded, though his thoughts looked far off. "I was the oldest child, and I had four younger sisters and a mother who depended upon me. I had to leave school and was sent to work at the factory where he died, reminded of his accident every day."

I was quiet as I waited for him to continue. People seemed to talk more when they had the space.

"My youngest sister, Michelle, was often sick. She was so frail and delicate and needed medicine we could not afford. So when I saw that there was a bicycle race with prize money that would take me weeks to earn at the factory, I entered the contest." He smiled, but it was a sad smile. "I won the race and was so proud to give my *maman* the money. I decided I would enter every race I could find, and I was very successful. When I was a bit older, I earned enough money to buy an automobile, and I began to race those, too. Eventually I quit working at the factory. But my maman was very angry with me. She said that the factory was good, honest, dependable income, that I was being ungrateful, and that I didn't care about our family."

His accent grew thicker with emotion, and I could see he still carried the pain from his mother's disapproval.

"I hated to disappoint her, but I had worked in my father's shadow at the factory for six years, and it had almost killed my spirit. I decided that if I was going to leave the factory and race for my family, I would have to be the very best in the world to make my maman proud."

"Is that why you take so many risks?" I asked him gently. For the first time since I'd met Lucas Voland, I felt like I was seeing the real man behind the celebrity. The vulnerability behind the façade of indifference.

"I have to be the best," he said, "even if that means risking my life."

"What would your family do if you died? They would have nothing."

"I have made enough money for Maman to be comfortable for the rest of her life."

"Then why do you continue?"

He pressed the brake at an intersection, bringing the automobile to a pause. "Because she still does not believe in me."

"She still thinks you should be at the factory?"

Luc nodded. "If it was good enough for Papa, then it should be good enough for me. She does not believe people should try to, how do you say, elevate yourself? Rise above your station."

"Did you see her when you were in Paris?"

"No." He pressed the gas pedal again, and we accelerated. "She refused to receive me. She says I have brought shame upon our family. She does not like to see my name in the newspapers. She told me it embarrasses her and our family."

"Is that why you avoid publicity?"

This time, he did not answer as he looked out at the sea of humanity on 42nd Street. But he didn't need to answer me.

I had misjudged him. He was not seeking fame for the sake of fame. He was trying to be the best, to convince his mother that he was worthy of her love and approval—and he was trying to do it without being noticed by anyone but her.

"My youngest sister died shortly after I left the factory," he continued, his countenance heavy. "It seemed no medicine in the world would save her, but somehow Maman blamed me for her death."

"I'm so sorry," I said again, though it didn't seem like enough.

His gaze was filled with emotions so deep, I could mine them for decades and not reach the bottom.

I looked out at 42nd Street, at the people walking into stores, the vendors hawking their wares, and the carriages rolling past, trying to understand what I was feeling—about Luc, about family, and about expectations.

We stopped at several of the addresses on my paper, but no one knew Tacy Barclay. Somehow, it didn't matter. My thoughts were consumed with the story Luc had told me. This was a new side of him, and it conflicted with the image I had created in my mind.

As the morning turned to afternoon, we stopped for lunch, and I shared bits and pieces of my own past growing up in Washington, DC. He asked questions about Hope, but they were for my benefit and not for his. Nothing he said indicated that his feelings ran deeper for my sister than friendly affection—and that, too, changed things.

We arrived at the last address on the Upper East Side late that afternoon. I was determined that if this was not the right one, I'd ask Luc to take me home and I'd try again tomorrow.

"Here we are," Luc said as he pulled up to a brownstone mansion.

I glanced at it, impressed with its size, though there were so many in New York that they all looked alike.

"I hope you find whoever you are looking for this time," he said as he came around to open the door for me.

I took a deep breath and stepped out of the automobile. I had to climb several stairs to get to the massive front door, where I rang the doorbell.

A few moments later, a butler answered. "How may I help you?"

"Is Mr. or Mrs. Barclay receiving callers?"

"Who may I say is calling?"

"My name is Grace Cooper. I'm looking for someone by the name of Tacy Barclay."

The name caused a flicker of recognition in the butler's eyes, and he nodded. "Please come in."

I stepped into the massive foyer and waited as the butler disappeared into the dark interior of the home.

There was an eerie silence and unusual stillness in the corridors of this house, almost as if no one resided there. A chill ran up my spine as I stood, rooted to one spot, my bag clutched in my trembling hands.

Was this Tacy's home? Did she live here now? Would I come face to face with a mother I had never met?

The sound of heels upon marble met my ears before I saw anyone appear. But then an older woman materialized from the dark hallway. She wore a long black gown, old-fashioned but expensive. Her white hair was piled into a bun upon her head, and she wore a long onyx necklace. She was regal in her bearing yet very cool as she looked me up and down.

"I am Mrs. Barclay. Parker said you've come asking after my daughter, Tacy."

I blinked in surprise. I could hardly believe it. *This* was Tacy's mother? "Yes. Is she here?"

Mrs. Barclay clasped her hands and pursed her lips. "We do not speak of Tacy in this home. She has not resided here in over twenty-four years."

Twenty-four years? It was twenty-four years ago that she had been hanged in Boston in my 1692 path. Had something happened to her here, as well?

"Do you know where she is?"

"Who are you?" Mrs. Barclay demanded. "Why do you want to know?"

I hadn't thought about how I would explain myself, so I simply said, "I'm Grace Cooper—I-I work for the *New York Globe*."

"Are you a reporter?"

"Yes." But how was I going to connect that to my interest in Tacy?

"Why are you looking for her?" Her eyes turned into slits. "Is this about her acting?"

Acting? I frowned but took a chance. "Yes."

"Tacy ran away from home twenty-four years ago, and the last I heard, she was in California, married to a movie director." She curled her lips in disgust.

California? My mind raced with the implications. If I made the cross-country flight, I could look for her in California. I would need to wire the *Los Angeles Examiner* and see if someone could locate an address for me. I only had her first name and a former last name, but it might be enough.

"Do you know her married name?"

"I've told you enough." Mrs. Barclay motioned toward the door. "You must leave, and do not say a word about me in the newspapers. I'll sue the *New York Globe* if you do."

"Thank you for your time," I said as I walked to the door. The butler appeared and opened it for me.

Mrs. Barclay did not respond as I stepped outside, stunned.

Luc got out of the automobile and walked around to open the passenger door. "That was fast. Did you find who you were looking for?"

I stood before him, amazed I had found Tacy's mother. "No, but I learned she might be in California."

A slow smile tilted up his lips. "Then that means you must go to California."

"Luc—"

"Come," he said as he offered me his hand and helped me into the automobile.

"Where are we going?"

He grinned. "Into the clouds."

It took us an hour to get to the airfield in Hempstead where Luc kept his Blériot two-seater—and I trembled the whole way. Even though I was determined to learn to fly, it still frightened me beyond reason.

"You are as white as a ghost," he said gently as he put the Model T in park and turned off the engine outside a hangar. There were dozens of aeroplanes on the field, next to the buildings, and in the air. Two mechanics looked up from their work, and both were shocked to see me. Did they think I was Hope?

"I'm not sure—" I began, but Luc put his hand over mine, and my entire body stilled.

He leaned close and said, "I know you are afraid, but I also know you are strong and brave and intelligent. You have what it takes to be a good flyer."

"My sister just died in an aeroplane," I whispered, my emotions making my voice quiver.

"All the more reason to overcome your fear and fly. She loved being in the air, and I know you will, too." He was very serious as he regarded me. "I will not force you to do this. At any time, you can ask me to stop. You can trust me."

He had said the same thing to me on our ride out of the city. But I had not stopped him.

I knew I would go through with it—because I owed it to Hope and to my parents. And I did trust Luc.

As he looked at me with those magnificent blue-green eyes, I suddenly wanted to do it for him, too.

"Let's go," I said.

He grinned, and we got out of the Model T. He motioned for me to follow him to the hangar.

The mechanics who had been watching us straightened as we approached, their faces ashen at the sight of me.

"This is Grace Cooper," he told them. "Hope's twin sister. She's come to fly."

Understanding dawned on their faces, and they smiled.

"Can you have my Blériot ready in ten minutes?" he asked them.

Nodding, they walked into the hangar and started preparing Luc's aeroplane for takeoff.

"There will probably be a lot of confusion around here until everyone knows who you are," Luc said. "You and Hope look a lot alike. I remember the first time I saw you standing together, I couldn't believe my eyes."

"I remember."

"Do you?"

I smiled. "Of course."

"You didn't like me." His eyes teased in a way I was starting to love. Here, at the airfield, away from the noise of crowds and people and responsibilities—and my sister—he seemed different.

"I didn't know you," I protested, "and I had just learned that my sister had kept a very important secret from me—one that you encouraged."

"Oui. I should have known you would be distrustful of me." He returned my smile. "It didn't take long to tell you apart, though. You are very different from your sister."

"She and I could not be more opposite."

"I realized that in Hardelot." He was quiet for a moment as he considered me, as if he wanted to say more, but then he took a deep breath and said, "Come. I will take you into the sky."

Ten minutes later, the aeroplane had been moved onto the field, and I stood before it as Luc finished preparing for the flight. This monoplane was very similar to the one Hope had used in Boston—which made me shake even more. Why had I let him talk me into this?

He came up beside me, putting his hand on the small of my back, and said, "Are you ready?"

"I'm scared," I whispered as I pulled my gaze from the aeroplane to his face.

"You *are* very different from your sister," he said, almost as quiet.

"She was fearless."

"No." He shook his head. "We are all afraid of something. She wanted people to believe she was fearless, but she just hid her fears better than most. And in the process, I think she started to believe it was true." He put his hands on my shoulders and turned me to look at him. "It's important to be honest with ourselves so we know who we are and who we are not. Only then do we become the best version of ourselves."

Warmth spread out from his hands and wrapped around my heart.

"You know who you are, Grace Cooper, and it's an admirable quality."

That was what made me different from Hope? For so long, I had been under her wing—yet here, standing on my own, Lucas Voland saw me, and he liked what he saw.

"I'm ready," I said, something sweet passing between us.

"Good."

He bent to one knee and told me to use it to step onto the plane. I had seen Hope do it a couple of times, but she was wearing a flying suit. In a skirt, it wasn't so easy.

We laughed as I attempted to maneuver into the machine— and it was exactly what we needed to overcome the seriousness of the moment before. After I plopped down on the metal seat, he climbed into the front.

He turned to hand me something. "Here is a hat for you." It was one of his flat caps.

I hadn't even thought about my voluminous hat—but I took it off now, removing the large hat pin first. I handed the hat and the pin to one of the mechanics, who treated it like a small infant or some other delicate creature that might break at any moment, then I looked at Luc's hat.

"Put it on backwards," he said. "The goggles will fit better on your face."

He watched as I did what he instructed. The hat was much too big for my head, and it slipped down my forehead, covering my eyes.

"Perfect!" he said with a laugh.

I made a face, though I couldn't see him.

He reached out and set the hat farther back on my head, a grin on his face as his hand brushed my cheek. The gentle contact surprised me and made me catch my breath.

His eyes met mine, and neither of us said anything for a heartbeat. Then he handed me the goggles. "Put them on," he said softly.

As soon as I had them in place, he turned around and settled into the metal chair in front of me.

And I finally realized how my sister had fallen in love with Luc so easily.

"Do not move—even a little," he warned over his shoulder, drawing my thoughts to something more serious. "Any movement can throw off the balance of the aeroplane."

"Is that what happened to Hope?"

"Oui—that is what I expect. Are you ready?"

"Yes," I said, determined not to look back now.

He told the mechanic to turn the propeller, and the motor started, causing the entire aeroplane to vibrate. I clutched the sides of the cockpit as the energy and momentum gathered.

Luc motioned for the mechanics to let go, and the aeroplane took off down the field. It was bumpy as the machine accelerated, causing my teeth to rattle—and then it left the ground and became smoother than anything I'd ever experienced.

My stomach fell as weightlessness took over and I became

breathless. The feeling was unfathomable—almost surreal. It sent a surge of energy racing through my body, yet a serene calmness washed over me.

Luc looked back, his goggles making it hard to see his eyes—but his smile was unmistakable.

And I knew, in that instant, that my life would never be the same.

19

HOPE

For the first time that I could remember, I woke up before Grace in 1692. The room above the kitchen was hot and humid, and I had been restless all night—something I had never experienced before. I had woken up with fitful dreams, sweating and exhausted.

But a new day was dawning, one that would hopefully bring a bit of joy to our lives. One of Susannah's cousins was getting married in Salem Towne, and her other cousins, Benjamin and Nathaniel, were heading back to Boston after the wedding. It had been an uncomfortable visit, but thankfully, neither had made an offer for Grace or me—at least, not yet.

The wedding would be a nice change of pace. Bethiah Putnam was an older bride, and she was marrying a widower with a small child. Her family's connection—and his—made this an important occasion, with all the wealthiest and most influential families in Massachusetts Bay Colony in attendance. It promised to be a reprieve from the harsh duties at the ordinary, and if I could manage it, I would use the opportunity to sneak away and find the cousin Pricilla had told us about.

Grace slept closest to the wall and was facing me. A hint of color tinted the eastern sky, outlining her cheek. Was her consciousness even now in 1912? What was she doing? Had she found Tacy? Had she decided whether she would make the trip for Armour and Company?

Did she miss me?

I couldn't wait another moment, so I tapped her on the shoulder. "Grace," I whispered.

She murmured something in her sleep.

"Grace," I said again, "wake up."

Slowly, she opened her eyes and blinked a couple of times before yawning. "Good morrow, Hope," she said with a lazy smile—and then her eyes opened wider. "Guess what I did?"

I sat up in our bed, bent over so my head would not hit the slanted ceiling above. "What did you do?"

Her lazy smile turned into a grin. "I rode in an aeroplane."

Elation rushed through me as I remembered what it had felt like to take my first flight.

"With Luc?" I asked.

She nodded. "There's so much to tell you."

"I want to know everything."

Grace glanced out the window behind her and said, "We need to get up. Father will expect breakfast before we leave for Salem Towne." She started to scoot around me, but I put my hand on her shoulder.

"What did you think of flying?"

She put her finger to her lips to quiet me. "What if Father or Susannah hears you? They'll think I was on a broomstick last night."

I couldn't help but smile. "Tell me!"

Grace let out a sigh. "It was magnificent—as you said it would be."

I bit my bottom lip to keep from grinning and saying *I told you so* as a surge of jealousy rushed through me. I pushed it aside, trying to be happy for her. "Did you decide to make the trip to California?"

"Yes. I will go back to Hempstead Plains tomorrow morning, and Luc will give me my first lesson."

A deep and lonely melancholy stole over me unexpectedly. I had to look down for fear I would steal Grace's joy. The last thing I wanted was to discourage her from learning to fly. She needed to do this for our parents—and I wanted her to do it for herself, too.

Thankfully, she was too elated to notice my unhappiness, and she continued.

"I almost forgot! I discovered that Tacy is in California, married to a movie director."

"A movie director?" I said in a stunned whisper. "Our mother is married to a movie director?"

"And," Grace said, fairly bouncing with her news, "she might be an actress—just like you. Maybe we saw her in a movie." She shook her head, her mood dipping. "But her mother was cold and unforgiving, which makes me very sad. She said Tacy left New York twenty-four years ago."

"Which is when she was hanged in this path."

"Yes." Grace nodded. "Her life here must have affected her life there."

"I imagine she was devastated to leave us. Can you imagine how difficult that must have been?"

"I can't wait to find her and ask what happened."

"In California?"

Grace stood and began to dress. "I decided to make the flight after talking to J. B. Thurston, but—"

"You went to Thurston? Daddy told you not to."

231

"I had to try—but I made it worse." She shook her head, as if to move past that bit of information. "I wired a newspaper in Los Angeles, asking if they can help me find Tacy Barclay, though I said she probably has a married name now. But how many Tacys can there be in California? It's not a common name. Hopefully I'll have an address for her by the time I get there."

"*If* she's still alive," I added.

"Yes, of course."

I also rose from our bed, not quite as eager as Grace to start the day but knowing I needed to be ready to serve breakfast. I pushed aside her comment about Thurston, hoping he wouldn't cause her more trouble, and began to dress.

"How is Luc?" I asked cautiously, watching Grace's response. "Does he miss me?"

She pulled on her shift—but didn't look at me. She was slow to answer. "Yes, he misses you."

"Did you talk about me?"

"A little."

"What did you say?"

Again, she took her time to respond. "He talked about how different you and I are."

I lifted my eyebrows. "That's all?"

She pulled on her skirt and secured it with her back to me. "Mm-hmm."

"What else did you talk about, then?"

After taking her waistcoat off the hook, she said, "A lot of things."

"Luc talked about a lot of things?" This I couldn't believe. He rarely spoke to me about anything other than aviation.

Grace seemed a little impatient with my questions, though I couldn't imagine why. "He told me about his childhood in Paris and how his father and sister died. He also told me how he came to be an aviator."

I stared at her. "He told you about his family?"

She turned to me, and there was a strange look on her face, almost like guilt. "I'm sorry, Hope."

"Sorry?" I frowned. "Why would you be sorry?"

"I—" She paused. "I don't know."

I took a deep breath and continued to get dressed. "You have nothing to be sorry about. You're simply doing what I asked you to do." I tried to sound convincing. "I'm happy you and Luc are finally becoming friends. It's what I wanted all along."

But was it? Really? I had tried to forget how Luc watched her on the train from Calais to Paris and how he had crossed the airfield in Boston to join her before I was thrown from my aeroplane.

Grace started to brush her hair, and I didn't ask any more questions.

Before I was finished dressing, she went downstairs to begin breakfast. I stayed above, wrestling with my sadness and my jealousy. I wanted Grace to fly with Luc—but I also wished it were me and not her. I wanted to be happy for her, but it was hard when she was enjoying something I would never do again.

But I struggled the most with my sister's growing relationship with Luc.

More than ever, I resolved to convince Isaac to fall in love with Grace and give her one more reason to stay with me. It wouldn't be easy, but I had to try. Hopefully I would see him at the wedding today, and I could start to put my plan into action.

⁂

The wedding was held in the groom's home in Salem Towne, off Derby Street. He was a sea merchant and lived close to the harbor in a large house, recently built for his first wife. Bethiah, his new bride, was radiant, standing beside her groom in an expensive gown and new satin slippers as they spoke their vows and signed the court registry. Magistrate William Stoughton presided over the ceremony. As one of the judges of the court of oyer and terminer in the witch trial, he was a powerful individual with deep ties to many of the colony's merchants, politicians, and ministers. He was connected to several of the guests through marriage and family, something that was common and hard to avoid in a small colony.

The wedding was much more subdued than those I attended in 1912. There was no dancing or singing, no decorations or music of any kind. There was a lavish meal, however, following the simple civil ceremony. Many people took their food out of doors where it was hot and humid but offered a slight breeze off the cool water.

I joined Grace, who sat on a bench in the corner of the garden. We hadn't spoken much since that morning, but there was little I could say to her about 1912 while we were here. Besides, I was watching for an opportunity to speak to Isaac.

"There you are," Benjamin Putnam said as he approached with a plate full of food. He'd been staying at the ordinary with his brother, Nathaniel, for the past three days, and he'd eaten more than anyone I'd ever met.

I sat next to Grace and was forced to look up at him.

"I'm happy to get the two of you alone without Nathaniel nearby," he said, looking over his shoulder. He came closer, his voice lowered as he smiled expectantly. "I'm willing to make an offer for either one of you."

I turned to Grace, and she turned to me. I couldn't hide the surprise from my face.

"I have no preference," he continued. "You're both one and the same to me, so I'll leave it up to you. I'm certain Nathaniel will take whoever is left."

My mouth parted—not only at his offer but at his callous comment. I could think of nothing else to say but "No, thank you."

Benjamin turned to Grace, appearing unaffected by my refusal.

She shook her head, looking between me and Benjamin like a cornered animal.

"And you—?" He paused, as if he wasn't sure whether she was Grace or me.

"Grace," she supplied.

"Yes." He nodded. "Do you prefer me or Nathaniel, Grace?"

"Neither," Grace finally said.

Benjamin frowned and pulled back. "Susannah led us to believe you two were desperate."

"Perhaps she is desperate to be rid of us," I said derisively, "but we are not desperate enough to marry you."

That did seem to insult him—but I didn't feel remorse. Not after his heartlessness.

I caught sight of Isaac as he walked up to us—but his eye was on Benjamin. Isaac had been at the ordinary the past few days, watching Benjamin and Nathaniel closely.

"Good day, Isaac," I said, standing at his arrival. "I was about to take a turn in the garden. Would you like to join me?"

He frowned slightly at my eager greeting but recovered quickly. "Of course."

I glanced at Grace, giving her an apologetic smile as I walked away with Isaac. Thankfully, Benjamin took our hint and excused himself. He joined Susannah, shaking his head.

She glared at me.

"'Tis a beautiful day for a wedding," I said quickly to Isaac, turning away from Susannah's anger to look at the garden and out at the harbor where tall, dark masts poked against the backdrop of a bright blue sky. A musty, fish-like scent wafted on the breeze, but it was subtle enough that it wasn't unpleasant.

"'Tis, indeed," he agreed as we came to a stop near the water's edge.

I had a lot to say and not much time to say it. "I was thinking about finding my cousin."

He frowned and spoke quietly. "Your Quaker cousin? Why?"

How did I explain this sudden need to feel connected to this time and place? Other than Grace, Pricilla, and my father, I had no other living relatives that I knew. "She is no longer a Quaker," I reminded him.

"She is a servant, if I remember correctly."

"Do you know who she works for?"

He straightened, and his blue eyes filled with disappointment. "You only sought me out to help you find her?"

I tried to offer him my most convincing smile. "Will you?"

He looked toward the ships and shook his head. "'Tis not wise, Hope."

"I must find her." I swallowed the emotions that threatened to clog my throat. I was not used to feeling so desperate or afraid. So lonely and uncertain. "Now that I know I have relatives, I want to meet them."

He must have heard the longing in my voice because he looked at me with apprehension. "Are you well?"

Shaking my head, I set my plate on a nearby bench, no longer hungry. I wanted to explain to Isaac about losing 1912, but I wasn't sure he'd believe me. Though if there was anyone in 1692 who might, it would be him. He had been such a dear friend for years. Always steadfast and trustworthy, even when I had brushed off his friendship. What would he say if I told him now?

I glanced toward the house to see if Grace was near. One of the bride's sisters had sat beside her on the bench, and they were talking. Would she advise me not to tell Isaac?

"If you want to find her," he said, concern in his voice, "I will help you. I would do anything for you."

Unexpected tears filled my eyes, and I saw myself as I truly was—selfish and thoughtless. After all the years I had ignored him, he would still do anything for me. "You have always been so kind to me, even when I have not been kind to you. Why do you persist?"

"Because I want you to be happy."

His words, so simple, warmed my heart.

"Thank you."

"She doth not live far from here. I'll take you there now, and we can be back before anyone misses us."

"Are you certain?"

Isaac nodded and motioned for me to walk with him along the garden's path.

I cast a glance toward the others, but no one seemed to notice as we walked toward the street and turned to the right.

"Your aunt told me your cousin is named Rachel."

"Who is her employer?" I asked.

"A merchant named Josias Reed. He is a very wealthy and influential man." Isaac looked back the way we had come. "He is at the wedding. 'Tis a good time to seek her out, while the others are celebrating and distracted."

The Reeds' house was only a few doors down. It was also on the water's edge. It wasn't as elaborate, but it was still substantial and foreboding, with slanted eaves and diamond-paned glass windows.

"I will wait here for you," Isaac said.

"You don't need to wait for me." He had already done so much, and I remembered my resolve to turn him toward Grace. "I can walk back on my own. Mayhap Grace would like some company."

He shook his head. "I would never leave you."

Something about the way he said those words made my heart pause. "I care for you deeply, Isaac, and always have." He needed to hear the truth. "But 'tis Grace who *loves* you."

He frowned, clearly baffled by my words. "Grace?" He shook his head. "Why do you tell me this now?"

"I—" I paused, not sure he would understand. "Susannah brought her cousins to the ordinary and wishes to see us both married and in our own homes. I do not want Grace to marry someone she doth not love."

His gaze was hooded as he regarded me, and then he finally said, "Do you wish to marry one of Susannah's cousins?"

"No." I shook my head, adamant.

"Do you ever plan to marry?"

He was so serious, so intent on my answer, I had to look away. "I know not."

A few seconds passed before he said, "I will wait for you."

I stared at him, wondering what he meant. He would wait to marry me—or wait for me to speak to my cousin?

Not knowing what to say, I turned and walked along the side of the house to the back door, my heart feeling funny.

After I knocked, it took a bit of time, but a young woman appeared behind the half-opened door. I could see the family resemblance in the blond hair and the slant of our noses. She wore a simple gray dress with a white coif, and had a large shawl over her shoulders, held together in front with her hands. She couldn't have been more than eighteen or nineteen, but she looked tired, as if she had been ill.

"May I help you?" she asked.

"Are you Rachel?"

"Yes." She glanced behind me, toward Isaac waiting on the edge of the property. "And who are you?"

"I'm Hope Eaton. I believe we are cousins."

She stared at me, a confused frown on her brow.

"Our aunt, Pricilla Baker, came to visit and told me about you."

Recognition dawned, though she looked skeptical. "And how are we related?"

"Through my mother." I paused, uncertain if I could trust her with my mother's name.

"Tacy?" she asked.

I nodded.

"I wondered about you. They told me you have a twin sister."

"Grace."

238

"Is she here?"

"She's at the Putnam wedding."

Rachel's pretty blue eyes filled with a longing I couldn't identify. "Mister Reed is at that wedding."

"That's what I heard."

She took a deep breath as she resecured the shawl over her shoulders. It was much too hot for such a large, thick shawl, but perhaps she was still recovering from her illness. "Is there a reason you've come?"

"I wanted to meet you. To tell you that you have cousins in Salem Village. My father owns the ordinary."

"Are you also a time-crosser?" she asked, her voice low, almost angry.

I glanced behind me, but Isaac was looking away. When I returned my focus to Rachel, I nodded. "My other path was 1912, but I recently died there, so this is all I have left. 'Tis one of the reasons I wanted to find family."

She dipped her chin and looked down at the shawl. "My other path is 1882." She shook her head. "'Tis a grand life there. Nothing like this one. There, I have servants. Here, I am one."

"Hope?" Isaac called to me. "We should return."

"If there is anything you ever need," I told Rachel, feeling a kinship with her that went beyond family ties. She understood what it was to be a time-crosser. "Or if you want to talk, send word, and I'll find a way to come."

She let out a weary sigh and shook her head. "I don't receive visitors."

It was all she said, and I wondered if it was because of her illness.

"Fare well, Rachel."

She simply nodded and then stepped back into the house and closed the door.

I slowly returned to Isaac, glancing back at the house, both curious and sad.

"Was it a good meeting?" he asked.

"I'm not certain."

There was a lot I didn't understand—about myself, about Salem, and about my family. The only thing that made sense was the one thing I couldn't have.

1912.

20

GRACE

AUGUST 19, 1912
HEMPSTEAD, NY

It was still dark when I opened my eyes to the sound of the telephone. I didn't have to glance at the clock to know it was four-thirty in the morning. The night before, I had asked the front desk for the wake-up call, knowing I would need to be on the airfield by five for my next lesson. And today would be the most important one of all.

Today I would fly on my own for the first time.

My mind was a jumble of thoughts and emotions as I tossed back the covers and stretched. Elation, trepidation, and expectation for today's flight mingled with grief and uncertainty about what had happened in Salem yesterday.

Five more people had been hanged. Four men and one woman, including the farmer John Proctor and the Reverend George Burroughs. Those who had been at the hanging in Salem Towne had come back to Salem Village visibly shaken. The five accused had claimed innocence to the last, begging God to forgive their accusers and praying that they would be the last innocent blood shed. George Burrough's final prayer had been so moving, people had begun to question his guilt. He finished with a perfect rendition of the Lord's Prayer, which some considered proof of innocence, but the afflicted who were there said they could see the devil's specter whispering the words into his ear.

John Proctor's wife, Elizabeth, had also been condemned, but she was pregnant, and her execution had been delayed until after she could give birth to the child. *If* she could survive childbirth in prison.

I tried to shake off the heaviness that weighed down my soul, needing to focus on the task ahead of me. We were only thirteen days away from leaving for the cross-country flight, and I had yet to fly on my own.

Turning on a light, I quickly dressed in the rented room at the Atlantic City Hotel near the airfield. Since I needed to be at the flying school every day, I had moved out of my apartment at the Victoria Hotel in New York City and into one that was close enough to walk to the airfield in Hempstead. I no longer needed the two bedrooms we'd had at the Victoria—and without Hope's income, I could not afford the weekly rent.

I'd had a flying suit created much like Hope's by the same dressmaker. On suggestion from Luc, it was dark purple to complement the Vin Fiz soda brand. It was surprisingly comfortable, and I didn't mind putting it on now. Mama had told us that women in the future would wear pants all the time, but it was hard to believe. I received many strange looks from those staying at the hotel, but thankfully, as I exited the elevator and entered the lobby that morning, the only person there was the night watchman, and he was used to seeing me in a flying suit.

"Good morning," Luc said as he came down the central stairs moments after me. No matter how early we rose, he still looked excited to face a new day on the airfield. "Are you ready for your flight?"

We had been working together almost every day for six weeks. Learning how to fly in the French style was slow and tedious, but Luc assured me it would set me up for safety and success.

After days of instruction about the mechanics of the aeroplane, I had graduated to what Luc called grass cutting—I had to guide the aeroplane back and forth across the field in a straight line without letting its wheels leave the earth. Then, after five or six successful rides—which meant over a week of lessons—I had moved on to jumping the aeroplane two or three feet into the air at a time as I rushed across the field. This had been affectionately called kangarooing. Each lesson lasted no longer than ten minutes, though I stayed on the airfield to watch the other students who were taking lessons with me.

Today I would fly for real.

"I think I'm ready," I said as we walked toward the front doors of the hotel. "I hope so."

"You're a natural," he reassured me for the dozenth time in the past few weeks. "You know everything there is to know about the mechanics of the aeroplane and the mechanisms for flying it. All you need to do is put them into practice."

I took a deep breath and tried to clear my mind of everything but flying.

It was still dark, and the sun would not rise until just after six o'clock. But there was a lot to do before I could take off for my solo flight, first being the dreaded weather test. If the wind was more than six miles an hour, aviation students were not allowed to fly. It was much too dangerous. I had risen this early several times and been turned away because of the weather. On those days, I would go back to my hotel room and write articles for the *Globe* or go into the city to meet with my editor.

It was impossible to make enough money to purchase the orphanage on my income from the *Globe*—especially when I learned that Mr. Thurston had made good on his threat and upped his offer. Everything rested on this cross-country flight.

The world was quiet as we stepped outside. Darkness blanketed the village of Hempstead, though a few lights glowed from the homes and businesses of early risers.

It was warm but not hot, and the morning stars sparkled with a brilliance that dazzled my imagination. I loved looking at the vast sky. It reminded me of the limitlessness of God. That He would love me, that He would call me His child and choose me for this time-crossing gift, was amazing to contemplate. It was a burden, to be sure, but it was also a blessing. I had heard Mama's stories of her paths and her mother's paths, and I believed, without a doubt, that God had orchestrated their stories for their good and His glory. I trusted He would do the same for me—no matter if I chose 1912 or 1692.

But I still had to choose—and that was the problem. I wanted 1912, but I didn't want to leave Hope. As much as I loved Mama and Daddy, Hope was dearer to me than anything else. Over the past six weeks, I had started to accept that I would choose 1692—and I would tell Mama and Daddy when we got to California.

A heaviness settled over my heart as I thought about leaving this path behind, but I lifted my face and decided to embrace the time I had left. I wouldn't worry about crashing my aeroplane today or any other day while flying to California. I would enjoy this experience to the fullest and be as fearless as possible so I could win the money for my parents. It afforded me a freedom I had never felt before. A place where fear did not linger on the edges of the unknown.

"I've come to love these morning walks," Luc said quietly beside me, breaking the stillness. His accent was deepest in the morning when his voice was sleepy.

"So have I," I said just as quietly as we turned down a side street with large Victorian homes. Ancient elm trees spread out overhead, creating a canopy that prevented us from seeing the stars.

"What will you do after the flight to California?" he asked.

"Assuming I make it?"

He put his hands in his pockets and didn't even hesitate. "You'll make it."

I didn't answer right away, my heart full of so many things. I would have less than two weeks before my birthday if I got to California by September 30th. What would I do with those two weeks? Spend it with Mama and Daddy, look for Tacy, and finish up any lingering articles I owed to the *New York Globe*? Was that what I wanted to do?

"I'm not sure," I said, honestly.

"Would you like to keep flying?"

Shaking my head, I sighed. "No."

"No?" He stopped and turned to me, his face shadowed by the darkness, though I could see him without trouble. "Perhaps today, after you've flown by yourself, you will think differently."

"Is this what you want to do for the rest of your life?" I asked. "If you continue, it's only a matter of time before something goes wrong. I hate watching you do the death dive." I looked down at my hands. Unlike Hope, if Luc died, that would be it. He would be gone forever.

"Does it bother you?" he asked, his voice low.

"Yes. I hate it."

"Why?"

"Why?" I studied him, trying to understand. "Because it makes me afraid."

"Afraid of what?"

"Afraid of losing you." The last word came out on a surprised breath.

He did not move as the first trills of a morning bird sang from the branches above us. "Why do you fear losing me?"

"Because," I said slowly, trying to understand my own

thoughts and feelings. At some point in the past six weeks, Luc had become a very dear friend. I had learned his habits, his mannerisms, even the way he spoke and how he thought. I had memorized his laugh lines and loved the way his accent changed the cadence of familiar words. Everything I had once assumed about him had been rewritten, and I had come to respect him deeply. "Because," I tried again, "you are dear to me, and I would miss you very much."

He regarded me in the darkness as a gentle wind rustled the leaves overhead and played with the tendrils of hair at my temples. "Thank you."

"Why?"

"Every time someone speaks about my death, they are sad because they would lose something I can *do* for them. For my mother, it's the money I earn. For my students, it's the education I give them. And for my fans, it's the thrill I provide." He reached out and removed the tendril that laid across my lips. "To know that you would miss me because I am very dear to you gives my life new meaning." He lowered his hand, but his gaze stayed on mine. "You are very dear to me, too, *ma chérie.*"

My heart started to flutter a new beat. When had I become his darling?

Affection for this thoughtful man had taken root within me weeks ago, but it was quickly turning into something more. Something much deeper.

Was I losing my heart to Lucas Voland? I couldn't love him—

"Come," he said, as he took my hand, "we will be late."

"Do not be afraid," Luc said to me an hour later as I sat in the cockpit of the Blériot aeroplane I would use for my first solo flight. He was standing beside me, his face level with mine. "Just remember all the things I have taught you."

"I'm not afraid," I told him—at least, not of flying. That was easy and far less frightening than trying to understand the complicated feelings churning within my heart since this morning's walk.

"Good," he said with a proud smile. "You are ready."

He backed up and motioned to the mechanics that I was prepared for takeoff.

The weather was ideal for my first solo flight. Light filled the morning sky, but the sun had not yet crested the horizon. The field was clear and level, and a mechanic stood at the far end, ready if I needed help.

It was my turn to fly.

With a deep breath and a prayer, I put everything else behind me and focused on my flight.

When I gave the front mechanic my signal, I flipped on the ignitor, and he turned the propeller. It whirred to life and began to tug at the men restraining it.

This was the moment I had been waiting for. If I failed, I had Mama and Daddy to think about. I had to do this and do it well. There wasn't much time before the cross-country flight. For the next thirteen days, I would need to practice as much as possible so I would be ready to tackle one of the biggest goals of my life. It was absurd even to contemplate that in less than two weeks I would be attempting to fly across the United States of America—and I had yet to fly solo.

I motioned to the mechanics, and they let me go.

This aeroplane was lighter and more powerful than the one I had been using for grass cutting and kangarooing. It raced across the bumpy field, causing my vision to bounce. When I pulled back on the throttle, the wheels left the earth, and the incessant jarring stopped.

My stomach fell, and everything became smooth.

I yelled with joy as I lifted the aeroplane higher still. I was flying! I could almost see Hope down below, cheering me on with

247

the others. Even though she wasn't there with me physically, she was there with me in spirit. I would tell her all about it tomorrow when I woke up in Salem. She would want to know every detail, and I would do my best to share them.

It only took me a couple of minutes to get to the end of the field, and there I moved the lever to warp the wings to bank the aeroplane and make a lefthand turn. The mechanic waved his white handkerchief as I arced over him and headed back toward the hangar.

The hardest part of the flight would be the landing. I would need to ease back on the speed and start to lower the aeroplane. The second my wheels touched the earth, I had to kill the engine, allowing enough space to let the aeroplane come to a complete stop on its own. There were no brakes in this machine, so I had to do everything with exact precision.

I began my descent, as Luc had instructed, and eased back on the throttle. The hangar was coming up quickly, so I eased back more and then lowered the machine until I felt the first jolt of the earth beneath me. As fast as I could, I switched off the motor and tried to keep control of my aeroplane as it bounced along the field.

Slowly, the wheels came to a stop, about fifty yards from the hangar.

Relief and exhilaration engulfed me as my fellow classmates and Luc rushed toward me, cheering and clapping.

I had done it—in less than five minutes. I had flown an aeroplane, and I wasn't looking back.

"Well done," Luc called to me as I stood from the seat and began to climb out of the aeroplane.

He reached up and grasped me around the waist, lowering me to the ground as if I weighed next to nothing. For a heart-stopping moment, he kept his hands at my waist and looked down at me with an admiration that went beyond the flight. I was breathless from flying—and from being so near him.

But in the next second, I was being lifted onto the shoulders of my classmates, all men, who proceeded to carry me back to the hangar, cheering.

I tossed a lingering look back at Luc, my heart and thoughts in a jumble.

There was much to tell Hope—and much more to keep to myself.

21

HOPE

All morning and afternoon, I thought about Grace's flight. She had told me everything she could think of, and it was still on my mind as I sat under the large oak tree on the side lawn of the ordinary, darning stockings.

It was a beautiful summer afternoon, much too nice to be indoors. Grace was in the kitchen, finishing her baking, but she'd said she would join me later. For now, I was soaking up the warmth and letting my mind drift into the bright blue sky and the billowing clouds up above. I ached to fly again—and that ache had turned to a pit in my stomach. I'd been stuck in 1692 for seven weeks, and with each passing day, I missed 1912 more.

A gentle breeze whispered across my skin as I lowered my gaze. A woman was walking toward the ordinary on the road to Salem Towne. She limped as if she was in pain, but nothing else looked unusual about her.

I concentrated on the stocking again, my mind slipping to Isaac. It had been weeks since he had come to the ordinary—not since the wedding in Salem Towne and my meeting with Rachel. I had heard he was away from the village on business in Boston, but that hadn't put my mind to rest.

I couldn't stop thinking about those few moments Isaac and I had spent together. They were the only thing that eased the constant pain in my heart, so I played them repeatedly in my mind. He'd said he would never leave me, and that simple statement had changed something inside of me. It caused me to think of him whenever I had a moment to myself—like this one. I thought of the past few months, how he had gone to Sandwich on our behalf, had orchestrated our meeting with Pricilla, and how he had taken me to my cousin.

I thought of his home, his servants, his farm, and his friendships. Everything Isaac valued was better because of it. He treated the people and the things in his life with treasured devotion, and because of that, they prospered. He was a man deeply respected in the village and beloved by everyone.

It was no wonder Grace was in love with him. He was just like her.

As my thoughts strayed to him, I was more determined than ever to convince him to love my sister. They deserved each other.

But I was running out of time, and he was nowhere to be found.

I glanced up again, and the woman was closer. Her limp was more pronounced, and her form had grown familiar.

The back door of the ordinary opened, and Grace appeared. She wiped her wrist along her brow and then stepped into the sunlight, closing the door behind her. "I believe I'm done until it's time to start supper." She walked over to her garden, which was flourishing, and surveyed it for a moment, her hands on her hips. "I should probably weed the potatoes."

"Grace," I said as I kept my eye on the approaching woman, unsure if I was seeing correctly. "Come here."

She walked over to me, her gaze traveling to the woman, and she put her hand up to shade her eyes. As the woman drew closer, my suspicions were confirmed. I set the darning in my sewing basket and stood.

I grasped Grace's arm and said in a hushed whisper, "That's our cousin, Rachel."

Grace turned to me, surprise and concern in her brown eyes. "Are you sure?"

"Yes." I looked toward the ordinary, my heart pounding. "If Father sees her, it will not go well for any of us."

"We need to stop her," Grace said, "but we don't want to draw attention from the watchtower or from anyone in the ordinary. Mercy Lewis and Mary Walcott were just here visiting Susannah."

"Let's go to the side of the ordinary, out of sight from the watchtower, and see if we can catch her eye before she goes in the front door."

I was already moving in that direction. There were no windows on the east side of the building except our bedroom window on the second floor. Grace followed, and we stood there until Rachel was within shouting distance. I glanced around the front of the building to see if anyone was there and then called out to Rachel.

She didn't hear me at first, but when I called her name a second time, she looked up.

I motioned her toward me, conscious of the customers who came and went throughout the day. I had told her to send word and I would go to her if she needed me. It was too dangerous for her to come here. We could not be seen with Rachel. There would be too many questions. And if Father found out we had learned our mother's identity and were in contact with family members, they would all be in danger.

Rachel hastened her steps, making her limp more pronounced, and joined us on the side of the ordinary. We were sheltered there, within the overgrown brush that grew on that side of the building.

She was dressed much the same as the last time I had seen her, with the oversized shawl held snug next to her throat, covering most of her body. She looked just as ill as before, though she was sweating, and her coif was askew.

"You're hurt," I said as I drew her toward us.

"'Tis just a twisted ankle," she said. "I fell outside of town, so I haven't come far with it hurting."

"You walked all the way from Salem Towne?" I asked. It was five miles, and though people walked it all the time, it wasn't wise to be out alone. The fear of Indian attacks or highwaymen was a constant threat, especially to single women.

"It was the only way I could get here." She looked from me to Grace and back to me. "Are you Hope?"

I nodded and then pointed to my sister. "And this is Grace."

"I'm pleased to meet you, Rachel," Grace said with a pleasant smile. "I'm happy you've come."

"Why *have* you come?" I asked. "I hope you're well." Though she didn't appear well.

Rachel looked down at her hands, which clasped her shawl about her like a vise. "I am not well—and I knew not where to turn."

"What can we do for you?"

Taking a deep breath, Rachel unclasped her hands and opened her shawl to reveal her midsection, which was large with child. I pulled back, both surprised and alarmed at her secret.

"The child belongs to Mister Reed," she said with her eyes cast down, her voice in a whisper.

Grace did not pull back but gently laid her hand on Rachel's arm. "Will he not marry you?"

She wrapped her arms around herself, closing the shawl once

again. "He's married to another. She lives in England with their children, but a letter arrived this very day telling him that she will be here by autumn."

Grace looked at Rachel with empathy and pain and asked the question that had been burning in my mind. "Was this child conceived in love or abuse?"

Tears came to Rachel's eyes, and she buried her face in her hands. "I met Josias before I moved to Salem Towne. I-I came because he asked me to live with him." She shook her head. "I'm not living as his servant, but as his kept mistress. His wife was supposed to stay in England."

"That's why you left your family?" I asked.

She nodded, but then the tears started in earnest. "I love him." She bent under the weight of her circumstances and crumpled to the ground, her back against the ordinary.

Grace crouched down and put her arm around Rachel's shoulder, murmuring encouraging words while I looked around to make sure no one had found us. When Rachel settled and had a better command of her emotions, she wiped her cheeks and looked up at me.

"I'm sorry to have come. I didn't know where else to go."

"Hath Mister Reed told you to leave his home?" Grace asked.

"No. But we don't know what we're going to do. We cannot imagine being away from each other."

As an unmarried pregnant woman, she was taking a risk to be seen in public. She could face fines, whipping, and even imprisonment. If it was proven that Mister Reed had committed adultery, he could face fines and whipping, as well. It was a very serious crime, one that would not go unpunished if discovered.

"What can we do to help you?" Grace asked, though there would be very little assistance we could give.

"If I need somewhere to live," she said to us, "once his wife arrives in Salem Towne, could I come here?"

Grace looked up at me, and I knew what she was thinking

as she let out a weary sigh. "Our father would never allow it. Perhaps you should go back to your family in Sandwich."

"I cannot," she said bitterly. "They would never take me."

"I think they would." I squatted next to her and laid my hand on her other arm. "They welcomed back our mother when she arrived with us on her hips."

"She was married," Rachel said.

"They love you," Grace told her, "and would rather see you safe at home than whipped and put in prison."

A noise at the corner of the house caught my attention the moment before Susannah appeared. Her gaze darted from one person to the next and then landed on me, a self-satisfied smile tilting up the corners of her lips.

"Uriah!" she called. "I've found them."

Rachel looked like she was about to bolt—but it was too late.

Father appeared, and he did not look pleased.

"What is the meaning of this?" Father asked as we all stood in the sweltering kitchen a few minutes later. "Who is this woman?"

I swallowed my fear and said, "This is Rachel." I didn't even know her last name—a fact that hadn't seemed to matter until now.

"Rachel?" Father stepped closer to her. His arms were crossed as he looked down his nose. "Rachel who?"

"Rachel Howlett," she said in a small voice, sweat dripping down her temples.

I could see the moment the name registered in Father's mind. Shock, fear, and then anger raced across his face. "Howlett?"

"Yes, sir." She clasped her thick shawl so tightly about herself, her knuckles were white.

Susannah stood off to the side, watching, her own growing babe just starting to show.

Father turned to her. "Leave us, wife."

Her eyes grew large as indignation rose in her face. "Leave?"

"Now!" Father commanded.

Susannah jumped, and then she began to cry as she ran up the back stairs.

Father's face had turned red as he stared at Rachel. "What are you doing here?"

I stepped forward. "I invited her to come." It wasn't quite true. I had told her to get word to us if she needed us, but it was an invitation, nonetheless.

"You?" He turned to me, and all the years of strife and anger we had pointed at one another seemed to come to a volcanic head. The rage in his face was frightening. "Do you know who this woman is?"

"She is my cousin," I said, unwilling to back down, though I knew the ramifications would be severe.

He ran his hands through his hair and said, almost to himself, "I should have silenced Ann Pudeator twenty-four years ago. She hath brought this curse upon my house. At least now she will pay."

"Curse?" I asked. "To know our mother? To know our kin?"

"What kin do you know?" He spun on his heels and stormed toward me. "Who else have you met?"

I would never tell him—not if he whipped me until I died. "I have met no one."

"How did you find this woman?" he asked, looking at Grace, probably hoping to find a more obedient witness.

"Ann told us," Grace lied. Ann was already in prison. What more could Father do to her? "Rachel lives in Salem Towne."

She made it sound like Ann had met Rachel through her connections there. It might be true, but it wasn't how we had met her. I admired Grace for not giving in to Father's demands. There was no telling what he would do to Pricilla or Isaac if he knew the truth.

"Why have you come here?" Father asked Rachel next.

She flinched and looked at each of us, terror in her eyes.

"Have you come to spread the destructive teachings of your Quaker beliefs?"

Rachel shook her head. "I do not follow the Quakers."

"But you have—you were born of Quakers."

"Were we not born of a Quaker, as well?" I asked Father in a steely voice.

He breathed heavily through his nostrils as he sliced his hand through the air and said to Rachel, "Be gone from here. And do not darken my door again. Do you understand?"

Rachel's face was ashen as she fled from the kitchen without looking back.

Father stared at me, and I knew I had pushed him beyond reason. "What hath she told you about your mother?" he asked through a clenched jaw.

I would not cower before him. "We know she was hanged and that you did nothing to help her."

Remorse and pain flickered in his eyes, but it was soon covered by righteous indignation. "You know not what you speak of, girl. She was warned—I warned her—and she heeded me not. She was headstrong and stubborn." He shook his head in disdain. "She was exactly like you. And if you do not heed my words, you, too, will hang at the end of a noose, and I will do nothing to stop it from happening."

I inhaled a sharp breath, his words cutting deep.

Grace cried out in shock and took a step toward me, but Father moved between us and turned to me.

"Do not see that woman again—or any of her family. This is my one and only warning."

Father turned and went up the back stairs, probably to console his wife, while I stood rooted to the spot, plagued by his words.

Grace wrapped me in her arms and held me tight. "Do not listen to him," she whispered.

"He would see me hang, like he saw his own wife hang. There

is no love in him, Grace. Just anger and bitterness and self-righteousness."

"There is fear," she said as she continued to embrace me. "He fears that which he cannot control—that is why he feared Tacy and why he fears you."

My tears came then—not only for what he had said, but because I was stuck here with no escape.

A knock at the back door made both of us jump. Rachel wouldn't have returned, would she?

As Grace left me, I turned my back to the door and wiped my cheeks with my apron.

"Good day, Isaac," Grace said, her voice strained.

Isaac?

I turned and our gazes met across the kitchen. His smile fell, and he stepped past Grace. "What's wrong?"

I'm not sure if he pulled me into his arms or if I fell into them, but in an instant he was holding me close. His arms were strong as they wrapped around me. His chest solid and comforting. I could feel the beating of his heart against my cheek, and I closed my eyes, certain that no one or nothing could hurt me here.

After a moment, I realized Grace was watching, and I pulled back, wiping my face.

"Why are you crying?" he asked, his voice low and gentle.

"I fought with my father" was all I would tell him.

"I'm sorry." He glanced at Grace and then back at me. "I brought something. Perhaps it will cheer you." He reached into the bag he carried and removed a round, shiny orange.

My lips parted in surprise as I looked up at his handsome face. "Where did you find it?"

"In Boston. It cost a king's ransom, but I knew it would please you." He took my hand and turned it over, then he placed the fruit onto my palm. "For you."

I swallowed the emotions that welled up inside me. I had

thought I'd never get another orange after dying in 1912—but Isaac had found one for me. "How did you know?"

"You told me once, many years ago."

Without another thought, I threw myself into his arms again, and this time I hugged him.

That evening, darkness fell over Salem Village, bringing with it a relentless storm that pounded against the windows of the ordinary. Isaac stayed for supper, and I made sure he had extra servings of the roasted turkey and stewed peas Grace cooked.

Susannah had not yet come down from her room, and I suspected she was both embarrassed and enraged at the way Father had treated her. He stayed abovestairs for most of the evening, and I could hear him pleading with her to forgive her.

He did not ask for my forgiveness.

As the storm wore on, Grace and I encouraged Isaac to stay and enjoy the orange with us. We drew chairs up to the hearth in the kitchen, and I peeled the orange, relishing the scent of the citrus. I wished I could tell Isaac what the gift meant to me, but I couldn't without revealing our time-crossing. So I showed him with my smiles and kind words.

I tore the sections apart and handed Grace and Isaac their pieces, then slipped one into my mouth and audibly moaned with delight.

"Had I known how much the gift would please you," Isaac said with a laugh, "I would have bought you one much sooner."

I laughed as juice dribbled down my chin. I hadn't been this happy since losing 1912.

I was just finishing my last bite when a strange noise sounded above our heads. Looking up, I frowned.

A moment later, Father appeared at the head of the steps, his face wild with fear. "Susannah is under affliction. She spasms like the others, and she is crying out in anguish. Come! I need help restraining her."

The three of us raced up the stairs, my stomach filling with dread at what we might see. The behavior of the afflicted was often gruesome and unhuman-like.

Susannah lay on the floor in a contorted position. Her body jerked this way and that as she cried out in pain.

"She afflicts me!" She grabbed at her arm. "She bites me and pinches me." A bitemark was fresh upon her forearm as she cried out to an invisible phantom in the room. "Leave me be! I beg of you!"

"Take hold of her," Father commanded us. "I fear this affliction will hurt the unborn child she carries."

Father knelt and put his hands on Susannah's shoulders, and Isaac secured her legs. Susannah still jerked and screamed, but she could no longer hurt herself.

"Who doth afflict you?" Father demanded as he looked into his wife's face.

"The woman who was here today," Susannah cried. "The one with the fair hair. She causes strife in my home and now afflicts me, causing me to suffer."

Father looked up at me, accusation in his gaze. "She speaks of Rachel Howlett."

I knew exactly who she spoke of—and exactly why she called her out. Either she was angry because of Father's treatment, or Father had convinced her that Rachel was a witch so he could be rid of her.

I left the room and ran down the back stairs. Did Father believe we would allow this plan to succeed? I needed to warn Rachel so she could escape Salem Towne—perhaps go to her family in Sandwich.

In the kitchen, I reached for my cloak by the door, but Grace appeared right behind me.

"Where are you going?"

"To warn Rachel."

"In this weather? How will you get there?"

Isaac appeared at the top of the steps next. "Who is Rachel?"

"Rachel Howlett, our cousin," I told him as I secured the cape about my shoulders.

"The one you met in Salem Towne? The one who serves Mister Reed?" He approached me, a frown marring his face.

I had no time to explain, but perhaps he would take me if he knew the truth. "She came here this afternoon, and Father was displeased. That is why Susannah hath accused her."

"You cannot go to Salem Towne in this storm," Isaac said to me. "'Tis too dangerous."

"Can you not take me?"

"You are going nowhere." Father came down the stairs, fire in his gaze. "I am going now to Salem Towne to make the arrest myself. By night's end, Rachel Howlett will be in the Salem gaol."

"No!" I reached for his arm, but he pushed me off, and I fell to the floor as he strode out into the night.

22

GRACE

SEPTEMBER 1, 1912
SHEEPSHEAD BAY, NY

For eleven days, Hope and I had pleaded with Father and Susannah to recant, but for eleven days, Susannah's afflictions increased, often coming on in the taproom or dining room, where she had the largest audience. As Father promised Hope, Rachel had been arrested that very evening, and it was quickly discovered that she was expecting a child. She refused to name the father, sparing Josias Reed, though everyone suspected the truth.

As I sat in an automobile moving toward Sheepshead Bay on the south end of Brooklyn, I forced myself to take several deep breaths. In just under an hour, I would take off for the first leg of the cross-country flight to California, and the last thing I needed to worry about was Salem.

"Are you nervous?" Mama asked as she sat beside me.

We were in the back of the automobile while my father sat in front with the driver. Luc would meet us at Sheepshead, where the Vin Fiz Flyer, as my aeroplane had been dubbed, was waiting and the three-car train was ready to go.

"Yes," I admitted. "But not just about the flight."

She nodded, taking my hand in hers. Mama and Daddy had come to New York two days ago, and I had told them all about what was happening in Salem. If anyone understood, it was Mama. She had lived in three troubling times and was a strength to lean upon.

"It will all work out," she said, as only a mother could. She spoke quietly so the driver wouldn't hear. "Try to be present in this moment and put aside thoughts of everything else. You can deal with Salem tomorrow."

I nodded as I took another deep breath. She had often told me not to let one path affect the other, though it was almost impossible, especially when Hope was stuck in 1692. My plan to tell my parents that I was going to stay in 1692 was foremost in my mind—but I wouldn't worry about that until we reached California and the trip was behind us.

We had enough trouble to contend with already. Papa had asked Mr. Lorenz if we could extend the deadline a little longer, in case I didn't make it to California in thirty days. But Mr. Lorenz refused the request. I had no choice but to reach California by September thirtieth if I wanted to save the orphanage.

The traffic was thick as we made our way south. "Will we be late?" I asked the driver.

"We should get there on time, Miss Cooper."

"Why are there so many people?"

"I think they're all here to see you." He nodded at the crowds moving along the boardwalk, heading to the beach.

I closed my eyes and said a prayer, wondering what I had gotten myself into. I had flown several times a day since my first flight on August 19th, but I still didn't feel ready. So many things could go wrong.

I would leave Sheepshead, New York, and follow the railroad

tracks as I flew west over the Appalachian Mountains toward Chicago, making several stops along the way. To avoid the Rocky Mountains, which would be much more treacherous, I would fly southwest over Missouri, Oklahoma, and into Texas, then head a bit northwest to California. Luc and I had pored over dozens of maps and made a route that should take twenty-six days. If we had trouble along the way or encountered bad weather, we would need to deal with it as quickly as possible so we could stay on track.

The driver turned down a side street and was able to pick up a little speed before doubling back and driving along the beach-side road. My eyes widened at the number of people who had come out to see the start of my trip. Mama squeezed my hand, and Daddy turned to smile, his dark brown eyes full of pride.

I hoped I wouldn't disappoint them—and everyone else.

But my real fear was embarrassing Luc.

We'd hardly had a minute alone since my first solo flight, and I was thankful. There had been something in his gaze—and something in my heart—that frightened me that morning. It was easier to stay busy and try to push the feelings aside than to face them and what they could mean.

Sweat ran down my spine as we finally pulled up to the roped-off area where my Blériot sat waiting. The word *Vin* had been painted under one wing and *Fiz* under the other. In smaller letters was "The Ideal Grape Drink." The awaiting train also had the Vin Fiz message painted on both sides with "Five Cents" and "Sold Everywhere" included. There was no question who was sponsoring this trip.

Luc stood next to the Vin Fiz Flyer, speaking to a group of reporters. He had told me that I would answer questions and then the governor of New York would make a speech. After that, I would take off, heading toward my first stop of Middle-town, New York, a flight of about seventy miles. It would be the longest flight I had ever made, and my pulse was racing.

Luc's smile was bright as I stepped out of the automobile to the sound of the cheering crowd. But despite the hundreds of people around me, he was the only one I saw. I was amazed at the confidence he inspired in me.

The next hour felt like ten as I answered endless questions from reporters and then listened to the governor drone on about the advancement of aviation and the historic journey I was about to undertake. William Randolph Hearst made a surprise appearance and handed me a large bouquet of roses, wishing me well. I gave them to my mother to take on the train.

Many people mentioned Hope and how proud she would be of me. I smiled at my parents, knowing Hope would be waiting for a full report tomorrow.

All I wanted was to get on with the flight, but I kept a smile on my face and endured the endless applause from the crowd.

Finally, it was time for me to leave. I put my canvas jacket on over my flying suit and then gladly climbed into the Vin Fiz Flyer just to be done with the questions. I waved at the crowd, blew a kiss to my parents, and took a deep breath.

Luc came up to the aeroplane and leaned close so I could hear him. He smelled good, and when he smiled, his eyes shone with pride and admiration. "I have nothing left to say, but Godspeed. You are ready for this day, *mon petit oiseau.*"

"What does that mean?" I asked, thankful for his calm reassurance.

He took my hand and brought it to his lips. Pressing a gentle kiss there, he said, just loud enough for me to hear, "My little bird." I smiled as he let me go and stepped away from the aeroplane. "I will see you in Middletown."

With that, he motioned to the mechanics to be ready, and I slipped my goggles over my eyes and pulled on my leather gloves. I signaled the front mechanic to turn the propeller, and the plane roared to life.

Everything else faded away as I faced the smooth, sandy

beach. The Vin Fiz Flyer pulled against the mechanics like a beast ready to be let loose from its cage—a beast I wasn't sure I could wrangle, though I would try my very best.

With another wave of my hand, the mechanics let her go, and I was off.

I quickly rose to the sky and banked the aeroplane to head northwest toward Middletown in the Hudson Valley region, at the foothills of the Shawangunk Mountains. Though I was anxious about flying the plane, it felt good to be away from the crowd.

Seventy miles would take me just under an hour and a half, if I had no delays or complications. The Vin Fiz Special, as the train had been named, would meet me there soon after landing. The Special was made up of three cars—a sleeper car, a diner car, and a mechanical shop on rails, filled with spare parts and tools to maintain the flyer at optimal performance.

I had memorized this leg of the journey and watched for landmarks. I flew between fifteen hundred and two thousand feet so I didn't miss any of them. Across Brooklyn I flew, then over the lower tip of Manhattan, where I could see thousands of people watching for me in Battery Park. The Statue of Liberty stood off to my left, raising her torch above her head like a beacon. No matter how many times I saw her, she still brought tears to my eyes.

I turned my attention to the Hudson River, which ran up the west side of Long Island, and flew low to see the crowds who had lined 12th Avenue.

The motor ran as smooth as ever, and the sunshine sparkled off the water below. Wind rushed past me, cooling my warm body. As I veered west and headed toward Middletown, the crowds behind me and California in front of me, I took a deep, cleansing breath.

I was only thirty days away from saving Mama and Daddy's orphanage.

The sun was fading behind the Shawangunk Mountains in the western sky as I stood beside the Vin Fiz Flyer and laid my hand on her fuselage. After a day of flying and weeks of nerves, I was exhausted—but exhilarated.

Behind me, the Vin Fiz Special was sitting on a side track in the Middletown depot yard, and the crew was celebrating our first day. Both reporters for the *New York Journal* and the *Los Angeles Examiner* were in the diner car, as were the two mechanics, the representative for Armour and Company, my parents, and Luc. The chef and porter had served an amazing meal, which I had eaten with enthusiasm. But after the meal, I had slipped away, needing a little time and space to process everything that had happened.

And to look at the telegram I had received upon arriving in Middletown.

Another reporter from the *Los Angeles Examiner* had found Tacy. Her name, according to the telegram, was now Tacy Bennet. She was married to Grant Bennet, a film director, and was co-owner of the aptly named Bennet Studios. I also had a home address for her. It was everything I needed to find her when I arrived in California.

I was thrilled—yet apprehensive. What if she didn't want to meet me? What if she turned me away? What if, like Daddy suggested, I shouldn't seek her out? Would I mess everything up?

Running my hand along the fabric of the fuselage, I didn't notice Luc's arrival until he spoke.

"You should not look so sad. Today was a success."

My heart sped at his gentle voice, and I turned. "I'm not sad."

He stood a few feet away with the setting sun behind him. I tried to still my heart, but it was impossible. Each time I saw him, affection overwhelmed me. Even in Salem, thoughts of Luc followed me—filling me with perplexing emotions I had never felt before. Happiness, joy, uncertainty . . . longing.

Guilt.

He put his hands in his pockets and slowly walked closer to me.

I had changed out of my flight suit and was wearing a simple skirt and blouse with a pair of heeled boots and a plain black ribbon around my head. My hair was in a long braid that rested over my shoulder.

When Luc stopped next to me, he reached out and lifted my braid, running his thumb over the strands of blonde hair. "*C'est doux.*"

I held my breath.

A smile warmed his eyes as he met my gaze. "It's as soft as I always suspected."

Slowly, he moved his hand from my braid to my cheek, pausing as he studied me. Waiting for me to stop him?

I had no desire to stop him.

Something had been building between us for weeks—something I had tried to deny and push aside. The tension was coiling deep within me, winding tighter and tighter, until I feared I might burst from the pent-up longing that filled my soul.

With a tenderness that made my heart ache, he laid the back of his fingers against my cheekbone and trailed them down to my jaw. A delightful shiver ran up my spine and made me tremble, so I reached up and put my hand over his. It was an anchor. Warm and strong.

Luc's gaze became very serious. The setting sun shadowed one side of his face while casting the other side in shades of rose gold.

"Grace." He said my name almost reverently as he drew closer to me.

He was going to kiss me—and I wanted him to, more than anything. Perhaps if he kissed me, this feeling in me would subside.

Even as I leaned into him, Hope's face appeared in my mind's eye, and guilt washed over me again. What would she think if she saw me standing here with the man she loved?

I wanted to let him kiss me, but I shook my head and swallowed my disappointment. "I'm sorry."

The look in his eyes instantly shifted, and I could see his old guards rising. He lowered his hand, but I reached for him, wanting him to understand. But how could I make him see?

I held his hand between both of mine. "I-I can't," I said, swallowing again. "But it's not because I don't want to."

His shoulders were stiff.

"Please," I said, bringing his hand to my lips. I pressed a kiss there as tears burned behind my eyes. "It's because of Hope."

"Hope?" He frowned and shook his head, clearly confused.

I briefly closed my eyes, forcing back my tears. When I opened them again, I lowered his hand. "Hope is—was—desperately in love with you."

He still looked confused.

"Didn't you know?" I asked.

"Of course I knew." He took a step away from me and ran his hands through his dark hair before putting them in his pockets again.

I pressed my lips together, needing to know the truth. "Did you love her?"

He looked at me, and there was no guile or pretense in his gaze. "No."

Relief filled me for reasons I wasn't ready to examine, but it didn't change the fact that Hope loved him.

Luc stepped closer to me again. "Are you afraid that you're my second choice? Because you are not—and never have been."

I shook my head. The thought hadn't even occurred to me. "I cannot betray my sister's memory."

"I know what it is to honor a memory. I tried to honor my father's for six long years, and in the process, it almost destroyed me. I finally had to stand up to his memory and to my mother's expectations and start living the life I wanted." He spoke plainly, with a rawness that cut me deep. "I care for you, Grace—very much. Do you remember the day on the *Amerika* when you spoke to Captain Barends about your writing?"

I nodded.

He lifted his hand to my cheek again, his fingers slipping into my hair as his thumb caressed my cheekbone.

"That was the day that I realized you were one of the most unique and beautiful women I had ever known—not only on the outside, but deep within, where your spirit and your soul collide. You are brave and fierce and determined. You care about injustice and seek after truth. And your loyalty to those you love is admirable. You never pretended with me—or anyone else. You are true to yourself, and that is a quality I admire above many others." He smiled and shook his head. "Do you remember when I asked you to dance the first night on the ship?"

I nodded again, unable to speak.

"When you refused me, I wished I had not been such a fool to treat you as I did in the beginning. I had great expectations for Hope and knew she could accomplish more for women in aviation than anyone I'd ever met—until you. When she introduced us and I saw the fiery passion in your eyes to protect her, I thought you would try to stop her. I misjudged you and was not kind. I quickly realized I was wrong, but it was too late, and you already disliked me."

My chest rose and fell in short breaths as I looked into his eyes.

"And every day since," he continued, his voice low, intimate, "I have hoped and prayed you would forgive me and see me for who I am—an imperfect man who is falling in love with you."

He looked at my mouth, and my heart stopped. I wanted his kiss—longed for it with every breath I took—but I knew I could not betray my sister.

"I need time," I said, though I'm not sure how I spoke. "Time to think and to pray."

He ran his thumb over my cheekbone again and said, "Do you care for me, even a little?"

I put my hand over his and nodded. "Oui."

A brilliant smile lit up his face, and he took my hand in his to place a kiss on my knuckles. "That is all I need for now."

I wanted to promise him more, but I knew it wasn't fair to him, to Hope—or to myself.

How could I face my sister in the morning? How could I look her in the eyes and keep this secret hidden—along with the other one that already weighed upon my heart?

23

※

HOPE

I sat outside the Salem Towne House, misting rain blowing against my hot face as I wept. The court of oyer and terminer had completed the weeklong examinations of six women, including Ann Pudeator and Rachel Howlett, and the grand jury had found them all guilty of witchcraft. They were sentenced to hang on September 22nd.

My heart twisted with guilt at the knowledge that Ann and Rachel suffered because of my father's actions—and their connection to my mother. Their innocence haunted me, yet I was powerless to save them.

The only consolation was that Rachel's pregnancy had stayed her execution. But her unborn child had also been used against her to demonstrate to the jury that she was a woman of immoral conduct. Her history as a Quaker had also come into play—one more reason I knew she would be condemned, though I had prayed hard that she would not.

Ann's accusers had come from all corners. As a midwife and healer, she was blamed by many who stepped forward to describe the death of their loved ones. Her husband's death, and the death of his first wife, were blamed on her, and it didn't help that she had twenty jars of unidentifiable greases—or potions—in her home. Those accusations, along with the claims of spectral affliction, were enough for the jury to convict her.

The street was empty, as everyone had left the courtroom and gone to their homes or to the prison. Grace had stayed at the ordinary to cook but had encouraged me to come so I could report on the trials. I had been here every day this week, walking the five miles back and forth on my own—heedless of the dangers along the road.

But now, with the final verdict cast and nothing left for anyone to do, I looked up at the gray sky, shaking my head at a God I didn't understand. "Why?" I asked as I fisted my hands. "Where are You? How can You watch this and not call out the injustice? These men speak in Your name—yet they misuse You and Your Word for their own purposes. Doth that not enrage You?"

The rain fell upon my hot face, though the answers remained locked away. Did God not care about my anguish and pain?

A wagon rounded the corner, disturbing the quiet. Isaac sat at the front of the vehicle, his hands gripping the reins, as rainwater dripped off the brim of his black, steeple-crowned hat. His face was so serious, so intent.

So angry.

I pulled myself from the stoop and met his wagon on the road.

He jumped down and in one fluid motion swept his cloak off his shoulders and settled it around mine. It was warm and smelled of him. "You will catch your death."

273

"I care not."

"The way you speak sometimes," he said as he tied his cloak about me, his work-roughened hands gentle and tender.

"Why have you come?"

"I went to the ordinary, and Grace told me you have been walking here every day." Sadness mingled with his anger—an anger that was not directed at me. "I've heard the verdict."

Shaking my head, I sniffed at my tears. "How can my father allow this to happen to Rachel and Ann? They are innocent."

"They're all innocent." He glanced up the street, then put his hand on the small of my back and led me to the wagon. "This madness must stop before more lives are taken."

"I thought you supported the magistrates and judges," I said as he handed me up into his wagon.

He climbed in next to me, lifting the reins. "I do not support prejudice, lies, and hatred. This is not witchcraft. 'Tis hysteria and terror. Mental turmoil and panic. Some are innocently following along, thinking it is real, uncertain what is happening, praying they will not be afflicted. They see everything through the lens of darkness and cannot imagine it is something other than witchcraft." His voice held conviction. "But others have begun to use this for power and control, to mete out personal justice for old feuds, boundary disputes, and grudges. Greed at its worst."

The rain soaked into his doublet and wet the sleeves of his white shirt. The fabric stuck to his forearms.

"You're cold," I said as I started to remove his cloak.

He stayed my hands and met my gaze. His eyes were filled with a righteous passion I had never seen before—one that filled me with awe. I was certain he didn't even notice the rain.

We drove through the streets of Salem Towne, heading north toward Salem Village.

"What will I do for Rachel?" I whispered in tears. "What if she gives birth to her child soon? She will be hanged in less than two weeks."

274

Isaac set his large hand over my clasped ones. It was warm and solid—just like him. I looked up and met his gaze.

"Pray," he said.

"I've been praying, but I do not know if God hears me." And I didn't know what I was praying for anymore. My prayers didn't seem to work.

"He hears the prayers of all His children."

"Then why doesn't He do as I ask?"

"Because praying isn't about getting what you want. He already knows. 'Tis about asking God what He wants."

"What if He doesn't want to save Rachel?"

"Then He hath a better plan than yours. Praying and seeking God means trusting that He will do what is best and taking comfort in His plan."

"What if I don't like what is best?"

"'Tis fine to tell Him your frustrations. Prayer is about a relationship with God." He tapped the reins against the back of his horses to get them to move a little faster. "Like we're talking now. 'Tis not about what you can do for me, or what I can do for you. We're talking to help each other better understand difficult situations. We talk to get to know one another and to enjoy each other's company. Sometimes we ask for help, but a loving relationship isn't always about what the other person can do for us. 'Tis the same with God. We pray and read the Bible to know Him better, to understand His nature. To take comfort. To be known."

"Do you think God changes?" I asked him.

"Never. Scripture says He is the same yesterday, today, and tomorrow. Our circumstances might change, people's beliefs might change. But He doth not."

I had so many questions as we turned onto the road leading to Salem Village. Isaac's voice was peaceful and comforting, unlike Reverend Parris's voice, which usually made me feel anxious and guilty on Sundays. I loved seeing God through Isaac's eyes—just like I loved seeing Him through Grace's eyes. They had so much faith and confidence. I wanted to feel that same assurance. It was there, right at the tips of my fingers, yet I wasn't sure if I could fully grasp it.

"Thank you for coming for me," I said as I nestled deeper into Isaac's cloak.

"I would never leave you, Hope."

Affection for him swelled within me, and I realized, with shame, that for many years I had not sought out Isaac for company or friendship—only when I needed something. It was how I had been treating God—only calling out to Him when I needed Him to perform for me or give me something I wanted.

What might happen if I treated both Isaac and God the way Isaac suggested? To spend time with them simply to get to know them better and enjoy their company?

The wagon jostled me closer to Isaac, and I didn't pull away. In a world full of men I couldn't trust, it was refreshing to know one I could. There were others, of course, but Isaac was the one who wanted to be with me. Who came for me, over and over again.

Sooner than I liked, he pulled up to the ordinary and jumped off his wagon to help me down. My dress was heavy with rain, but my heart was heavier still.

"Will you come in?" I asked him.

"I need to return home. 'Tis Judith's birthday, and there's to be a celebration tonight."

The reminder of Isaac's gentle, soft-spoken servant made me pause. She was close to Isaac's age and running his home like a wife might do. Why hadn't he fallen in love with her?

"Hath Judith thought to marry again?" I asked, trying not to sound obvious as I untied his cloak and removed it from my shoulders.

"Yes."

I waited, but he didn't say more as he took his cloak.

"Doth she have someone in mind?"

"I believe so." He slipped the cloak over his shoulders.

I put my hands on my hips, a little annoyed by his brief answers. "Do I know who she intends to marry?"

"You do, indeed."

"Isaac Abbot! Are you trying to rile me?"

He grinned. "'Tis Jabez."

A funny kind of relief went through me. Of course. Jabez was another of Isaac's servants.

Isaac's smile softened his eyes, as if he was pleased with my response. "Fare thee well, Hope."

"Fare well, Isaac."

He stepped into his wagon and then rode off, turning once to smile at me as he drove down the road toward his farm.

I entered the ordinary feeling like a wet rag doll—though Isaac's smile warmed me. John was behind the bar, serving the patrons, while Father sat at a table in the corner with several of his male Putnam relatives. He didn't notice my arrival, and even if he had, he probably wouldn't have greeted me. Ever since the night Rachel came, I had hardly said a word to him except when I was begging him to recant.

I wanted to change into something dry before helping Grace in the kitchen. Since starting her cross-country flight at the beginning of the month, she had been distracted and quiet. We were so concerned about Rachel and Ann that I hadn't pressed her about what bothered her. Perhaps it was the worry from the flight. They had already lost a day to a slight crash she'd had in Ohio, and I knew she was anxious. She answered my questions but didn't elaborate on her time with Mama and Daddy, how the journey was going, or how Luc was getting along without me. It wasn't like her to be so distant, but I chose not to press her. She was doing this for our parents, and I wanted her to succeed.

I also didn't press her for an answer about where she would stay on our birthday. I suspected she had chosen 1692, but I was half-afraid to ask.

Disappointment wrapped around me as I realized I had done nothing to encourage Isaac's feelings for Grace on the ride home from Salem Towne. I'd been too preoccupied with my own thoughts and feelings.

I took the front stairs and walked through the hallway between the two rooms on the second floor. A door led to the smaller hallway between mine and Grace's bedroom and Father's. The ceiling was lower here and the space more crowded.

Voices drifted out of Father and Susannah's bedroom, where Susannah had been staying more often. I suspected her public afflictions took a toll on her and were too tiresome to keep up for long. It was easier to hide away in her room.

"Neither of your cousins offered for them?" I heard the voice of Mary Wolcott through Susannah's bedroom door.

"Benjamin tried," Susannah said with scorn. "But they both turned him down. Nathaniel didn't even try. Neither Grace nor Hope seems to have any interest in marriage."

"No wonder," said another voice that I recognized as Mercy Lewis. "They act as if they are the mistresses of this ordinary, doing as they please. They ignore your authority and treat you as if you're a visitor. Why would they want to leave and be under the authority of a husband?"

"I cannot abide their presence," Susannah spat. "Especially Hope. She's a thorn in my flesh."

"She'll remain so, unless you get rid of her," Mercy warned.

"Have you considered your options?" Mary asked.

"If they will not marry, what options do I have?"

I held my breath as I leaned a little closer to the door.

"You know what you must do," Mercy said, her voice going lower. "When you're in the taproom and an affliction comes upon you, simply call them out. With their strange markings,

278

rumors about their mother, and Leah's testimony, no one would doubt you."

My pulse started to thrum. Leah's testimony?

"Even their father will support your claims," Mercy continued. "He is loyal to you, Susannah."

"He *is* loyal," she agreed. "And he's angry enough at Hope to see it done."

"Then get it over with and move on with your life," Mercy insisted. "It can be done this very night."

I stiffened.

"I'm so tired," Susannah complained. "'Tis not an easy thing to do with a babe growing inside me."

"It will be worth the trouble," Mercy assured her. "I could do it for you."

"No. It will be better if I do it. The magistrates will trust me as Uriah's wife who has seen things firsthand. Besides, Leah will speak for no one but me."

"If you do it soon," Mercy continued, "perhaps they'll speed up the trials so they can hang with the rest on the 22nd."

I stumbled back, panic choking me. If Susannah called out Grace and me, we would be arrested immediately and taken to the gaol. We would be questioned soon after and then put on trial. There was every possibility we could hang with Rachel and Ann in twelve days.

I had to find Grace. She had to know what they were planning.

The day I had feared was finally here.

The smell of roasted venison and woodsmoke filtered up the back stairs as I raced down into the kitchen. Grace stood near the hearth, using her apron to lift a lid and stir the bubbling contents.

She looked so comfortable—so at home in this space—even

if her thoughts were centuries away. What would I do if she was sent to the gaol? It would be miserable in that rat-infested building. No one deserved to be chained there, least of all an innocent person.

"Grace," I said, looking around for Leah. Thankfully, there was no sign of her. She could not overhear our plans—even if I didn't know what our plans were yet.

"You're back." Grace's face was lined with worry and sadness as she took in my wet appearance. We'd had little time to talk this week, as I had gone to Salem Towne each day. "I heard the verdict. I'm heartbroken."

I took her arm to lead her to the corner of the room, as far away from the stairs as possible. The spoon she held dripped sauce upon the floor, but I didn't care. "I just overheard Susannah speaking to Mary Wolcott and Mercy Lewis."

She made a face as she held her free hand under the spoon. "They've been here all afternoon."

"Susannah is going to accuse us," I said to her. "I just heard her tell Mercy. She's going to have a fit of affliction and call us out—and she knows Father will not deny her."

Grace's face went pale as she shook her head.

"She's going to do it, Grace. She wants us gone and doesn't care how it happens."

"How can they be so callous and cruel?" she asked, setting the spoon on the worktable. "'Tis murder, plain and simple."

"'Tis sport to Mercy, as she said."

"How can this be sport?" Grace paced away from me but then turned back. "What will we do? Run away?"

"That won't work. Look at how many people they have dragged back to Salem." There were only a few who had run away and succeeded, and most of them were wealthy with means to travel and lodge far from Massachusetts. Where could Grace and I go that we wouldn't be found?

"What about our Quaker relatives?" she asked.

I shook my head. "That's the first place Father will look, now that he knows we've been in contact with them. And we can't put them at risk."

"What of Isaac? He will help us."

I couldn't ask Isaac for one more thing. Our conversation from before filled me with shame. I had used him far too much. I needed to take care of myself.

A thought took root in my mind, growing with intensity, until I knew it was the only possible way we would both come out alive.

I took Grace by the shoulders and turned her to look at me. "You will need to accuse me."

Her mouth parted, and she looked as if she had seen an apparition herself. "What?"

"'Tis the only way, Grace. There are no afflicted people in prison. You must act afflicted, like Susannah and the others, and then call me out. It will spare you from the gaol."

"That's—that's—" She shook her head, speechless, and took a step back.

"'Tis brilliant," I said. "When you accuse me, I will be taken to prison, and when they question me, all I need to do is confess."

Her speechlessness turned to confusion. "What are you saying?"

"Those who confess have not gone to trial. The magistrates accept their confession and then move on to those who maintain their innocence, like Rachel and Ann."

"You would confess to something so heinous?"

"I am confessing to nothing. 'Tis not true, so I have nothing to be ashamed of."

She looked even more confused. "But everyone will think 'tis true."

"Who?" I shrugged. "No one we care about believes any of the people who have confessed are witches. We all know why they confess."

She continued to shake her head. "I cannot send you to the gaol, Hope. 'Tis unlivable."

"I will survive. This cannot go on for much longer."

"I don't know how long it lasts," she said. "You could be in there for months."

"It matters not to me. Either you send me there or Susannah will. And if you accuse me, at least you'll be free. There's no reason we both need to be there."

"You could accuse me." She nodded, as if this was the better idea. "I can be there. I have another path to break up the monotony."

"No." I shook my head. "I will not hear it. You need to focus on your journey to California. I don't want anything to hinder your effort to help Mama and Daddy."

"You don't think the knowledge that you're in gaol would hinder me?"

"This is the only way, Grace. Besides, I know you. Once you're being questioned, you'll decide you need to tell the truth, and you won't admit to the charges. You'll be hanged with Rachel and Ann."

She dropped her gaze, and I knew she couldn't argue with me. It was true.

When she looked up again, there was remorse in her gaze. "I'm sorry, Hope, but I cannot do it. We'll need to find another way."

There was no other way.

24

GRACE

SEPTEMBER 10, 1912
SPRINGFIELD, ILLINOIS

The rooster's crow echoed across the empty Illinois State Fairgrounds. I slowly opened my eyes and blinked away the sleep as I looked out the long, narrow window of the sleeper car. A lone piece of paper blew across the barren fairground and hit the wheel of the Vin Fiz Flyer, just in front of the grandstand. It stayed there, flapping in the wind for a second before it continued.

Rolling onto my back, I looked at the ceiling just above my head. The sleeper was comfortable—surprisingly so—but it was strange to know that just beyond the curtain there were eight other people sleeping. And one of them was Luc.

But my thoughts were on something else entirely. I still couldn't believe Hope's suggestion last night. All these years, I had been tormented by the ominous words of a dusty history book—and it was Hope herself who told me I needed to accuse her.

I put my forearm over my eyes and stifled a groan. How could I fight against Hope *and* history? Her final words to me before we went to sleep last night were true.

"We're running out of time."

Susannah had not come out of her room the night before, but she would probably be rested enough to pretend affliction in the morning or afternoon—and then both of us would be hauled away.

At least I had today to contemplate my options—which were few.

It didn't pay to try to sleep any longer, so I quietly pulled on my robe and went to the washroom at the end of the hall, where I completed my toilette and rebraided my hair. Breakfast wouldn't be ready for another hour, so I went back to my berth to write a little before the others woke up. I had promised at least a few lines every day to the *New York Globe*, which would be wired back to New York before we left Springfield to head southwest.

"Grace?" Mama whispered through the closed curtain a few minutes later. "Are you awake?"

I set down my pad of paper and pencil and pulled the curtain aside, offering her a smile.

We hadn't had as much time together as I would have liked since the trip started. Every day, I made three legs of our journey. Each one was about sixty miles in length and took me a little over an hour to complete. The train was usually close behind, since I followed the tracks, and at each stop I would get a refueling, as well as any maintenance that was necessary. On these breaks, I also ate, made public appearances for Vin Fiz, and took care of other needs. It made for a long, busy day, and when night fell, I was usually exhausted and ready to sleep.

But Mama was here now, and I motioned for her to climb into my berth with me.

"I was hoping you'd be awake," she said quietly as she sat

on the bed and closed the curtains for privacy. She was still in her nightgown and robe, her hair up in a night kerchief.

"Do you need something?" I asked.

"No. I just wanted to talk. I know we have a later start this morning, so I thought it would be a good time."

I smiled as I leaned against the headboard. "What do you want to talk about?"

She looked down at the quilt on my bed and touched one of the loose threads. "Shall we start with Luc," she asked quietly, "or end with him?"

Even though she wasn't looking at me, I still dropped my gaze. "Is it that obvious?"

"It's hard to hide the look of love on a young woman's face."

I covered my warm cheeks with my hands, surprised Mama had seen it so easily. For years, when I thought I had been in love with Isaac, no one had noticed. Perhaps what I had felt for him wasn't the kind of love I felt for Luc.

That thought stopped me in my tracks. Wasn't I in love with Isaac anymore?

"Don't worry," Mama said with a smile. "It's written all over his face, too."

I groaned and pulled my knees up to my chest, hugging my legs close.

"What?" She laid her hand on my knee. "What's wrong? Your father and I love Luc. He's kind, respectful, intelligent, and his faith runs deep. We've had wonderful conversations with him on the train as we've followed your flights. What else could you want?"

"It's not that," I said. "I think Luc is wonderful."

She nodded, and her smile fell. "You've decided to stay in 1692? Is that the trouble?"

"That's not it—I mean, it is part of the problem, but—" I paused, not wanting to admit the truth. "Remember? Hope is in love with him."

"Ah." Mama bit her bottom lip and sighed. "I had forgotten. I can see how that would be problematic."

"Even if she wasn't in love with him, there is still the matter of my upcoming birthday." My shoulders drooped. "I was planning to tell you when we got to California, but I-I think I should stay in 1692 for Hope. I can't imagine being away from her or leaving her there alone. We've been together all our lives. There's no one else who could possibly understand what we've been through." I shook my head and lowered my gaze again. "Last night she told me I need to accuse her of witchcraft."

"What?" Mama's voice betrayed her surprise.

I quickly told her how Hope had overheard Susannah's plans.

"Will you follow through with it?" she asked me.

"That's the strange part. For years, I've known I would accuse Hope."

"What?" she asked again, frowning.

"I saw it in a history book and kept this horrid secret locked away in my heart. I had no idea how it would come about. But the ironic thing is that it's Hope's idea! I've been plagued with this knowledge, and I'm not as guilty as I thought I would be."

Despite the situation, Mama smiled. "It's proof that we spend far too much time worrying about things we don't understand." She studied me for a moment. "Perhaps Hope has the right idea. I'm not an advocate for lying to the authorities or admitting to a crime you didn't commit—but it might be the only way to beat them at their own game."

"But she'll have to stay in prison, and I don't know how long she'll be there."

"If it's something she's willing to do for you, then you might need to let her." She studied me with her clear, blue eyes. "Sacrificial love hasn't always come easy for Hope. She's so single-minded, she often only thinks of herself. It heartens me to know she has made this offer for you. Perhaps being stuck in 1692 has softened her."

I thought about Hope's behavior the past few months and nodded. "I have seen a change in her."

"Brokenness changes our hearts. We either become bitter and angry, or more compassionate, selfless, and loving. I'm happy to know she's letting her brokenness change her for the good."

"Me, too." I leaned my head against the backrest and let out a deep sigh. "I don't think I can accuse her, though. It's not in my nature to do something so horrible."

"Pray about it. You don't need to make your decision right now."

"There are so many hard choices to make."

"I know."

"And I need to stay focused on what I'm doing here. I really want to finish this in thirty days or less—and I want to find Tacy."

Mama nodded. "And somewhere in all of that, you have to decide where you're going to stay—and," she said more quietly, "if you're going to tell your sister that you've fallen in love with Luc."

I lowered my eyes.

Mama placed her hands on either side of my face. "I love you with all my heart and soul, Grace. You and your sister." She lowered her hands and put them on my upraised knees. "I had accepted the fact that I would never have my own children, so when I became pregnant with you and your sister, I was overjoyed. But from the day I knew you were on your way until this one, I have always known that your times are in God's hands.

"I want to give you the same gift my parents gave me—and that's the freedom to make the best decision for you. If that means 1692, then you have mine and Daddy's blessing to stay there. I will miss you every day of my life, but I will know you are where you belong. If it's 1912, then I will cheer you on and support your decision. Whatever you decide, I will love you for the rest of my life."

"Thank you, Mama." I leaned forward and gave her a hug.

"And tell Hope I love her," she said, her voice just above a whisper. "She's exactly where she's supposed to be, and the twenty-four years I had with her were a gift from God."

"She loves you, too."

"I know she does." She patted my knee. "If it's any help, I think you should tell her that you're in love with Luc—and let her help you decide which course to take. You might be surprised." She smiled. "I should probably get dressed. Everyone will be up soon, and we must get going if we want to make it to California on time."

"Okay."

As she pushed aside the curtain, I looked up, and my gaze collided with Luc's.

He was standing in the aisle, wearing a robe over his pajamas, holding a small towel and his toothbrush in his hand. His dark hair was damp, and his face looked freshly shaved.

My heart fell as I pulled my sheets up to my chest, though my nightgown and robe were as decent as my regular clothes. But it was more than my lack of dress that made me feel exposed and vulnerable.

It was all the things I had just said.

Mama paused as Luc and I stared at each other.

"Perhaps I should leave you two with some privacy," she said as she moved away and climbed into her berth.

I could almost see the questions racing around in Luc's mind—yet I wasn't unhappy he had heard us. Perhaps I had wanted him to. I hated keeping the truth about my time-crossing from him.

As Mama closed the curtains on her berth, I climbed out of mine and stood face to face with Luc.

He stared at me, but it was impossible to know what he was thinking.

"Should we go outside?" I whispered.

Nodding, he set his things aside and followed me down the aisle to the door.

The morning sun was low on the eastern horizon, painting the fairgrounds and train in muted reds, yellows, and pinks.

I had forgotten to put on my slippers and didn't realize it until I stepped out of the sleeper car. The metal was cold and rough on my bare feet, so I took a seat on the steps, my legs weak from all the emotions running through me. What would Luc think about what he had heard? Would he believe me?

Luc followed me silently, coming out of the train a little slower.

"Will you sit with me?" I asked him.

He took the spot next to me, though it was tight. He smelled of soap and aftershave. "Are you going to tell me what you and your mother were discussing?"

I took a deep breath. Outside of Mama, Daddy, and Hope, I had never told anyone else the truth about my time-crossing.

"My family and I have a special gift," I began slowly, watching him for his reaction. "My mother has it, her mother and father had it, their parents, and so on. This gift means we are born as time-crossers."

He frowned as he stared at me, confusion in his gaze.

"I have a mark." I turned and lifted my braid to show him the sunburst birthmark on the back of my head, then faced him again. "It marks me as a time-crosser. Every night when I go to sleep here, I wake up the next day in 1692. And when I go to sleep there, I wake up here—without any time passing while I'm away. I only have twenty-five years to decide which path I want to keep and which one I'll forfeit."

He continued to stare at me, and I could see he was processing everything I said, though he made no attempt to ask questions.

"I have two identical bodies and one conscious mind that goes between them." I paused, knowing this part would be even harder to believe. "Hope has the same mark, and until she died at the air meet, she and I traveled back and forth together. Now she is only alive in 1692."

Luc's face revealed nothing—no indication if he believed me or not.

"On my twenty-fifth birthday, on October 12th, I must decide if I am going to stay here—or if I will stay with Hope in 1692. If I decide to stay in 1692, my body will die here, and my consciousness will remain there."

I finished speaking and waited for him to respond.

It took a few moments, but he finally said, "Grace, I have no idea what you're talking about."

"I'm explaining what you heard."

"I heard your mother say, 'I think you should tell her that you're in love with Luc.'"

My eyebrows lifted high. "*That's* what you heard?"

He nodded.

"You didn't hear us talking about the problems I'm having in 1692? Or what Hope suggested we do?"

He looked really confused as he said, "No."

I moaned as I lowered my face into my hands. "I can't believe I told you all of that."

He was so quiet, I lifted my head to look at him.

"It's really true?" he asked, this time with less skepticism and more amazement.

I nodded. "Do you believe me?"

He tucked a tendril of hair behind my ear. "I have never known anyone I trust more or believe in so completely. I have nothing but respect and admiration for you, and I know your heart is pure and good. It might take me a little while to wrap my mind around something so fantastical, but I know you would not lie to me. I believe you."

Tears threatened as I pressed my lips together. To know that he believed me and trusted me meant more than almost anything else. "I've kept the secret my whole life," I said in a hushed voice. "You can't imagine how hard it is."

"I can imagine it would be very difficult. Does your father know?"

"Yes." I smiled. "He guessed the truth when he and Mama were just falling in love. She saved a man's life in 1861 with medical knowledge she had from 2001, and he became suspicious. Then he noticed other strange things about her that couldn't be explained any other way."

"Your mother lives in 2001?"

"Lived—she had to make her choice, too, and she chose my father."

"She chose this life for him?"

"Yes."

"Have you decided which one you're going to choose?"

I wanted to tell him yes—but I couldn't bear to say it. I had grown to love Luc, but I wasn't sure if it was the kind of love needed to sustain a marriage—or to take me from Hope. And I didn't know how deep his feelings ran, either.

"I'm not sure." I looked down at the fabric of my robe and picked at a piece of lint.

Luc took my hand in his, drawing my gaze back to him. "About the other thing I heard . . ."

Warmth filled my cheeks, but I wouldn't deny it. I wanted to be completely honest with him. "That I'm in love with you?" I whispered.

His eyes were full of longing as he said, "Is that true, as well?"

The morning sun was so calm, so new, that it felt warm and promising. Shadows from the nearby grandstand stretched lazily across the open field where the Vin Fiz Flyer sat, waiting. But all I could think about right now—all I wanted to think about—was telling Luc what I knew to be true.

"I am in love with you," I told him, though I knew it would cost me. But even if I couldn't choose him, I couldn't live with myself if he didn't know.

He lifted his hand to the side of my face, his fingers slipping into my hair. I leaned into it.

When he set his forehead against mine, he whispered, "*Et je t'aime.*"

I didn't even need to ask what it meant, because my heart knew. A deep well of affection overflowed within me. The longing that had been building for weeks pushed against my better judgment, wanting to be released.

I went into his arms, and he embraced me.

Perhaps I was being selfish, but I didn't care about anything else in that moment. All I wanted was Luc. His arms, his lips, his heart.

So when he lifted my chin with his fingers and questioned me with his eyes, I nodded. I loved him, and I wanted to feel his love surround me.

He lowered his lips to mine, and the longing I had felt for him flooded me with warmth. I felt like I could drown in the sensations.

It was the most spectacular kiss that had ever been.

Yet as I reveled in Luc's embrace and marveled that he loved me, all I could think about was waking up next to Hope and trying to explain my betrayal.

25

HOPE

The creaking of a door brought me to awareness as I opened my eyes on a new day. Rain slashed against the small window. Our bedroom was unusually cold for September, causing me to shiver under the thin blanket.

"Grace," I called to my sister, but she didn't hear me or heed me as she left the room.

I quickly got out of bed and scrambled to get dressed, my hands and feet feeling like icicles.

Yesterday I had begged Grace to go along with my plan, but she had refused. If we didn't act quickly, Susannah would send us both to the gaol.

I finished dressing and went to find my sister. She was laying a fire in the kitchen hearth as the wind and the rain rattled the windowpanes.

"Have you given my suggestion any thought?" I asked, rubbing my hands together for warmth.

She startled and turned at my arrival. Her countenance was heavy, and I instantly knew something was wrong—more than what was happening in Salem Village.

"What is it?" I walked across the kitchen and stood near her. "Has something happened in 1912?"

The fire was just starting to come to life as she faced me. I knew my sister almost better than I knew myself. Just by looking into her eyes and seeing how she held her mouth, I knew she was carrying something troubling in her mind.

My heart fell as I realized what it was.

"You're not staying here with me, are you?" I asked her.

"What?" She frowned. "What are you talking about?"

"Something's wrong—something you don't want to tell me." I took her hand as panic settled into my heart. I tried not to sound desperate, but I couldn't live here without Grace. "The only thing that would make you look so guilty is that you decided not to stay here."

"No." She shook her head. "That's not it."

My shoulders sagged with relief. "Then what's wrong?"

"I—"

She paused as the door to the lean-to opened and Leah entered the kitchen. Leah looked at both of us but did not say a word as she began her morning chores.

"Start with laying the fire in the front rooms," I told her, my voice harsher than I intended. I needed more time with my sister.

Leah nodded and left the kitchen.

I turned back to Grace. "Please tell me what's wrong."

She shook her head as she looked at me with something akin to pity.

I pulled back, surprised. Grace had never pitied me—even after I died in 1912.

There was movement on the stairs, and we both turned to

find Susannah entering the kitchen. She looked tired and cross six months into her pregnancy and was starting to show signs of discomfort and impatience—though that shouldn't surprise me.

She stared at us as she made a face. "Haven't you started breakfast? I'm starving."

"I'm starting now," Grace said as she turned back to the hearth.

Susannah's gaze held mine, but I wouldn't shy away—no matter what she planned to do to me.

"Hurry," she said as she walked through the kitchen and entered the dining room.

As soon as she was through the door, I turned back to Grace. "You have to accuse me," I said. "We can't wait another moment. As soon as she's fed and there's an audience in the dining room, she'll start one of her afflictions and call us both out. We'll be in the gaol within hours."

"I can't." Grace shook her head.

I grasped her shoulder and turned her to look at me, desperate. Angry. "You would rather have both of us in gaol? Please, Grace."

She shook her head, tears in her eyes. "I'm sorry."

Something about the way she said it made me wonder what she was sorry about. That she wouldn't accuse me—or something else?

Leah reentered the kitchen, and I couldn't find another moment to talk to Grace alone. Every time I met her gaze, I pleaded with my eyes, but she looked away.

Panic made me tremble as the dining room began to fill with customers and Grace finished breakfast. I wasn't sure how she appeared so calm as she fried bacon and made bread pudding from yesterday's penny loafs.

"Grace," I said in a frantic whisper as she finished filling several plates that I would take to the dining room. "Please." I glanced at Leah, who was leaving the kitchen. "Tell me what is wrong."

295

Grace waited until Leah was out of the room. "Now isn't the time. We need to get the meal served."

"I must know. What is bothering you—besides Susannah? I know there is something."

She finally let out a breath. "It's about Luc."

"Luc? Did something happen to him?" I grabbed her arms. "Did he die?"

She shook her head.

"Tell me—I don't care if this isn't the time. I need to know."

"I-I'm in love with him."

My breath caught as I stared at her, confused, certain I hadn't heard correctly. "What?"

"I love him," she said with a little sob. "I didn't mean for it to happen, Hope. It just did."

I took a step back from her, hurt and betrayal tearing at my heart. How had I not known this was coming? They had spent months together. I asked the question I had suspected in July. "Does he love you?"

She swallowed and nodded slowly.

"He—he told you?"

"Yes."

I stared at her, seeing the telltale signs of guilt, and whispered, "Did you kiss him?"

She looked down at her hands and nodded.

I turned away from her. This was the final crushing blow to the disappointments I had endured the past few months. First, to lose 1912 and the man I loved—and then to have him fall in love with my twin sister?

"Hope," she said as she reached for me.

I pulled out of her grasp, not wanting to talk to her or look at her or even acknowledge what she had said. Luc wasn't supposed to love her. Nothing had gone as I planned.

Picking up a few plates, I walked blindly into the dining room, holding back the torrent of emotions wreaking havoc in my heart. The storm was still blowing against the ordinary, and more people than usual had come to hear the latest gossip and spend the dreary hours with others.

As I aimlessly set the plates in front of customers, the front door opened, and Isaac entered.

I met his gaze and could see his concern immediately. He knew me better than I had realized.

The reality of Grace's confession brought tears to my eyes even as I acknowledged that my heart had started to soften toward another man—one who was now approaching me. It didn't change the fact that my sister knowingly fell in love with a man I loved—in a devastating time when she knew it would only add to my pain.

Yet wasn't that what I was doing? Falling for a man Grace loved?

My heart constricted with guilt and shame. Did she still love Isaac?

"Is all well?" he asked, searching my face.

I shook my head, but there was no way I could tell him.

Grace entered the dining room, and our gazes collided. She looked miserable—and though I wanted to despise her for capturing Luc's heart, I couldn't. The truth was, I had never been good for him. I had pushed him to be someone he wasn't. Grace probably drew out the best in him. She did that for everyone, except perhaps me, who was selfish and spiteful when I should have been happy for her.

And this shouldn't have come as a complete surprise. I saw the way Luc looked at my sister on the train and at the air meet. He'd probably been in love with her a lot longer than she with him. Could I blame her? Could I blame him?

"Did something happen between you and Grace?" Isaac asked.

Seeing the concern in his gaze, I nodded, but before I could say more, a commotion in the corner of the room drew our attention.

Susannah, who was sitting at a table with Mercy, started to spasm like she had so many times before.

Father was on the other side of the room, but he dropped the cup of cider he was filling and raced toward her. He put his arms around Susannah from behind, holding her steady as her body trembled.

"They afflict me!" Susannah cried in a wretched voice as she looked up into his worried face.

I turned to Grace. This was the moment—the one I had warned her about.

She was crying, and her eyes filled with an intense sadness that broke my heart.

I mouthed the word, "Please."

Tears spilled down her cheeks as she dropped her chin, and then she began to cry out—louder than Susannah—in a voice that was wracked with such anguish, I knew she was not faking her emotion.

"She afflicts me!" Grace cried. "She pinches me and bites me and torments me."

Everyone turned their stunned gazes to Grace. Even Susannah stopped spasming and stared at Grace, her mouth slipping open.

The tears cascaded down Grace's cheeks as she began convulsing, twisting her body in painful contortions. Her heart was breaking—and it wasn't just about this moment and sending me to the gaol. I knew my sister. She would not have fallen in love with Luc to spite me. She had probably fought it, forsaking her own feelings, her own happiness, for mine.

As she cried out in pain, I knew she was sacrificing for me yet again.

Tears gathered in my eyes as I watched her, knowing this went against her nature—but she was doing it for me, because I had asked her. Begged her.

And she loved me.

"What are you crying about, daughter?" Father asked as he left Susannah's side and put his hand on Grace's shoulder.

Grace opened her eyes and grabbed his doublet, sobbing so hard she couldn't speak.

Father looked truly concerned—as did all the others who watched her. This was not an act. Grace was being afflicted by guilt and fear. Terror flashed in everyone's eyes, and more than one person looked behind them to see what—or *who*—might be causing Grace such anguish.

Isaac stood close beside me, stiff and uncertain.

I wept silently as I watched her, knowing she *was* in anguish. Our souls were two halves of one whole, and I could feel the pain she endured. I wanted to call out to her to stop—but I knew it would mean she would end up in the gaol with me. And I wouldn't let her. This might hurt for a time, but in the end, she would be free from chains.

"She pinches me and—and chokes me," Grace finally said as she fought for air, clawing at her throat.

"Who pinches and chokes you?" Father asked, his voice severe.

There was silence as everyone waited. I held my breath.

And then my sister lifted her shaking hand, sobbing—and pointed at me.

It didn't take long for Father to force me upstairs and into the room where the others had been held for questioning. He didn't even ask me if I was guilty of the charges. The look in his eyes told me he believed it was true—perhaps had suspected it all along.

He'd said I was just like my mother, Tacy, after all.

An hour later, I sat alone in the cold room, looking out the window at the storm-tossed front yard. Across the way, guards were changing shifts at the watchtower. Always watching for the enemy's arrival. What they didn't realize was that the worst threat to Salem Village had come in the form of fear—a timeless adversary that stole through the recesses of the mind and heart. There was no guard, no watchtower, and no magistrate who could protect the people from the greatest enemy of their soul.

As soon as the magistrates could be summoned, my questioning would begin. Tonight, as I had planned, I would probably be in the Salem gaol.

A shiver ran through me as I closed my eyes. My first inclination was to ask God to protect me, to give me the right words, to open the eyes of the court to see the foolishness of their ways.

But then I remembered what Isaac had told me. God knew what I needed more than I did. So I simply asked if He would sit with me, to be my Comfort, my Peace, my Rock amidst the storm. A gentle warmth filled my heart as I envisioned sitting in the presence of God, not worrying about what would happen, but trusting Him.

A knock came at the door, and I opened my eyes, surprised that the magistrates had come so soon. But when the door opened, it was Isaac who entered.

I stood, my heart pounding at his arrival. He took two giant steps across the room and engulfed me in his embrace. I pressed my cheek against his chest, tears coming to my eyes as I wrapped my arms around him. He was warmth and strength and all that was good in Salem Village.

"How could Grace do this to you?" His voice was choked, desperate.

"I told her to."

"What?" He pulled back, his blue eyes filled with confusion.

I explained what I had heard Susannah planning and how I had begged Grace to accuse me. "'Tis the only way to keep her out of the gaol."

He put his hands on either side of my face and shook his head. "My beautiful, impetuous girl. What have you done?"

"I couldn't see her suffer."

He ran his thumbs over my cheeks, wiping away my tears. "I've never loved you more than I do right now, Hope Eaton."

I inhaled as he lowered his lips to mine, kissing me with an intensity that left me dazed. My hands went to his waist, and I grasped his coat, trying to pull him closer, wanting to be fully enveloped by this courageous, loving man.

He deepened the kiss at my prompting but quickly pulled back, drawing a ragged breath. "I'm sorry."

I shook my head, holding on to him. "Don't be."

"I can't stay long," he said. "The magistrates will be here soon."

"I know." I felt a calmness that defied understanding. "I'll be fine. God hath given me peace."

He shook his head in wonder as he ran a thumb over my swollen lip, tender from his kisses. "I will do whatever I can to free you. I promise."

"I plan to confess."

"Confess to what?"

"To witchcraft. 'Tis part of my plan."

He frowned. "What are you saying?"

"Don't you see? 'Tis the only way to be safe from the gallows. Everyone who confesses is allowed to stay in the gaol and hath not been called before the grand jury."

"For now—but what about later?" He was adamant. "'Tis not worth lying about something so evil, Hope."

"But they won't believe the truth, so I must tell them what their itching ears want to hear. They are the ones in the wrong, not me."

"How will you stand before God if you do this thing?"

"He will understand. He knows I am innocent and they are guilty."

There was movement on the road in front of the ordinary.

"The magistrates have arrived," I said.

Uncertainty clung to Isaac as he pressed his lips to my forehead. "I long to see you free, but I also long for you to have a clean conscience before the Lord. Do what you feel is best, and I will trust that it is the right decision."

"Thank you," I said, though doubt plagued me. *Was* this the right way to go?

He left the room, and a few minutes later, Father appeared. Had he allowed Isaac to see me? It didn't seem like something he would do.

"Come," Father said. "The magistrates are ready to question you."

I took a deep breath and followed him out of the room and down the stairs.

The magistrates sat at a table in the dining room, their backs to the outside wall. Susannah, Mercy, Mary Walcott, Elizabeth Hubbard, and Grace were seated to their right. All but Grace looked at me when I entered, and on cue, they began to spasm and convulse.

Leah sat near Susannah. She stared at me as the others writhed in pain. Her gaze told me that she did not need to act, because she had real evidence the magistrates would want to hear.

The room was overflowing with onlookers who sat at the tables or stood against the walls. The wind and rain blew outside, swirling around the ordinary like a wild beast. Magistrates John Hathorne and Jonathan Corwin sat behind the table, watching me, while Reverend Parris sat ready with a piece of paper and a quill.

Isaac stood in the corner behind the magistrates, taller than most. I focused on him as the afflicted women made such a ruckus the magistrates had to ask them to quiet themselves.

Father left me standing in front of the magistrates while he took a seat next to Susannah.

Grace did not look at me.

Magistrate Hathorne stared at me with cold, calculating

eyes. "There have been charges set against you, Hope Eaton. What say yourself?"

I took a deep breath, ready to go along with the ruse. I had been an actress—I could play the part.

"What are the charges?" I asked.

The magistrate looked toward Leah while Susannah nudged her to stand. My heart beat hard.

"Leah Smythe," Magistrate Hathorne said, "repeat what you have heard and reported to your mistress."

I had never heard Leah speak—would she now? To condemn me?

"I have heard many troubling things in the lean-to at the back of the ordinary," Leah began, her voice quiet and timid.

I looked at Grace, and she met my gaze, just as surprised as me. Would Leah condemn us both?

"Tell us what you have heard," John Hathorne said again.

Leah trembled as she clasped her hands. Her face was pale under her white coif, but she continued. "She had secret meetings with the accused witch, Ann Pudeator, at all hours of the night. Hope and Goody Pudeator left to attend gatherings in Reverend Parris's field with all the other witches."

I opened my mouth to protest but remembered that I was going to agree to all their accusations.

"She also met the other accused witch, Rachel Howlett, visiting her home in Salem Towne and calling her to the ordinary to afflict my mistress."

"Is that all?" Magistrate Hawthorn asked.

Leah shook her head and swallowed. "I also heard her speak of flying—many times."

All eyes turned to me. Flying was a serious accusation.

"Do you deny these claims?" the magistrate asked me.

I shook my head honestly—at least about the flying. "I do not."

Isaac briefly closed his eyes as the afflicted girls stared at me in surprise.

"Do you deny the other accusations?" he asked. "That you afflict your sister, Grace Eaton, and that you have met with a coven of witches in Reverend Parris's field?"

I opened my mouth to say I did not deny the charges, but the look on Isaac's face—pain and disappointment—made me hesitate.

And when I hesitated, the afflicted girls came to life.

"There are familiars all around her!" Mercy cried. "They swarm her, doing her bidding for the devil's work." She started to swat at the air near her, as if fending off the little beasts. Others in the room became uncomfortable as they looked for the invisible demonic creatures.

I stared at the magistrates, refusing to acknowledge Mercy.

"Her specter bites me!" Susannah called out, showing a fresh bite mark on her wrist.

"And she sticks me with pins," cried Elizabeth Hubbard, showing pins stuck into the pads of her fingers.

The magistrates looked disturbed as they spoke amongst themselves. The claims were so preposterous. Could they not see that?

I couldn't help it. I shook my head, letting out a frustrated breath.

All the afflicted—except Grace—also began to shake their heads, but with greater force. Even Leah shook her head, her voice rising with the others.

I crossed my arms—and they crossed their arms.

Mercy cried out. "Make her stop! I cannot unclench my arms. She holds us prisoner and doth not want us to speak."

I slowly lowered my arms, and they finally lowered theirs.

"What do you say for yourself?" Magistrate Hathorne asked me. "Do you not see what you do to these women?"

My gaze returned to Isaac. He looked so sad that as I opened my mouth to confess that I was bewitching these women, the words stuck in my throat.

How could I stand before all these people—and God—and say that I was controlling their behaviors? That I had sold my soul to the devil and was now doing his bidding?

I could not.

I glanced at Grace, panic starting to creep into my heart. Her face was pale as she clutched her hands together and didn't meet my gaze.

I looked at Isaac, remembering his embrace and his words of love and encouragement. Could I speak such vile things in his presence?

"Well?" Magistrate Hathorne asked. "What say you to these claims, Hope Eaton?"

"She cannot speak, because the devil holds her tongue!" Susannah said. "I see him there, beside her. He controls her like she controls us."

Revulsion turned my stomach, and I shook my head.

They shook their heads.

Tears of indignation rose inside me, and I swallowed as I faced the magistrates. "I say I am innocent. They lie for attention and wish to see me hang. I heard Susannah and Mercy planning it last night."

The racket the afflicted girls caused became so great, Susannah fell to the ground, her body twitching with spasms that looked as if they would break her spine.

Father rushed to her side as he glared at me. "You lie!" he said as he pointed at me. "You have hated her from the moment she came here, and you signed a deal with the devil to see her and the unborn babe dead."

"No." Tears fell down my cheeks, but my defense was lost in the chaos.

"Have her taken to the Salem gaol to await trial," Magistrate Hathorne said. "We have seen and heard enough. We are done here."

Someone grabbed my arm from behind as my breath caught.

Grace stood, horror on her face as they started to pull me out. I looked at Isaac, and he was on his way across the room, but someone held him back.

The reality of the situation hit me like a blow to the face.

I would hang.

26

GRACE

SEPTEMBER 30, 1912
LOS ANGELES, CA

The Pacific Ocean appeared on the horizon, and despite the problems that had been weighing on me for over a week, my heart leapt at the glorious sight.

After thirty days, five accidents, three days of inclement weather, and over fifty appearances along the way, the West Coast—and sixty thousand dollars—was finally within my grasp.

I had made it, just in time to collect the prize money from William Randolph Hearst—and the ten thousand dollars from Armour and Company. It was a fortune. It would be more than enough for my parents to live comfortably for the rest of their lives and would also guarantee that their orphanage would thrive.

I only wished my heart was light enough to enjoy this moment —and not mourning what Hope was enduring in Salem.

I banked my aeroplane to head slightly south, following the

train tracks, with the Vin Fiz Special just behind me. The lush California landscape looked warm and inviting below, making me long for Hope even more. She would love to be here. If it wasn't for her, none of this would have happened.

But she wasn't here. She'd been stuck in the gaol in Salem Towne for the past nine days since claiming her innocence at the ordinary. Every day, Isaac had taken me into Salem Towne to visit her and beg her to let me recant.

But she refused, reminding me that even if I did recant, the others would not. They would probably cast me in shackles, as well.

I also wanted to talk to her about Luc, but she refused to let me say his name.

The conditions in the gaol were abominable. Cold, moldy, and infested with lice and other vermin. The worst part was that she would be required to pay for each day she was incarcerated, as well as for the shackles used to transport her. Thankfully, the gaoler allowed me to bring her food and blankets, though Hope shared them freely with the others. The accused had reached such a number that they were spread between the gaols in Salem Towne, Boston, Cambridge, and Ipswich.

On September 19th, Goodman Giles Corey had been pressed to death with heavy rocks across the road from the Salem gaol because he refused to stand trial for witchcraft. On the 22nd, Ann Pudeator and seven other men and women, including Giles' wife, Martha, had been hanged. It was the darkest day so far, and had only added to the pain and uncertainty of seeing Hope in the gaol. Rachel was still pregnant with her unborn child, sparing her from the noose—but for how long?

A sharp wind rocked my aeroplane, tearing my thoughts away from Salem to focus on this important moment.

The plan was to land in Long Beach, California, just outside of Los Angeles. It was about noon, which meant I would still have time to look for Tacy this evening. Mama had said she'd come with me, and though I was eager to end the flight, I was most excited about meeting my other mother.

I finally found the beach where I would land. There were at least a thousand people lining the runway that had been marked out for me. The train wasn't far behind, so I passed over the crowd a few times, waving at them, until the train was near the beach. The reporters on board wanted to be present for the landing, and I wanted Luc and my parents to be there, as well.

In the past week and a half, Luc and I had had many conversations about my time-crossing gift, and he had talked with Mama and Daddy about it, as well. I told him what was happening in Salem with Hope, and he was beginning to accept everything he'd learned.

But what he didn't understand—and what I was struggling to accept myself—was the distance I had put between us. I couldn't continue to offer him my heart if I wasn't staying in 1912—and the more I saw Hope suffer in 1692, the more I knew I couldn't leave her. I didn't want to leave her. Life without Hope was unimaginable.

She was my sister, my dearest friend in the world. The very thought of never seeing her again—or worse, leaving her in Salem when she was in the gaol, awaiting her trial—tore at the very fabric of my being.

A strong wind blew off the ocean, making my descent onto the beach a bit rocky. The last thing I needed was to plow into the crowd. Sweat beaded on my brow as I slowly lowered the aeroplane to the beach, fighting every second of the way. When the wheels touched the ground, I killed the engine, allowing the aeroplane to come to a stop.

The roar of the crowd was deafening.

For a second, I just sat in the cockpit, staring at the sky. There was a sense of accomplishment—but more relief that it was over. I was happy I had done it, though I had no desire ever to fly again. It was stressful and nerve-wracking on the best days. Terrifying and miserable on the others.

Several people moved past the barricade, including Luc, as I finally pulled myself together and stood in the cockpit. I waved at the crowd as Luc stopped beside the aeroplane, grinning up at me. With a smile, I reached down to accept his help, and he put his hands at my waist. He lowered me to the ground and then wrapped me in his arms.

"Congratulations," he whispered for my ears only. "You were magnificent, my little bird."

"Thank you." I held him tight. "I couldn't have done this without you."

He pulled back, his eyes shining with admiration. "I will tell you this a hundred times, but you will not believe me: you are a natural-born flyer. You flew brilliantly, and I am very proud of you."

My cheeks warmed under his praise, but before I could respond, I was bombarded by dozens of people vying for my attention. The mayor of Los Angeles had arrived, as had the president of the California Aeronautical Club. My parents were ushered to my side for a brief picture, and then I was brought to a makeshift stage to receive the key to the city of Los Angeles by Mayor George Alexander. I was also presented with a check from one of William Randolph Hearst's employees, and another from Armour and Company. Money would be wired to Mr. Lorenz in the morning to pay for my parents' orphanage.

But all I wanted now was to find Tacy.

The Los Angeles subdivision of Westmoreland Place was a gated community of beautiful, stately homes that were elegant but not as glamourous as their East Coast counterparts. I looked out the cab window as we pulled into the neighborhood around the supper hour. The sun was setting low in the west, and shadows elongated the tall palm trees.

Mama sat next to me, holding my hand. She squeezed it as we drew closer to 59 Westmoreland Place.

"I hope she's home," I said. I hadn't even considered whether Tacy would be there until we were almost at her front door. "I'll be so disappointed if she's not."

"We can come back another time," Mama reassured me. "Perhaps we'll need to set up an appointment."

I hoped we wouldn't have to wait any longer. Not only was I thirteen days from my birthday, but I had waited months for this meeting.

The cab pulled up to the curb of a beautiful Tudor-influenced home with dark timber framing and cream stucco. A thick, green ivy grew up the side of the elegant two-story house, and the landscaping was expertly groomed with an inviting side-walk meandering to the wide front porch.

"Shall I wait?" the cabbie asked.

"Just for a moment," Mama said, handing him his fare. "If the family is at home, I'll wave you off."

"Very good."

I stepped out of the automobile, and Mama followed. I was wearing one of the best day gowns I had brought. It was a pale blue linen dress with blue embroidery and a lace chemisette and cuffs. My oversized hat kept the sun out of my eyes as we walked up the concrete steps and onto the sidewalk. Mama was also dressed well and was so gentle as she encouraged me with a smile. I wanted to make a good impression on Tacy and was much more nervous than I had anticipated.

"Just breathe," Mama said. "Life is full of twists and turns. We can't always predict which way it will go, but it's a magnificent journey when we let it take us where it wants."

I returned her smile, thankful she was there with me.

When we reached the front door, I took a deep breath and

pressed the doorbell. A maid in a black dress and white apron opened the door and greeted us.

"May I help you?" she asked in an Irish accent.

"Is Mrs. Bennet at home?" My voice caught on my nerves.

"May I ask who is calling?"

"Miss Grace Cooper and Dr. Margaret Cooper."

The maid's eyes widened. "Grace Cooper, the aviatrix?"

I nodded, surprised she had heard about me.

"Won't you come in?" She opened the door wider and stepped aside for us to enter the cool receiving hall. Her wide-eyed gaze followed me as Mama waved away the cab driver. "I will tell Mrs. Bennet you're here."

"Thank you."

We waited in the tasteful foyer as the maid disappeared into a room off to the left. My heart was beating hard, and I tried to take another steadying breath.

"She's here," I whispered to Mama. "What if she doesn't want to meet me?"

"She will want to meet you."

"Is this strange for you?" I asked. "Meeting my other mother?"

Mama's chuckle was sweet and tender. "What do you think?"

I took her hand and shook my head. "This is a strange existence, isn't it?"

"It seems to get stranger and stranger. I can't imagine how Tacy will feel when she learns who you are. It will be a complete shock."

The door opened again, and a woman entered the hallway. She was beautiful, in her mid-forties, with blond hair and that familiar nose. She resembled Pricilla so much, it took me by surprise—though it shouldn't have. They were sisters.

"You look like her," Mama whispered.

Tacy was wearing a simple but elegant house dress of dark plum with a long necklace. She had a pleasant, if somewhat curious, smile on her face.

"Hello," she said as she extended her hand to Mama first and then to me. "I'm Tacy Bennet. How do you do?"

"Hello, I'm Maggie Cooper," Mama said, "and this is my daughter—" She paused, and I wondered if she had almost said, *and your daughter*. "Grace."

"It's a pleasure to meet you both," Tacy said. "I've read all about your flight across America, Miss Cooper. You can imagine my great honor and surprise to welcome you into my home. Won't you come into the parlor?"

My pulse thrummed as we followed her into the beautiful front room, which had large windows facing the street and the manicured side lawn. The room was gracefully decorated with expensive furnishings, though it was not ostentatious. Large potted ferns adorned the corners of the room.

"Please have a seat. I've asked Katie to bring us tea."

"We're sorry it's so close to the supper hour," I said as Mama and I took seats next to each other on the sofa, while Tacy sat on the chair opposite from us. "I just arrived in Los Angeles at noon and had a few things that I needed to do before we could come."

Tacy smiled, but her brow came together in confusion again. "You just completed your cross-country flight at noon, and you came here? Am I to assume you'd like to discuss making a movie with our film company?"

I glanced at Mama and then leaned forward, not wanting to make Tacy wait another moment. "This may come as a surprise—actually, I know it will." I tried not to get emotional and had to stop for a second. "Are you Tacy Barclay of New York City?"

Her frown deepened, and she started to look more suspicious than curious. "Yes."

"And—" I paused, hoping I had not gotten this terribly wrong, because if I had, she would think I had lost my mind. "Are you the same Tacy Howlett who once lived in Massachusetts? A very long time ago?"

Tacy's face became completely still and devoid of confusion. In its place was shock—pure and complete. "How do you know?"

I briefly closed my eyes as the truth sank deep within my soul. This was my other mother. When I opened my eyes again, tears rimmed my lashes and fell down my cheeks.

"I'm one of the twin girls you gave birth to in 1667."

Her mouth slid open, and her chest rose and fell on short, quick breaths. She stared at me, shaking her head. "What did you just say?"

"I'm Grace, one of your daughters."

Tacy stood, her face pale. "You're *that* Grace?"

I also stood, nodding. "This is my second path. Maggie is my mother and is also a time-crosser."

Mama rose, wiping her cheeks, as she extended her hand to Tacy once again. This time meeting her in a way that could not be expressed but only felt.

Tacy took Mama's hand—almost like an anchor—as she continued to stare at me. "You're my daughter? How is this possible? I had no idea what other path you occupied, so I had not even tried to look for you here."

"We only just realized ourselves," I told her as I wiped at my tears, "or I would have come much sooner."

Tacy let go of Mama's hand and took a step toward me. We were the same height. She looked me over with awe and then pulled me into her arms.

I closed my eyes as I embraced the mother I had never known. So many emotions swam through my heart. There was so much to say—so much to hear. But all we could do was hug each other. The irony was that her physical body had given birth to my physical body in 1667—the bodies we were not currently occupying. But our hearts, our souls, our very spirits were the same, and that was all that mattered.

When she finally pulled back, her face was washed in tears, but she was smiling. "Thank God He brought us together." She briefly glanced at the ceiling, a grin on her face as she shook her head. "He has such a way, doesn't He?"

I laughed. "He certainly does."

"Sit. There is so much I long to know. Where is Hope? How did you learn about me?"

"Sit beside her," Mama said as she moved out of the way, giving Tacy space to sit on the sofa with me.

"And you!" Tacy turned to Mama. "You're also a time-crosser? When I died in Boston, my biggest fear was that the girls would have no guide. I knew that Uriah would remove them from my family, and it has plagued me for twenty-four years. But the entire time, they had a guide—right here. I'm shocked—and so very pleased."

"We think that's why they are twins," Mama said to Tacy. "Because they have two time-crossing mothers."

"This is unbelievable." Tacy studied me as if trying to memorize every detail. "Tell me, where is Hope?" But then something dawned in her eyes, and she leaned close to me. "Is she *that* Hope Cooper? Who flew over the English Channel and died in Boston in July?"

I nodded, the truth still stinging with an intensity that made me catch my breath. "She's in 1692—and wishes she could meet you herself. She sends her love and is eagerly awaiting my report tomorrow." I glanced at Mama, my mood falling. "But she's being held in the Salem gaol under accusation of witchcraft."

Tacy closed her eyes and took a deep breath before she opened them again. "I feared such a thing might happen to you both, knowing that your time would align with the trials. But I did not look for your names in the history books. It was too painful."

"We didn't even *know* your name until we went to Ann Pude-ator and asked her." I paused, not wanting to burden Tacy with Ann's fate. "And then a good friend of ours went to Sandwich on our behalf and found the rest of your family. Pricilla came to visit us."

Tacy grabbed my hand. "My sister?"

I nodded. "She told me that if I found you, I was supposed to say she is sorry."

Pain passed over Tacy's face as she said, "I forgave her a long time ago. She has nothing to be sorry about." She turned to Mama to explain. "I was a Quaker in Massachusetts—am a Quaker still—but when I met Uriah, I left the faith and followed the Puritan ways. My family was angry, because I had not yet made my final decision and was still living in New York in 1888. Our time-crossing mother had always encouraged us not to marry or have children before we chose our final path. My sister, Pricilla, denounced me and refused to speak to me—until I came back to my family. Then she embraced me and the girls and encouraged me to keep sharing my faith. She tried to fight for me when I was arrested and sentenced to hang, but there was nothing she could do. I knew she would feel guilty, but it wasn't her fault."

"How very sad," Mama said. "How was it that you were hanged?"

"It didn't take me long to return to the Quaker faith. I hated that women were not treated as equals in the Puritan community. When I stood up to Uriah, his real character appeared, and our relationship deteriorated. I knew I had made a dire mistake, so I returned to my family, took back my old name, and tried to make up for the time I had lost. I began preaching equality and freedom to those in Boston who would listen, but I was arrested and sentenced to hang. Uriah was so angry at me and so worried about what others in his community would say if they knew he'd married a Quaker that he let them hang me without a fight. He took the girls away from me in prison, and that was the last I heard of him before I died."

"I'm so sorry," Mama said.

"I was impetuous and headstrong," Tacy continued as she looked at me. "I should have tried to fight for my marriage because I did love Uriah. But I could not abide his treatment of me. I would have stayed in the 1600s forever, if I could, to be with you and Hope."

"You remind me of Hope," I told her. "She's also impetuous and headstrong."

Mama laughed and nodded. "She is, indeed."

"I will pray for her," Tacy said. "And you." She frowned. "It's been twenty-four years and you're still crossing? How is that possible?"

"I inherited a different mark from Mama," I said. "Marks on the back of your head give you twenty-five years. I'll need to make my final decision in less than two weeks."

"You must be torn, especially with Hope stuck in 1692."

"Very torn. I love Hope and want to stay with her, but—" I looked down at my hands, thinking of this life—but especially about Luc.

"I miss my family in Massachusetts," Tacy said, still holding my hand. "And I have a very poor relationship with my mother here—but that is another story. When I came to Los Angeles in 1888, I didn't think I would ever find happiness again. But I met Grant Bennet, and he has been such a blessing from God. We've built a very good life for ourselves. You have three younger sisters here, and only one of them is a time-crosser. I haven't even told them about my life in the 1600s because I don't want to burden them." She let out a sigh. "I tell you this to let you know that no matter what you choose, God has blessings in store for you that you can't even imagine. So don't be afraid to take the life you want."

A noise on the porch indicated that a group of people were entering the house.

"Speaking of your sisters," she said with a smile, letting go of my hand. "They're just getting home." Her gentle gaze rested on my face. "I hope you won't mind that I cannot tell them who you really are."

"Of course not. I didn't come here to complicate your life."

"I know, dear. But they will be thrilled to meet you as the daring aviatrix, Grace Cooper. And I will welcome you any time you want to come. There is still a lot I want to know, and I'm sure there is a lot you want to know, so we will meet often. And no matter what you choose on October 12th, I will be forever grateful that you found me and that God blessed me with the knowledge that you were guided with this special gift. I love you Grace—and I love Hope, too. Very much. Please tell her."

I nodded. "And we've always loved you."

Her eyes crinkled at the edges as she smiled at me, and then, in the next second, three beautiful young women entered the parlor with parcels from a shopping trip in hand. Their excited chatter came to a halt when they realized there were guests present.

Mama, Tacy, and I rose as Tacy said, "Girls, you'll never guess who has come to visit."

And they wouldn't. But it was enough that Tacy knew.

27

HOPE

There was nothing to mark the endless hours in the gaol except the appearance of Grace and Isaac each morning. As I sat near the barred window at the door, waiting for their visit, I tried to inhale as much fresh air as I could—though the outside was almost as rank as the inside.

Cold nights were followed by unusually warm days. Illness ran rampant through the small room, and a community toilet in the corner offered putrid smells and no privacy. The boards at our feet were stained with years of unhappy memories, and the odor of unbathed bodies and unwashed clothing made my eyes water. All I could think about was a hot bath and a warm meal among the white linen tablecloths at Delmonico's.

For some, like little Dorothy Good and Tituba, who had been transferred to other gaols, their imprisonments were going on seven or eight months. They had probably not had a bath, a change of clothes, or even a hairbrush in all that time. Add to that the constant fear of the unknown, watching friends, neighbors, and family brought out for hanging, and the horrors of such surroundings—and I knew they would never be the same again. The mental anguish was far too great. Someday Dorothy would also have to live with the knowledge that she had aided in her mother's execution. Though she wasn't to blame, no doubt she wouldn't see it that way.

"Move aside," young Abigail Hobbs said as she pushed her way up to the window. "You're taking all the light and fresh air."

There were eighteen women in a room that should only hold four at most. Three of them were so ill they could not rise from their pallets on the ground, including Rachel Howlett. The blankets Grace had brought were the only thing they rested upon.

I went to Rachel now as she sat with her back against the wall, her head down and her knees drawn up. She grimaced.

"Rachel? How fare you today?"

She looked up at me, and there was both fear and resignation in her blue-eyed gaze. "The pains have started."

I knelt beside her and put my hand on her knee. Guilt suffocated me when I thought about how Rachel had ended up here. If she hadn't come to the ordinary, Father and Susannah wouldn't have known about her. She had come because she was desperate—yet she had found no sanctuary in our home, only condemnation.

"How long have they been paining you?"

"Only an hour or so." She grasped my hand, anguish in her gaze. "Promise me you'll take care of my baby if something should happen to me. See that she's brought to my mother in Sandwich."

"I promise," I said without hesitation, though what could I do if I was still in the gaol? "But you will survive to care for the

320

baby on your own. There has been no talk of another hanging since the last."

"'Tis only a matter of time."

"Then I will pray for God's peace to surround and comfort you."

What used to sound like a platitude had become my constant prayer for myself and for those who were incarcerated. And He had been a comfort, whether through Grace and Isaac's visits, the kind words of an inmate, or even in the thoughts that occupied my mind. I'd found a measure of peace, though I'd like to be anywhere else but here.

"Hope?" Grace called from the bars at the door.

My heart leapt at the sound of her voice.

"I'll be back to help you," I promised Rachel. "Tell me if you need me sooner."

She nodded as she bent her head, grimacing with more pain.

I went to the window, where the crossed bars were so small, they didn't even allow a hand to slip through.

"Grace," I said, my tears ever-present. As much as I had insisted I should be the one in this gaol, I had not anticipated the horrors of its reality. "Is Isaac here?"

"He is." She nodded. "He's speaking to the gaoler."

"Rachel's pains have started," I said. "The babe will come soon."

Grace's empathy softened her gaze, and she nodded. "I've made some things for the baby. Cloth diapers, a sleeping gown, and warm slippers. I hope it will be enough for now."

"It will be better than what we have." I glanced behind me to see if anyone stood close, then turned back to Grace, a different topic foremost in my mind. "Did you meet Tacy?" I whispered.

Grace's smile transcended this time and place as she nodded. "She was so surprised. You're so much like her, Hope. In almost every way."

"Is that good or bad?"

"'Tis wonderful." Her smile did not dim. "She's married and has three beautiful daughters who are eighteen, seventeen, and fifteen. There's so much to tell you, but I can't—"

"I know." There were too many people who might hear. Everything we said had to be said carefully. "What about the flight?" I whispered. "Did you make it?"

"I did—and we wired the payment to Washington. The building belongs to Mama and Daddy forever. They'll have nothing to worry about."

Relief overwhelmed me, and I grasped at the bars with my fingers, wanting to weep with joy. "Thank you, Grace. I will sleep easier."

I wanted to ask her about Luc, but I couldn't bring myself to mention him. My jealousy and resentment had subsided, but a new fear had developed. Would Grace choose Luc over me?

Isaac appeared in the small courtyard with the gaoler. He saw me behind the window, and a tender smile tilted his lips. My heart leapt at seeing him, just as it had leapt at hearing Grace's voice. The fact that he came each day and brought my sister was a testament to his love for me—a love he had finally professed in the upstairs room of the ordinary. I had thought about that profession—and his passionate kiss—every day since. On cold, lonely nights, it warmed me more than the blankets they'd brought.

Goodman Dounton, the gaoler, unlocked the door to our cell, allowing us into the sunshine for a bit of exercise. He didn't do this every day, but on occasion, when Isaac and Grace came to visit, he would let us out. I wondered if Isaac was paying him a handsome fee for this privilege, but I would never ask. Isaac didn't do things for attention or praise.

As soon as the door opened, I left the horrid smells behind and threw myself into Grace's arms. Thankfully, none of the accusers or magistrates were present, or they would question why my sister would accuse me and then visit me in gaol every day. I suspected that Isaac also paid Goodman Dounton to keep Grace's visits a secret so the others wouldn't question her. The fact that Father knew she came to me but did not stop her was a mystery. Was it that Susannah simply wanted me gone and didn't care what happened now?

It felt good to embrace my sister, even as I looked over her shoulder at Isaac. He stood near the brick wall, a basket at his feet, and simply watched as Grace and I greeted one another. It would not be acceptable for me and him to embrace, though I wanted his arms around me again. I wanted to see if it felt the same a second time. Had that moment in the upstairs room been special because it was charged with emotion—or was it something that I would feel every time?

I finally pulled away from Grace and tore my gaze from Isaac.

"There are so many things I want to tell you," Grace said to me.

"And so many things I want to hear. Hopefully, when I'm out of here . . ." I let the words trail away, because I didn't know how long I would be in the gaol. Would our birthday come and go in that time? Would Grace still be here? I needed to know but had to speak quietly and in a way that no one would question. "Have you made your final decision?"

She swallowed and nodded. "I think—I think I will stay here."

I closed my eyes, trying not to weep as I embraced her again. We just held each other without saying a word as we both cried. No one understood what I was feeling like Grace. The pain of loss was so deep, and the fear of losing her was so profound, it robbed me of words.

I pulled away from my sister, trying to control my emotions.

Grace struggled to look at me. "I told Mama and Daddy—but I haven't told Luc yet."

"He knows about—us?" I stared at her, stunned.

"He overheard Mama and me talking, so I told him everything."

323

"And he believes you?" I continued to whisper, though it was difficult with the shock I felt.

Grace nodded.

"He knows about me?"

"Yes."

Luc knew I was still alive—somewhere—and he believed Grace. I looked at Isaac, who waited quietly several feet away. Would he believe me if I told him the truth? Somehow, I suspected he would.

But none of that was as important as Grace's earlier comment. She was going to stay with me in 1692. Her words were the sweetest I had heard all week—and she had agreed to stay even though the man she loved was in 1912. But did she still love Isaac?

A sinking feeling hit the bottom of my stomach. I had thought I needed to convince Isaac to fall in love with Grace so that if she stayed here, she would have the man she loved. Yet I had done the opposite. I had welcomed Isaac's kisses in the ordinary, pulling him closer. It was my heart that fluttered at his arrival, and it was his gaze that warmed me now.

Things I had not told Grace.

With her staying, I would need to step away from Isaac. Allow her to pursue him and win him over, as I knew she could.

I didn't realize there was more of my heart left to break, but as I thought of Grace in Isaac's arms, the little part that remained unbruised was torn in two. Yet it was the sacrifice I could make for Grace, as she had sacrificed so much for me.

"Time's up," Goodman Dounton called, though we'd only had a few stolen moments in the sun. "Everyone back to the cell."

"I love you," Grace said as she handed me the basket she had brought. "And as soon as this is over, we'll find a way to move on." She took a step back, giving me space to approach Isaac.

Instead, I stayed near her and nodded my thanks to Isaac

from across the courtyard. It hurt too much to speak to him or be so close yet not be able to touch him.

I saw the longing in his gaze but turned back to the cell, trying to keep my composure.

As I waited in line to return to our prison, there was a touch on my arm. I looked down as Isaac slipped his basket into my hand. My pulse raced when I glanced up into his beautiful blue eyes.

"For you," he said.

"Thank you."

And then I was in the cell with the door being locked behind me.

I couldn't bring myself to watch him leave or look into the basket that he'd brought for me. Instead, I set the baskets down so I could sit with Rachel as her labor pains increased.

I wasn't sure how much time had passed before I heard the gaoler call my name from the window. "Hope Eaton?"

"Yes?"

"You'll be brought before the grand jury for questioning tomorrow. Be prepared."

All the other women looked at me. Some with fear, some with pity, and some with apathy.

My fate was sealed. I knew what the grand jury meant. I could not confess to witchcraft, as I thought I could, which left one alternative. Everyone who had claimed innocence and gone before the grand jury was dead.

For a long time, I sat in the corner, helping Rachel through her labor. The hours slipped away as I tried not to think about the grand jury summons.

It was starting to grow dark when Rachel finally gave birth to a tiny baby girl.

I caught the infant in my hands as she took her first breath in this world. The moment should have been full of joy and expectation, but it was clouded by fear and uncertainty.

Rachel lifted her head, exhaustion lining her face, and said, "Does she have the mark?"

A sunburst birthmark sat over the baby's heart, marking her as a time-crosser. Slowly, I nodded.

Rachel didn't even reach for the child. There was no happiness to be had in this birth.

I cleaned the baby as best I could and placed her in the clothes and diaper Grace had brought, swaddling her in a small blanket.

When she was calm, I held her out to Rachel—and realized that in the time it had taken me to clean and clothe the baby, Rachel had died.

I stood for a long time, shock and sorrow making me mute.

One of the older women came to me and bent to examine Rachel. "Bled to death."

"No." I shook my head as the baby began to squirm, nuzzling for its mother's milk. Why hadn't I paid attention to Rachel?

Even as the question plagued me, I knew I couldn't have stopped the bleeding. I had no experience birthing babies.

Another woman called for the gaoler to take the body away—but I couldn't move or think. I was numb.

The baby started to cry, and some of the women grumbled about the noise—and still, I stood in shock.

When the gaoler came, he brought his wife, and she reached for the baby.

I shook my head. "Let me keep her, please."

Goody Dounton snorted. "You're not her mother—and a prisoner at that. I'll see to the baby's needs better than you."

"But I promised her mother—"

"You should never make a promise to a dying woman," Goody Dounton said. "Especially in a place like this." She removed the baby from my arms and left the cell.

I watched in silence as the gaoler and his son hauled Rachel's body away, and I wondered why I wasn't crying. Had I used all my tears? Would I always be this numb?

The cell door slammed shut with finality, and darkness enveloped me. There were over a dozen women in the gaol, but I had never felt so utterly alone.

I pulled Isaac's basket onto my lap and sat against the wall, hugging it close, wishing it were him. When I finally removed the blanket from the top of the basket, my gaze fell on the gift he had brought.

Somehow, from somewhere, he had found a perfect, round orange.

And I discovered that I had tears left, after all.

The night was especially cold as I lay in the corner of the cell, Isaac's blanket wrapped around my shivering body, holding his gift in my hands. I could not stop thinking about Rachel and the promise I had made. When Grace came in the morning, I would tell her to get word to Pricilla to come for the baby. Surely the gaoler would give the baby to Rachel's family.

I had slept very little since coming to the gaol, so I spent my time in prayer, focusing on God's promises, remembering that even now, He had not left me nor forsaken me.

I recalled countless stories of His faithfulness to those He loved in the Bible. Each person faced moments of uncertainty, when they were in their darkest hour, but God had not abandoned them. And He would not abandon me. He'd had a plan for their good and His glory—just as He did for mine. Even if my story didn't end the way I wanted, I would still trust that it would end the way He planned.

And perhaps, if I was meant to die here, that would free Grace to stay in 1912, as I knew she wanted.

The sound of rats scurrying just outside the cell made my skin crawl, and I tried to dig deeper into my blanket.

Yet—had that sound been a rat?

I removed the blanket from my head and listened a little harder. No one else moved in the cell. A few of the women were snoring, but I could still make out the noise. Sitting up, I pressed my ear to the timber wall and thought I heard metal on metal.

It was the sound of a key slipping into the lock.

As quietly as I could, I stood and moved closer to the door, trying not to step on anyone as I tiptoed across the room. The moon was bright, casting shadows over the courtyard. It had to be the middle of the night, though how late, I wasn't certain.

My breath caught when I heard the telltale click of the lock, and I glanced through the window to see that the gate to the courtyard was slightly ajar.

Someone was bent low, opening the cell door.

My pulse thudded against my eardrums as it squeaked on its hinges. One of the women in the cell snorted and said something unintelligible in her sleep.

Then a man rose from the crouched position he'd been in to open the lock, and I almost fainted in relief and shock.

It was Isaac.

He saw me at the same moment and reached for my wrist, tugging me gently out of the cell.

I wanted to shout his name and throw my arms around him, but there was no time. He didn't even bother to lock the door again as he pulled me through the courtyard and out the door to the street. My heart was pounding so hard, I thought it would burst out of my chest.

We ran through the dark street, and he didn't say a word to me. He held my hand, urging me to go faster, though it didn't take much convincing. My legs were weak from sitting in the cell for so long without much exercise, but I pushed them as hard as they would go, still clinging to the orange with my other hand.

When we rounded the corner, there was a lightweight wagon waiting with two horses pawing the ground impatiently. Isaac helped me into the wagon and jumped up beside me. He tapped the reins against the horses, and we pulled away with a jolt.

Isaac put his arm around me to hold me on the seat. I was at once aware of his nearness, of the press of his large, powerful hand against my waist, the fresh smell of his clean clothes—and my utter filth. But I didn't care. The filth could be washed away.

"You came for me," I whispered on a sob that tore up from my soul.

He pulled me closer and said, "I will never leave you, Hope."

I wrapped my arms around his waist. The love I felt for him was more powerful than it had ever been. Isaac had broken every rule, defied every authority to rescue me, and stood up to injustice. I had never respected and admired anyone more than I did him. He had pursued me with unconditional love, even when I was unkind and unwelcoming. I was not worthy of being loved by a man like Isaac Abbott.

"Why do you love me," I whispered, "when I have done nothing to deserve it?"

His hand splayed against my waist as he placed a kiss on top of my head. "My love for you does not depend on your love for me. And if I were to live to be a hundred, it wouldn't be enough time to tell you all the reasons I love you." He held me close. "Your courage, fierce determination, and your loyalty inspire me. The way you stand up to injustice and defend the defenseless humbles me. And your questions challenge me." The passion in his eyes burned deep into my soul. "But it is your bold and authentic heart that draws me, over and over again, Hope. You make me want to be a better person, to fight alongside you—but at the same time, to cherish and protect you."

Tears burned my eyes as I thought of all the heartache I had caused this good man. "I'm sorry I have hurt you, Isaac."

He kissed me, his lips warm and possessive against mine, and when he pulled back, there were tears in his eyes. "You don't need to apologize. God has sustained me while I waited for you, and though I am far from perfect, I have learned to be patient and forgiving as I trust Him."

"I love you," I whispered, though the force of my emotions felt as if the one simple sentence had exploded within me.

The look of wonder on Isaac's face made all the pain and heartache from the past months evaporate. He kissed me again. "It was worth every prayer and every day apart to hear those words. I want to marry you, if you'll have me, and spend the rest of our lives together."

I had never felt more loved or valued in my life, and I realized that no matter what I did, Isaac would never love Grace the way he loved me.

This feeling I had for Isaac went beyond attraction or emotion—it went to the very core of my being and filled me with a desire to please him and honor him for the rest of my life.

"Yes," I said without hesitation or uncertainty.

Isaac's smile could light the darkness—and it had many times.

I realized that what I'd felt for Luc had been mere attraction and nothing more—I hadn't been in love. I had been enamored with the idea of Luc—the international hero. Grace was in love with the man behind the façade—the real Lucas Voland. Yet even in the glow of this understanding, pain darkened the edges as I thought of my sister. If her love for Luc was as strong as my love for Isaac, how could I ask her to stay with me in 1692?

Grief settled over me like a cloak, enveloping me completely in the darkness as I realized what I needed to do.

28

GRACE

OCTOBER 2, 1912
LOS ANGELES, CALIFORNIA

The moment my eyes opened in the Hollywood Hotel, I slipped out of my bed and put on my robe. It was early, and the sky was still pale with the first hint of daylight, but I couldn't wait to tell my parents what had happened.

We were sharing a suite in the lavish hotel overlooking Hollywood Boulevard. William Randolph Hearst had reserved rooms for us, wiring his staff to treat us to anything that money could buy. The Hollywood Hotel was the cultural center of the emerging movie industry and the place to see and be seen in Los Angeles.

I rapped on my parents' bedroom door, knowing they wouldn't mind the early wake-up.

"Come in," Mama called in a sleepy voice.

I entered the room and found them still in bed. Daddy was

yawning as he sat up, and Mama was just blinking her eyes open.

"What's wrong?" Daddy asked as he took his glasses off the nightstand. "Did something happen to Hope?"

"She escaped the gaol!" I said, relief making me want to cry.

"How?" Mama was now wide awake as she, too, sat up.

"I don't know—but I think Isaac Abbot had something to do with it. If it wasn't him, he would have come for me yesterday morning, like usual. But he didn't, so I suspect he broke her out."

"How did he do it?" Daddy asked.

"From the report I heard, he slipped into the gaoler's home and simply took the keys off the hook near his door. When I was there with Isaac the day before this happened, he went into the gaoler's house to pay him to let the prisoners out into the courtyard for a few minutes. I suspect he did it in order to identify where the keys were kept."

I was breathless with excitement—but then the reminder of the other news sobered my thoughts.

"Rachel Howlett died giving birth to her child. I sent word to Tacy's sister that a child was born, and I pray they can retrieve her from the gaoler's wife."

"I'm so sorry to hear that," Mama said. "How awful."

"I think it happened before Hope escaped," I added, "so she was with Rachel until the end."

"A small consolation," Daddy said. "What about the others in gaol?"

"Several escaped, since Isaac left the door open, but the gaoler discovered what had happened before they could all leave. A few of them were brought back, but Hope is still not found."

"Where do you think he took her?" Mama asked.

"I'm not sure—and the less I know, the better. I was already questioned by Father and the sheriff, George Corwin. But I honestly told them I have no idea what happened to her."

"I'm so relieved," Mama said. "We'll pray Isaac keeps her hidden until it all blows over."

"He won't be able to show himself in Salem for a long time," Daddy said. "He risks losing everything to help her."

I took a seat on the end of their bed. "I suspect Isaac heard that Hope was supposed to go to trial yesterday, so that's why he snuck her out when he did. If she had stood trial, she would have been found guilty, and who knows how quickly they would have hanged her."

Mama shuddered. "It's one thing to know she's not here—but it would be another entirely to know that she was gone completely. They are not safe yet. I'm sure people will be looking for them."

Daddy took Mama's hand in his own. "Let God take care of her, Maggie. He always has, and He always will."

I loved my father's reassurance. His steady, calm voice had eased many of my worries and fears over the years. But there was another fear I hadn't faced yet—and that was the fear of saying good-bye to them.

"I don't know if I'll get a chance to see Hope before our birthday," I said slowly, "but I told her I would choose 1692." I lowered my gaze, not wanting to see the pain in their eyes.

"Are you sure that's what you want?" Daddy asked.

"I want both. But I think I would have more guilt if I abandoned Hope now—especially if I didn't get to say good-bye."

"We should never be driven by guilt," Mama said. "Conviction, yes—but not guilt. Guilt implies you did something wrong. Conviction is the knowledge that you need to do something right, even if it's hard. You are not doing anything wrong if you choose 1912."

I closed my eyes, both sad and frustrated.

"I'm sorry," Mama said. "I don't mean to pressure you. I just want you to know that either way, you're not doing anything wrong."

I nodded. "I know you understand what I'm going through."

"Unfortunately, I do. And despite my parents' advice and wisdom, it was still very difficult for me to decide."

"Except," Daddy said with a teasing gleam in his eyes, "you were choosing between me and that Navy doctor in 1941—so we know the choice was easier than you let on." He winked at me.

"All that to say," Mama said with a side-eyed smile at him, "I know how hard this is, but don't let guilt play into it. Make your choice based on conviction and love, not guilt and fear."

Conviction and love. I loved Hope in a way I would never love another human. We had experienced things no one else would ever understand. Yet I also loved Mama and Daddy— and I loved Luc, in a way I would never love another. And there was also Tacy to consider. We'd only scratched the surface of knowing each other. I wanted time with her, too.

But I had told Hope I would choose 1692. If I didn't see her before our birthday, I couldn't leave her without saying good-bye and explaining myself.

"I should get dressed," I told them. "I'm supposed to meet Luc at seven to drive back to Long Beach to take pictures with the aeroplane."

"Do you want us to wait to eat breakfast with you when you get back?" Mama asked.

"I'm not sure how long it will last."

"Remember, we've been invited to a luncheon at Tacy's."

I nodded. "I won't forget."

I left their room and was soon dressed in the same blue linen gown I'd worn to Tacy's house. I brought my flying suit along—since we were taking promotional photos—so I could change into it at the hangar.

Luc was waiting outside the Hollywood Hotel near a beautiful white Oldsmobile. He leaned against it, wearing a pinstripe suit and a straw boater on his damp hair.

The moment our gazes met, my stomach filled with butterflies and warmth spread into my cheeks. I would never tire of the way he made me feel—both attractive and desirable. He saw me—truly saw me—and wanted more of me.

If only I could give him what he wanted—what we both wanted.

"You look beautiful," he said, as he opened the automobile door for me.

"Thank you."

He closed the door and leaned against it—his face close to mine. He smelled of shaving soap and the warmth of sunshine. His countenance grew serious, and for a second I thought he would kiss me, right there on Hollywood Boulevard for everyone to see.

And I would have let him.

Instead, he walked around the vehicle and cranked the motor, jumping into the Oldsmobile a second later.

We pulled away from the stucco-covered hotel, and I was thankful for my wide-brimmed hat. The sun was already bright as we drove toward the ocean, palm trees swaying in the breeze.

It was over thirty miles to Long Beach, but I didn't mind. Everything about California felt new and invigorating. I closed my eyes to enjoy the warm wind as it rushed past—and felt Luc's hand engulf mine.

We didn't speak for most of the ride. The motor made it difficult to hear, and I didn't mind the silence. It was enough just to hold his hand.

When we finally reached the ocean, Luc pulled over to the side of the road and turned off the engine. The waves crashed against the shore and rolled toward the beach in a never-ending pattern, running along the sand, creeping toward a family who sat on a picnic blanket.

Luc lifted my hand to his lips, tearing my gaze from the ocean. My pulse soared, and I had to swallow the rush of emotion welling up inside me. I had never wanted to offer my heart to anyone like I wanted to offer it to Luc. I trusted him completely—to be tender with me, to love me, to cherish me. I'd watched him care for the things he loved in those ways, and I knew he would do the same with me.

If only.

"I've made a decision," he said, his accent thick. "I'm retiring from flying."

I sat up straighter, surprised. "What?"

"I've had a lot of time to think about it, and you're right. You told me several months ago, after Hope died, that if you fly, you know your time will eventually come." He shook his head. "And I've decided I don't want my time to be up yet. I want to start a flying school and invent things and travel the world. There is so much more I want to do with my life." He put his arm around my waist, drawing me closer to his side. "And so much more I want to live for."

I didn't resist him as he pulled me toward him—I yearned to be in his arms again—but even as he did, I knew it was only prolonging our agony.

"I love you," he whispered, his mouth a breath away from mine. "And I want to marry you, Grace."

My heart beat wildly as he laid his lips against mine. I responded to his kiss, inviting him to deepen it as I laid my hands against his face, drawing him closer to me. If desire and longing could have stopped time and made everything else disappear, I'm certain it would have happened then.

But when I pulled back, breathless, the reality of the situation crashed upon me.

"I promised Hope I would stay in 1692," I whispered, a sob in my voice.

He leaned his forehead against mine, his arms still around me. His voice was strained as he said, "You will take my heart, *mon amour*."

I kissed him again with tears in my eyes.

"I always knew you and Hope could not be separated," he said as I pulled back. He ran his thumb down the side of my face with aching tenderness, heartbreak in his gaze. "I would never ask you to give up your sister for me." He shook his head. "But, oh, how I want to."

I leaned into his touch and closed my eyes. I wanted to say more, but what was the point?

For a long time, I sat there with my head against his chest, listening to the beat of his heart and the crashing waves.

When we finally arrived at the hangar, the reporters were already waiting. I went inside and changed into my flying suit, but nothing felt right. My limbs were heavy, my thinking was foggy, and my heart wasn't in flying.

But I had a job to do and commitments to fulfill, so I forced myself to smile.

After the pictures were over, one of the reporters asked if I would take up the flyer for a set of publicity photos. I looked to Luc, whose countenance was as heavy as mine, and he nodded. Twenty minutes later, I was in my aeroplane again.

I glanced at Luc, wanting him to know how much it broke my heart that I couldn't have him, but somehow I knew he understood. It was in the way he smiled at me, in the way he continued to love me, even when I was breaking his heart.

I took off from Long Beach, the sunlight blinding me with its brilliance.

From the second my wheels left the sand, I knew something was terribly wrong.

One moment I was feeling the rush of weightlessness in my stomach, and the next, my world went black.

I woke up with a jolt—and inhaled a deep breath.

The room above the ordinary was cold and filled with an inky blackness that suffocated me. I reached through the darkness to where Hope usually slept but was reminded her spot was empty.

A shiver took over my body, and I tried wrapping myself in the blanket, but it was no use.

Something had woken me up with a start—and something had sent me reeling back to Salem with a force I had never experienced before.

I slowly sat up in the bed, ducking my head to avoid the slanted ceiling, as memories from Long Beach started to surface.

After the reporters had snapped a few pictures, I stepped into my aeroplane and took off from the beach. But something had felt wrong—and then there had been nothing.

And now I was back in Salem, with no other memories from yesterday.

Panic started to tighten my chest as the reality of what had happened hit me. Memories of Hope's accident in Boston engulfed me. The rush of air she'd inhaled when she woke up in Salem after her death—the loss of memories—the shock of it all.

The slanted ceiling closed in on me, and my throat tightened. I wanted to cry out in disbelief and anger, but the sound was lodged in my throat. I put my fist to my mouth as my body began to tremble uncontrollably.

And then I wept.

The memory of sitting with Luc by the ocean filled me with a longing so intense, I couldn't breathe. I had known I would lose him, but I had been hoping for a miracle. Instead, I had gotten the opposite. God had made the choice for me and taken me away weeks before I was ready to say good-bye.

The pain smothered me, and I began to hyperventilate. I clawed at the blankets, trying to find a foothold on reality. I needed Hope. I needed to know where she was and what had happened to her. I needed her reassurance that everything was going to be fine—because right now, I was terrified.

Something hit the window. At first I was too overcome with my emotions to pay attention—but then it hit the window again, and I realized it was the thing that had woken me up in the first place.

The distraction pulled me from my despair. I looked out the window and saw a man standing in the side yard. He was hidden in the bushes, but I could still see him—and I knew instantly who it was.

Isaac.

I had never known a heart could break and be filled with hope all at the same moment. I dressed as quickly and quietly as possible, my limbs weak and unsteady, then snuck out of my room and down the back stairs into the kitchen. My cloak hung on the hook near the door, so I grabbed it, hoping and praying that Leah would not hear me.

My heart was pounding as I quietly opened the back door and then closed it behind me, not wanting a draft to wake anyone. The moon was high and bright, telling me it was still early morning. I tiptoed around the back of the ordinary to where Isaac was waiting, close to the spot where Hope and I had been discovered with our cousin Rachel.

My relief at seeing Isaac was so keen, I rushed into his arms, tears streaming down my cheeks.

He held me for a moment, then pulled away. "We must hurry," he said as he drew me toward the road in front of the ordinary.

"What if the watchman sees?"

"I've paid him. Now, come, and do not ask any more questions until we're away."

I did as he instructed, not even looking back at the ordinary as we ran down the road that led to Salem Towne.

Isaac's wagon was waiting with his two horses attached. After he helped me up, he climbed aboard, and we were off.

I waited as long as I could before I asked, "Where are we going?"

"I'm taking you to Hope. She won't rest until you're by her side."

"Where is she?"

"In Boston with friends of mine. We will not tarry long but will continue our journey tonight and make our way to New York."

"New York?" It was a journey of over two hundred miles. It would take us days to get there.

"'Tis the safest place I can take her." There was confidence in his voice—but there was fear, as well.

"Thank you," I said to him. "For everything."

He glanced at me and nodded. "I would do anything for her."

"I know."

There was a time when I would have been jealous of his statement, but now it brought me comfort—even if it pierced my soul, making me long for Luc.

We drove in silence most of the way, Isaac pushing the horses as fast as he could without tiring them. My mind and heart were on Luc, and if I had not been sitting beside Isaac, running for our lives, I would have been weeping.

It took over three hours, but we finally arrived in Boston, and Isaac took me to an imposing home on the harbor. It was dark within, but as soon as we pulled up to the front, the door opened, and Hope appeared.

Isaac leapt from the wagon and helped me down. My feet were barely on the earth before I was running toward my sister.

She met me halfway, on the street, and we embraced. The force of our hug was so intense, it took my breath away. I felt whole again—even if my heart was being torn in two.

"You're here," she said.

"Oh, Hope." Tears cracked my voice. "Something horrible has happened."

Isaac moved past us to the people in the house who had bags for him.

"There was an accident," I whispered, unable to comprehend what I was even saying. "I died in California. One moment, I was taking off—and the next, I woke up with a start in Salem."

She pulled me close again, her arms more comforting than any other. I melted into her embrace, drawing strength from her. "I'm so sorry, Grace. That was how it happened to me, too."

I wept against my sister's shoulder, not caring what Isaac's friends thought of me. It was still dark, and the sky was filled with countless stars.

Hope whispered soothing words to me, but all too soon, Isaac was there with his friends, speaking softly.

"We must hasten away."

Hope led me to the wagon, and we climbed into the back, where some blankets covered a bed of hay. Isaac instructed us to lay on the wagon bed, and his friends moved some of the trunks around us to create a barrier. Then they laid several warm blankets above us, cocooning us in a safe little haven.

I lay facing my sister, my eyes adjusted enough to see her. I was certain my face was red and splotchy, but I didn't care. Hope had seen me at my best and my very worst, and she loved me no matter how I looked.

The wagon began to move, bouncing over the uneven road, as Isaac took us away from Massachusetts and all the madness.

"You love him dearly," Hope said as she reached out and put her hand on my cheek.

A sob shuddered through me. "I do, with all my heart."

"I'm so sorry, Grace." She was crying, too. "I wanted to talk to you—to tell you—" She paused.

"What?"

Shaking her head, she said, "It doesn't matter now. It will only hurt more."

"Tell me, Hope. I don't want any more secrets between us."

"'Tis not a secret, and you will soon know. Isaac has asked

me to marry him, and I've agreed—but only if you give us your blessing."

"Do you love him?"

She nodded. "More than I thought possible. I was wrong about him. He's not boring or a rule-follower. He's passionate and adventurous and so very faithful."

"I would never come between you," I said, tears in my eyes. "You have my blessing."

"You—" She paused and then tried again, "You do not love Isaac anymore?"

Despite my heartache, I clutched her hand. "I do love him, very much. But I'm not in love with him." My heart belonged wholly to Luc.

She let out a soft cry. "I realized that I was being selfish to ask you to give up what you have with Luc to stay with me. I was going to tell you that you had my blessing to choose him."

She was right. It didn't matter now. The words were bitter-sweet, knowing Hope wanted my happiness above her own. Her sacrificial love meant more to me than any other. Mama would be so pleased to see this side of Hope blossom.

Thoughts of Mama and Daddy made my sorrow deepen.

All I could do was lay in my sister's embrace and try not to think about everything I had lost.

Because I still had Hope.

29

HOPE

It was quiet and cool in the little stone church within the walls of Fort William Henry on the southern tip of Manhattan Island. Grace walked beside me as we made our way up the aisle. The only noise was the tapping of our shoes against the wood floor and the beat of my heart as I met Isaac's tender gaze.

He stood tall and proud at the front of the church with the minister, Henricus Selyns, who had agreed to marry us in a small, private ceremony. Our marriage vows would be witnessed by Grace and one of Mister Selyns's sons. There was not time, or extra money, for new clothes or fancy shoes. Though I had insisted upon a warm bath that morning.

The stone church was the tallest structure on the island, with its spire and weathercock rising high above the fort. Mister Selyns had told us it had been used for over fifty years by the Dutch Reformed Church and was dearly loved by all. It was a far cry from the Meeting House in Salem Village, for which I was thankful. Isaac and I had agreed that a marriage with a Minister of the Gospel was more important to us than a civil ceremony with a magistrate, as the Puritans practiced. Thankfully, Mister Selyns did not ask too many questions and was willing to see that we were properly married in the eyes of God and the Church.

Grace was withdrawn and pale, though she tried to rally with a smile for my benefit as I stopped beside Isaac and we faced the minister.

Mister Selyns spoke in broken English, but it was enough for us to understand. The ceremony was very simple as we shared our marriage vows, promising to honor one another, to be faithful, and to care for each other, so long as we both lived.

After we signed the register and Isaac paid the minister, the ceremony was finished.

"Congratulations," Grace said as she hugged me just outside the church's front door. "I'm so happy for you."

She didn't sound or look happy, but I knew she was trying.

It had been eight days since she'd died in 1912. Each day, as we traveled to New York, she had gone to sleep, only to wake up the next morning more and more anguished over what she had lost. I tried to talk to her about Luc, but she didn't want to discuss her pain.

As much as I had mourned losing 1912 and Luc, it was nothing like Grace's grief, and it made me realize how deeply she loved him.

We had arrived at Fort William Henry, formerly Fort Amsterdam, just two days ago, and Isaac had secured a little house for us to use while we waited for the madness in Salem to die down. With almost five thousand occupants in the fort and living nearby on the southern tip of Manhattan Island, it hadn't been easy to find a place to live. New York was a bustling, thriving colony—though it was a far cry from what it would be in 1912.

Now, as I walked away from the stone church as Isaac's bride, I couldn't wait to be his completely. My love for him grew every day. If I was given the choice between him and 1912, I would choose him over and over again. But God, in His infinite wisdom, had known I needed my eyes to be opened and had orchestrated our romance in a way that left me in awe.

Isaac reached for me, and I slipped my hand into his. I wished Mama and Daddy could be with us today, but I was thankful for Grace.

When we returned to our little cottage, Grace started to prepare our wedding supper. With her back turned to us, Isaac drew me into his arms and kissed me. Warmth filled me from head to toe, and if Grace hadn't been there, I would have allowed him to kiss me as long as he wanted. But I didn't want to make her uncomfortable, so I pulled back and smiled at him. It was difficult to wait, but it would make our time together later even sweeter.

Isaac let out a little groan for my ears only and then said, "I've heard Philip English is living on the other side of the fort." Philip and his wife had been accused and had fled Massachusetts with their daughter. "I think I'll go speak to him while supper is being prepared."

I glanced at Grace, who seemed lost in her own thoughts, and nodded. There were things I needed to say to my sister, things best said without Isaac present. On the long trip to New York, we had told him about our time-crossing gift, and he had accepted the truth without question. But I knew Grace wouldn't speak as freely with Isaac at hand.

He left the small house, but not before giving me another kiss. It would be hard to be newlyweds with Grace underfoot. The house had one room on the main floor and one room above. Isaac and I would sleep upstairs while Grace slept on a cot near the hearth.

"I'm sorry," I said to Grace after Isaac was gone. "I know this day is hard for you."

She turned from the carrots she was cutting and shook her head. "Don't be sorry for being happy, Hope. This day isn't hard because you've married Isaac. 'Tis better because of it."

"I wish there was something I could do for you."

"You and Isaac have freed me from life in Salem. I cannot ask for more."

I put my hands on her forearms and said, "You can ask for so much more, Grace. I know you're miserable—I was, too—but I believe there is a life waiting for you here. God has a plan, and though it looks dark and uncertain right now, it will be bright again. I promise."

She smiled, though her eyes were still sad. "It heartens me to hear you say such things, but please let me mourn for now. I cannot mend my heart in a day or even a week. 'Tis broken and might take a lifetime to heal. But I will trust in God's plan." She nodded, as if trying to fortify herself. "And this was what I was going to choose anyway. Remember?"

Would she have chosen it? If I had been able to talk to her—to tell her that I would let her go with my blessing. If she had not died in that aeroplane, would she have chosen this path?

The answer was plain to see in the sorrow in her eyes.

"I will pray for you," I told her. "That God will give you His peace and comfort, as only He can."

She put her hand on my shoulder and smiled. "He has already. But peace and comfort don't always take away the pain. They just dull it a little."

I hugged her tight, and she hugged me back.

"Now," she said as she pulled away, forcing a smile, "let's make the best wedding feast we can manage. Today is a day to celebrate, and the day after tomorrow is our birthday. We have much to be thankful for."

I helped her make a chicken pie with carrots and beans on the side. She patiently taught me how to make the puffed pastry and how to clean the chicken and season the meat just right.

Then she helped me make a pound cake for dessert. By the time Isaac returned, we had a delicious feast prepared, and I knew a few more recipes. In the past, I had not enjoyed cooking and baking, but I had never had a husband to feed. I wanted to please him more than I wanted anything else, and it made me proud to serve him good food. The work didn't feel like a chore when I had his pleasure to anticipate.

After the meal was finished, we sat at the hearth with apple cider. I nestled close to Isaac, wanting to be as near him as possible. Every chance I could get.

Grace sat opposite us, looking into the flames. I had worried that it would be difficult for her to see Isaac and I together because of her old feelings for him, but she seemed hardly to notice us. She was so caught up in her own grief and memories.

"Tell me about flying," Isaac said yet again. He never seemed to tire of hearing about 1912, and I never tired of telling him.

"'Tis unlike anything you can imagine," Grace said before I could answer him. "'Tis a sort of weightless freedom. Thrilling yet dangerous. Effortless yet extremely difficult. A miracle, really."

Isaac and I both looked at her, though she still stared into the fire.

"You flew, as well?" he asked.

She turned to him and nodded. "After Hope died, I learned to fly and made a trip across America, from New York to California."

"California?" he repeated.

"There's so much to tell you," I said to him, leaning closer. "So very much."

"Luc taught me to fly," Grace continued, as if she hadn't heard us. "He taught me many things."

"Who is Luc?" Isaac asked.

"The man I love," she said with a simple shrug and tears in her eyes.

Isaac looked at me, questions in his gaze, and I nodded. He had to see that Grace's grief went deeper than losing our parents and her life in 1912. She was grieving the loss of a lifetime.

"I'm sorry," he said. "I wish I had known him."

Grace turned her gaze back to the flames and nodded. "I wish you had, too."

Isaac asked other questions about automobiles, telephones, and things we would not live long enough to see. We talked for over an hour as the sun disappeared and the stars filled the vast sky.

Finally, it was time for bed.

Isaac went up the ladder first and smiled at me before he disappeared into our room. My heart raced with anticipation, and my nerves hummed with energy.

Grace blew out all but one candle, which she left on the table for me.

"Good night," I said as I gave her another hug. My joy was dimmed by her melancholy, and I wanted to ease her pain. But the only thing that could heal her broken heart was time. "Thank you for helping me with supper."

She nodded and then turned, almost blindly, to her cot, where she began to undress for bed.

With a trembling hand, I took the candle and made my way up the ladder. Grace and I had slept in the loft the past two nights before the wedding, but it would now be just mine and Isaac's until we returned to his farm in Salem Village.

He stood near the lone window, his back to the ladder. When he heard the boards creak beneath my feet, he turned and extended his hand to me.

I set the candle on a small table near the bed and joined him at the window. He put his arm around me, drawing me into his warmth. I looked up at him, my nerves settling. This was Isaac, the gentle, kind man who had loved me so well for so long.

"Is there anything we can do for Grace?" he whispered. "Anything at all?"

"We can pray."

He smiled at me and nodded. "We will pray."

"But not right now," I said as I stood on tiptoe and kissed my husband. "For now, I have something else in mind."

He grinned and lifted me into his arms, which had become my favorite place in the world.

30

GRACE

Before I opened my eyes the morning after Hope's wedding, I lay for a moment, allowing the warmth of the sunshine to bathe my face. The melancholy I'd felt for the past eight days filled my soul even before I was fully awake. A constant reminder of everything I'd lost.

But I didn't want to ruin Hope's happiness. She deserved so much better from me.

I started to get out of bed, but a strange pain shot through my back, and I moaned.

Why did my back hurt?

I tried to open my eyes, but they were heavier than usual, and it was hard to focus. I blinked several times, but I couldn't seem to wake up.

"Grace?"

I froze, my heart pounding a strange rhythm at the sound of that voice.

"*Mon amour*, can you hear me?"

"Luc?" I said his name, but my throat was dry, and my mouth felt like cotton. I forced my eyes to open, and they slowly cleared.

Luc rose from a chair near my bed and took my hand in his. "Grace!" He knelt beside me and lifted my hand to his lips, tears in his eyes. "Thank God you've come back to us."

My gaze traveled around the large room, confusion clouding my mind. The tall ceiling was white and rounded, and large bright windows were positioned between each bed.

I was in a hospital.

In 1912.

"Your mother just left for a moment," he said as he held my hand between his, using his shoulder to wipe a tear from his cheek. "She will be so relieved."

"What happened?" I whispered, my voice not wanting to work.

"Your aeroplane malfunctioned on Long Beach nine days ago. You've been unconscious ever since."

"Unconscious?" Realization dawned, and I stared at him, breathing hard. I hadn't died. My physical body had been unable to wake up here, so my conscious mind stayed in 1692 until I was well enough to wake up again. "What day is it?"

"October 10th."

Which meant tomorrow would be the 11th when I woke up in 1692. I still had time to make my final decision.

"The doctors didn't know if you would ever wake up again." Luc blinked away his tears. His smile was brilliant as he said, "But your parents and I have not stopped praying for or believing in a miracle."

Tears of relief and love dripped down the side of my face into my hair. "You have no idea how happy I am to see you. I have been living in 1692 for the past eight days, believing I died here and that I would never see you again."

"I'm here, mon amour." He gently wiped away my tears, love in his voice. "I will always be here."

351

"Grace!" Mama's voice traveled across the distance of the large hospital ward. There were at least a dozen other beds and many female patients, but the beds were spaced far enough apart that I felt some semblance of privacy.

"Mama." I cried happy tears as she rushed up to my bed and gently kissed my cheek.

"Thank God you're awake."

She called the doctor over to examine me, though she could have done it herself. He said he believed I would make a full recovery, though I needed to give myself time to heal. I was given some water, which helped my dry throat, and was promised something to eat soon.

"May I sit up?" I asked.

"If it doesn't hurt too much," the doctor told me. "Take your time."

"You'll be dizzy and probably nauseous," Mama cautioned.

They helped me sit up, though the movement did make me dizzy. There was pain in my back, but the doctor told me it was only bruising. Miraculously, I had no broken bones, just a very serious concussion that had left me in a coma for the past eight days.

After the doctor left, Mama said, "The body is a beautiful, miraculous thing. You are going to be fine, Grace. Better than fine." She smiled. "I'm going to call your father and Tacy. They've both been here every day. They'll be so happy."

"Wait, Mama." I held her hand, thankful Luc knew about my time-crossing so I could speak freely in front of him. "I want to tell you what's happened."

Mama nodded, her expression eager.

"Isaac took Hope and me to New York."

At the sound of Isaac's name, Luc sat up a little straighter.

I put his heart at ease by adding, "Hope and Isaac were married yesterday, and they are very happy. They will wait out the hysteria in New York."

Mama pressed her lips together, more tears coming to her eyes. "I'm so happy for her," she managed to say. "I can't wait to tell your father."

She wiped her cheeks with a handkerchief and then left to phone Daddy, leaving Luc and I alone again.

He pulled his chair closer to my bed and took my hand in his again. "Is Isaac a good man?"

"One of the very best," I said with a smile. "But only one of them."

Luc also smiled, his eyes looking bluer today than green. He was even more handsome than I remembered, his accent dearer, his presence more comforting.

"I've been miserable these past eight days," I said. "My grief was crushing."

"Mine, too." He looked down at our hands, and I saw the anguish lining his eyes and mouth. It had taken a toll on him, just as it had on me. "All I could think about was our last conversation, when you told me you had chosen 1692. And I worried I would never get to speak to you again. I have never known such heartache in my life, Grace."

"I made a mistake." I choked on the words, trying to gain control of my emotions, wanting him to understand. I knew what I was giving up with Hope, and my heart was breaking—but if anyone could understand, it would be her. She would tell me to do this. "When you asked me to marry you, I should have said yes without hesitation. I've had a glimpse of life without you, and it was bleak. I believe God has given me a second chance to do the right thing. To choose the life that is right for me."

"Even if that means giving up Hope?"

I smiled through my tears. "I won't ever give up Hope. She will forever be a part of me—even if we can't be in the same place and time. Our life together prepared us for the lives we'll lead apart—and I think that was God's plan all along."

He stood, holding my hand, and leaned forward to kiss me.

It was tender and brief—but heartfelt and hopeful. "Does that mean you'll say yes if I ask again?"

"Will you, please?"

He laughed, and it was the most joyful sound I'd ever heard. "Will you marry me, Grace Cooper?"

"Yes." I nodded. The motion made me dizzy, but I didn't care. I was already starting to feel stronger.

"I will spend the rest of my life trying to make you happy."

"You already have."

"We can live wherever you want—New York, or near your parents in Washington, DC. We can live here, too, if you want to be close to Tacy—or even in Paris, if you'd like. I don't care where we are, as long as we're together."

Was it possible that I could have Luc *and* my parents? "It would be nice to be near my parents."

"Done." He smiled, but it was a different kind of smile, one that was filled with reverence. "I lost my father when I was very young, and my relationship with my mother has not been good for a long time. Your parents have treated me with so much love and kindness. They have taken me under their wing these past eight days, caring for me as much as they have for you. We've had wonderful conversations, and they've taught me so much." He shook his head. "My greatest joy is in marrying you, but second is knowing that I will have parents again. I could not ask for more, Grace. Truly."

I gently squeezed his hand, wishing I were healthy enough to walk out of this hospital with him right now. But that would come in time, and we would be married and start a life together near my parents. I would write, and together we would start a flying school. "I could not ask for more, either."

He kissed me again, and this time I put my hands up to his cheeks to hold him closer a little longer.

It would take time to understand all that had happened, but I knew one thing for certain: I would not take this life for granted.

And tomorrow, when I woke up in 1692, I would tell Hope that I had made my final decision. As much as I loved her, my life—my love—was here in 1912.

A new kind of pain pressed against my heart—the pain of saying good-bye.

31

HOPE

OCTOBER 11, 1692
NEW YORK

A rooster crowed somewhere in the fort. It woke me up, but I didn't want to get out of bed. Not now—maybe not at all today.

Isaac lay behind me, warm and strong, his arms around me. I had slept deeper and longer than ever before, my dreams sweet for the first time since losing 1912.

He must have felt me stirring, because he pulled me closer, nuzzling his face into my neck. A shiver of pleasure ran up my spine, and I let out a happy sigh.

"Do you think Grace would notice if we stayed here all day?" he asked.

I smiled. "I believe she would."

He groaned. "How many hours until 'tis acceptable for us to go back to bed?"

I laughed and rolled over to face my husband. "Thankfully,

the days are growing shorter, so a few seconds earlier than yesterday."

He joined in my laughter but eventually let me go to get dressed. The smell of frying bacon and something sweet wafted up the ladder, telling me that Grace had been awake for a while. She would never come looking for me, but the longer I stayed upstairs, the more my cheeks would color when I finally made an appearance.

"Take your time," I told Isaac as I started down the ladder.

Grace was busy at the hearth, turning the bacon on the griddle. There was a lightness in her step as she moved from the hearth to the cupboard to take out the plates.

But it was the smile on her face that stopped me in my tracks.

All thoughts of being embarrassed faded as I stared at my sister. She was happy, glowing, vibrant. Grace had returned to me.

When she finally saw me standing there, her smile grew even more brilliant. "I woke up in 1912!"

"What?" I frowned, stunned. "What do you mean?"

She set the plates on the table and rushed across the room to me. She took my hands in hers. "I was unconscious from the aeroplane crash—I wasn't dead. Because my body couldn't wake up there, my conscious mind stayed here. Until yesterday. Mama explained that my brain had swollen but had finally returned to normal, which allowed me to wake up."

"You didn't die?" I couldn't believe it.

"Luc was there when I woke up." Tears sparkled in her eyes, but they didn't spill over her cheeks. She was too happy. "He asked me to marry him, Hope."

My legs felt weak, and I took my hand out of hers to grab the back of a nearby chair. Though I knew she was unhappy, I had thought she would be here with me forever.

Her smile slipped and was replaced by concern. "Do you not think I should marry him?"

My heart broke as I faced the truth. I couldn't fathom life

without Grace. Yet how could I ask her to give up the man she loved? Especially when I had such happiness with Isaac. I could make her choose me—but I didn't want to force her. God had given us the gift of choice, and it wasn't my job to withhold it from my sister.

I mustered a smile, though my heart wept. "You must stay with him."

Sorrow was written all over her face. "I'm so sorry, Hope."

"No." I shook my head, though tears ran down my cheeks. I tried to remember every line and detail of her beautiful face. The shade of her eyes, the sound of her voice, the cadence of her words. "Don't be sorry." I wiped my cheek, impatient with my tears. "You belong with Luc, just as I belong with Isaac. God gave us the past eight days to realize what we both truly want and need. This is good." I said it even though I didn't believe it—not yet.

She pulled me into her arms, hugging me tight.

We held each other for a long time. Emotions and memories flooded my mind and heart as I thought about all we had lived through. I had never imagined a day when Grace might not be by my side—yet I was facing a lifetime without her.

"I will miss you with every breath I take," she whispered. "I love you more than life itself."

I clung to her, tears burning my eyes. "And I will miss you." It was all I could manage to say, though there was so much more. Even if I had forever with my sister, I could never say all I wanted or needed to say.

I couldn't wrap my mind around losing her—never seeing her again and not knowing how her life would turn out. Yet I trusted that God would be with Grace, just as He was with me, and that one day we would see each other again. The hope of that reunion kept my heart beating.

When Isaac finally came downstairs, our tears were shed, and we pulled apart. He looked between us, confusion on his brow.

"Grace woke up in 1912 last night while we slept," I explained as I wiped the last remnants of my tears with my apron. "She wasn't dead—just unconscious."

He still looked confused, so I wrapped my arm around his. "Grace is going to stay in 1912, Isaac. Tomorrow will be her last day here. She'll go to sleep before midnight on our birthday and will not wake up here ever again."

His gaze sliced to hers. "You're leaving us?"

She nodded, a sad smile on her face. "Luc has asked me to marry him, and I've said yes. I'll be there to help Mama and Daddy as they age and make sure the orphanage continues."

Isaac seemed almost as shaken as me. He opened his arms, and Grace went into his embrace.

I stepped back, watching my husband hug my sister, and more tears streamed down my cheeks. Isaac had been the most important man in our life here—and would continue to be so for me. Grace had spent years loving him, and she would miss him dearly. He would miss her, too, and we would grieve together.

But I was not jealous of their love. I was thankful they cared so deeply for each other.

"I'm sorry you will start your married life in mourning," Grace said as she pulled out of his embrace. "I never imagined this would happen."

"Don't worry about us." Isaac reached for my hand. "I will love and cherish Hope just as you have always done."

Grace's beautiful face was still glowing as she wiped her tears. "That is the only consolation I take in leaving you. The only one." She took a deep breath and then smiled at both of us. "Enough tears. We only have two days left together, and I don't want to spend them crying. We have a wedding and a birthday to celebrate."

I used my free hand to capture hers, nodding in agreement. "And an engagement."

She smiled at me—as only Grace could—and a lifetime of

words seemed to pass between us. Those we had said and those we longed to say. Our relationship had not been perfect, but I had no regrets. I loved Grace completely, and she would always be a part of me.

We would make the most of our time together—and once she was gone, I would make the most of my life with Isaac. Time was a gift—one of the greatest we would ever be given—and I wouldn't take it for granted.

And one day, if we had children, they would learn all about Grace.

Epilogue

GRACE

AUGUST 1, 1914
NEW YORK CITY

Sunshine beat down upon our heads as Luc and I stood on 5th Avenue. I wore a large hat with a wide brim to shade my eyes, but it was still bright. There were no clouds to mar the beautiful blue sky or offer relief from the glare to those on the street. My lavender gown was soft and lightweight, helping with the heat, which I was thankful for as I had recently entered my seventh month of pregnancy.

"Mr. Hearst seemed pleased with your latest article," Luc said as he held my hand. He looked handsome in a black suit and tie with a black fedora on his head. He had to speak loudly over the noise of the crowd. "But are you certain you should cover this story?"

I grasped the strap of my brown leather bag, making sure I didn't lose it in the melee outside the church. Hundreds of people had gathered to watch the event unfold, and I had been sent by Mr. Hearst to take pictures and report back to his newspaper. Luc and I had arrived nearly an hour ago to get a good place to stand, and my feet were aching—but I was too excited to think about it for long.

"I didn't ask for this job," I said, feeling a little sheepish, "so I saw no reason to turn it down when it was offered."

"No reason?" he asked with a laugh. "There is every reason to turn this one down. You could have made an excuse to Mr. Hearst."

"No one says no to William Randolph Hearst." Even as I said the words, I knew it was just an excuse.

I wanted to be here today.

Ever since I'd recovered from the accident, Mr. Hearst had been paying me to write articles for his newspaper, the *New York Journal*. I still wrote for the *New York Globe* and had begun writing for *The Washington Times* after we moved to DC. Writing for two New York newspapers required regular trips to the city, but I didn't mind coming back. New York would always feel like home.

"I'm not sure how many trips I'll be able to take once the baby arrives," I told him as I laid a hand on my growing midsection, "so I'm taking advantage of this opportunity while I still can."

"Mr. Hearst capitalizes on sensationalism, which is often at the expense of people's privacy," Luc said, his voice reflecting his dislike of Hearst's business practices. "That's why he sent you here. Are you sure you want to add to her misery by writing this article?"

I looked down the street at the approaching carriage and tried to contain the feelings surging within me. Anticipation, excitement, fear—but it was nothing compared to what she was feeling right now.

"Whether I'm here or not," I said, preparing my camera, "she must endure today. She won't even notice me. I'm simply a face in the crowd." I couldn't contain my eagerness, and I smiled at him. "I don't know if I'll ever get another chance to see her."

He smiled as he put one hand on the small of my back and kissed my temple. "Who knows what adventure life will throw at us next?"

"A baby. That's our next big adventure."

He grinned. "I can't wait."

For the past eighteen months, Luc and I had been busy establishing our careers. While I had been writing for three newspapers, he had started a flying school in DC and had begun advising the government on use of aeroplanes in the military. His business had grown faster than we anticipated and occupied much of his time. But he was happy to be done with exhibition flying, and I was happy to know he would never perform the death dive again. Years ago, Mama had mentioned that WWI was on the horizon, and though I hadn't mentioned it to Luc, I knew he would be instrumental in developing aviation for the war effort. He would be invaluable as a consultant and instructor for the US government.

As for me, I hadn't flown an aeroplane since the accident in Long Beach, but Luc had convinced me to go up with him as a passenger on several occasions. I loved the feel of the air and knew it would always be in my blood—I just had no interest in piloting an aeroplane ever again.

I was thankful Luc was able to be here with me today. When Mama heard what I had done, she'd probably scold me. Luc would be a buffer between us, though she wouldn't stay mad for long. Not once I gave her a copy of the picture I was about to take.

The beautiful black carriage drew closer to St. Thomas Episcopal Church. Yards of white flower garland had been draped on the sides of the carriage. As it passed through an intersection, a police officer stopped the cross traffic and doffed his cap at the bride and her father, who sat within.

My heart pounded as the carriage came to a stop in front of the church. The crowds cheered, and the bride's father waved his white-gloved hand at the onlookers. The driver stepped down from his perch and opened the door, allowing the bride's father to exit first. He turned and offered his hand to his daughter. She took it and stepped out of the carriage.

She wore an exquisite gown of white silk with a long train embroidered with flowers along the scalloped edges. Her veil covered her face, but she was so close, I could make out her features clearly—and though I couldn't see them, I knew she had tears upon her cheeks.

Women tossed flowers onto the bride's path as her mother pulled up in an automobile and was escorted into the church without looking at her. A servant arranged her train and veil and then handed her a bouquet of flowers before offering a gentle smile and disappearing into the church.

As the bride took her father's arm and looked up at the imposing Gothic façade of the church, I lifted my camera and snapped a picture.

Her gaze slipped to mine, and I held my breath.

For a heartbeat, I looked into the beautiful green eyes of my grandmother Libby. She was only twenty and just embarking on her own journey. She didn't know who I was—would never know me—but it was enough that I knew her.

Just as quickly, she looked down at the ground and allowed her father to walk her into the church. Someone closed the heavy doors behind her, and the moment was over.

Several people began to walk away while others stayed, waiting for the bride and groom to exit the church after the wedding.

But I had what I needed, and I was ready to leave.

I had no desire to see Libby's husband, Lord Reginald Fairhaven, the Marquess of Cumberland. Especially knowing he would make my grandmother's life miserable—until she found her happily-ever-after with my grandfather Henry.

"Ready to go?" Luc asked as he offered me his arm.

I set my camera in my leather bag and then wrapped my arm through his and nodded.

As we walked away from St. Thomas's, Luc asked, "What are you thinking about, ma chérie?"

"Hope."

He smiled as he set his hand over mine. "When do you not think of Hope?"

"I wish she was here with me."

"You say that every day."

"I wish it today, most of all."

He lifted my hand and kissed it. "You also say that every day."

I smiled up at him. My heart would never be the same without my sister, but I took pleasure in knowing that she was happy. Because even though we were parted by centuries, I knew, without a doubt, that she had found peace with Isaac. Hope lived on. I could feel her, as if she were standing beside me.

And that made me happiest of all.

My only wish was that she knew about the baby I carried, but as I set my hand on my rounded stomach, marveling at my active child, I had a feeling that somehow, some way, she would.

HOPE

AUGUST 1, 1694
MASSACHUSETTS BAY COLONY

The day was warm, but not overly hot, as I sat beside Isaac on the wagon. One of my hands was wrapped around his arm, while the other lay gently on my rounded stomach. I had just entered my seventh month, and the child was active. Each time I felt it, I smiled.

"Happy?" Isaac asked me. "Even though you're a farmer's wife and you live in Salem Village?"

I chuckled, recalling my words to Grace two years ago, when the witch hysteria had just begun. How wrong I had been about Isaac.

"He's a rule-follower. He bows down to the elders without question. He is content to stay on his farm, attend meeting, and work himself to death. I would shrivel up and die if I had to submit myself to such a life. I want more than Salem Village can give me."

Yet I had everything I had thought I would hate—and I was completely and utterly content. My struggle to find a place on the Broadway stage and my daring flights seemed so foreign and unwelcome. The hustle and bustle of New York City in 1912 felt loud and crowded now.

"I'm very happy." I filled my lungs with the pure New England air and knew I would not take back the life I had once known, even if I were given the choice. I had found purpose and joy in being Isaac's wife, in caring for our home, and in growing our farm. I still hated cleaning—but I enjoyed cooking and baking. It made me feel closer to Grace.

There wasn't a day that went by that I didn't think about my sister. Her death in 1692 had been harder than I had anticipated, and I had spent months in deep grief. But slowly, the grief had dulled, and I could think of her with joy again.

"Are you ready to meet the rest of your family?" Isaac asked.

"I have longed for this day for many months." I was especially curious about Rachel Howlett's child. I had thought of her often, praying for her as I did my own unborn child.

My hand settled on my stomach as I thought about the growing babe. If he or she was a time-crosser, I would deal with the reality, though I prayed they were not. There were blessings that came with crossing time, but the difficulties far outweighed the joys.

We entered the outskirts of Sandwich, and Isaac turned down a winding lane. He'd been there once before and knew how to find Pricilla's home.

I thought of our own home, which had suffered while we were in New York. The servants had done their best to keep the farm running, but many things were out of their control. It hadn't taken long for the authorities to realize that Isaac helped me escape the gaol, so a warrant for his arrest had been issued, and Sheriff Corwin had confiscated all his livestock under justification of the law.

It had taken us a year to rebuild what was lost, but Isaac was a good manager, and we were thriving once again.

In October, on the day Grace left us for good, Governor Phips had halted all court proceedings in Salem and ordered an end to the arrests. By January, while we were still in New York, the charges against me had been dropped, as were those against many others. By May, Governor Phips had pardoned the rest, and everyone who could afford their debt to the gaol had been released. To pay for Tituba's debt, Reverend Parris sold her, and she was sent out of the colony. John Indian soon followed.

By the end, almost two hundred men, women, and children were accused. Fourteen women and five men were hanged; one man was pressed to death; and three women, one man, and one baby died in prison. But every person in Salem Village and the surrounding communities had been scarred with emotional and mental wounds that would never go away.

It was something I both feared and hoped would never be forgotten.

"There," Isaac said as he pointed at a simple brown house up ahead. "Pricilla Baker's home."

It was a charming property with large trees all around and a split-rail fence encircling the generous yard.

As we came to a stop, the front door opened, and several women stepped outside. I recognized Pricilla instantly but wondered who the others were.

"They're your family," Isaac said as if he knew my thoughts. "All of them."

Delight bubbled up inside me as people poured out of the house and into the yard, waving at me as if I were returning home after a long journey.

And perhaps I was.

"Hope!" Pricilla cried. "Thee hath finally come."

I had written to her several times, telling her about Grace and asking if I could come to visit. She had written back with a resounding yes.

Isaac stepped out of the wagon and helped me down. The child I carried made the process a little more difficult. The moment my feet were on the ground, I was engulfed in hugs.

"This is Virginia and Esther and Joanna and Alice . . ." Pricilla's introductions continued, but I could only laugh, knowing I would never remember everyone's names the first time. There were aunts, uncles, and cousins to greet, and they all looked so much like me—so much like Grace—that I felt completely at home.

"Come inside," Pricilla said. "There are cakes and doughnuts and more food than thee could ever eat. And bring thy good husband."

I took Isaac's hand as one of the cousins led the horse and wagon to the barn. Isaac seemed just as pleased with all the family as I was. When his mother died, he had been alone in the world—until he'd married me. I also felt orphaned in a way. Since our return to Salem Village, I had not spoken to my father or Susannah. I saw them at meeting and admired their little boy, but we acted as if we were strangers. It was easier that way, after all we'd been through. I didn't know if we'd ever reconcile, but I trusted that God would find a way for us to move on.

Now we were surrounded by family who loved us, and nothing else mattered.

As we ate, I asked for the introductions again and discovered that my mother Tacy had been one of eight sisters and two brothers. All but one aunt was married or widowed, and there were dozens of cousins.

And they spoke openly about their time-crossing.

"Two of our sisters, Abigail and Hannah, chose their other paths," Pricilla said.

"Are all of you time-crossers?" I asked.

"No." Buela shook her head. "Damaris and I are not."

I looked around the room, and one of the sisters raised her hand. "I'm Damaris."

Laughing, I shook my head. "I'm sorry. It may take me some time to learn everyone's names."

"Don't worry," Pricilla said as she touched my knee. "Thee hath time."

Isaac stood behind me and put his hand on my shoulder. I reached up and rested mine on his. I did have time.

"And who are Rachel's parents?" I asked, looking around the room.

Everyone turned to John and Patience, whose quiet sadness gripped my heart. I recognized their grief.

"I was with her until the very last," I told Patience, who had married into the family and was not a time-crosser.

Tears rimmed Patience's beautiful blue eyes, and she nodded. "Thank thee, Hope. It brings my heart comfort to know thee were with her."

"Do you know what happened to the baby?" I asked quietly.

"Yes," Patience said. "We've inquired after her and learned that her father, Josias Reed, took the baby with him to the Carolinas. It seems his wife died on the ocean crossing and never made it to Salem Towne. He is raising the child, and we have no right to her."

"I'm sorry."

"He named her Anne," Pricilla said, "and we are praying that God sends her a guide, just as He provided one to thee and Grace."

I had written to Pricilla about Tacy, as well, and all that Grace had told me about her life in 1912.

"And what of my cousins?" I asked as I looked around the large room at dozens of men, women, and children, all different ages.

Pricilla smiled. "Not all are time-crossers, but there are many, and they span the ages both past and future."

The child in my womb rolled, reminding me that he or she would be joining this strange and wonderful family. And for the first time, I felt at peace knowing that if they were a time-crosser, it would be okay. Somehow, Pricilla made me feel as if this was a normal experience—something that had never felt normal before now.

"Thank you," I said to Pricilla and the others as I met their loving gazes. "For welcoming Isaac and me into your family. You don't know how much it means to us."

Isaac gave my shoulder a comforting squeeze—and I knew I was exactly where I belonged. The only thing that would make it better was having Grace here with me—but she was where she belonged, as well. And I knew, deep within, that Grace was happy.

If I had learned anything, it was that God's plans were far better than our own.

Historical Note

The Salem Witch Trials are the most intriguing, horrifying, fascinating, and daunting thing I have ever researched. As a descendent of individuals on both sides of the hysteria, including the Putnams and the Proctors, I have always felt a personal connection to the events in Salem Village in 1692. Like most people, I thought I knew the history—but when I started to dive deep, I realized I was woefully uninformed.

Those who want to make sense of such a senseless tragedy chalk it up to prejudice, religious fervor, or even ergotism (poisoning from spoiled grain)—but the truth is much too complicated to blame on one or two factors. A perfect storm of fear, trauma, and hatred was brewing over Puritan Massachusetts in 1692, and it unleashed a hurricane of devastation that no one fully understood then—or now. There are countless theories about why the hysteria became so widespread, but the difficult reality is that we will never know for certain. It wasn't the first mass witch-hunt the world had seen, but thankfully it was one of the last.

Regardless of the theories, there are concrete facts surrounding the people and events in 1692, and those are what I set out

371

to share in this book. It was a challenge to decide what part of the history to include, how my characters would interpret it, and how to communicate my own thoughts without misrepresenting or maligning the truth.

A few things to note. I set the main part of the story in the Eaton Ordinary, which is patterned after the Ingersol Ordinary, owned by Richard and Ann Ingersol. Most of the initial events in 1692 happened in or near the ordinary, so I thought it would be an ideal place for Hope and Grace to live. Almost all the people mentioned in the 1692 path are real, apart from Hope, Grace, Uriah, Leah, Isaac, Susannah, and Tacy's family, though they are inspired by real people. I tried to keep the timeline, afflictions, and accusations as accurate as possible, though I only included a fraction of the historical accounts. For a complete overview, I highly recommend a book called *The Salem Witch Trials: A Day-by-Day Chronicle of a Community Under Siege* by Marilynne K. Roach. The book is almost seven hundred pages long and simply relays the facts.

As I've noted, historians have several theories about the hysteria, but they all agree that almost everyone in 1692, regardless of religion, believed that witches did, in fact, exist. How to identify them—or punish them—was up for debate. And almost everyone in 1692 agreed witchcraft was something that needed to be eradicated from the earth. Many of the theories about Salem are examined in a book called *A Storm of Witchcraft: The Salem Trials and the American Experience* by Emerson W. Baker. This book was, by far, the best source of information about the events that transpired. Mr. Baker's commentary and interpretations are concise and easy to understand. He references other similar events, called mass psychogenic illness, that took place before and after 1692 (most recently in Le Roy, New York, in 2011–2012) which sheds light on what might have happened in Salem. The book also discusses conversion disorder and post-traumatic stress disorder as possible psychological conditions that the afflicted might have suffered from, making their experiences very real and troubling for them. Without modern understanding about mental illness, those around them—and they themselves—would have turned to witchcraft as an explanation. Historians also agree that there were some who used the hysteria to perpetuate fraud, revenge, or simply for "sport," as Mercy Lewis said on March 28, 1692, at Ingersol Ordinary.

I had to condense some timelines and facts to make the story work, but I tried not to change anything significant. One change I made involves Quaker history. In the story, Tacy Howlett is hanged as a Quaker in Boston in 1668. However, it became illegal to hang Quakers in Massachusetts by 1661. That didn't stop people from accusing Quakers of witchcraft—which was a hanging offense until after the Salem Witch Trials in 1692.

My hope is that I have given you enough information to understand what happened in Salem while stirring your desire to learn more.

Much of Hope and Grace's experiences in the 1912 path were inspired by the fascinating life of Harriet Quimby, the first woman to receive her pilot's license in America. Harriet was a stage actress, a journalist in New York City, a film screenwriter, and an aviation pioneer. She learned how to fly at the Moisant Aviation School in Hempstead Plains, New York, where Hope and Grace learn, and was an exhibition flyer for several months before her death. She was the first woman to fly over the English Channel on April 16, 1912—the day after the *Titanic* sank—but didn't receive much publicity because of the *Titanic*. Harriet died at an air meet near Boston on July 1, 1912, in almost the same fashion as Hope. Her remarkable life is told through the story *Fearless: Harriet Quimby, a Life Without Limits* by Don Dahler.

Lucas Voland is also inspired by a few different early aviators, including Lincoln Beachy, an American who was known for his death-defying stunts and record-breaking skills. It is estimated that 30 million people (30 percent of the population) saw him fly during his career.

Though the aeroplane was first invented by the Wright brothers in America (something heavily debated by aviation historians!), the French began to perfect the machines and techniques used in flying. By 1911, when Harriet learned to fly, it was believed that the French were the best aviation teachers in the world. She was taught by a Frenchman named André Houpert, another inspiration for Luc, at the Moisant Aviation School.

One more thing to note: The first successful trip by aircraft from New York to California took place in 1911. It was completed by a man named Calbraith Perry Rogers in answer to William Randolph Hearst's offer to pay fifty thousand dollars to the first person to make the trip in less than thirty days. The flight was sponsored by Armour and Company, and Rogers's aeroplane was called the Vin Fiz Flyer. He had a support team, including his wife and mother, who followed on the Vin Fiz Special, a three-car train, much like Grace's in the story. It took Rogers three months to complete the trip, and he missed out on the prize money, but he still gained notoriety. Sadly, he died in a plane crash six months later.

It is said that outside of war, aviation is the deadliest endeavor in human history. Most believed that death was a necessary sacrifice toward safe aviation for everyone. From the first death in an aeroplane in 1908 to Harriet Quimby's death in 1912, it's estimated that one aviator died every ten days. To learn more about early aviators, I highly recommend *Birdmen:*

The Wright Brothers, Glenn Curtiss, and the Battle to Control the Skies by Lawrence Goldstone.

If I have gleaned anything from history, it's that humans still have a lot to learn.

Author's Note

As part of my book research, I visited the Salem area on two separate occasions. My mistake on the first trip was to go at the end of October near Halloween. The small town was crowded beyond imagining! I was just beginning my research and thought it would be a good place to start. Unfortunately, a lot of the history in Salem has been commercialized, and it was very difficult to learn anything useful. By my second trip a year later—this time in November—I had read several books and came armed with more knowledge. I knew that I needed to go to nearby Danvers (previously Salem Village) to find the original locations where the hysteria began. And it was there that I connected with many people who are preserving the raw, heartbreaking, and uncommercialized history of the Salem Witch Trials.

One of those men is Richard B. Trask, who works at the Danvers Archival Center at the Peabody Institute Library. Mr. Trask was a wealth of knowledge and so very kind to talk to me. He has written several books and articles, which you can find by visiting DanversLibrary.org and clicking on *Archives*.

Danvers is a small town, and like most small towns, everyone seems to know everyone else. I stopped at the local historical society to see if I could find information about the Ingersol Ordinary, part of which is still standing today, and while I was chatting with one of the staff members, a volunteer poked her head out of a door and said, "I used to live in that building!" Joyce Cranford introduced herself and told me everything I wanted to know. Later she emailed pictures of the interior, and her husband, Doug, drew me a floorplan from memory. A heartfelt thank you to everyone I met in Danvers!

Speaking of that trip, I want to thank my niece, Madelyn VanRisseghem, for hosting us, and my husband, David, and my daughters, Ellis and Maryn, for putting up with my un-quenchable appetite for more history as we traipsed through Danvers in the rain.

I knew that writing a story about twin sisters would be dif-ficult. I wanted to make sure that each sister sounded unique and had a distinctive personality. I didn't have to look far for inspiration. I have a set of fourteen-year-old twin boys, Judah and Asher, so I understand the special bond between twins. But Hope and Grace are definitely more like my teenage daugh-ters, Ellis and Maryn—though only in the best possible ways. Ellis is my daring, goal-oriented daughter with big dreams and strong convictions. She will tell you what is on her mind and passionately pursues her God-given talents. Maryn is my gentle servant, eager to keep the peace, though she's a mighty warrior when it comes to injustice. She always digs for the truth, dislikes arrogance, and believes in second chances. Both are remark-able young women with loyal hearts and beautiful souls. Girls, thank you for showing me (and telling me—with much debate sometimes) how Hope and Grace would handle the difficulties they were given.

I'm honored and blessed to work with one of the best teams in the business at Bethany House Publishers. I love that my ac-quisitions editor, Jessica Sharpe, is one of my biggest fans, and that my copyeditor, Bethany Lenderink, asked to be assigned to *For a Lifetime*. It's a joy to know that the staff at Bethany House are eager for more TIMELESS stories. Thank you to the fabulous art department and the rockstar marketing team for all you do to make my stories stand out. I'm grateful to partner with all of you.

Thanks also go out to my agent, Wendy Lawton, and the whole team at Books & Such Literary Agency. I love being part of the Bookie family. I want to give a special shout-out to my friends at the MN NICE ACFW writing group, as well. Thank you for your encouragement and support each step of the way. And thank you to my newly formed mastermind group of ladies who have come alongside me to do this writing life together.

For a Lifetime was one of the hardest books I've ever written. Not only because of the subject matter, but because our family faced many challenges this year, some I've shared publicly and some I've kept private. I'd love to think that I learned valuable lessons along the way or that the challenges made me stronger, but the truth is that sometimes life is just hard—not Salem Witch Trials or death-by-aviation hard, but hard nonetheless. One of the truths I clung to was the same truth Hope embraced: God doesn't always give us what we want, but He never abandons us, and He desires for us to draw near to Him in both the good and the bad. He has a plan, even if I don't understand it or see it clearly. I pray you cling to that truth, as well.

If you enjoyed *For a Lifetime*,
read on for an excerpt from

Across the Ages

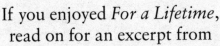

Available in November 2024

One

MAY 21, 1727
MIDDLEBURG PLANTATION
HUGER, SOUTH CAROLINA

My bare toes dug into the hardpacked earth as I clutched my diary close to my chest and looked up into the ancient oak tree overhead. The setting sunlight flickered through the drooping Spanish moss as I tried to still my anxious thoughts and calm my fearful heart. I took a risk writing the truth into my diary, but there was no other place where I could unburden my soul or try to make sense of my existence. The words I wrote in this sacred book were the deepest and darkest secrets I possessed, and I had to keep them hidden.

Everythig about my life was one secret built upon another. A fortress of mysteries, too high to breach. Some were the secrets I kept, and others were the secrets kept from me.

"Caroline!" Grandfather's stern voice drifted through the oak trees and the magnolias on our small tobacco plantation.

I turned away from the Cooper River and quickly lifted my overskirt to slip the diary into a hidden pocket in my petticoat. Though the words were shut away in the tattered book, the reality of my life was still with me—or rather, my lives. I didn't know what to call my existence, or why it happened to me. When I went to sleep tonight in South Carolina in 1727, I would wake up in Paris, France, in 1927 tomorrow. And when I went to sleep in Paris, I would wake up in South Carolina again the next day—with no time passing while I was gone. I had been going back and forth since I could remember. Perhaps from the very beginning of my strange life.

"Caroline!" Grandfather called again, this time with impatience.

I lifted the hem of my homespun gown and made haste over the roots and rocks toward the plantation house. The simple, two-story white clapboard building came into view through the thicket of trees. My grandfather, Josias Reed, was standing on the edge of the lawn, his arms crossed in disapproval as he waited for me.

"Where have you been?" he asked as I slowed my steps. His gaze fell to my bare feet, and the disapproval in his brow deepened. "A woman of twenty should know better. And today, of all days."

"I'm sorry," I told him. "I lost track of time."

"Our guests have arrived." He shook his head, looking at me from my uncovered head to my dirty hem. "You should have been preparing. Governor Shepherd is an important man, and he will not look kindly upon his oldest son marrying a hoyden."

"His son?" I frowned, confused. "I am not marrying the governor's son."

"What do you think this meeting is for?" he asked, his frustration mounting. Grandfather took a step forward and lowered his voice, no doubt worried that the governor and his son might hear. "Thomas Shepherd will inherit five thousand acres of the best rice plantation in America one day." He shook his head with disappointment. "I could make nothing of your fickle mother, but I will make something of you."

I had heard this threat my whole life. My mother, Anne Reed, had been a hoyden, as well. A motherless child with a penchant for recklessness and rebellion. She'd run off with the first man who had shown interest in her, and a year later she'd left me on my grandfather's doorstep.

Her recklessness had led to all our pain—and I vowed to never be wild and thoughtless like her. Yet how could I marry a man I didn't love?

"I do not want to marry Thomas Shepherd," I said, trying to appeal to his compassion, though I'd not witnessed it often. "I do not love him."

"You will obey me," he said. "If I can secure a marriage between you and Thomas, and we can join our plantations, we will be the richest planters in South Carolina. I will not have you thwart my plans." He turned and walked toward the back of the house. "Come. Dress for supper."

As I walked down the stairs and into the central room of our home, I felt all eyes upon me. I was wearing my best gown, my hair was properly restyled upon my head, and shoes covered my feet.

As my gaze met Thomas Shepherd's, my heart fell with disappointment and dread. He looked me up and down, assessing me with a coolness that was all business. He did not smile or offer any warm welcome but analyzed me as if he were purchasing livestock or seed.

"Caroline," Grandfather said as he lifted a hand to beckon me. "May I present Governor Shepherd and his son, Mister Thomas Shepherd?"

I curtsied as I'd been taught, and the men bowed. "How do you do?" I asked them, trying to hide the revulsion from my face and voice. Thomas was at least ten years my senior, and he did not bear the look of a man who worked his own land. He was thick about the middle, and his skin was pale, telling me he spent his days indoors. There was no depth to his gaze, no sign of intelligence or character.

"'Tis a pleasure to finally meet you, Miss Reed," Governor Shepherd said. "Thomas and I have been eagerly awaiting this day."

"We've been working through the details of the betrothal," Grandfather said to me. "But I believe we've finally arrived at an agreement."

"Indeed, we have," Governor Shepherd said, smiling at his son.

I left the men to their cigars and brandy the moment I could be excused. It had been an unbearable supper as Thomas stared at me. Grandfather and Governor Shepherd spoke of farming and politics, though neither man included Thomas in the discussion. The longer I sat in his presence, the more I worried Thomas was simpleminded. Was he even capable of inheriting such a large plantation? Or taking a wife?

My pulse thrummed as soon as I left the room, needing to be free of the confines of my life. I couldn't marry Thomas Shepherd and be forced into loveless servitude to a man I didn't know. I shivered just thinking about him touching me or living with him day after day for the rest of my life.

Panic began to overwhelm me, and I felt breathless as I raced up the stairs, an oil lamp in hand. Tomorrow I would be in 1927 and could have a reprieve from this life—yet I would wake up here the next day and it would be waiting for me.

There had to be an answer—a way out of this nightmare.

The house was long and narrow, with three rooms on the main floor and three above. Grandfather slept in one room on the far end of the upstairs, and I had the middle room. The room on the opposite end had belonged to Mother but had been locked my whole life, a reminder of all the secrets that had been kept from me. Twice, I'd tried to break into that room, but both times I had been discovered and thoroughly disciplined with the rod.

I stopped at her bedchamber door. What was my grandfather hiding from me? Was my mother still alive? Would she help me if I could find her?

I didn't think twice but went into Grandfather's bedchamber in search of the keys. Setting down the lamp, I began to look through his bureau drawers. My heart was pounding so hard, I could hear the beating in my ears.

Finally, I found a key ring, and then quickly replaced everything I had dislodged in my search. I returned to my mother's bedchamber door, and with shaking hands, I slipped several keys into the lock until I found the right one.

When it clicked, time felt like it stopped.

Tossing a glance over my shoulder, I slowly turned the knob and then slipped into the room, closing the door behind me.

My breath was shallow as I looked around, holding my lamp high. The room was nondescript. A four-poster bed, a bureau, a washstand. Disappointment weighed down upon me. I had hoped this room would reveal the answers to my questions. I opened each of the drawers and looked under the bed, but it was all empty. Nothing remained of my mother.

As I turned, the lamp in my hand cast a shadow over the wall across from me, and I noticed a slight variation in the wainscotting. Frowning, I moved across the room. When I reached the wall, I ran my hand over the wainscotting and felt a piece shift.

Slowly, I removed the panel and sucked in a breath.

There was a hole behind the wall, and within was an envelope.

With trembling hands, I lifted the envelope and brought it back to the bed. I opened it and pulled out the paper within. My mouth slipped open as I skimmed the page.

It had been written by my mother, and she had dated it New Year's Eve, 1707. It was three months after I was born, about the time I had been brought to my grandfather. I had assumed she left me on the doorstep and didn't show her face—but how had this letter found its way inside the wall?

I leaned closer to the lamp to see the words my mother had penned twenty years ago.

> *I suspect you will hate me, Caroline. As much as I hated my mother for abandoning me and leaving me in the care of my father. He tells me she died in Salem in 1692 but refuses to tell me how or why. There can only be one reason a woman of her age died there that year and it is kept a secret. She was a witch. Did she curse me? Is that why I must suffer through two lives, because she hated the child she bore?*

My pulse thrummed in my ears. Did my mother have two lives, as well? Had I inherited her curse? I continued to read, filled with both panic and exhilaration to know I wasn't the only one.

> *I hate myself for leaving you with my father, but the difficult life you'll lead with him will offer you more advantages than the difficult one I've chosen for myself. You might wonder why I don't abandon my life in Nassau, but that is the trouble with love, isn't it? We give up anything that makes sense to be near the one who makes us feel the most alive. That is what your father does for me. That is why I am returning to him. I left before my pregnancy was obvious and will never tell him of your birth. You would not be safe if he knew you existed.*
>
> *I write this to you now because I wish my mother had left me something. I wish I could explain why I've left*

you—why I left South Carolina in the first place—but it will only hurt you more. I've never told anyone the truth about my lives, and I wouldn't expect you to understand it, either. I shall carry the secret to my grave, though that inevitable day feels closer and closer. Mayhap, when you read this, I will no longer be alive. But that might be best for you and anyone else who knows me.

The letter ended on that final, fatalistic, note.

My mind spun with all the implications. My mother had two lives, just like me. She'd brought me to South Carolina to protect me from my father—but why? Would he have harmed me if he knew she was pregnant? Grandfather said the sea merchant my mother ran off with was a cowardly, weak man. Surely, he wouldn't have wanted to harm his own daughter. Why would my mother need to keep my birth a secret from him? And why was she living in Nassau? The only thing I knew about Nassau, Bahamas, was that it was the Republic of Pirates until nine or ten years ago—and it still had a reputation for depravity and crime. Pirate leaders like Benjamin Hornigold, Blackbeard, and Charles Vane had either been pardoned by the king or killed, but there were still some pirates who plied the Caribbean.

Had my mother been associated with the pirates? Was she still living in Nassau? Could she tell me why we were burdened with two lives? I desperately wanted to understand what was happening to me. Did she hold the answers?

And could she keep me from being forced to marry Thomas Shepherd?

I heard a footstep on the stairs and quickly turned out my lamp. It was Grandfather's tread, slow, heavy, deliberate. My heart beat hard as I held my breath, praying he would not suspect I was in Mother's room. Because if he found me with her letter, and knew what I was planning to do, he would keep me under lock and key.

His footsteps didn't even pause or hesitate by Mother's room, and a few seconds later, I heard his door open and close.

After waiting a few moments, I slipped out of Mother's bedchamber and locked the door. I would need to work fast if I was going to get away without notice.

Nothing would stop me from finding my mother.

Gabrielle Meyer is an ECPA bestselling author. She has worked for state and local historical societies and loves writing fiction inspired by real people, places, and events. She currently resides along the banks of the Mississippi River in central Minnesota with her husband and four children. By day, she's a busy homeschool mom, and by night she pens fiction and nonfiction filled with hope. Find her online at GabrielleMeyer.com.

Sign Up for Gabrielle's Newsletter

Keep up to date with Gabrielle's latest news on book releases and events by signing up for her email list at the link below.

GabrielleMeyer.com

FOLLOW GABRIELLE ON SOCIAL MEDIA

 Gabrielle Meyer, Author   @Gabrielle_Meyer   @MeyerGabrielle

More from Gabrielle Meyer

Libby has been given a powerful gift: to live one life in 1774 Colonial Williamsburg and the other in 1914 Gilded Age New York City. When she falls asleep in one life, she wakes up in the other without any time passing. On her twenty-first birthday, Libby must choose one path and forfeit the other—but how can she possibly decide when she has so much to lose?

When the Day Comes
TIMELESS #1

Maggie inherited a gift from her time-crossing parents that allows her to live three separate lives in 1861, 1941, and 2001. Each night, she goes to sleep in one time period and wakes up in another. She faces a difficult journey to discover her true self, while drawn to three worthy gentlemen, before she must choose one life to keep and the rest to lose.

In This Moment
TIMELESS #2